Deep Sea Feline

Dave Hurlow

Library and Archives Canada Cataloguing in Publication

Title: Deep sea feline : a novel / Dave Hurlow.
Names: Hurlow, Dave, 1984- author.
Identifiers: Canadiana (print) 20230460224 | Canadiana (ebook) 20230460232 | ISBN 9781988989709
  (softcover) | ISBN 9781988989716 (EPUB)
Subjects: LCGFT: Novels.
Classification: LCC PS8615.U747 D44 2023 | DDC C813/.6—dc23

Printed and bound in Canada on 100% recycled paper.
Cover Artwork: Wenting Li
Author Photo: Annie Briggs

Published by:
Latitude 46 Publishing
info@latitude46publishing.com
Latitude46publishing.com

We acknowledge the generous support of the Ontario Arts Council.

ONTARIO ARTS COUNCIL
CONSEIL DES ARTS DE L'ONTARIO

an Ontario government agency
un organisme du gouvernement de l'Ontario

Deep Sea Feline

A Novel

Dave Hurlow

PRAISE FOR *DEEP SEA FELINE*

Hurlow's written one hell of a book. It's weird, wild, funny, thrilling, fun, deep, operatic. I just don't get what he has against birds.
  —Morgan Murray, author of *Dirty Birds*

Deep Sea Feline is mesmerizing and exhilarating. It sneaks into your psyche and sticks with you throughout the day, the month, the year... just like a great song you just cannot get out of your head.
  —Jennifer Morrison, filmmaker/actor/Jen's Bookshelf

Deep Sea Feline is a wild bag of an opera, full of digital piano tracks, art gallery visits, and musicians on tour in mid-life. There's a train running through a Manitoba landscape -- a mysterious connection between science and art. Dave Hurlow pierces the membrane that separates this world from another world that runs under it: a lake of ice and, below, a world where mothers depart, friends question life choices while still attempting to reach a truth, through both figurative and sonic art. You might have to be on ketamine to read Hurlow correctly, or maybe just a long sleepless night on Nyquil, but you'll learn how to live inside a painting and a piece of music. Deep Sea Feline is funny, adventurous, and a break from the reality we know as the normy 9 to 5 – everyone will agree the more interesting hours in life usually occur between six in the evening and eight the next morning.
  —Michael Winter, author of *The Death of Donna Whalen* and *Minister Without Portfolio*

Serious fun. Loved it. Dave Hurlow is one of those rare writers who can dig deep into the bag of weird but still somehow engineer a brilliant plot with lovable characters. A bright crackling sparkler of a mind.

—Charles Spearin, musician (Do Make Say Think, Broken Social Scene)

In a Toronto of the not-too-distant future, robotic pets have replaced cats and dogs, birds have turned into Hitchcockian homicidal maniacs, and potholes have become portals to another enigmatic realm. In David Hurlow's Deep Sea Feline, the line between reality and fantasy is washed away in this remarkably imaginative read, epic in scope, and filled to the fringes with a bustling menagerie of opera singers, musicians, and painters battling to save the world from a mean-spirited pelican god. Yet, for all its offbeat humour and fantastical layering, at its core, Deep Sea Feline is a wake-up call for humanity.

—Rod Carley, award-winning author of *Grin Reaping* and *Kinmount*

Prologue:

The Sixth Door

It was the disgraced philosophy professor, Campbell, who'd come up with Zarathustra. Whenever the wild-eyed Fin concluded one of his apocalyptic rants – and this was, at the very least, a weekly occurrence – Campbell would raise his drink and bellow cheerfully Thus spoke Zarathustra! Over time the nickname was shortened to Zee, which stuck for the remainder of his days.

For as long as he could remember, Zee had stood at the same stop on Queen Street every morning, waiting to board the streetcar and join the undesirables lounging near the front. Like most of his peers, Zee never had anywhere in particular to be. He had no family and subscribed to a heavy regimen of alcohol as a means of quieting the perverse acrobatics of his mind. Travelling across the downtown core, he'd peer through the shimmering skyscrapers and imagine he was trespassing in a cavernous land inhabited by giants.

On a good day, he'd ride all the way to the Beach and back. He'd get off at Rainbow Cinema and perform Chopin's Nocturnes on the piano in the lobby for change, then scour the garbage for stale popcorn and half-eaten chocolate bars. In this manner, he'd collect enough food to live and enough money for a bottle of vodka to get him through another night in the park or the men's shelter.

On a bad day, Zee suffered at the hands of the Chaos Signal. He was burdened with the knowledge that every sentient being on Earth was hardwired with a receiver, which could be matched to a Universal Frequency. The ability to tune into the Universal Frequency was imperative to an individual's quest for harmony and inner peace. In his lifetime, he'd felt the Chaos Signal grow increasingly powerful, scrambling the channels.

As a result, on certain days the entropy of Zee's mind made way for sinister currents. He ranted about the coming apocalypse: a gargantuan pelican the size of the Sun was going to swallow the earth down through its cold antimatter digestive system, into the belly of oblivion. Often these rants got him kicked off the streetcar as they escalated. At unfamiliar intersections he was reduced to begging like a common bum. If he managed to make it to the piano in the cinema lobby on a Chaos day, he'd end up performing complex, atonal Schoenberg compositions that people mistook for random key mashing. On Chaos days, he'd be lucky if he could afford a couple cans of strong beer.

There was, however, a foil to the Pelican and the Chaos Signal, a vision that struck Zee in moments of extreme clarity, often when he was performing music by one of his heroes: Béla Bartók. In the vision there was a lake of pure white, beneath which lay a dark, vast ocean. Several cones of light shone out from the belly of the ocean, lighting up a series of large spheres, which hung in the air like toys on a baby's mobile. The spheres were hemmed in by a circular waterfall, cascading out of the darkness above. When he was transported to this place, a calm came over him and he felt as though he'd donned a cloak that shielded him from the Chaos Signal.

If it was Bartók that triggered this vision in him, there was an obvious correlation. In Bartók's celebrated opera, Bluebeard's Castle, Bluebeard's wife opens the sixth door of his palace to discover a still, silent lake. This had always been Zee's favourite scene: the beauty of Bartók's composition – the glimmering harp and swirling clarinets – flashed in his mind whenever he visited the ocean beneath the lake.

In the spring he performed themes from the music of Jean Sibelius, which invariably conjured disjointed flashbacks from his birthplace: a small town near the southern coast of Finland, just outside Helsinki. How he'd ended up in Canada, he could no longer recall. He had scattered recollections of a woman he'd loved deeply, an irreparable rift and, finally, grief so severe it had driven him partway mad.

He remembered the great capitals of Europe more clearly: the domed cathedrals, the strong coffee, the pigeons and the fountains. He recalled the feeling of a starched tuxedo, the thunderous applause of the audience, the cold champagne and the soft, dimly lit hotel rooms. The many women he'd made love to visited him in his dreams, accompanied by the music of the Gershwin Brothers. He spoke with the women, but they were never physical. When they left he cried, awakening wet faced in the cool, grey dawn.

Shortly before his death, Zee was visited by a pleasant lightness of body, accompanied by a vivid sense that he was speeding towards a euphoric experience that would elude him as long as he resided in the battered vehicle of his own body. Finally, he resolved to destroy himself, just as soon as he completed his final project: an ambitious one-act opera with a libretto based loosely on a tale from Finland's ancient folk epic, The Kalevala.

The opera was, in essence, a theatrical portrayal of the ocean beneath the lake, contrasted against the dreaded Chaos Signal. The score itself was a faultless, mind-bending work resulting from Zee's lifelong ambition to reconcile the dissonant, labyrinthine music of Bartók with the heroic, romantic symphonies of Sibelius. Against all odds, the interludes and recitativo flowed together as well as anything by either composer, treading the strangest of aesthetic lines with virtuosic grace.

It was, above all else, a humanist opera, written as a last-ditch attempt to stifle or divert the Chaos Signal, to create a temporary asylum from the madness of the age and the ever-encroaching chaos that would finally – Zee knew, despite his noble efforts – swallow everything up.

It was a very hot day in September when Zee finished his opera. The clouds had parted in the early afternoon, precipitating a radical shift in the weather. Those who'd left the house wearing sweaters tore them off in frustration. Zee was wearing black boots, white pants, a dress shirt and a khaki trench-coat, all smeared with dirt. Beneath the layers, he'd worked up a lather of perspiration. As the Queen streetcar rapidly approached, he stepped into the road. He took a three-point stance in the middle of the tracks, his grey hair falling in tangles down through his beard, partially obscuring his icy blue eyes.

The streetcar operator was, at that precise moment, distracted by a commotion. A man had begun masturbating in one of the rear seats, and passengers were screaming and rushing forward in a miniature stampede. By the time he saw Zee, planted in his path like a linebacker, it was too late. He slammed the brakes, but the tracks were sweating from the heat. Perched nine-feet up in his seat, the operator watched Zee disappear beneath him as a rammed car of commuters groaned, swayed and gradually slid to a bloody halt.

Part One:

The Cocoon

CHAPTER 1

"It's kind of... I don't know how to say it. Desolate? Hopeless? It sounds like the soundtrack to a recurring nightmare where my ex fucks Joe Stalin and then knifes me."

Charlie Potichny was sitting in the office of Oliver Noodles at Enemy Airship Headquarters in downtown Toronto. They were discussing the demos that presently constituted Antidotes for Manic Toads, Charlie's sixth record for Enemy Airship under his pseudonym Cave Music. At present the label had an option to renew Charlie's contract or drop him. Noodles, leaning towards the latter, was resorting to the ugly practice of issuing ultimatums.

The storied record exec wore thick framed glasses and a bright blue suit with a pocket square. Above the impressive creases of his forehead he was badly balding. Charlie had pale, almost translucent skin and grey-green eyes the colour of a cold ocean in a Dutch painting. His blonde hair, sticking out at every angle, always seemed too long and too short at the same time. He had on jeans, a hoodie and dirty, white sneakers.

Noodles' third storey office in the heart of Chinatown was adorned with washed out posters of eighties post-punk bands; there was a bottle of bourbon open on his desk and random liquor strewn about the office. Several bottles of prescription pills were nestled amongst facsimiles of record contracts and legal files. Noodles took a swig of bourbon.

"Charlie, have you ever considered putting some vocals on your record? A hook maybe? You know, something melodic?"

Charlie squirmed uncomfortably in his chair. "I think there are a lot of earworms on the record," he offered. "Just give it a couple more spins."

"I've listened to it several times. It never repeats itself. A hook traditionally repeats itself."

"Look, you and I have always seen eye to eye. I feel like you understand what I'm trying to do. Can you just trust me on this one? I always get good reviews and make the year end lists. I promise, Manic Toads is no different from any other Cave Music record."

"Your records always end up on year end lists in the egregiously overlooked category. You won't even tour. Listen, I'm not trying to be an asshole, but this is business. I have our staff to think about. Fucking. . . alimony payments. Your sales have declined steadily since When Your Shoulders Are Like Cannon Balls. Please, Charlie, work with me here. I'm trying to help you."

"Record sales in general are in decline!" Charlie protested. "Stop being a record label douche, Noodles. Just sign another folky poser in a cowboy hat and let me keep putting out weird ambient music."

Noodles sighed and, lamenting the complications that arose when he befriended his artists, played his ace in the hole: "Charlie, I love you, and I respect your artistic integrity, but if you don't find a way to make this record more palatable we're dropping you. Period."

A strained silence settled atop the din of midday traffic. If Charlie was especially defensive about the record it was because, on some subconscious level, he knew it was mediocre. He took a sharp breath and rolled his eyes. "So that's what this meeting is? After everything we've been through you're fucking threatening to drop me?"

"Threatening is not the word I would use."

"Because I won't put hooks on my record?"

Noodles nodded.

"Because I won't make the record you want me to make?"

"That's about the jist of it."

Charlie reached for the bourbon. "Fuck you dude." He took a big sip, immediately regretted it. "Fuck this," he coughed.

Noodles, having anticipated an outburst, was unruffled. "Let me lay it out for you: you're the product, I'm the investor. Your job is to be as true to your vision as possible; my job is to distort and monetize that vision. Right now, that involves bullying you out of your comfort zone. Additionally, as your honest friend, I'll tell you something: Manic Toads is boring. Make it a little livelier, get some drums on there maybe. I don't know, do something. Your contract is on the line. If you don't want to take my advice you can put it out independently and work your own promo."

Noodles, feeling guilty despite carrying through in his resolve, picked up the bottle of bourbon, walked over to an expensive stereo and pressed play on Wowee Zowee. He stood at the window taking in the cyberpunk grandeur of Chinatown in silence and sipped the bourbon.

Charlie stood to go out, but Noodles piped up again.

"There's one more thing. I got a call from someone at the AGO," Noodles flicked his head towards the venerable art gallery up the street. "They're doing a big retrospective on your mother next year and they want to commission you for some music. The proposal is kind of. . . eccentric."

"Why didn't they contact me directly?"

"You have a landline that's unhooked most of the time. Sometimes I get calls from Errol asking if you're alive." Charlie nodded. "Anyway, they want to hang a bunch of your mother's work in that cabin where she. . . worked."

"Where she died. You can say it."

"They're offering to drive you up with your gear. The idea is that you'd cultivate a vibe or whatever. The music would soundtrack the exhibit, playing on a loop. They'll pay all your expenses and a small honorarium; of course, the exposure would be great. Frankly it sounds like the premise for a Stephen King novella, but from a business perspective it's an attractive gambit." Noodle paused, then looked at Charlie. "I'll take this opportunity to remind you that your future here is tenuous."

"I would have expected you to go for the low hanging metaphor there – something with thin ice."

"I'm a sick fuck Charlie, but I draw a line at making jokes about the grizzly death of a friend's mother."

This last proclamation restored a touch of warmth to the room. Charlie looked past Noodles and let his vision blur.

"I'll need to think about it," he said, finally.

"Of course, but please let me know as soon as possible, and stop leaving your phone off the hook. Take care of yourself, alright?"

"You too."

✧

Charlie stepped out of the building onto Spadina Avenue, a wide artery running through the centre of the city. He'd heard that in the nineteenth century, horse drawn streetcars had galloped up and down the thoroughfare. A century and change later, sinister looking space-age vehicles slid up and down the metal tracks, superseding Toronto's iconic red and white antiques.

In the paved margins of the artery, Charlie struggled to slip through the powerful current of humans on his way to the streetcar platform. He'd always found the intense energy of Chinatown unsettling, and the unseasonable heat was suddenly oppressive. The high density of human bodies made him feel claustrophobic. He rarely left his apartment and had no concept of the ebb and flow of rush hour – the rhythms that drove the movement patterns of the human organism.

Climbing aboard one of the glimmering new cars, he was confused by the fact that the operator was sealed off behind a glass partition. He had relegated two chunky coins to his back pocket for fare, but there was no obvious slot to push them through. He almost never drank anymore, and the whisky had momentarily befuddled him beyond his baseline standard of befuddlement.

A group of teenage boys observing his confusion waved him into the car, which somehow seemed to validate his unintentional flouting of the rules. He returned the coins to his pocket and slumped into an uncomfortable seat across from a beautiful, elegantly dressed woman reading a copy of Goethe's Faust. Her dark skin glowed with a healthy sheen of carefully selected ointments and her voluminous, curly hair spilled out of a bright green headscarf. All this caused Charlie to consider the state of his own scaly, eczema-addled skin and impossibly messy hair.

The new streetcars were divided into four-seat sections, with pairs of patrons facing each other in close proximity. It was terribly awkward and Charlie, not having a book of his own to hide behind, gazed determinedly out the window. Outside it spat rain for a moment despite the sun. The flashing neon signs popped and blurred. For a moment Charlie was lost. When he came back to himself the woman had set her book down and was staring straight at him. He cast a cautious glance towards her and something odd happened: her eyes, which had been downturned when he initially looked at her, revealed a burst of emerald green with slivers of glowing hazel, causing a wave of electricity to course through his nervous system.

"I know you," she said. "You're Charlie Potichny. You went to Saint Augustine's."

Charlie reflexively pulled his hood back and ran a hand through his hair as he struggled to place her.

"I'm Sophie Rénard, remember?"

He was drawing a blank.

"I went to Saint Mathilda's. Saint Augustine's sister schools."

Distant memories crackled, fractured images and foggy notions.

"You got drunk at my house one time and threw up on the lawn. You even left your shoes behind. It was brilliant."

Charlie's ghostly skin turned a light pink colour. "Hello," he croaked, and then cleared his throat. "That seems like forever ago. I think I remember you. Didn't you date my friend Greg for a couple months?"

"Yes! I lost my virginity to him in a garden shed at Daniel Schlepfer's kegger, in Grade Eleven. It's a bit surreal that we both ended up in the opera world, kind of awkward, really. Ah well, let bygones be bygones. What is a bygone anyway? I've never been clear on that."

Charlie cracked a smile, tickled by the speed and content of her speech. "You don't really mess around with small talk, do you?" he asked.

"Talk about the weather, you mean? Stifle what's really on your mind because you're worried what people will think of you?"

"I genuinely enjoy a good chat about the weather," Charlie said, loosening up a bit. "And I happen to have made a fine hobby out of worrying what people think of me."

Sophie narrowed her eyes. "You're sentimental, aren't you? You like to linger on the past."

Charlie took a second to think about it. "I don't know that I like to, but I can't say that I don't. It's a powerful reflex."

"I've made a pretty good hobby out of worrying about the future," Sophie said. "I suppose we're opposites."

"I'll make an effort to connect with the present moment,"

Charlie said. "But I'm almost always uncomfortable in the present moment unless I'm working. If I could ever learn how to sleep I could retreat into dreams, I suppose."

Sophie gasped. "I was in a plane crash in my dreams last night, and then a whale swallowed me. It was a small whale, maybe an orca, and it didn't use its teeth, I was just sucked down into its soft, silky belly."

"Gross!"

"Oh no, it was quite lovely."

They both got off at Queen Street to transfer to the westbound car. Sophie continued talking as Charlie stood, temporarily transfixed by the swirl of pedestrians and traffic. The combined aroma of sausages, exhaust, and tempura wafted through the soupy humidity, assaulting his olfactories. A van sailed nonchalantly through a red light, and a chorus of honks erupted violently. He was lost, once more, to a case of sensory overload.

" – and he gets off on all charges because he can afford an expensive defense lawyer whose strategy is to attack the victims' character? It's a farce. That guy is such a creep. Have you ever met him? Charlie?"

"What? Oh! Yeah," he snapped out of it and fumbled for the coins in his pocket as an ancient streetcar screeched to a halt and flung open its accordion doors. "Total creep. I was on his show once, and he kept asking me if I thought his assistant was hot during the breaks. And his hand was too soft and slippery when I shook it."

As they boarded, Charlie popped his coins into the fare slot – a gesture that brought him great comfort. The operator, not even paying attention, lazily passed him a transfer ticket. Sophie gave him a funny look. "Why did you just pay?" she asked.

"I didn't pay before," he shrugged. "Now I've paid."

"Christ you're innocent," she said. "It's probably terminal."

They found seats together at the very back, squished between a dusty construction worker drinking a bottle of beer and an overweight college student watching television on a tablet.

"I can't believe Greg never mentioned that we sing together," Sophie said. "The three of us used to hang out once in a while. Remember when we smoked weed and went to see The Lord of the Rings and Greg made us leave because he thought Sauron was real? Then he insisted we go to Burger Shack and he ate four servings of onion rings? He can be quite a handful, that one."

"He's always needed a lot of looking after. I guess it's good that he's got a wife and a litter of kids now, keeps him grounded. Well, more grounded than he might be. He's still a bit of a wild man."

Sophie grinned. "No shit. I was in a production of Aida with him in Leipzig last year – he got completely naked at the after-party on closing night and did a lap around the block. One of the violin players gave him some very strong absinthe, so he's not completely to blame. But yeah, he still parties. What about you? You still vomiting on peoples' lawns and walking home barefoot?"

They shuddered to an abrupt halt behind another streetcar, sparks burst from the cables overhead. "I don't really party these days," Charlie said. He considered telling Sophie about his condition, but it was too complicated. "I mostly just hang out with my cat and read. If I'm feeling adventurous I'll throw on Lawrence of Arabia or The Third Man and eat a bag of Doritos."

"Cool Ranch or Classic?"

"Sweet Chili Heat."

"Freak."

They were stuck in a growing traffic jam with no sign of relief. An ambulance flew by, sirens blazing. There was a commotion in the street up ahead.

"Motherfuck, I'm late for therapy," Sophie said. "Gonna have to catch a cab."

She stood up abruptly and started towards the doors.

"Are you on Facebook?" she asked.

"No. I'm allergic to technology."

"Terminal!" Sophie repeated, shaking her head. "See you around, then."

After she was gone, Charlie pulled a battered notebook and a tiny pencil out of his pocket and wrote:

population destiny

absinthe makes the heart grow fonder

He sat in the motionless streetcar for a long time before he realized he was outside his own building. He stood up in a daze and walked out into a sun shower. Down the road a body was being loaded into an ambulance. There was blood on the tracks and in the streets. The short excursion had taken a heavy toll and he could not muster the appropriate reaction to the strange scene of violence. A chill he'd suppressed on the streetcar ran through him now, and he allowed his body to shudder and spasm, releasing the energy. He had the distinct impression he was standing several feet in front of himself until he was pulled forward, his body merging with his perception, or vice-versa. He was having a great deal of trouble pinpointing the precise physical location of himself, which was not at all uncommon. He took a breath, gathered himself up, and made his way inside.

CHAPTER 2

CHARLIE HAD BEEN living in a perpetual state of loneliness for as long as he could remember. His main source of consolation was a tubby, stub-tailed, ornery Manx cat called Goblin. The ownership of Goblin had been transferred to Charlie when his first and only serious girlfriend, Gwendolyn, had left Canada to work as a midwife in Africa: a turn of events that Charlie had coped with by recording a moody album entitled You Can't Take a Cat to the Congo, which was received poorly by fans and critics alike.

Charlie made a modest living scoring nature documentaries and subsisted mostly on boiled eggs, stir-fries, and takeout pizza. He left his apartment so infrequently that he'd taken to calling it the cocoon. Occasionally it occurred to him that he was failing to achieve the metamorphosis inherent in the concept of a cocoon. The conspicuous beauty of butterflies – depicted immaculately in the films he scored – invariably triggered strong feelings of melancholic envy in Charlie.

The second storey apartment sat above a dive bar and a cavernous junk shop run by the landlord, who specialized in vintage stereo equipment. The building was on a fashionable strip of Queen West, bridging the city's core and the rapidly developing fringe. Breaking up the parade of gentrification, residents of the men's shelter across the street emitted a low hum of idle chatter throughout the day and night, erupting into occasional arguments over thefts and betrayals.

Shortly after he moved in, Charlie bought a pile of old stereo equipment from his landlord and rigged it up to emit a subtle, but effective, white-noise loop through a dozen carefully placed speakers. This initiative provided a relaxing atmosphere for his overtaxed nervous system and helped facilitate irregular snatches of sleep.

Beyond recording music and feeding himself, Charlie typically had just enough energy left over to take a long walk in the evening. His doctor recommended that he walk as much as he could every day without fatiguing. For years it had been about a hundred feet: to the pizza shop and back. These days it was a few kilometers round trip.

Walking west he would duck into second-hand shops, searching for Brian Eno records and vintage editions of Asimov paperbacks, then do a loop through Trinity Bellwoods Park where handsome professionals walked their fashionable dogs.

To the east, he'd end up on the more central, touristic part of Queen West, marked by the legendary Horseshoe Tavern and the Much Music building, where teens from the suburbs loitered, hoping to meet rockers and popstars. He liked this part of Queen Street for the strange, sci-fi architecture of City Hall and the weather beacon on the Canada Life Building, flashing red for rain and blue for snow, as if summoning precipitation down on itself. The skyline, dominated by the pulsing lights of the CN Tower and the automated ivory tortoise shell of the SkyDome, created the impression of a city designed by a futurist from the 1970s whose bold ideas had been rendered anachronistic by decades of architectural evolution.

On these walks, Charlie fed off the energy of the world without interacting with it. To engage with it would have been like touching wet paint on a canvas. He moved through the world as if he were invisible, wearing the city like a cloak. Every night he brought the city home with him and endeavoured to translate it into sound.

The day after his meeting with Noodles and his unexpected encounter with Sophie, Charlie returned from his evening constitutional, took a hot shower and changed into pyjama bottoms and an oversized t-shirt. He brewed a pot of Sleepy Time tea and spiked it with a shot of cough syrup. He pulled open the sessions for his new album and listened intently, hunched over in a rickety desk chair. After a few minutes he tore off his headphones in frustration. Noodles was right; he was stagnating.

He needed to reset his mind, shake things up. He pulled a dusty bass guitar out of his storage closet and plugged it in.

He sat down again, hugging the bass to him. Goblin sat motionless behind him, roosting in a hoodie he'd left strewn on the couch. He clicked the playback on his recording suite: a piano loop and the deep drone of a synthesizer oozed from his monitors. The mix was sparse and threadbare, it needed something more. Not some crude hook, as Noodles had suggested, just something to make it more substantial. Something beguiling.

The room was dim save for the glow of the computer and the Christmas lights strung up against a cotton sheet that hung above the couch, dyed in psychedelic patterns. He observed the bustle of the intersection below: streetcars floating past each other; drunken students laughing and dancing; aging punks sulking next to their lethargic dogs. The streets were alive, but he couldn't fathom it.

Charlie tried out several different patterns on the bass, but nothing stuck. He worked steadily for an hour, refilling his mug with tea at intervals until his senses dulled and reconfigured. He stared at a painting on the wall above his electric piano and tried to hypnotize himself- tried to lose track of what his hands were doing. He felt the cough syrup soften his perception of reality. Behind his eyelids he observed aristocrats in a scene from Tolstoy spinning gracefully across a ballroom. Opening his eyes, he saw the painting anew and his fingers began playing notes with an intelligence of their own.

Aside from a modest sum of cash and the cabin up north, the painting was the only thing his mother had left him. It depicted a train going over a bridge somewhere in Manitoba. There were clusters of massive spruce trees on either side of the bridge, branches bowed beneath thick slabs of snow. It was dusk and the sky was an explosion of soft pinks and bluish purples.

As his fingers continued to move of their own accord, the images in the painting blurred and reconfigured in an unsettling manner. Goblin hissed loudly – hackles up, claws out. She was tracking something with a predatory gaze. Something moved in the painting, rustling the trees slightly. As Goblin's hiss intensified into a series of shrieks, Charlie took back control of his hands and tossed some catnip on the carpet. She rubbed her face in it, rolling around wildly until she grew sedate, assuming a pose like a beached whale. Charlie shook his head and stared at the picture, reassuring himself that it had been a trick of the light. And yet, as he stared soberly into the picture, he perceived further rustling, accompanied by noises of scraping snow and ice. Something was moving behind the glass frame, in the painting.

A figure emerged from the trees and stood on the bridge, next to the motionless train. Charlie leaned forward, squinting. The figure was wearing a dark, hooded cloak, obscuring most of its features. Brown, furry hands peeked out from under the sleeves and a pair of glacial eyes glowed in the dark recess of the hood. Charlie reached out without thinking to kill the music, but the visitor whapped a snowball against the picture frame and let out a shrill bark. He heard the bark more in his head than in his ears and started with fright. The visitor pointed at him and pantomimed playing a guitar.

Understanding nothing, he resumed the bass part he'd stumbled upon. The visitor let out an ethereal cry that blossomed into a gorgeous lead melody. Once again, Charlie felt like he was hearing it more in his mind than in his ears. This went on for about an hour. Every once in a while, Charlie would loop the bass and swivel to the synthesizer, adding another textural layer. The piano loop was the steady beating heart of the piece, the visitor's melody was the dancing spirit. Everything else was sonic pudding.

Eventually the visitor gently brought the singing to rest. Charlie wrapped up his bass part, faded the other channels and clicked stop in the recording suite. He stared into the painting and a faint chill crept through him. There was something eerily familiar about the little creature. Charlie sensed it smiling from beneath the hood. The visitor bowed solemnly and trudged back into the forest, knocking snow from the spruce trees as it went. The painting was still once more.

Charlie stood up and poured the Nyquil down the drain. He emptied the box of herbal tea into the toilet and flushed it. Before he had a chance to brush his teeth, he was struck by a wave of paralyzing fatigue and collapsed on his bed fully clothed. As he was pulled down into sleep he finally made the connection between his mother and the visitor. Before he had a chance to explore this connection he was sucked down into a crevice so dark that he had the strange sensation he was floating in a trench of the ocean that lay buried beneath another body of water. He clicked on the light bulb that hung from his forehead only to remember, for the millionth time, that he was not, in fact, an anglerfish. For the first time in as long as he could remember, he remained in darkness and slept, absorbing the healing effects of a full night's sleep.

When he checked the playback the following morning he was simultaneously astonished and disturbed to discover that the alien sound was still in the mix.

CHAPTER 3

"I AIN'T A killer but please don't push me
    When I don't need my glock, I'm up in that tushy
    to the side, to the side, pull those panties to the side
    When I'm deep in my zone I just can't be denied"

Greg Chest was belting it out astride a weightlifting bench
with the full force of his million-dollar voice. Unfortunately,
his voice did not lend itself as well to hip-hop as it did to the
operatic works of Wolfgang Amadeus Mozart. Also regrettable
was the discomfort and annoyance he'd ignited in his fellow gym
members.

Either Greg was ignorant of the stir he was causing or he
simply didn't care. He was wearing noise-cancelling headphones
with the volume cranked, in addition to being incredibly high
from the electric vape-pen he'd recently purchased. The problem
with vaping was that he couldn't gauge when he'd had his fill and
erred reliably on the side of excess. His voice coach had insisted
that if he continued consuming cannabis he would need to
switch to vapour or edibles. He'd acquiesced grudgingly, though
he missed the tactile sensation of smoke in his lungs.

Greg laid down and slid beneath the bar, loaded with four
heavy plates, and heaved his way through another set. He sat up
again, dizzy from the exertion and blacked out for a split second,
forgetting his own identity and the most basic circumstances of
his life. As these details slowly reasserted themselves, a concept
emerged that he immediately seized upon as an irrefutable truth:
the place that human consciousness resides must be the cavern of
the mouth. Delighted by this revelation, he let his voice ring out,
a perfect note at the low end of his range. Every single person in

the weight room stopped what they were doing and became, for an instant, lost in the velvety depth of the vibration.

✧

At six-foot four-inches, weighing in at two hundred and thirty pounds, Greg cut an imposing figure. The premature sagging of his handsome, open face was thrown into relief by his light brown eyes, which still shone with a rapt sense of childlike anticipation. He was generally clean-shaven – his facial hair grew in patchy and uneven – and pampered his skin with expensive moisturizing products. A very large man to begin with, Greg built up his muscles in the gym and consumed a tremendous amount of food and booze, building up his gut, as well. Whenever he napped on the couch (which was often), his three children would jump on him, clinging for dear life as he rose and lumbered around like a bear awakening from hibernation.

Greg's iPhone vibrated in the pocket of his shorts between sets at the squat rack, interrupting Big Poppa; it was Errol. He'd been dodging his father's calls all morning, but between the weed and the endorphins he was ready to deal with him now. He jogged out of the conditioning room and up the stairs to the rooftop garden. He suspected for a second that the central Y was a Mesopotamian ziggurat, but he shook it off and answered the phone before it went to voicemail.

"Gregory?" Errol boomed. "Well, what'll it be? Did you get it?"

"Get what?" Greg was spinning in circles, taking in the tall buildings surrounding the rooftop garden, almost positive now that he was not in Mesopotamia.

"The role, dammit."

"Right. I got the call this morning. I didn't get it. They offered me Cosi Fan Tutte instead. Guglielmo."

The other end of the phone was silent.

"And you're content with that?" Errol asked eventually, his passive aggressive tone disintegrating Greg's buzz.

"It doesn't really matter how I feel about it, I'm just dealing with reality."

"And Dietrich Eichelberger will play Bluebeard?"

"Who else?"

Once more there was silence.

"Can I ask you something Gregory? Aren't you sick of being pigeon-holed as the opera buffa guy, the clown? Are you not sick of singing Mozart? Have you no love for Wagner? For serious opera?"

The word buffa evoked an image of soft cheese drizzled with warm oil. Greg's mouth started to water. "I like Mozart, Dad, I like buffa!" Greg held the phone away from his face, yelling into it. "Why are you so obsessed with Wagner?"

"Because it means something, Greg, it actually means something. It's important."

"You think Mozart doesn't mean anything?" Greg yelled, tripping over a stray solar panel.

Errol ignored the question. "Greg, I corralled the board in your favour, I made every recommendation – I just don't understand what you could have done to blow this."

"You think that helps?" he howled. "The general director is German, the musical director is German, if they felt like a board member was meddling on behalf of their son don't you imagine they'd feel compelled to give the beefier role to a guy with a name like Dietrich-fucking-Eichelberger."

"So, you think it's because of some nationalist conspiracy rather than your lack of experience with serious roles? They're not racists Greg, Jeezus. Sophie Rénard is co-starring." Greg threw the phone on the ground, smashing the screen.

"Ass Panda!" he screamed at the top of his lungs.

Sitting in the steam room, Greg tried to calm down. Why his father had this much power over him at this point, he did not know. He was his own man, was he not? Had he not travelled the world over, singing in the greatest opera houses, charming critics and audiences alike? His stage presence was legendary, his voice had been likened to an orgasmic tsunami, and his agent had more offers coming in than he could keep up with. Sure, all the good offers were for comedies, but so what? He liked comedies, he was funny. His father made it sound as if he were some sort of hack, but that was crazy; he was a specialist.

If Errol had his way, Greg would be playing Odin in Wagner's Ring Cycle. And what did that say about Errol? How insanely solipsistic did you have to be to entertain fantasies wherein your son was king of the gods?

I'm no Odin, Greg thought, but being typecast as Don Giovanni's not so bad. Then he frowned, remembering that every time he tried to be more than Don Giovanni, there seemed to be a Dietrich Eichelberger-shaped object in his way.

An hour later, having performed his intricate toilette, Greg climbed into his dark-purple PT Cruiser and piloted it towards Queen West where he was meeting Charlie for dinner. He was slightly calmer, but still ruffled enough to spark one of the pre-rolled joints he kept in the glove box, voice coach be damned. He merged with slow traffic on Dundas, chugging water out of a squeeze bottle between tokes.

By the time he was engaged in the near impossible act of parallel parking on Queen West during rush hour, Greg had just about forgotten his fight with Errol. To hell with Eichelberger, he thought, cutting the steering wheel and waving calmly at an ocean of homicidal drivers and cyclists. He can keep his precious Bluebeard and his Odin; those roles suck ass anyway.

He was just about to kill the engine when an ad on the public radio station caught his attention: "This Saturday, spend the afternoon with opera's hottest star, Dietrich Eichelberger, as he takes you backstage around the world."

Then, unexpected and uninvited, Eichelberger was in Greg's car, his thick, sophisticated voice seeping through the speakers. "And when I told him I'd been born to sing Don Quixote, ze director said to me, 'Don Quixote? But my dear boy I wouldn't even trust you to play ze donkey!' And of course, years later when I sang the role in Paris we had quite a laugh about zis."

He turned off the car, took a deep breath, counted to ten and then beat the shit out of his steering wheel. He allowed himself to say combinations of words much worse than ass panda.

CHAPTER 4

CHARLIE AND GREG had been best friends ever since they both wore the same Teenage Mutant Ninja Turtles sneakers to school on the first day of kindergarten. The two were joined at the hip throughout elementary school but hit a speed bump when it became clear that Greg was destined for an all boys' private school starting in Grade Seven. Charlie was obliged to wage a fierce campaign in defiance of his mother's scorn for private education, and after a tumultuous year of crying and yelling matches, he prevailed.

In the testosterone charged environment of St. Augustine's, Greg and Charlie were subjected to relentless bullying. Charlie's diminutive stature, shyness, and eccentricities (he mumbled and sang to himself and was perpetually lost in daydream) made him an obvious target. Greg, on the other hand, was persecuted partially due to the visible traits of his Japanese heritage, but more so on the basis of his association with Charlie: the freak. It was not uncommon for the lacrosse team to fold Charlie's tiny body into a plastic garbage bin and roll him down the stairs. Greg could have beat them up easily, but since the nefarious jocks could coordinate a false testimony, he almost always ended up landing in detention when he fought back. The oppression further cemented the duos' reliance on each other, to the exclusion of a more balanced social life.

As a boy, Charlie lived with his mother, Yana, on a residential street in Corso Italiano, a short streetcar ride west from uptown central. His childhood was relatively happy and as normal as one could expect in the context of being raised by a socialist artist. As Charlie reached adolescence, however, his mother's moods, which had always been mercurial, evolved into a diagnosis of manic depression. From time to time, Yana would check herself into a mental hospital on Queen West, and Charlie would stay with Greg and his convivial parents, Errol and Aoi, at their nearby house in Wychwood Park.

By this time, Charlie was already in the habit of accompanying Greg and his family to their chalet for winter vacation and to their cottage in the summertime. As the boys grew into teenagers, they would raid Errol's liquor cabinet and go woolly bagging (an activity that consisted of stripping the safety pads from chairlift pillars to sled down the ski hill), or paddle out to the middle of the lake and smoke pot as shooting stars washed over the sky.

When the boys were fifteen-years old, Yana fell through the ice near her small cabin on Canoe Lake and drowned. It was deemed an accidental death, but given her struggle with manic depression, suicide couldn't be ruled out. The following month, Aoi served Errol divorce papers, leaving him for a tech billionaire she'd been having an affair with.

Charlie was staying with the family on a temporary basis as this melodrama unravelled, and was officially adopted by Errol in the aftermath. The trio of abandoned men all found different ways of coping with the trauma: Errol continued to work but drank himself into oblivion at every opportunity; Greg continued going to school as if nothing had happened; and Charlie immersed himself in a cloud of dissociative pot smoke, cutting class to mess around on the neglected piano in Errol's living room.

As they sped towards graduation, Charlie sealed himself off from the world, marinating in anger and sadness. Greg took the opposite route, diving head-long into conventional pursuits: he became the star singer in St. Augustine's renowned choir and fostered a serious relationship with a girl from St. Mathilda's named Maggie, who eventually became his wife and the mother of his children. Upon graduating, Greg accepted a scholarship to a prestigious vocal program in London and embarked on an enviable career in the opera.

As Greg entered the bustling restaurant, Charlie noticed that his fists were clenched and swollen. His concern grew when, after a perfunctory hello, Greg flagged down their waiter and ordered a Negroni, a bottle of Montepulciano, eggplant stuffed with buffalo mozzarella, a plate of calamari, and a white pizza topped with anchovies and truffle oil.

Charlie smiled at him awkwardly. "You smell like a Rastafarian fraternity," he said. Greg did not laugh. "And what's up with the white pie? It's not pizza if it doesn't have red sauce on it."

Greg grunted. "My wrist is still fucked up from falling off that moving platform in Doctor Atomic. Physio says I'm going to have arthritis in my left wrist. According to Maggie, nightshade vegetables cause inflammation, so tomato is out."

"I hate to be the bearer of bad news, but eggplant is also in the nightshade family."

Greg's Negroni arrived and he drank it in a single gulp. "Life without aubergine," he pondered aloud. "That's a bleak motherfucking prospect."

Charlie eyed him suspiciously. "Have you been playing Nintendo again?"

"Yeah sure, just a little."

"It's never just a little with you, you're a maniac. I thought Maggie smashed your SNES."

Greg cringed at the traumatic memory. "I bought a used one from the internet for, like, five hundred dollars. I sneak out back to the gardening shed with a couple beers and go buck wild playing Contra whenever I can manage."

"Garden shed? What kind of a life are you living? What does Maggie think you're doing back there?"

"I don't know," said Greg, listlessly. "Jacking off?"

The food began to arrive, and Greg set about meticulously removing the buffalo mozzarella from the eggplant. Buffalo Buffa Mozzarella Mozart. The words ran through his mind rhythmically – a compulsive new mantra. Charlie sipped his sparkling water and munched on the calamari. He considered telling Greg about the creature that had visited him earlier that week, but determined that his friend would only conclude that he was losing his mind.

"I ran into Sophie Rénard on the streetcar the other day. How come you never mentioned you two sing together? She said she lost her virginity to you in a garden shed?"

Greg almost did a spit take. He managed to swallow the wine, but it went down the wrong tube and he coughed violently. "My relationship with garden sheds has changed," he finally croaked.

"Anyway," Charlie pushed on, "she and I really hit it off but she left abruptly before I had a chance to get her number, do you have it on you?"

Greg stiffened at this request, took a moment to wipe his mouth carefully and consider his words. "I don't know, Charlie, everyone in the opera community is obsessed with Sophie. She's a handful. You have a hard enough time already, the last thing you need is to have your heart broken."

"Don't be an asshole, just give me her number. Is it weird because you slept with her a million years ago?"

"That's not – Jeezus, we were basically children. Don't try to make a pimp out of me, it's uncomfortable."

"Whatever," Charlie said, rotating his glass in frustration. "I guess I'm just sick of being alone."

Greg swirled his wine, sipped it, and lifted an eyebrow. "Are you kidding me? Alone time is a luxury. Your life is amazing. You get paid to make music, you're signed to a hip record label, you can eat snacks in bed and watch Tarantino movies whenever you want. I have three kids who live to eat and shit and contradict me, a marriage that is – to be quite frank – probably falling apart, and a father who thinks I'm not good enough no matter what I do. I don't even remember what it's like to be alone. Plus, that fungal infection I had a few months ago is making a wicked comeback," he concluded, shifting uncomfortably in his seat.

"Well, at least you've got a nice voice so you can sing yourself a sad, sad song," Charlie said, stealing a slice of Greg's pizza. "Grass is always greener."

"Grass is always greener," Greg repeated, holding his glass up. "I'll drink to that."

"You'll drink to anything." Charlie clinked his glass against Greg's and they each took a sip, maintaining ludicrously intense eye contact and screwing up their faces.

A bowl of gnocchi and a grilled lamb shank arrived. "I completely forgot to ask," Charlie said. "Which role did you get?"

Greg hesitated. "Guglielmo."

"I bet Errol wasn't too happy about that."

"He talks to you about that shit?" Greg was turning a deep shade of red with anger and also from eating and drinking too fast.

"Hey, at least you know the role, right?"

"I can't win," Greg whined. He started eating the deflated eggplant carcasses but Charlie didn't call him out. "In Canada, everyone sees me as Errol's kid, and in Europe – Eichelberger is the king of Europe! Either he steals all the serious roles or the directors think I'm a clown. I just got an offer for The Flying Dutchman in Bulgaria. It's not exactly Salzburg, but at least I'd get a chance to flex some dramatic muscles."

When they finished their mains, the waiter brought out raspberry tarts with mascarpone and a glass of grappa for Greg. "Is it mascarpone or marscapone? I can never remember," Greg said, not really caring what the answer was. "Hey, did you hear about the hobo that got hit by the streetcar last week?"

"What? No."

"It was practically outside your apartment."

"Did he die?"

Greg nodded. "It was a huge news story."

"I don't look at the news. Since when do the media make such a big deal over one dead hobo."

"It wasn't just some rando," Greg paused for dramatic effect, "turned out it was Luka Lampo, the famous pianist and composer."

Charlie stared blankly.

"Seriously? For your birthday last year, I gave you a record, remember?" Charlie looked down at his plate, embarrassed – Greg's unsolicited attempts to 'elevate' his musical tastes were mostly in vain. "Beethoven's Emperor Concerto, Kyoto, nineteen eighty-nine. Lampo destroyed on the piano. He was one of the only guys who could throw down a really solid Rachmaninoff. No one had seen him in years; his last public appearance was like twenty years ago." Charlie's gaze drifted to a busy waitress covered in mesmerizing tattoos. "Anyway, once the body was I.D.'d the Finnish government flew him home, there was a huge funeral in Helsinki, a tribute concert with the best pianists in Europe. I mean, what are the chances? Here, look."

Greg took out his phone and pulled up a picture: a handsome man with a big, jowly face and a fat, red nose; a light sheen of stubble and a vertical shock of curly hair; cigarette hanging from the side of his mouth. Charlie turned white and pushed his mascarpone away.

"I used to see that guy every day."

"What!?"

"He lived at the shelter across the street, I gave him change sometimes and we talked about the weather. Well. . . I talked about the weather. I think he was mute."

"You're sure it's the same guy?"

Charlie stared at the picture. "He had a wild beard and he was filthy, but the eyes are unmistakable. Same guy."

Greg sat back in his seat. "Well that's fucking interesting."

By the time they left the restaurant, Charlie was turning into a pumpkin. In order to weather even a brief evening of conversation he was obliged to rest all day, sheltering himself from any form of stimulation. When Greg suggested a walk in the park he resolved to push on through the fog, knowing that he'd pay for it later.

The sun was setting as they entered Trinity Bellwoods. It was still hot for late September and the park was littered with packs of hipsters huddled in circles drinking beer. Someone had written WHEN WILL YOU COME HOME in bright yellow fabric on the tennis court fence. Greg and Charlie walked along the edge of the dog bowl, watching a Great Dane wrestle an English Mastiff. They settled on a bench.

"Do you ever have sex dreams about your dad?" Greg asked, out of nowhere.

"What? No," Charlie replied. "You mean my dad or your dad? Errol? I don't even know who my dad is."

"I've just been reading about psychology and Freud on the internet. Apparently it's quite common."

"Don't read Freud, read Jung. He's groovier. Hey, can you talk to Sophie for me, but actually?"

"Oh boy. You're really not going to let this one go, are you?"

Charlie shook his head. Greg stretched a bearish arm out behind Charlie.

"You sure you're up for this? When was your last entanglement? Gwen? Five years ago? You were pretty fucked up after that. Please understand, I'm just trying to get your back."

"Don't," Charlie said, growing irritated with fatigue. "Don't baby me, it's offensive."

A fraction of the sky was painted pink beneath a bright, cuticle moon.

"I'm not babying you, I just don't want you to get hurt. Look, I'll give her your number, okay? If she's interested she'll call. Just remember not to leave your phone off the hook, alright stud?"

"Okay. Fine," Charlie said. "Thank you. I can't stay in the cocoon forever, it's depressing. I'll lose my mind, end up like my mom," Charlie sighed, he knew he was being melodramatic. "I need someone in my life. My D'Angelo records are getting dusty."

"At least you have your music."

"It's not enough, you know that."

"Wish I could take some of that lonely off your hands. Seriously, I'm gonna do a reverse Lampo one of these days, run off to Scandinavia, find myself a flaxen maid and learn how to yodel."

"I think yodelling is Swiss."

"I'll be remembered as the man who brought yodelling to Finland."

They dissolved into laughter and then yodelled at the top of their lungs, setting off a chain reaction of barking throughout the park.

After Greg went home, Charlie sat alone in the park staring at the WHEN WILL YOU COME HOME sign. He could not remember Beethoven's Emperor Concerto and instead a song from Stereolab's Emperor Tomato Ketchup flowed through some loose, flapping corner of his brain. He pictured the homeless man from outside his building at a piano in a pristine tux playing along with a furrowed brow. After a time, he tried to get up, but a massive weight pulled him down. He fell briefly to sleep on the bench and woke at midnight, teeth chattering violently. He shuffled home in confusion, the streetlamps of Queen lighting his way. Having deposited himself on the bed, he lay wide awake through the rest of the night enveloped in a forcefield of melancholy.

CHAPTER 5

ACCORDING TO THE doctor, the diagnosis of fibromyalgia came down to a small piece of the brain called the hypothalamus: A major control centre integral to sleep, hormonal function and the regulation of the nervous system; life without a functioning hypothalamus often seemed like a life not worth living at all. And maybe, just maybe, if his doctor wasn't so confident that this morsel of brain matter was merely hibernating – rather than dead – Charlie would have chugged down a cocktail of sleeping pills and bourbon by now and drifted blissfully into the great blue yonder.

Without the cooperation of his hypothalamus, Charlie could barely sleep. His most lucid and productive hours tended to be between 10 p.m. and 4 a.m., on account of an inverted circadian rhythm. If he clocked five hours of sleep at night, he was elated. His pituitary gland was blind to its purpose, which meant that he suffered from low adrenaline and testosterone. He often found himself drenched in sweat as a wonky nervous system jacked his pulse up, causing his heart to bang like a club anthem.

Worst of all was the chronic pain, which slithered around his body willy-nilly. Sometimes it would relent for weeks at a time, only to return with a vengeance the moment he became hopeful. When he rubbed an afflicted muscle, the dull pain morphed into a sharp, stabbing sensation. It felt like he was rubbing a sack of angry marbles, as if some sinister insect had laid brittle eggs inside him that possessed a life of their own.

In addition to this shit storm of unpleasant sensations, his mind would go completely blank from time to time, leaving him utterly disoriented once it rebooted. He'd come to in the aisle of a grocery store – spinach in hand, classic rock on the stereo, fluorescent lights humming overhead – and have no idea what to make of it all. He might end up staggering into the street with a plastic basket of food, ELO trailing after him: there's a hole in my head where the rain comes in.

His experience of the world felt like a puppet show. He recalled Plato's allegory of the cave from high school philosophy and empathized deeply with those poor souls, mistaking shadows for reality. What he craved more than anything was clarity, an even continuity of experience, a 1:1 correlation between what was perceived and what truly was. Like anyone else, he had good weeks and bad weeks, but his bad weeks were torturous and his good weeks, 'fine' at best.

Despite his struggles, Charlie felt that he had some small understanding of the world outside of his cocoon, namely that it was completely backwards and insane. Once, while visiting Errol, he'd flipped through an issue of The Economist and learned that the Chinese government was employing a process called quantum entanglement (Einstein's term was "spooky action at a distance") to send uncrackable code via a satellite launched from the Gobi Desert, which fired a laser beam through a specially designed crystal. Charlie despaired to live in a world where humans launched satellites that shot communication lasers through special crystals. It was simply too much.

He mostly avoided the news, but he knew that the bees were dying, along with thousands of other species; shiploads of refugees were drowning in the cruel, cold seas; corporate villainy was rapidly decimating the earth. Meanwhile, most North Americans had been lulled into slumberous apathy by the Netflixitization of culture, by cheap access to sophisticated media.

Peeking through the shiny glass facades of the sleek cafés that populated Queen West, Charlie became an amateur anthropologist studying the ubiquitous pod people, inhabitants of the laptop villages jacked into a stream of media that seemed to be turning their brains to a dull, grey porridge. With very few exceptions, the pod people's faces rested in lazy frowns. As an outside observer, Charlie had developed a talent for reading people's inner experiences through their faces. The pod people's faces most often betrayed a mix of loneliness, longing, and disappointment.

The way they moved through the world bumping into each other, yammering with invisible interlocutors, betrayed a high degree of alienation from their own bodies and material environments. Most of the people in his culture, he concluded, did not have a 1:1 relationship with reality, but interacted with it through a thick static that clouded direct experience. He simultaneously hated and envied them.

As far as Charlie understood, the 1:1 had rarely been within his own mother's reach. Yana's labour-intensive youth, split between schooling and farm work in rural Saskatchewan, had been punctuated by a mental breakdown. Through a therapeutic practice of painting, she'd slowly pieced herself back together, producing her first significant body of work. Shortly thereafter, she'd gone to art-school in Toronto on a scholarship (much to her parents' dismay) and then travelled to Europe where she achieved a great deal of fame.

After a decade of bouncing between Paris, Berlin, and Amsterdam, Yana had moved back to Toronto, and Charlie was born some five months later. Thus, Charlie surmised, it was during this European chapter that she must have met his father. Although it upset him, it was impossible not to wonder if her decision to leave Europe wasn't motivated by the pregnancy.

For the first decade of Charlie's life, Yana was stable and relatively content. She painted every day, gave guest lectures at the art college, read voraciously and socialized with a small number of intimate friends. He grew into a young adolescent untouched by the dark patterns hibernating beneath the surface of her mind. Those years of clarity, between the creation of Yana's initial works and her rapid slide into manic depression, constituted a section of her life that might have been titled The Good Years: a period of lucid engagement had emerged out of chaos only to be enshrouded in darkness once more.

When they were thirteen years old – Yana was in pretty bad shape by that point – Greg and Charlie took mushrooms for the first time, at Errol's cottage. Having no point of reference, they ate the whole bag and spent the day navigating trips that seasoned psychonauts would have found challenging. Lying on a bed of lichen on a rock near the water with his eyes closed, Charlie felt an asteroid crash and saw the crust of the world tossed up into space as lava spurted everywhere, quickly drying to a black crust. Reality turned over, and he was a bee flying through a serene meadow on a new, rejuvenated planet. He landed on a beautiful orange flower, honing in on its sensual piston. He came out of the trip in the throes of arousal, but the feeling quickly turned to nausea and he was sick off the end of the rock, disturbing a troop of ducks swimming along the shoreline.

As the mother duck guided her ducklings away from the vomiting, hairless ape, Charlie connected with her, and his attention turned to his own mother. He felt a peculiar kind of knowledge expanding in his veins: his mother was a beacon of authentic wisdom, and she was not long for this world.

It was just a few months after the mushroom trip that Yana died. In the final years of her life, her direction as an artist had taken a drastic and puzzling turn. Yana had initially become famous for her abstract style: geometric patterns dancing across the canvas; alien objects in outer-space; panoramic dreamscapes and blocks of textured colour. She subscribed to Kandinsky's theory that truth in art was dictated by an inner need, that you could always recognize honest art by the subtle ripples and vibrations it stirred up in the subject's soul.

Above all else was the principle that whatever element of a painting could not be expressed in language was by nature its most valuable component. Once, Charlie overheard Yana telling a friend that music was probably the noblest art because its expression was independent from form. Long after he'd lost the explicit memory, this pious devotion to the abstract became the cornerstone of his musical career.

In her final years, however, Yana completely betrayed this conviction. She renounced everything she had ever painted as a pack of skillful lies and re-invented herself as a stylized landscape artist in the vein of The Group of Seven. Before she lost her life in the icy depths of Canoe Lake, she produced a staggering body of new paintings that baffled and perplexed the art world. She never bothered to respond to the hubbub, by that time she was in a manic tailspin, squirreled away at her cabin working like mad or recovering in the hospital.

Before Yana's death, visiting artists regarded Canoe Lake (the scene of Tom Thomson's mysterious death) with a sinister superstition. Afterwards, they avoided it like the plague. Ask anyone and they'd tell you: you'd have to be insane to paint on Canoe Lake, genuinely bent on your own destruction. Yana had stipulated in her will that Charlie offer up the cabin to emerging artists free of charge when he wasn't using it (he never used it), but no one ever responded to the ad that he diligently posted on local community boards every spring. The fact that no struggling painter was desperate enough to take up residence there spoke volumes.

Several years after his mother's death, when Charlie started releasing music under the name Cave Music, he generally dodged questions from the press about his mother and her influence on his music. Her landscape works had been validated by general consensus as the years tumbled by, increasing her posthumous fame. The family connection was too juicy for most interviewers to pass over, and Charlie had become adept at the art of stonewalling, which he found easy. In any case, his music followed the principle of expression without form and resisted biographical interpretations. He wasn't about to give the press some tearful anecdote they could turn into a sound bite. It would've gone against what Yana stood for; it would have been cheap.

On the topic of his father, not much can be related. At a certain age, Yana explained to Charlie that she'd only known the man for a brief time and that even if she wanted to, it would have been impossible to track him down. Despite her iron will on the subject, Charlie had seized on something Yana said to him the year he'd grown enthusiastic about playing the piano: It's alright if you want to become a musician, she'd told him, just promise me you'll never fall in love with one, no matter what.

He wouldn't have thought this strange, except that his mother tended to shy away from categorical judgments – she favoured a case-by-case system that allowed for flexibility. Thus, Charlie came to believe that whoever his father was, he must have been a musician. Once Yana was beyond the veil, however, Charlie had to accept that he would never know his father. He was an orphan in a strange land, not quite ready to die but not quite living either. His compulsion for creating and capturing squiggly vibrations – expression without form – was simply a way to pass the time until he died or (he dared not hope) until some strange event jolted his hypothalamus back to life.

CHAPTER 6

THE DAY AFTER his dinner with Greg, Charlie was in bad shape. The expenditure of energy required for social outings always left him feeling drained, but it was a price he was willing to pay to feel normal once in a while. He spent the afternoon on the couch listening to Arthur Russel as Goblin purred consolingly on his chest. Around sundown he defied the force field of fatigue and stood up abruptly, frightening the overweight cat who'd forgotten she was perched on a living creature.

A streaming service had commissioned Charlie to score a series documenting the behaviour of sea creatures such as vampire squids and giant tube worms. They'd re-edited it on a whim a month before it was scheduled for release, consequently rendering the score that Charlie had prepared next to useless. To meet their demands, he'd have to spend his precious ration of daily energy laying down hazy synth tracks, setting the tone for the mating rituals of cuckolding cuttlefish.

After two hours of solid work, he staged an unsuccessful attempt to play with Goblin. She'd resumed dozing on a heating vent behind his record collection and clearly had no intention of doing anything else for the foreseeable future. To persist would have meant risking a nasty scratch.

He gave a quick listen to an updated mix of Manic Toads, which now included the otherworldly sonic stylings of the mysterious visitor. These additions had completely revolutionized the record, turning it on its head so that it was now bursting with vitality. It sounded unlike anything Charlie had ever recorded, but in such a way that was still consistent with his catalogue. He emailed the new demos to Noodles, threw on a flannel and walked two blocks to grab a slice and a soda.

On the walk home, a bright glow down an unfamiliar laneway

caught Charlie's eye. No sooner had he glanced at it that he was tugged – half-walking, half-floating – towards it. He felt he was caught in a tractor beam with folded pizza in one hand and ginger ale in the other. The light was coming from a sign emblazoned with the logo of the Toronto Transit Commission. Beneath it was a set of stairs leading underground. Charlie finished the pizza and walked into the mouth of the stairway. After a time, the light diminished and then disappeared.

He clung to the handrail and descended slowly, feeling out the steps as he went. He should have been frightened, but he felt as though he was precisely where he ought to be, that the night was proceeding in a logical and orderly fashion. For how long he descended those steps he could not have said; time had taken on a fluid and reversible quality. When he finally reached the bottom, he found it uncomfortably bright, owing to an ornate chandelier that hung from the panelled, metallic ceiling. The floor was made up of glistening terra cotta tiles, the walls were adorned with patent leather and regal floral patterns.

As his vision returned, Charlie made out a tree sprouting from a patch of soil, breaking up the tiles. It was a small zelkova tree, with little purple branchlets and rough orange inner bark peeking through in a couple places. He took a deep breath and found the air to be especially fresh and fragrant, as though it were being pumped in from an outside source. On the other side of the room there was a creepy statue of a bird the size of a large, adult human.

As Charlie walked further into the room, he was transfixed by the statue: the bird was a pied raven with bright orange rings around its glistening dark eyes. It was hyper-realistic, like a taxidermy specimen, and it was moving now, hopping towards him with little wing flaps. Charlie panicked and turned to run, but found he could not move. He was paralyzed. The bird gave him a reassuring look (his face was strangely expressive) that mildly assuaged his panic. When it opened its beak, it was the deep voice of a macho 1950's movie star rather than a feeble chirp that echoed through the large subterranean chamber: "Mr. Potichny, I'm glad you finally found your way down. I've been waiting here for some time. My name is Mizza, pleased to meet you." The bird placed a wing to his chest and gave a little bow. "I can see by the expression on your face that you're surprised and frightened by the situation. I understand that in your world avian beings of my size are uncommon and possess neither the intelligence nor the proper biological equipment to communicate with you, let alone in your own language. Well Mr. Potichny, I am not from your world."

"Where the fuck am I?" Charlie said. "What are you doing to me?" He still couldn't move.

"Please Mr. Potichny, relax, I'm not going to hurt you. Quite the contrary, I'm here to help you."

"Who are you?"

"I'm a diplomat from a reality that lies on the other side of a small crack in the spacetime continuum. Our worlds are joined by a subtle strand that up until this point has borne no relevance. Up until this point. Please Mr. Potichny, you look rather pale, try to relax, breathe. Why don't you have a seat in the chaise and gather your wits, we have much to discuss. You see, a situation has arisen."

Mizza gestured to a luxurious chaise longue that had materialized near the zelkova tree. Charlie found that he could move again. He walked cautiously to the chair and sat down on its edge. He placed his hands over his eyes and massaged his face. He wondered if he was experiencing a prolonged hallucination. Maybe his body was still up in the pizzeria, planted in front of the glowing soda fridge. The bird called Mizza spoke up again, and Charlie tried his best to follow along.

"Mr. Potichny, I'll be blunt, for the first time in the history of our two worlds there has been a breach. A vile creature by the name of Philip – what your people might call a terrorist – has escaped from captivity. He is neither bird nor man, rather, he is a sinister amalgam: a creature born of misguided experimentation. Something akin to the creature in your popular fable, The Modern Prometheus by Mary Shelley."

"You mean Frankenstein?"

"Whichever title pleases you, Mr. Potichny, the moral is the same: going against nature is tantamount to playing with fire. We learned that the hard way."

"Tantamount," Charlie repeated.

"Let us return to the crucial issue – Philip, that is. Given the appropriate circumstances he will be able to access and open something called a StormBox: an invisible stress point between dimensions that can activate catastrophic chain reactions when disrupted. If that happens. . ." Mizza trailed off and stared solemnly at the ground. "Mr. Potichny, have you ever had the feeling you were waiting for your life to begin in earnest, that you were destined for something more?"

Charlie had to admit that he'd often felt that way. At the same time, the question felt like a palm reader's trick and stirred his sense of cynicism.

"We've been tracking his movements, and we're inclined to believe that Philip contacted you recently. You are most certainly our best option."

"The creature in the painting," Charlie said in a low voice. He was beginning to suspect that what he was seeing and hearing was correlated, in some remote sense, to reality.

"That's absolutely correct. Having been in contact with Philip, you are in a unique position to help us capture him. He moves through your world in works of visual art and seems to have a predilection for your mother's paintings as well as your sonic transmissions – your music, I should say. We are confident that he will visit you again. When he does, you are to pull the painting in which he appears from the wall, this will deprive him of an escape route. At that point I will contact you with further instructions. In return, you will be cured of your lethargic disease, your. . . fibromyalgia, as the medical books would have it. In fact, as a token of good faith, we will lift your condition presently, also that you might complete your assigned task with added vim. There may be a slight delay, no more than a single rotation of the planet."

"I don't understand. If you have the power to cure me, why can't you capture Philip on your own?"

Mizza's beak curled slightly into what Charlie thought might be a smile. "Make no mistake my good man, Philip is a cunning foe. If we came straight after him he'd smell us a mile off. Besides, navigating your world would be rather awkward due to our unusual appearance. Given the situation, you are most certainly – excuse the reiteration – our best option. Perhaps our only option."

"Okay." Charlie finally lay back in the chair. "I'll think it over. To be honest I'm hoping that this is a dream, because otherwise I must be insane, or maybe I've been drinking cough syrup again. I hate to be rude, but I don't think you're really real."

Mizza puffed out his spotted breast and spoke with a stern tone. He appeared vibrantly alive, more so, in fact, than the world above. "I assure you Mr. Potichny, as mad as this all seems, it is very, very real. Our respective worlds hang in the balance. I've got sixteen eggs in the nest back home and a beautiful wife. I intend on protecting them. I imagine there must be something in this world that you feel is worth protecting. I urge you not to treat the situation lightly. Take an honest look inside yourself Mr. Potichny, I trust you'll know just what to do. And in the meantime, beware Philip's tricks. His song is sweet, but there is blackness in his heart. You'd do well to remember that."

"Sure thing Mizza," Charlie mumbled.

A speck of light appeared in the air behind Mizza and rippled out, tearing at the empty space until it formed a perfectly symmetrical black hole big enough for the feathered diplomat to hop through. Just before he disappeared into it he turned to Charlie, raised a wingtip to his brow and saluted.

"Godspeed Potichny. Heavens knows how many lives rest on those frail shoulders."

And then he was gone. The horizontal pancake zipped shut instantaneously and Charlie finally laid back in the chaise.

He stayed down in the chamber with his thoughts for long enough that the experience took on a real feel, and the flow of time righted itself. He hollered and yodeled, testing out the acoustics, and found them to be most satisfactory. Finally, once he'd admitted to himself that he was in a real place and discounted the possibility that he was experiencing a prolonged hallucination, he gathered himself up and made for the exit.

Later that night, after Charlie had climbed the interminable stairs in exhaustion and tumbled into bed next to Goblin, he began twitching wildly in his sleep. It was not Philip or Mizza that he dreamed of, but the multi-coloured carnival comprising the creatures of the deep. Most of these creatures were diaphanous and without sight, lonely lost beings shrouded in depth and darkness. In many ways Charlie felt he could relate, and although there was sadness in this pathos, he found there was also a surprising element of comfort: the stubborn pride of creating an identity based on exclusion, rather than participation. As he slept, he realized that the comfort of exclusion was a sickness, not exactly part of his condition but an accidental by-product.

He sunk to a depth where giant tube worms fed on microscopic bacteria growing on the heat valves from an underwater volcano. Passing through the largest valve, he was massaged and sucked by the hungry red worms that were like hundreds of sentient flowers. He emerged in the darkness of nowhere, the worms had cleaned his body of all superfluous organic matter – in fact his consciousness seemed to have shuffled loose from his cumbersome bag of bones entirely. There was something huge swimming around him, but it chose not to show itself. Or perhaps he refused to see it. Now and then its warm scales brushed against him, but rather than unsettling him, the contact comforted him, so that he began to fall asleep within his own dream.

He came to understand that this creature was bigger than anything that existed in reality – bigger than a blue whale, whose arteries are big enough for a human to swim through. The creature was like a snake or an eel the size of a dinosaur and possessed a remarkable grace and precision of movement that was ancient and poetic. In his dream, Charlie went to sleep, tumbling through a trapdoor in his unconscious to a silent, secret place.

And in the secret place he was repaired.

CHAPTER 7

HE WOKE UP the following morning feeling like a new man. There was no pain, no fatigue; he was actually smiling as he got out of bed and reached for his bathrobe. He ran towards Goblin, wanting to dance with her, but she shrieked and dove behind a bookshelf.

Charlie fixed himself a bowl of granola and switched off the white noise loop, allowing the raw din of Queen Street to enter his apartment for the first time in years. He poured a glass of juice and swallowed some vitamins. The sound of life outside the cocoon was inviting rather than hostile. He closed his eyes and felt his heart beating, observed the gentle rise and fall of his breath. He felt clear. It was only 9:30 a.m. and yet he wanted to go outside. His mood darkened suddenly, as he recalled his encounter with the giant bird.

Could it plausibly have been a dream? The walk to the pizzeria and the strange encounter? At very least, the visitor in the painting, Philip, had left some evidence of his existence. Judging by the unprecedented energy with which Charlie had awoken, Mizza had made good on his promise, but at the same time there was the possibility that it was just a coincidence.

As the ancient grains crunched between his teeth, Charlie constructed a theory that dismissed a deeper concern: being of an especially artistic, imaginative nature, his unconscious mind was weaving a constellation of symbols and episodes, guiding him towards a higher expression of his own art and a wholeness of his fractured psyche. Perhaps there was no Philip, no Mizza, he was simply tapping into a part of himself that had been compartmentalized for so long that it could only express itself as other, as characters and environments that appeared strange and foreign.

He must have created the track attributed to Philip – he'd work out what combination of instruments and effects he'd used later on. Likewise, his discipline and dedication to recovery were to thank for this sudden improvement in mood and energy, not some giant bird. He felt good, he actually felt happy, why complicate things with unanswerable questions? It was too early to trust the good feelings, but he resolved to take advantage of it while it lasted.

Congratulating himself for formulating such an intelligent and plausible explanation, Charlie threw on his shoes and flannel, scarf and cap, made a funny face at Goblin and sprang down the stairs, out into the blustery day.

Fall was in full swing that week, and Charlie took advantage of the agreeable weather, walking as far as he pleased as the red and yellow leaves drifted down around him, turning to mush in the streets. He walked north to Casa Loma, a genuinely impressive, probably haunted castle overlooking the city from the north, then east to the Allan Gardens Conservatory where he wandered through the humid foliage and stood transfixed by dozens of baby turtles piling on top of one another, and then west to Roncesvalles village where he sampled a variety of Polish delicacies and scoured vintage shops for old books and records. Each day was blissful and strange, tinged with subtle hues of longing and contentment that swirled together, blending into something complex and altogether new.

Each day, when he arrived home from his outings with fresh groceries in tow from the market, he'd throw on an Art Tatum record he hadn't touched in years and listen to it over and over again. It wasn't even Tatum's playing that he was listening for, but the sounds produced by Buddy DeFranco on the clarinet. His life had taken on a feeling of brightness and lightness that he could not distinguish from the dazzling flutter of those virtuosic fingers, the melodies and tone which represented, at a ratio of 1:1, the texture of life unshackled from fatigue and chronic pain.

Late in that autumnal week, on a sunny, breezy day that would herald a full moon, Charlie resolved to visit the Art Gallery of

Ontario. The Gallery was not far from his apartment, and yet he had avoided it since he was a schoolboy, most likely out of a deep-seated aversion for anything associated with Yana. He could feel a part of himself going cold at the prospect, but he couldn't hide forever, he had to push through the discomfort.

The light from outside took on a viscous, honeyed quality as it passed through the massive glass panels of the gallery's exterior, spilling into the foyer. Clipping the bright metallic tag onto his shirt, he headed up to the second floor and entered a room dedicated to the works of Artemis Gwillimbury. Gwillimbury was a landscape painter – perhaps the most famous Canadian artist in the world – and a total recluse. He'd never made a public appearance, and he refused to sign or date his paintings, supposedly on the principle that they should be judged on their own merit. Gwillimbury's style was so iconic, however, that a signature would have been superfluous.

His favourite subject was the arctic portion of the Canadian west coast. As Charlie gazed at a painting of a mountainous, snow-capped island protruding from the Pacific Ocean, he felt, for a moment, as if there was no one else in the gallery. And then even Charlie himself seemed to disappear and all that was left was nature, unseen and untouched, not a soul around for miles: the intelligent, self-sufficient shades of blue retreated inward at a nearly imperceptible rate, the white of the snowcaps suggested a lifeless ice age, a canvas of infinite possibilities.

He spent an hour in the Gwillimbury room, taking in every square inch of every canvas, letting it wash over him. Eventually, he arrived at a rare black and white photograph of the artist himself, wearing a paint stained dress shirt unbuttoned to the solar plexus, eyes burning out of his handsome, square jawed face like sapphires. The photo was accompanied by text: The enigmatic Artemis Gwillimbury was born in Toronto in 1956. In the only interview he ever gave he stated that the guiding principles of his art are borrowed from the occult philosophy of Theosophism. When asked what Theosophy is, Gwillimbury replied "I couldn't really say." His current whereabouts are unknown.

From the Gwillimbury room, Charlie turned a corner and found himself in the presence of several of his mother's abstract works. He was surprised to find that he had no love whatsoever for the paintings; he couldn't see past the smears and splotches. Yana had invented her own visual language, dedicating a painstaking amount of effort to honing form and style. These paintings had no shortage of admirers. For Charlie, however, who had never actively engaged with them, their abstract nature distanced them from a universal experience, rather than eliciting some profound vibration of the spirit.

An awful thought struck Charlie: what if his music was the sonic equivalent of these obtuse paintings. His mother's phrase, "expression without form," came loose in his memory. He thought of his music as a sanctuary for the lonely, but this sanctuary was exclusive by nature. He spoke to a select few, expressed the deeper feelings of the loners and shored up their collective sense of being disconnected. Maybe accessible art wasn't so bad after all. Everybody loved Gwillimbury's work, for example, and he'd just had a transcendental experience because of its simplicity, its effortless beauty.

He walked back into the atrium lost in thought and ascended the spiraling central staircase. The glass exterior provided a view of the rooftops of Kensington Market, a neighbourhood so well preserved that Charlie temporarily had the sensation that he was looking at a version of the city from the middle of the 20th century. Sun poked through the clouds, creating a cinematic effect; swallows raced around church spires in harmonious swells; a skein of geese appeared, skimming the bottom of a silver cloud.

Resuming his journey up the winding staircase, he came upon an alcove featuring a solitary painting. It was one of Yana's landscapes, a panorama of the Canadian prairies. Separate weather systems could be perceived in the sky, traces of red and gold from a sun veiled in a light haze that gradually transitioned into dark menacing clouds and a yellow web of lightning striking against the blackened sky. She'd captured the effect of rain falling at various speeds and densities on a curving horizon that was faithfully depicted through some phenomenal trick, as if the canvas itself was convex.

The picture caught him off guard, and he began weeping uncontrollably, tremors sweeping up and down his nervous system. A group of patrons passed behind him, and he hunched over, trying to muffle his sobs. Whatever frozen blockage had been holding him back all these years, physically and emotionally, was beginning to thaw. He decided that he would work with the gallery and soundtrack Yana's exhibit.

CHAPTER 8

THE BRUCE PENINSULA Royal Trillium Oil Concern was a huge brick building on the eastern edge of the downtown waterfront, adjacent to the towering condos of the Distillery District. The Toronto Opera had purchased it in 1972 for a meager sum. Previously, it had lain dormant for a decade, and by the present day, most people could not comprehend what the words Oil and Concern meant in relation to each other.

When more than one production was in rehearsal, mock stages were marked off at either end of the space. In between the makeshift stages lay heaps of props, costumes and monolithic sets from mothballed productions. At the eastern edge of the Concern, Dietrich Eichelberger quietly slipped in (early as always), proceeded to the halfway mark, leaned against the wall, frowned at his script and began scribbling notes. Every so often he glanced up at the rehearsal in progress. His imposing frame (he was the only man in the opera scene taller than Greg) was draped in a cashmere V-neck sweater, exposing his waxed, muscular chest. He wore loose fitting woolen trousers and black deck shoes with no socks.

Greg had tried wearing shoes with no socks one summer, but it had led to a severe case of athlete's foot. He was plainly jealous of Eichelberger's effortless style. His square jaw was padded with a full, neatly trimmed beard. Greg, in a sudden fit of jealousy, wondered if he'd been denied the Bluebeard role because he couldn't grow a good beard. His thoughts wallowed in insecurity as he waited for the musical director, Otto Von Strohn, to finish lecturing the musicians: "No, no, no, no, no, you're playing it like daa-da-daa-da-daa, slightly behind the beat, but what I'd really like would be for you to play it da-da-da-da-daaa. Come in on top of the beat, even a hair early is good, and really emphasize that last beat."

Who fucking cares? Greg wanted to yell. No one's going to notice. Not one fucking person in the audience will be able to tell the difference. His thoughts swiftly shifted to single malt Scotch, and he was by and large lost to the rehearsal.

From the time he'd first seen it performed, to the first time he'd performed in it, Greg had always found the second act of Cosi Fan Tutte tedious. Now, in his reprisal of the role of Guglielmo, he grew exasperated and irritable as the opera stretched on interminably. Rehearsal was a drag. As he bellowed out the lines by rote, his mind drifted from Scotch to ketamine.

Sunday meant church. Sunday meant Sunday School and the Holy Trinity. Sunday meant ketamine. Greg had been raised Anglican, but beyond singing in the choir he'd never found anything reassuring or helpful about church or the Christian faith. His wife Maggie, on the other hand, came from an observant Catholic family and still clung to some vague notion of religion. Mostly out of respect for Greg's in-laws' wishes, every Sunday the children were loaded into the minivan and carted off to church. Greg agreed to subject his children to organized religion on the condition that he could forego the ritual.

After the van departed, Greg would sing along to the weekly edition of Choral Concert and luxuriate in his pyjamas over a pile of comic books. Once he'd slipped into a state of relaxation, he'd cue up some ambient music on an iPod and head to his sanctuary: the garden shed. With the help of his library card, he'd divide a portion of pulverized ketamine crystals into two lines, inhale the massive dose evenly through a piece of drinking straw, press play and lie back on a picnic blanket.

As the drug took effect, the little piece of pink and white straw typically rolled from his hand as he was sucked down several stories beneath his own body, into the multi-dimensional playground of the k-hole. Usually the imagery was a cross between ancient Egyptian and 60's sci-fi; Greg spent a lot of time engaged in activities such as building pyramids in space, riding conveyor belts through the sky, and saluting various alien incarnations of the Sphinx. But last Sunday had been radically different. Last Sunday's k-hole had been vivid and distinct in a way he couldn't shake.

Charlie had sent him a demo version of Antidotes for Manic Toads, which he'd selected as his k-hole soundtrack. At first it seemed like a good choice. As the deep bass slowly leaked into his ears, Greg's body and mind melted like butter in a frying pan. He became a trans-dimensional robot that resembled a lion and made a sport of colliding with stars, rattling unharmed at the root of the explosions.

Then something strange happened. A sound ripped through the fabric of the false reality. Greg was plucked from space and flung through a forest. He landed in a cold, picturesque lake and was quickly pulled down into an underground chamber where the current spat him over a waterfall, into a sheer drop.

It was strange that he was falling; he'd never experienced gravity in a k-hole. He almost smashed into a giant violet orb. As he corkscrewed through the air, he was amazed to see a network of these orbs, held in place by beams of rich, opaque light. The orbs drifted out of sight as he smashed into another layer of water and was sucked into a darkness so all-encompassing that he suddenly wanted to cry. He started to shout, but no noise came out. He shouted louder and louder until he was sure he was doomed, but then, out of the darkness, a light in the distance.

When he came to, he was yelling at the top of his voice. The twins were running around the backyard singing and screaming, and he could hear Esmé playing on the swing set. Maggie had switched on the light and stood over him in her Sunday best with a look of confusion on her face. Luckily, he'd hidden the paraphernalia behind some planters and the piece of straw had rolled into the shadows.

"What in the heavens are you hollering about back here?"

Greg rubbed his face with both hands, forced his eyelids to lift and sat up slowly.

"Just singing along to my favourite Swedish speed-metal band," he said, his voice gruff and groggy.

"Since when do you listen to speed-metal?" Maggie asked.

"Charlie's recommendation. It grows on you, y'know?"

"Oh God, anything that Charlie tells you is hip – hey! Is that a Nintendo?"

This episode, which ended in his console being confiscated rather than outright destroyed, had set a very poor tone for a very poor week. For one thing Greg was so sick of Mozart he could hardly bear it. Furthermore, he'd been named Eichelberger's understudy for Bluebeard and had to learn the entire role, which was in Hungarian: a language of which he had no knowledge. This was a tremendous amount of work for what promised to be zero payoff; it was well known that Eichelberger had never missed a performance in his life on account of his robust constitution and disciplined lifestyle.

As Greg sang his final lines, he could have sworn he saw Charlie strolling across the Concern. As rehearsal broke up, he spied his friend in the flesh, leaning where Eichelberger had been moments before. Charlie looked like he'd gone shopping: he had on brand-new skinny jeans, a freshly pressed mint green button down, and a black, slim cut blazer.

What struck Greg more than anything, however, was the vitality that emanated from his friend, visible even from a distance. Charlie did not look up as Greg approached, he was distracted by the tiny screen that lit up his face.

"Is that Charlie fucking Potichny playing with a smartphone? What is the world coming to?" Greg asked as he approached his friend. Charlie smiled self-consciously and held out the fancy gadget.

"Nobody told me about all the vintage games you can get on here. They've got Final Fantasy IV for this thing. I'm never going to get any work done again. Or bathe or eat."

"I thought you were a dedicated luddite. I don't object to you joining the age of information and infinite pornography, but aren't you allergic to technology?"

"Some allergies go away. You had that fatal nut allergy that cleared up after puberty, remember?"

"Thank fuck. Chunky PB is like half my diet."

"Right? Anyway, I'm feeling really good! Better sleep, more energy, virtually no pain. I'm actually going out to a concert tonight, I swung by to see if you're game to tag along."

"A concert? With drinking? And staying up late?" Greg was elated at the prospect, marvelling at Charlie's transformation. "Shit," he said. "It's my night to take the kids –"

"You're off the hook. I called up Maggie, you've got a free pass tonight."

"Dope! What's the plan?"

"There's this band called Milk Prison I want to check out, show's in Kensington Market."

"Sweet. My car's out this way. Let's go ditch it, so we can get loaded." Greg started towards the western exit, but Charlie made a bee-line to the east, towards the Bluebeard rehearsal where Sophie had just come in and begun warming up with Eichelberger.

"What's up sweet chili heat?" Sophie called out to him as he approached, and then, nodding to Greg, "it's like a high school reunion up in here. This is bringing back so many memories! Remember that Halloween rager when you were dressed as Mario and Luigi, and I dared you to make out with each other and you totally did!"

Charlie and Greg smiled uneasily at each other. "We were pretty high on mushrooms," Charlie said.

"What sort of trouble are you two getting up to this evening?" She asked.

"Going to see a band called Milk Prison," Greg said.

"Milk Prison, eh? Sounds exhilarating. I'd love to join, but unfortunately I'm stuck rehearsing with the schnitzel gang all night." She cast a glance at Eichelberger and Von Strohn who rolled their eyes in turn. "Don't be so sensitive boys, schnitzel is a well-loved delicacy around the world. As Germans you could do a lot worse by way of cultural references."

"Sophie, I think we'd better get started," Von Strohn said. "You came in late and we've got a lot of work to do."

"You see what I'm saying? These boys are very serious about the opera and very efficient. I wish a night at the opera was more like a fun, chilled out party. You know, Charlie, up until the twentieth century everyone gossiped, smoked and drank at the opera, all sorts of shenanigans! Now it's all quite aristocratic and cheerless. But I digress. I bought one of your records last week: Hawaiian Something? I loved it, you should come to our opening next month. Greg, will you bring him please, make sure he gets the royal treatment?"

"Charlie doesn't really go in for opera," Greg said curtly.

Charlie looked at him incredulously. "I'd love to come," he said. "Thanks."

"Good. Then it's settled. We'll have a drink or several at the afterparty. And at that I will bid you good day and turn my attention to zee Germans."

They said goodbye to Sophie and the unamused Germans and walked the length of the Concern back in the opposite direction. They got into Greg's aubergine cruiser, the colour of which now reminded him of his favourite forbidden vegetable. Charlie put on the hip hop station and sang along to Ja Rule as Greg piloted them up a long winding highway that ran through a ravine.

"So let me get this straight," Greg said, dialing the radio down, "After more than a decade of the chronic fatigue thing, you just suddenly get better?"

"I wouldn't say it was sudden," Charlie replied, notching the radio back up a hair. "I've been making progress for the past year or two, this last doctor actually knew what he was talking about. It's a big deal, I know! I'm so overwhelmed I could laugh and cry, but here we are, this is simply the new reality, no use overthinking it."

Greg teared up from joy and tousled his friend's hair, "I'm so happy I could laugh and cry, you beautiful bastard. I mean, all those years. . ."

"Let's just proceed with cautious optimism," Charlie said. "It still feels too good to be true."

Eventually the uptown streets became an indistinct blur of sushi joints and Italian restaurants, and finally they were pulling into Greg's driveway.

Inside the house the twins jumped on Charlie. He lifted them into the air one-by-one, twirling in circles until they were all dizzy and sick and collapsing in laughter on the floor. Greg and Maggie had a tense conversation in the kitchen and then the kids were being herded up to bed as Charlie and Greg knocked back Scotch. When the taxi arrived, "Any Major Dude Will Tell You" by Steely Dan was on the stereo and Charlie didn't want to leave.

"But this was your idea!" Greg said.

"I know. Okay. Let's chug these whiskies."

They chugged the whiskies and went out to the cab feeling buoyant and bright and alive.

CHAPTER 9

THAT AUTUMN, CHARLIE built himself a life. A dreaded backslide into fatigue seemed less likely as the days sped by, and after several weeks he'd unconsciously adjusted to his new baseline. Like most people who have their health, he learned to take it for granted.

He got Oliver Noodles to put him on the guest list for any and every show affiliated with Enemy Airship. He hob-knobbed, attending afterparties in dilapidated buildings that had been transformed into art spaces. He drank all night with musicians and industry hangers-on, discouraged by a scarcity of thoughtful conversationalists in the vast ocean of name-dropping drones that flocked backstage. Although he remained somewhat aloof to the industry scene, there was something addictive about being out in the sweaty chaos of people. On several occasions he saw the sun come up, half-drunk and giddy from watching miniature dramas unfurl all night. Coming home, he'd black out the windows and tumble into a viscous slumber, only to be awakened in the early afternoon by Goblin, screeching angrily for her organic food.

On a dreary evening in November, Charlie and Greg stepped out of a cocktail bar and jaywalked across University Avenue, passing a hash joint back and forth on the way to the opening night of Bluebeard's Castle.

"Sticks and stones have never broken my bones, but names actually do really hurt me," Greg croaked, exhaling. The first major review for Cosi Fan Tutte had just come out, declaring that it was a brilliant show aside from Greg's uninspired performance.

Hounslow Hathaway had written in Token magazine, "It's almost as if he doesn't want to be there."

"At least he's not saying that you're bad," Charlie said. "He just says that your performance was lazy, that you're not living up to your potential."

The Four Seasons Centre for the Performing Arts was a massive glass cube that lit up the corner of Queen and University. Charlie and Greg stood outside finishing the joint as droves of people swirled around them in beautiful clothing. In all the years that Greg had been performing, Charlie had not once come to see him, partly because of his condition and partly because he did not care for opera. Now he saw that more than half the fun was in the ceremony of the event: the spectacle created by the eccentric and the wealthy, drawn out of their homes to converge on an anachronistic art form.

For Greg, on the other hand, it was business as usual; he was burnt out on the scene and rarely enjoyed openings. He puffed heartily on the hash and flashed fake smiles at friends and regulars. He gave a strong impression of not giving two fucks.

"Hey, if Eichelberger has an aneurysm or shits his pants or something on stage, would you just jump up there and start singing in Hungarian?" Charlie asked as they walked into the atrium, bathed in glittering light.

Greg considered the question. "I don't think so. Pretty sure they'd cancel the performance." He fished a throat lozenge out of his pocket and popped it in his mouth. "Wait, why would he shit his pants?"

"I mean like if he sharted really bad."

"I've sharted on stage before. The show goes on."

"You sharted?"

"Yup. Marriage of Figaro, right in the middle of the wedding. I ate carbonara for dinner. Looking back, it was a poor choice."

"Carbonara is never a mistake."

Greg narrowed his eyes and cracked the lozenge in half with his teeth. "It was a mistake that time."

They made their way up to the Glenn Gould Lounge on the third floor. Greg ordered two double Johnny Walkers and passed one to Charlie.

"Any more news on the cabin?" Greg asked.

"Yeah, it's all set, they're driving me up next week."

"Have you thought at all about what you want to record?"

"I've been looking through Yana's work. I think I'll just do some ambient soundscapes, keep it simple."

"Is it just the landscapes? Or the abstract works as well?"

Charlie was temporarily hypnotized by a stream of light from the traffic below, bouncing off a massive pane of glass. The reflection created the impression that there was a second layer of vehicles floating above the first.

"Abstract also."

A tri-tonal ringing had begun echoing through the glass box. Charlie and Greg were so buzzed that they thought it was just in their heads. Then, at the same instant, they realized it was the five-minute warning.

They made their way to a private box adjacent to the second mezzanine and sat down behind Errol and Melody Greyhound, the oldest and wealthiest member of the opera board. Errol turned around, grasped Greg by the knee and gave him a look of condolence. This was part of his father's way of making peace over the Guglielmo casting, but Greg also read a look of I told you so on his face and had to resist the impulse to tell him off.

The curtain came up, revealing a golden, glowing castle suspended in mid-air. The effect was trippy, so seemingly designed for stoned people that Charlie and Greg began giggling. Errol snapped his head back towards them with a chastising gaze. Charlie was in the act of passing a flask of brandy to Greg, who raised his palms, feigning innocence. Charlie froze and the flask just hung between them. They found this even more amusing than the floating castle and burst out laughing again. Errol rolled his eyes and shushed them with the subtle touch of a seasoned opera fanatic.

The performance was breathtakingly beautiful, by any standard. Even Greg had to admit that Eichelberger was in top form. The orchestra played with passion and restraint in the appropriate instances. The remarkable acoustics of the building, the chemistry between Eichelberger and Sophie, and the visual feast on stage created the atmosphere that opera enthusiasts fantasize about but are rewarded with only on the rarest of occasions.

In the section where Sophie opens the sixth door to discover the lake of pure white, Greg experienced a sudden flashback to the anomalous k-hole from a few weeks back. He'd come to suspect that his strange experience had been tied up with Charlie's music, but now the visuals of the frozen lake, the violet orbs, and the ocean of light were inexplicably conjured by Bartók as well. He glanced over at Charlie to see how he would react, but his eyes were closed and he appeared to be fast asleep.

Back in the Glenn Gould Lounge, they ran into Oliver Noodles. He held a glass of sparkling in one hand and an ice cream bar in the other.

"Hey Noodles," Charlie said. "I didn't know you were into opera."

"I'm not. My ex-wife is. She made me buy a pass for the season but now she's fucking some tech billionaire on the Amalfi Coast."

"Harsh," Charlie replied. "Did you like it at least?"

"I guess the singing was okay, but I thought the orchestra was pretty weak. And the timpanist totally fucked the dog."

"Jesus, take it easy," Greg said.

"Greg, Noodles; Noodles, Greg," Charlie said. The two men shook hands.

Noodles grinned, "I'm just kidding. It was decent."

All around them opera goers were singing praises about the performance: "The timpanist was a revelation. . ."; "But surely you'll agree, the woodwinds stole the show. . ."; "Goodness, that Rénard girl is stunning. . ."; "Her and Eichelberger are quite a team. What chemistry! I think he must be the best baritone in the world right now, maybe the best of all time. . ."; ". . . heard he spent a year in total silence, contemplating the shape of his voice. . ."; ". . . so handsome! Such good hair. . ."

Greg turned to the reflective glass and inspected his receding hairline. He pulled the flask out and poured some into his flute.

"Did you just pour brandy into your champagne?" Charlie asked.

"What? It's just mixing wine with wine," Greg drained the glass and grimaced. It was disgusting.

"That's disgusting," said Noodles, laughing. "You guys aren't sticking around for this Schoenberg bullshit, are you?"

Errol appeared out of a nearby crowd in a classic tuxedo. He looked very fine at that moment with his full moustache and moussed mop of hair comprising a curious blend of grey-white and reddish-brown. Errol was eleven-years sober, but always arranged for the bar to serve him ginger ale in a champagne flute at intermission for appearance's sake.

"Gentlemen, gentlemen, quite a triumph, quite a triumph wouldn't you say? What an incredible evening. Are you all as excited as I am for Schoenberg one-act? I'm very excited."

Greg and Noodles both made farting noises and gave a thumbs down.

"You know I don't fuck with Schoenberg, Errol. . . atonal piece of shit," Noodles said with gravitas.

"Please, please, speak your mind Oliver. No need to sugarcoat the truth," Errol huffed. "If you can't enjoy dissonant music, frankly I pity you."

Charlie looked back and forth between Errol and Noodles, confused. "How do you two know each other?"

"I told you, Errol calls me sometimes when you go all Brian Wilson. We have a lot in common. Our wives both left us for tech billionaires. We play squash once a week."

Greg was unsettled by this information and grew impatient. "Dad, you're hosting the afterparty right? We might head up there now and preview the catering. Grab a few canapés and watch the end of the basketball before the riff raff arrives."

"I suppose that's fine," Errol said. "But if you obstreperous young lads eat all of the ceviché there'll be hell to pay. Mark my words!"

CHAPTER 10

ERROL'S RESIDENCE WAS located at the heart of a wealthy, heavily forested neighbourhood called Wychwood Park. It was a grand, rustic old house with a large front yard and three fireplaces. As Charlie, Greg, and Noodles walked through the front door, a massive, wolfish dog charged them, leaping up on Greg.

"Cujo! Hey buddy!" Greg grabbed him by the paws and dropped to his knees, slow dancing with the dog and humming a famous melody.

"I don't think he likes that," said Noodles.

"Sure he does!"

Cujo yipped and gripped Greg's forearm in his maw. Greg released him and the beast jumped on Charlie, nearly knocking him over. A caterer burst out of the kitchen and gave them a stern look. "Keep that beast out of here," she said. "He already ate half the ceviche."

They went down to the basement, raided the beer fridge, and caught the final quarter of the basketball game. Afterwards they shot a game of cutthroat on the snooker table. Noodles pulled out a baggie of cocaine and cut up some lines for him and Greg. Upstairs the guests started arriving. Greg had connected his phone to the high-tech sound system and Enter the Wu-Tang Clan (36 Chambers) was pumping through every room in the house.

"Have you heard Charlie's new track? Have you heard that shit?" Noodles was asking Greg excitedly. "It sounds like it's from a different world. I don't mean it's otherworldly, I mean it actually sounds like it's from another world. How did you do it, you brilliant son of a bitch?"

"I meant to ask you about that," Greg said. "Noodles is right. That noise, the lead melody, it's like... it's like Mozart says, about how music is from heaven and musicians are just conduits. It's so much better than Hawaiian Eyes, and you know I love Hawaiian Eyes, so please take that as a compliment."

Charlie shrugged uncomfortably as a rapid series of slaps on the basement steps announced Errol's approach.

"Gregory," Errol bellowed. Noodles swiftly pocketed the baggie and paraphernalia. "Turn off this racket and put on something more appropriate. You're upsetting the guests."

"Why don't you change it?"

"I don't understand how to work the bloody thing. You promised you'd teach me last Christmas, but you drank too much eggnog at brunch and slept all afternoon."

"Best. Christmas. Ever." Greg said, tapping at his phone. The divine beats of the 36 Chambers abruptly gave way to Dave Brubeck. Visibly relieved, Errol fetched himself a Club Soda from the fridge.

"Well," he said. "Come up and mingle. This isn't junior high. You can't just hide out down here and play video games. I'm not ordering you a pepperoni pizza. Tuck in your shirts, straighten your ties and come up young lads, come up and be sociable."

Upstairs, the party was in full swing. Plentiful trays of canapés were gliding around the living room, and champagne cocktails were being passed out faster than they could be replenished. Hounslow Hathaway – the critic who'd accused Greg of being a lazy Guglielmo – was engaged in a conversation with Melody Greyhound over the function of opera. "I'm good for one or two acts at most," Hounslow was saying. "I've never met a third act I've much liked. It's usually some poor, heartbroken wretch dying of consumption and repeating the same lines over and over for an hour. It makes for poor story-telling and the resolution is always disappointing."

"Good opera is not about storytelling," Melody replied. "I'll be the first to admit, the plot of any opera can be summarized in ten minutes or less. It's about the feeling of the thing: the way the poetry and music cooperate to create a transcendental experience. When I resist the urge to look at the surtitles I can feel more deeply. It's not about the words, it's about the feeling. If you want good storytelling, head to Stratford."

"Agreed," Errol cut in. "Some Wagner operas are four hours long and it's hard to find a discernable plot. I'll find myself in tears at times, in ecstasy at others. If you give yourself over to the feeling of the thing you become lost in the beauty. When the Ring Cycle ends I want to stand up and shout at the bastards to keep singing, I feel like I'm just getting started."

Greg, who had been listening closely to the conversation, found his moment to jump in: "I'm with Hounslow. Most people would prefer to watch some billion-dollar superhero extravaganza over people in costumes singing music written by dead people for four hours. Opera companies are in the red all over the world and it'll only get worse. My generation doesn't give a shit about opera. Ticket sales are plummeting and significant donors like Melody are literally a dying breed – sorry Mel. I don't think there's a place for opera in the future. Why can't we all just admit that we're the final crew on a sinking ship? Wouldn't it be a relief?"

The room fell silent. Finally, Hounslow spoke: "I don't mean to throw you under the bus old chap, but that wasn't exactly my point. I think you're on your own."

"Gregory, my dear boy," Melody said. "I'm afraid you know nothing of what you speak. Younger generations evolve into opera lovers. You couldn't have paid me to attend a performance when I was a young girl, but in one's later years one undergoes a blossoming: a calm that allows the magic of opera to seep into the deepest chambers of the soul. I thought you might understand that by now. . . then again, judging by the impotence of your recent performances, one might suspect you've lost your ability to cast a decent spell."

Suppressed laughter and gasps rippled through the living room, but Greg only smiled, waiting patiently to speak. "Come on Mel, how much did you donate to the opera this year? Twenty million? And without that money where would the company be? In the toilet, that's where. As much as I love opera, I have to ask, couldn't that money have found a better home as, shit I don't know, earthquake relief in some crumbling nation? Funding programs for street youth or the mentally ill? How important is opera, seriously? I'll tell you what, in the grand scheme of things:

opera doesn't fucking matter." He looked Errol straight in the face, "Wagner doesn't fucking matter. Why don't you all get a real hobby," he said, addressing the room.

"You'd do well not to bite the hand that feeds you," Melody said as Greg stormed out.

The partygoers mumbled uncomfortably: "I donate to a number of charitable foundations. . ."; "The younger generation has no respect for tradition. . ."; "Just sore over the trouncing Hounslow gave him in Token. . ."; "Needs to re-evaluate his career. . ."; "Is there no more bloody ceviche? I'm drowning in a sea of canapés!"

Greg found Cujo dozing on the couch in the library. He sat down and rubbed the top of his head. The dog let out an appreciative growl without opening his eyes.

The brisk high from Noodles' cocaine was already wearing off and Greg sank back into the aching sadness that had defined his life of late. He'd begun to feel as though his career and family life were not the results of calculated decisions he'd made, so much as things that had accidentally happened to him over time. This feeling of powerlessness caused him to act out more and more as time went on, since courting disaster was always easier than initiating a conscious change. If he'd been especially agitated lately, it was because Maggie and him had finally admitted how miserable they were together and begun discussing the sticky logistics of a trial separation. Whether or not they split up, he knew his life would not improve until he initiated difficult changes, started shedding the familiar persona he wore out of habit, like an old, moth-eaten bathrobe riddled with holes.

Charlie and Noodles had snuck into the kitchen, narrowly missing Greg's outburst. Noodles, coked out as all hell, was talking about his big plans for Charlie's new album. He said he was going to drop some serious coin on promotion and light a fire under his staff's asses to really work the record. After a time, they were cornered by a drunken bassist from the orchestra hell-bent on describing his folk-rock project, hoping, undoubtedly, that Noodles would be interested in signing him. Charlie pretended to listen as he polished off the last of the ceviché, but as soon as he saw an opportunity he plucked two Bellinis off a passing platter and declared that he had promised to bring someone a drink.

He walked up to the third floor, hoping for some peace and quiet. He had a notion to drink both Bellinis and fall asleep on his old bed, it had been a long day and he was feeling drowsy. Opening the door to his old bedroom, he was startled to find Eichelberger and Sophie sitting on a deep-set windowsill. They abruptly broke off what seemed like a very intense conversation.

"Close the door," Eichelberger said.

"No way, this is my room," Charlie replied firmly. "Find some other room to have a sketchy argument in. Trust me, there are plenty."

"Hey! It's Potichny!" Sophie said, turning on a smile. "Dietrich, why don't you go back downstairs; I'll catch up with you later." Eichelberger stomped out of the room, apoplectic in lieu of his usual cool.

"I brought you a drink," Charlie offered, passing one of the Bellinis to Sophie. He walked over to his old stereo and hit play on a random disc. Return to Hot Chicken drifted out of the speakers.

"I Can Feel the Heart Beating as One," Charlie said.

"Oh, can you now?"

"It's the name of the album."

"Oh. I never listened to much popular music. I'm sort of missing a century of references."

"I'm not sure you'd call this popular music."

"Well, it's nice anyway," she said.

Charlie joined her on the windowsill.

"I don't understand," she said. "How is this your room? This is Errol's place, right? I know you and Greg are friends, but it seems more like you're –"

"Brothers? We are, well, sort of. My mom died when I was fifteen, and I never knew my dad. Since me and Greg were inseparable anyway, Errol took me in."

"You poor thing," Sophie said. "How did your mother die?"

"It's pretty brutal," Charlie said. "She fell through the ice outside her cabin in Algonquin Park and drowned. She'd been depressed for a long time, but she'd never..." he trailed off.

"My father was a brilliant jazz pianist," Sophie said. "Got in a terrible cycling accident when I was twelve. He went part-way mad afterwards trying to regain his former glory, but it was no good – some people cling to the half-baked notion that they're on this earth for one single purpose. Anyway, he got addicted to prescription pills and slept around. Eventually my emotionally repressed mother divorced him. He's still alive, but basically he's gone."

"You want to go splits on a shrink?" Charlie asked.

"Or we could just talk to each other."

Outside the window, plump, bright snowflakes had begun to fall.

✧

Five minutes later they snuck out into the frosty streets with a bottle of Chianti in tow. Wychwood already resembled the setting of a fairy-tale with its big brick houses, narrow streets and towering trees, and the glittering snow added to this impression.

"The only way I could connect with my mother was to read about war and revolution – she's a history professor and a hardcore activist," Sophie said. "At first, I found it all very boring, but I came around in time. It's just a century and a half since slavery ended in the States, seventy-odd years since the Holocaust, since Hiroshima and Nagasaki. Most people already think that's ancient history, but if you look at the whole of human history, really it's just – " she held up a hand and snapped her fingers.

"Just think: a hundred years ago most people in the 'civilized' world would have been working all day under brutal conditions, making barely enough to survive, some of them starving and going to war, dying of influenza. Now we're furious if the internet is broken for two minutes."

"I know what you mean, my maternal grandparents lost most of their families to the Holodomor, the man-made famine in Ukraine, in the thirties. It's why they came to Canada. My grandpa died before I was born, but the few times I met my baba I remember feeling like she was carrying the sorrows of the universe. The best she could hope for was survival. We all demand self-actualization, a heavily variegated, shame-free sex life, and total enlightenment."

"That could be part of honouring baba – pursuing the kinky sex and self-expression that she never got to experience. As for enlightenment. . . whereof one cannot speak – "

" – thereof one must be silent."

"Oh, you're good!"

Charlie felt a warmth spreading through his body, a profound relaxation.

"So, what about your dad," Sophie continued. "Where does he fit in?"

"Mom was always tight lipped about that. She'd change the subject when I pressed, it seemed to make her sad. Who knows, maybe she'd have been better off if she'd never met him."

"But then you wouldn't exist. And that would be a shame." Charlie blushed, couldn't find the words. "When my dad left I coped by reading Marxist theory and discussing Frederick Douglas with my mom," Sophie said. "What was your method?"

"I was so out of it. I barely knew what was going on."

"And now?"

"Lately I'm all right. Things are better than ever, but at the same time. . ."

"What?"

"I don't think I can explain it."

"Try me."

"Lately I'm not sure what's real and what's fake. Like somewhere along the way reality was swapped out for something nearly identical but not quite the same. I can't figure out when it changed or what the difference is. Sometimes I think I might be losing my mind. I don't know why I'm telling you all this. You must think I'm insane."

"No," she said. "I don't. I think I know what you mean."

"I think you're beautiful," Charlie declared, meeting her eyes.

They were on a slope at the southern gates of Wychwood, by a pond layered over with fresh, fizzing ice. She pulled him to her and kissed him, their frozen faces warming in a rosy blush.

They walked back up to Errol's arm in arm and kissed some more, and then Sophie hopped in one of several taxis that had gathered in front of the house – the party was winding down.

Charlie found Greg in the library cleaning up a pile of vomit. "Overdid it on the Bellinis did you?"

"Hilarious. No, it was Cujo, he ate something funny."

"Didn't that caterer say –"

"Do you think of me as a happy person?" Greg asked, focusing on the vomit.

"What? Why would you ask that? Of course I do, you get to live your dream every day. You're a pleasant, fun guy, people like you, you've got a great wife and a bunch of offspring to ensure your legacy. What's not to be happy about?"

"I don't know, man," Greg said wearily. "Opera was my dream when I was a kid. I'm a completely different person now. Maybe this isn't for me anymore."

"What a bunch of horseshit," Charlie said, sitting down on the sofa. "Of anyone I've ever known I always thought you were the one guy who had it figured out. Whatever internal crisis you're having, don't worry about it, it'll pass. Besides, for my money, you can sing Eichelberger under the table any day of the week."

Greg got up and slumped onto the couch holding a clump of soiled rags. He started weeping. "That's not true, but I appreciate you saying it." Charlie took Greg's massive torso in his little arms and hugged him. His hands barely reached all the way around his back.

"Errol's going to be so pissed at Cujo," Greg said, between sobs. "This is his favourite Persian."

"It's okay buddy, it's okay," Charlie said and rocked him until he was all cried out.

CHAPTER 11

YANA'S CABIN, BURIED deep in Algonquin, had been deserted since her death and was barely accessible by car. November had been exceptionally cold and now, in the first week of December, the northern lakes were frozen over and blanketed with snow. The cabin was surrounded by birch trees, up a steep embankment from the water. Almost all of the wildlife was in hibernation. The cabin had power, but was fully reliant on a wood stove for heat. The art gallery supplied Charlie with a significant load of logs and kindling, a couple of space heaters and a week's worth of groceries from a list that he'd emailed them: bacon, beans, beer, bread, and coffee. In the middle of the first night, Charlie woke, startled to find that he was not in his own bed, and then fell instantly back to sleep.

In the morning he poured himself a large mug of coffee, put on several layers of clothes, and walked down to the lake. The snow crunched under his boots; he marveled at how still and quiet the world was. It was sunny, and the frozen crust of ice on top of the lake looked inviting. Delighted by his solitude and by the folly of the act, he stepped tentatively out onto the solid ice and walked a couple feet. Much to his surprise, a human voice called out behind him. He turned and saw a woman standing on the shore, long grey hair spilling out from beneath her toque. "Get off the ice," she called.

Feeling embarrassed and offended by what he felt to be an intrusion, Charlie walked back onto the land.

"I thought I was all alone," he said sheepishly. "Where did you come from?"

She pointed to a cabin forty yards from his own. It was camouflaged by the coniferous branches that hung around it.

"I guess we're neighbours for the week," he said, holding out a mitt to shake her hand. "My name's – "

"I know who you are," the woman snapped. "Stay off the ice. It's dangerous." She turned briskly and crunched towards her home.

Charlie walked back up to his own cabin and threw a log in the furnace. He thought for a brief moment about the strange woman, wondered why on earth she was living here in the winter and why she was so intense about the ice. He opened a beer and sat under a blanket reading Buddenbrooks. He quickly forgot about the woman. In the afternoon he went back to sleep for several hours. As darkness fell he ate some nuts, pressed some coffee and set to work at the keyboard. He'd brought his black bass and a small synthesizer as well. He started building loops purposefully and found some chords and rhythms he liked. He'd thought that Yana's pictures would make him nervous, but instead he was inspired – he knew exactly what to do.

It wasn't until well after dark that Philip showed himself. Charlie had been studying a picture that he interpreted as an animal skull floating in space, playing distorted bass over heavy piano chords. He noticed a low hum, subtle and sumptuous, shifting hypnotically with him whenever he changed chords. It felt so good that Charlie didn't even look around to see which painting Philip was in, instead he closed his eyes and leaned over the piano, executing leads with his right hand that he usually wouldn't have been able to pull off.

The longer it went on, the better it got. Charlie had never played so well; he floated above the room and watched himself switch back and forth between bass, synth, and piano, sculpting an ambient, progressive masterpiece. Philip stayed with him the whole way, creating harmonies so rich Charlie could hear colours in them – midnight blue and electric purple.

By the time it was over, Charlie was drenched in sweat. He took a beer from the fridge and caught sight of the furry virtuoso perched high on a range of the Rocky Mountains in one of the frames. The quiet was total now as Charlie and Philip sized each other up. Charlie still couldn't make out much beyond those glacial blue eyes and furry hands peeking out beneath the darkness of the cloak. Philip's sound was integral to capturing the essence of Yana's paintings and brought out a level of musicianship and confidence that Charlie heretofore had never been able to access.

After a time, Philip turned his back and trudged down the mountain he'd been standing on. Charlie was alone. The sweat dried and grew cold. He threw another log in the furnace, pulled on a wool sweater and sat down with his book. He could not read; the words sat lifeless and inaccessible before his eyes. He grew hot again and pulled the sweater off. He listened to the playback on the recording suite and grew excited – this was, without a doubt, some of his best work. As he listened, he found that it was Philip, more than himself, who was guiding the composition – he'd been following rather than leading. This discovery troubled him, though not greatly.

The days that followed were so similar and so effortlessly pleasant that they blurred together. After a late breakfast, Charlie would drink beer and read until he fell back to sleep. He'd wake up as it grew dark, brew some coffee, and then record into the early hours of the morning.

Each night Philip would appear in a different landscape painting, instinctually providing Charlie's composition with whatever it lacked and sometimes leading him into uncharted territory. As they became more familiar with each other's quirks and habits they were able to anticipate what the other was thinking to the point of near telepathy. These sessions went on for hours but never felt directionless. Both parties knew when it was time to call it quits, and together they would fashion an elegant conclusion. Early in the morning, flush and exhausted, Charlie would crack a well-earned beer only to fall asleep on the couch before he could finish it.

By the second to last night of his stay, Charlie felt like he never wanted to leave the cabin. After he finished recording with Philip, he smoked a bit of hash out of a tiny glass pipe and listened to the playback. He thought about Mizza, the giant bird with the mellifluous voice. If all this fantastical madness was somehow "true" after all, how was Charlie to know that Philip was a terrorist, that Mizza was an agent of justice. He'd become entwined with Philip in a process of profound beauty, of spirituality even. He couldn't just kidnap him and hand him over without first seeing solid evidence against him. Even if Philip was a supernatural being from a parallel universe, he deserved due process. He was innocent until proven guilty. Charlie was so proud of his admirable ethics that he opened a second beer.

When the playback finished he thought he heard music coming from outside the cabin, as if the wind had begun to sing. He threw on his flannel jacket and went out into the clear, still night. He realized it was Philip he'd heard singing just then, not the wind. The singing was coming off the lake.

It was an exceptionally bright night, a sharp, silvery sheen glossing the sky. As he walked away from the cabin, Philip's Windsong grew louder. He felt that he was moving towards the sound, towards a place where he would be directly beneath the stars. The Windsong blew outside of his head, and then inside of it. He grew disoriented and spun around. He was way out on the lake.

As the ice beneath him cracked and gave way, he understood that he'd done something horribly stupid. The understanding coincided with the shock of the frigid water as the lake swallowed him up.

CHAPTER 12

THE NEXT THING he knew he was tumbling around in the swirling whitewash. The water was salty and warm, unlike that of the frozen lake. His body corkscrewed into a narrow opening that seemed too small for him to fit through, but eventually the immense pressure forced him headfirst through the passage. It was tight, dark, and claustrophobic; it felt like the muddy tunnel was going to pull the skin off of his body as he was forced through. He thought he must be dying.

Eventually he slipped out the other side of the tunnel into a calm pool, through which the streaming water tumbled off a cliff. He caught himself on the jagged edge of a rock and dragged himself onto the floor of the cavern, the mouth of which was obscured by yet more water tumbling from an unseen source overhead. He tried to shout but could not manage to produce a sound. He reached the disturbing conclusion that he no longer had a mouth. He took a breath through his nose and smelled wet dog. Looking down, he saw that his hands and feet – his entire body, in fact – were covered in sleek brown fur. He shook himself vigorously in an attempt to shed the damp.

Trying to keep from freaking out, he walked to the mouth of the cavern. He found the end of a narrow suspension bridge fastened to the rock, leading through the waterfall. He grabbed hold of the handrails and put his weight on the bridge, passed through the curtain of water and out into the vast, dazzling Cathedral on the other side.

Charlie gripped the rails tightly out of a concern that he'd lose consciousness. The vision that lay before him was so intoxicatingly beautiful that he feared he might pass out and slip over the edge. Water rushed out of the darkness above the entire circumference of the massive, cavernous space. At the end of the long suspension bridge, a large, violet sphere was floating in the air. It was one of many such spheres of varying size, connected by a network of bridges and ladders.

The spheres themselves appeared to be held in place by thick cones of light emanating from the tumultuous body of water kicking up hay bales far below. As Charlie slowly made his way across the swaying bridge, dozens of furry creatures came into view, going in and out of the orbs, some of them engaged in wordless exchanges, some of them staring at the ocean below.

As he grew closer to the structure at the end of his bridge, one of the creatures caught sight of him. In the absence of a murmur, Charlie had a sense that a murmur was spreading through the crowd. All eyes were fixed on the newcomer.

One of the creatures climbed onto the bridge and approached Charlie. They approached him slowly, with amazement. This one was slim, with long limbs: a biped with padded paws. Dark brown-green eyes glowed in their furry face above a leathery black snout. A tuft of hair shaped a point at the back of their head.

Just as the creature reached him, a rumble spread through the Cathedral. The pillars of light flickered, and the network of orbs sank for a split second; everything went dark. Charlie nearly fell over, but the creature with the brown-green eyes caught him. There was a loud roar below; a hungry roar. When the lights came back on, the spheres were noticeably lower, sinking towards the ocean.

Charlie looked into the creature's eyes and convulsed violently.

The creature was his mother.

The fact seized him so suddenly that he fell again, only to be caught once more. He reached up and felt his own furry face, his wet nose. He called out reflexively but could not make a sound. He looked again into the creature's brown-green eyes, the eyes that were quite precisely the same shade as his mother's. Again, the roar came from below, ferocious and desperate. Inside his head, Charlie felt something burrow and expand. A living thing was blossoming in his mind; he started slapping his own head in terror, but his mother seized him by his arms and held him. He let it blossom with a sigh of relief, and only then did he understand.

✦

When he came to, he understood nothing. His body had gone numb in the freezing water and somebody was shouting at him. He could see the glint of a flashlight towards what he imagined was the shore. He'd swallowed a lot of water and began coughing violently. A length of rope landed on the edge of the hole. He managed to get a grip on the line, despite the fact that his arms were like frozen hot dogs.

He flopped up on the edge of the ice as his rescuer began tugging the line. He was dragged slowly across the ice, teeth chattering, eyes rolling wildly. His breath was short and laboured, he was drifting in and out of consciousness. He slipped onto his back and saw the faint stars in the bright sky. He wished for warmth, for fur; Don't I have fur, he thought. The stars blurred and faded into light, every inhale felt like he was being stabbed in the chest.

The old woman helped him up the embankment to her cabin. She poured a lukewarm bath and helped him get his clothes off. He felt pain and saw colours and shapes, but he could not process anything beyond the simplest impressions.

He came back to himself under a pile of warm blankets on a green sofa. His muscles ached, and he was shivering uncontrollably despite the warmth. He was wrapped in a bathrobe, his clothes drying by the fire. When he'd finally gathered the strength to raise his head he saw a woman with grey hair – the woman who'd shooed him off the ice – sitting in an armchair staring back at him.

"A lesser woman than myself might ask the gods, 'Why? Why have you burdened me with the chronic idiocy of the Potichny family?' However, unbelieving as I am in the existence of sentient gods with a sense of justice, I accept this burden grudgingly as part of the greater idiocy of the world at large."

Charlie gawked at the woman, an unflattering look of complete confusion on his face. The woman sighed. "Well. Are you alright boy?"

"Yeah," Charlie croaked. "I think so. Do you have any whisky?"

The woman fetched a bottle of rye from the pantry and

poured them both a glass. Charlie sat up tenuously, testing out his sore, protesting body.

"Shouldn't you take me to the hospital or something?" he asked.

"Hospital?" She laughed, passing him his glass. "Neither of us has a car. We're in the middle of Algonquin. The only option would be to airlift you out of here, but that seems like quite a to-do at the moment – especially since you seem to have your faculties and health intact. Your faculties and health are intact, yes?"

Charlie studied himself uselessly and sipped his whisky. "I think so, yeah." He looked around the cabin, it was almost identical to his own except for the art that hung on the walls. There was a hyper-realistic painting of a caterpillar that struck him as familiar, though he knew he'd never seen it before.

"Hey, where did you get that caterpillar? It looks like –"

"One of your mother's? Beautiful isn't it? It was a gift to celebrate the arrival of spring in ninety-six."

"You knew her?"

"I did. We were contemporaries, friends, neighbours."

"You're a painter as well?"

"You'll have to excuse me, with all the commotion I somehow failed to introduce myself. Artemis Gwillimbury, at your service."

"The Artemis Gwillimbury?"

"Yes, the. As far as I know I'm the only human on the planet to wield this ridiculous name."

"But I thought Artemis Gwillimbury was a man."

"Then you thought what I wanted you to think. Makes it easier for me to sell my paintings at the price they deserve."

"What about those iconic pictures of you? With the giant moustache and the messy hair?"

"My brother Tennyson posed for those. He worked as a longshoreman in Labrador most of his life. Not much chance of a scandal on his account."

"Isn't that sort of sexist? Lying about your gender to make more money?"

"Please, please, extrapolate dear boy, there's nothing I love more than being lectured on gender politics by young white men."

Charlie was silent.

"Tell me, young master Potichny, now that you're hip to the fact that I have a vagina, have your feelings towards my work changed?"

"Well, now that you mention it, a lot of it is rather phallic. I always loved the way you painted icebergs as these epic shining monuments. There's something religious about your work, but also something very masculine, like Superman's fortress of solitude."

"If my work comes across as masculine, it is precisely because my primary task has been to find God in the land. Mother Earth as God is a particularly feminine notion, but specific encounters with the divine in nature, for me at least, usually involve some sort of volcano or a mountain or an iceberg. In short, yes, some sort of naturally occurring monolithic cock. I'm sure there are a number of feminist art critics out there who would take issue with my depiction of the divine, but it's simply how I've always felt. It's also coherent with the popular idea that God is a dick."

Artemis took a breath and furrowed her brow. An unpleasant memory passed through her mind, and her tone turned serious.

"Chuck, you've had a hell of a night. Why don't you get some shuteye. Your clothes should be dry by tomorrow, and you can go back to the haunted cabin and finish whatever it is you came here to do," she pointed at Charlie, "just don't go out on the damn lake again, okay? It's bad enough I lost my best friend that way. If I let her son drown too I'm going to end up in the psych ward."

When she called him Chuck, a warmth spread through his body. No one had called him that since his mom died. "How come you trust me?" he asked. "You didn't have to tell me who you are."

"You're Yana's kid. I'm not going to lie to you. Besides, I saved your life. Tell anyone my secret and I'll take it away." Artemis winked at him and headed for the bedroom.

Beware Philip's tricks, his song is sweet but there is blackness in his heart. Mizza had warned him, but he had not listened. Evidence? Due process? What the hell had he been thinking?

He'd exonerated Philip of all suspicion based on the fact that he liked to jam with him, and he'd almost lost his life. Charlie was disturbed by what he'd seen in the Cathedral beneath the ice, but it must have been some sort of illusion conjured by the sinister Philip. The feeling that he had been with his mother just the night before had opened up old wounds. He was fragile and angry. He was officially throwing his lot in with the Big Bird: Philip had to go.

He wasn't sure if Philip would show after the events of the previous night, but sure enough, around midnight, he appeared amidst the grain elevators of Saskatchewan in a painting of a sunny summer day in the prairies. Charlie built a loop on the piano and left it on for the entire session, playing three note patterns on the bass and improvising leads softly. Philip was singing quietly and sadly in the middle register, as if he knew what was coming. The song that night was the shortest. They never strayed from Charlie's initial chord progression, and the arrangement was sparse. It was much simpler than anything they'd recorded in the previous sessions: fluid, understated, and slightly paranoid.

As they landed on the resolution, Charlie approached the painting of the grain elevators. He felt Philip smiling from beneath his cloak, tried not to meet his glowing eyes. Then, in one swift motion, he reached out and plucked the painting from where it hung. One of Philip's shrill barks rang out in Charlie's head. He ran out the left side of the painting and appeared immediately on the right side, next to a tractor. He repeated this exercise until he had exhausted himself, Charlie's eyes tracking him from right to left and back, over and again. Eventually he slumped onto the golden field of wheat. Charlie thought it was over now, but a loud shriek erupted, more painful and powerful than anything he'd ever heard. It rattled his brain so violently that he dropped the painting, smacking the corner of the hand carved frame on the ground.

The shrieking continued, Charlie felt like his brain was being eaten from the inside out by starved larvae. He grabbed the painting and stuffed it in a gym bag he'd brought for this explicit purpose. The shrieking was only slightly muffled. He startled rifling through drawers and cupboards, searching for something, anything he could use to put a buffer between himself and the torturous noise of his captive. He found a roll of duct tape and set to work wrapping the painting. Once he'd administered three layers the sound was slightly dulled; he went on wrapping until all the tape was gone and the painting resembled a grey throw pillow. It no longer fit in the gym bag, so he simply set it aside, head throbbing.

He replaced the Saskatchewan painting with the one from his apartment, of Manitoba in winter, that Philip had first appeared in months ago. He opened a beer and sat down on the couch, but he did not fall asleep. One beer turned into four and then the sun was coming up. He might have dozed for a moment, but his nightmares mixed indiscriminately with reality so that by the time Artemis knocked on his door the next morning he could not say for certain whether he had slept at all.

"Charlie, I don't know what you were doing over here last night, but it was not good," Artemis said. "I woke up in the middle of the night to what sounded like hippos being tortured. I understand that you're an experimental artist, but please promise me you will never, ever make that sound again. Charlie? Are you listening to me?"

Charlie was sitting on the couch, bleary eyed, staring blankly at nothing in particular.

"Jeezus Christ, you look like hell. Let's get some fresh air."

They poured themselves piping hot cups of coffee from the French Press and sat outside in the morning sun. A light breeze was ruffling the trees, and the sky was a soft, cool blue. The cold air was clean and refreshing, and after a couple sips from his mug Charlie felt a bit better.

"Why do you stay here?" he asked Artemis. "Don't you get lonely living all by yourself?"

"No. I get really lonely when I'm around people. I find it difficult to relate to them. That's why I loved your mother. She was fierce and true and funny. Like no one else, really."

"Yeah, to be honest I can only remember her as a sort of elemental mother figure. Just as I started to mature, she lost it, became evasive and unreliable. I can barely remember a single day we spent together."

"I'm sorry. Depression is an awful thing, and horribly misunderstood. You know, I thought of you over the years – wondered how you were doing."

"Thanks for wondering," Charlie said. "You could have taken a day or two from your busy schedule to come see me if you actually cared."

"I'm not proud of a lot of the decisions I've made in my life. I'm sorry you've had to figure everything out for yourself. But this place, this lake, there's something about it – "

"Let me guess: something divine?"

"Yes. Something divine. I feel like part of me has grown into the land here, like if I left I'd be torn in half and die. Maybe I've been here too long and I'm losing my marbles, but I do know I'll never leave this place again."

"How come you painters are all psycho?"

"Yana had her own thing with the lake," Artemis laughed. "She was always on about a bird, a pterodactyl or something, that was poisoning humanity. She said there was a giant catfish beneath this lake that had the antidote, said the catfish told her to switch to landscape painting."

"See what I mean?" Charlie replied in exasperation. "Psycho!"

"Your mother was a rare and beautiful specimen, and the world is a much worse place without her." Artemis took a deep breath, closed and opened her eyes. "I'm going to tell you something I think she'd want you to hear: it's okay to be a little bit crazy, Chuck, it's necessary for good art, just keep an eye on the crazy if it starts to hurt you, get some therapy or learn to meditate. Eat lots of vegetables."

"Thanks, but I think I'm good. I'm nothing like Yana."

"That's comically untrue – you were doing a pretty good impression out there on the ice the other night. What was that all about anyway?"

"Honestly, I have no idea. It was an accident."

"Just be careful, okay? Your family history reads like a Greek tragedy. I'd love for you to live a long and happy life."

CHAPTER 13

FOR A WHILE after he got back from the cabin there was nothing from Mizza. Charlie shoved the painting containing Philip in a closet and forgot about it. Soon it was the week leading up to Christmas and the city was going bonkers. He spent almost every night with Sophie, taking her to concerts, going to plays, staying in with Thai food and watching old movies. They went shopping for gifts in the cinematic snow, bought second-hand books, stylish coffee mugs and bluish antique mason jars for friends and family. Sophie was an assertive partner in the bedroom and it took a while for Charlie to get up to speed. One night when she was riding him, she shouted at him to say something: "Anything, say anything, I'm about to come."

"I bought a new shirt today,"

"Fu-uck," she moaned, writhing with pleasure.

"I bought a new shirt today?" she said afterwards.

"It's organic cotton."

"Just call me a whore next time, okay?"

"I'm not going to call you a whore, I have too much respect for you."

Sophie laughed. "It's just a game. I like it, okay? If you ever called me a whore outside of coitus I'd castrate you."

"Jeezus," Charlie said, sitting up on the side of the bed. "This is complicated."

"But worth it," Sophie said, biting his neck.

When he asked Greg about this, he only laughed: "You better give her what she wants, stud. I told you she was going to be a handful."

✧

Two nights before Christmas, Charlie was happily frying pineapples and beef in black bean sauce. Sophie was visiting her mom in Montreal, and he was taking a much-needed night for himself. It was dusk and he had Count Basie with Joe Williams on the stereo. He was stirring rice noodles in boiling water to make sure they didn't stick. He took a sip of his beer and then splashed some into the frying pan. It was that critical point in the cooking process where several things needed to happen in quick succession. He was bent over, fumbling with the Lazy Susan, searching for the strainer, when the phone rang. The noise startled him and he smacked his head on the edge of the counter. Goblin meowed, sprinted the length of the apartment and hid behind the wall of records.

Rubbing the back of his head with one hand, Charlie pulled out his phone, but it was dark and silent. He remembered that he had a landline, walked over to the rotary phone hanging next to the fridge and lifted the receiver.

"Hello?"

"Mr. Potichny, hello."

"Mizza? Is that you?" He pinned the phone between his head and his shoulder and rushed back to the stove to stir the food. The cord barely stretched.

"Yes, Mr. Potichny, it is indeed. Sorry I haven't been in touch; things have been a bit hectic."

"How did you get this number? I meant to have this thing disconnected."

"It's listed Mr. Potichny. In the phone book."

Charlie scooped a piece of pineapple out of the pan and ate it. It burned his tongue. He cursed and dropped the phone, which flew across the room and smacked against the wall. He poured cold beer in his mouth and retrieved the receiver. Goblin meowed again, loudly.

"Is everything all right Mr. Potichny? Sounds rather chaotic on your end."

"Everything's fine. Sorry, just burned my mouth on a piece of pineapple."

"A most versatile fruit."

"Yeah, I guess so. Anyway, I assume you're calling about Philip."

"Your assumption is correct."

Charlie dumped the steaming rice noodles into a strainer in the sink and poured cold water over them. "Well, I've got him here. To be honest I'd prefer to get rid of him sooner rather than later. Kind of creeps me out holding a prisoner. This is a personal residence, not Guantanamo Bay."

"Very well, Mr. Potichny, then our agendas are in alignment. I'm down at the station right now, why don't you join me."

Charlie hung up the phone. He took out a pair of scissors and cut the rice noodles several times at different angles. He dumped the contents of the frying pan into a pot with the noodles and poured sesame oil on the smorgasbord. He took a swig of beer, splashed the last sip in the pot and put a lid on it. He donned a coat, grabbed the taped-up painting and headed out the door.

The lit up TTC sign was just around the corner, exactly as it had been before. Charlie descended the steps quickly, using his phone as a flashlight. He was annoyed by the timing of Mizza's call and anxious to get back to his dinner. Reaching the bottom of the stairs, he found the lavish room exactly as it had been.

Mizza was waiting expectantly beneath the zelkova tree. His black, shining eyes shifted and fixed on Charlie, and he hopped towards him, flicking his wings slightly.

"How did you hold the phone to call me?" Charlie asked, fixating on Mizza's huge wings. "You don't even have any hands."

"Mr. Potichny, this is not the time for irrelevant questions. How was your stay at the cabin? Was it enjoyable? Productive?"

"I'm pretty eager to get back to my dinner, Mizza, so why don't we dispense with the small talk. Just take Philip and go home, alright? I'm done being your errand boy."

Mizza was visibly offended by Charlie's tone, and his large avian eyes filled with water. "I thought that by this stage we would have developed a mutual respect for each other, Mr. Potichny. This hasn't been easy for me, you know, navigating your complex world and dealing with everything else back home. I would have liked to think of you as a friend, but perhaps you find me to be a mere nuisance. My mentor always said diplomacy was a lonely, thankless endeavor."

"Mizz, I'm sorry, I really appreciate everything you've done for me, but Philip almost killed me, and I'm still a bit sore over it. I hope everything works out for you. Sorry for being a dick, I've got low blood sugar. Here's the painting. Seriously, thanks for everything."

"I told you there was darkness in his heart. You'd do well to listen to me next time. But hopefully there won't be a next time. Not that I don't enjoy your company, but once we close the book on this jokester I'm hoping to settle into a cushy life of semi-retirement."

Mizza executed a neat little hop and glide movement and plucked the package from Charlie's hands with his beak. No sooner had he taken the painting when a low hum began sounding through the chamber. It grew louder and heavier, causing the whole room to vibrate. Suddenly the thick layers of tape on the painting split open and an ungodly shriek shook reality. Behind Mizza, a portal opened up, but as the diplomat shifted towards it with laboured movements, his feathered mass expanded grotesquely. He stopped in his tracks, jerking around like an epileptic. The painting dropped to the ground. Mizza doubled in size, his eyes ballooned outward, and he began malting rapidly. Then, just as the shrieking hit its highest pitch and reality seemed to fold back on itself in terror, the diplomat burst in a blast of feathers and guts.

The painting lay on the ground, splattered with blood. Charlie moved towards it in a trance, covered in entrails. As he leaned down to pick it up, another shriek burst forth, giving him that awful larvae-in-the-brain sensation. He screamed back at the painting, shouting straight into Philip's glowing face and then hurled it through the portal which promptly zipped itself shut, leaving Charlie standing amongst a pool of blood and feathers in merciful silence.

He trudged back up the stairs and out into the night air. When he reached Queen, he looked back and saw that the lit-up sign and stairwell had vanished. He went up to his apartment, undressed and took a long shower. The rice noodles sat forgotten on the stove.

CHAPTER 14

"FIRST YOU NEED to download this app, then turn on Bluetooth, see? Then you can adjust the volume in every individual room in the house. Pretty cool, right?"

Errol stared enviously at Charlie's sleek iPhone and took out his ancient Blackberry.

"I don't think this has Bluetooth. Can't I just play CDs?" Errol gestured towards his massive collection of classical compact discs.

Charlie laughed. "Why did you install this elaborate setup if you just wanted to listen to CDs?"

"It was his idea," Errol pointed to Greg, asleep on the couch and snoring loudly.

"Well, if you're dedicated to your Blackberry you might need to get a tablet, and I'll help you transfer your CDs to MP3. In the meantime, do you want me to stream something on my phone?"

"'The Messiah' would do quite nicely."

"Okay... who's that by?"

"Handel, for Chrissakes Charlie, George Frederic Handel! Is it really possible that in all these years under my wing you failed to absorb even a modicum of culture?"

It was Christmas at Wychwood, and Errol was in fine form. He had on his Union Jack apron and was busy preparing the holiday meal. Greg and Maggie had driven over for brunch with the kids, who were now building a snowman with Cujo in the front yard. Maggie was reading in the library and Greg – who'd drunk several glasses of strong eggnog at brunch – was passed out cold.

Charlie had happily taken on the role of kitchen helper, slicing celery, julienning carrots, chopping onions. He obeyed Errol's expert instructions as they danced around each other with gleeful holiday cheer. Charlie was grateful for any assigned task. He'd been jumping from one distraction to the next since the incident with the exploding diplomat.

He wanted to put the supernatural events that had punctuated the past months behind him – starting with the first visit from Philip and ending with Mizza's death. But he could not help but feel that these had been the most significant events of his life. The portal had zipped shut with Philip inside; Mizza had died in the line of diplomatic duty; the secret passageway to the underground chamber was sealed and paved over. End of story. And yet he was left with souvenirs and questions.

Philip had made tremendous contributions to both Manic Toads and the recordings for the art gallery. Mizza had somehow lifted the curtain of fatigue that had hung between Charlie and the rest of the world for so long. He could not shake that disturbing image of the feathered diplomat – who he had been rather fond of after all – expanding and exploding in what looked like an intensely painful death.

As thoughts of Mizza churned repetitively in the back of his mind, the choir burst forth into Hallelujah.

"Hey, I know this song!" Charlie said.

Errol rolled his eyes. Greg sat up on the couch and joined the chorus, bellowing loudly. He came into the kitchen and poured himself a hefty glass of wine. He'd taken a package wrapped in golden paper from beneath the Christmas tree, and now he handed it to Errol. "I got you something special this year," he said, eyes lit up with anticipation.

Errol's face loosened and then tightened into a scowl, sensing some sort of mischief. He tore the paper off, revealing a thick sheaf of musty paper. It was a manuscript with a handwritten musical score scribbled onto it. Underneath the music, words had been written in some strange, unrecognizable language.

Errol stared at the papers, completely at a loss, Greg was smiling a demonic smile. "Out with it!" Errol cried, "What in the hell am I looking at here?"

Greg let a beat pass for dramatic effect. "The last lost work of Luka Lampo."

Errol stared at the filthy manuscript, bewildered. "But how on earth?"

When Luka Lampo disappeared just before the turn of the millennium, it was rumoured that he'd been working on something big, perhaps his magnum opus. The work was said to be an opera based loosely on a Finnish folk tale, borrowing freely from the music of Béla Bartók and Jean Sibelius. Many opera lovers, feeling that the art of romantic composition had been mortally wounded in the sonic explosion of the 20th century, were hungry for a consonant production of Wagnerian proportions. There were whispers that Lampo's tantalizing opera might fit the bill, but rumours gradually died out following the disappearance of the brilliant Finnish composer.

On June 6, 1999, Lampo performed a series of piano concertos at a ceremony for members of the International Court of Justice in The Hague. A few months earlier, he'd learned of the death of the only woman he'd ever truly loved. His heart was shattered to pieces, his mind, a muddle of despair.

Immediately following the concert, he slipped out into the fog and rain, the pages of his unfinished opera stuffed roughly into the pockets of his tuxedo. He wandered down to the shipping yard and bribed a sea captain to smuggle him to Nova Scotia amongst a shipment of furniture. As he waited for the boat, he smoked cigarettes, soaked to the bone, and observed a multitude of herons soaring above the harbour. The birds were a deep crimson colour from beak to tail-feather, unlike any herons he'd ever seen before.

He arrived in Halifax five days later, a shade of dirt had darkened his tuxedo. The sky was a silvery indigo, dabbed with a tiny spot of flame from an oil refinery on the horizon. He found a restaurant and accidentally ordered a donair: the sweet white sauce, onions and spiced meat were delicious. Later that night he found himself curled up on the floor of a freight train clutching his stomach and cursing the spicy meat that was burning away the lining of his stomach. He went unconscious, and when he woke he was aware of another presence in the boxcar. He saw the amber glint of a whisky bottle and heard a greedy glugging as some pungent creature turned the bottle up. The glint of white teeth flashed in the dark as the man grinned.

"Why is there something instead of nothing at all? If nothing means anything then everything means everything. I've often penetrated the nubile flesh of young, impressionable women. In pagan cultures my leanings would be considered healthy. People say it isn't good. They say there's an imbalance in my brain. The dinosaur brain, the lizard brain, the primordial force that pummels my intellect time and time again. It's too strong. Like Hulk Hogan fighting Stephen Hawking. No contest. What about you? What do they say about you?"

Lampo was in a fever now, sweating profusely. The burning in his stomach twisted and evolved into the most intense pain he'd ever known. What was this man asking him? Why wouldn't he leave him alone?

"What do they say about you!?" the man bellowed, slamming his bottle against the side of the train. "What the fuck do they say about you!?"

He passed out from the pain, woke up in a bright room surrounded by medical staff. The loudest voice was the drunk man from the train.

"I told you, he's my cousin, the cops beat him up and robbed him. You fucking calling me a liar? My lawyer's going to come to your house and steal your fine china. That man in there? He used to play the 'Singing Saw' for Stompin' Tom, okay? He used to be a world champion log driver. Is it a sport? Sure, it's a fucking sport! I told you, he's my cousin. Goddam, let me see him already."

It hadn't been a heart attack, as the symptoms suggested, but a severe bout of indigestion brought on by the donair. The foulmouthed stranger had paid for a cab, and taken him to the hospital. Back on the street the man berated him.

"I'm down to my last kopek because of you, you disgusting yeti. I'd blame you completely if I wasn't so conscious of my weakness: the profound depth of feeling I possess for my fellow man. But now we're stranded in New Brunswick. I wouldn't wish that fate on my worst enemy. We need to get to Toronto, Hogtown, the Big Smoke! I heard the recycling bins are spilling over with empties there. Man could stay drunk for a truncated lifetime! You got any busking hustle? Any good at devil sticks? Oral sex? I've got a PhD. in philosophy. I could blow your mind all the way from Xenophon to Zizek and back again. But folks won't pay for that. Folks think I'm nuts! Well? You got anything stranger? Stroke the shaft? Carry a tune?"

Despite his decent English, Lampo found himself unable to speak. From the time he landed in Halifax up until his death, he became a selective mute, opening his mouth exclusively to describe aspects of the Chaos Signal and the Ocean Beneath the Lake. In this instance, he mimed playing a violin. Campbell took him to a pawn shop and haggled with the clerk for an old beat up fiddle. Outside of a liquor store near a college campus Lampo played eastern European folk tunes while Campbell slam danced, hammered on rye, and rapped badly:

> Çeci n'est pas un pipe, je sais, je sais
> The French girls love me 'cause I'm so cliché
> Pump My own gas when I hit up the Irving
> East coast women hate me say I'm so self-serving

They stayed in the town, which was called Fredericton, for about a week before they moved on. Campbell recounted the series of events that had led to his current state of squalor. The man had been a respectable university professor up until recently, when an unconquerable lust for cocaine, alcohol, and sex had sent him into a brutal tail-spin that had cost him everything. He'd been caught making love to a young co-ed on the altar of the campus church, doing bumps off a small statue of the Virgin Mary, incense burner up his ass. Oddly, the man maintained a positive outlook on life. As long as he could fuck, get fucked up, and listen to Bob Dylan, he said he would always be happy. He had no regrets, he said, he was just glad to be out of the house.

On the cargo train to Toronto they lived on cans of chili and strong beer. Entering the city from the east, Lampo was astonished by the silhouette of the giant tower in the distance. The landmarks of Europe – Big Ben, The Pantheon, L'Arc de Triomphe – were grand and beautiful, but none of them compared to this in scale in the way that it dominated the skyline so completely and in doing so seemed to express an ownership over the city. What is it for? he wondered.

Later, when he found out that its primary purpose was simply to be very tall and impressive, he was disturbed. What was the meaning of anything in this culture? People built and bustled, but it never seemed to be for any purpose in particular. North Americans, he concluded, were obsessed with distraction as a means unto itself. He started to sense the Chaos Signal, the insidious force that scrambled the minds of the general population, causing them to run in circles without a purpose. It expressed itself as fine veins running through the clouds and strong winds blowing straight out of the ground, kicking up dirt and newspapers – the flooding winds of madness. He could sometimes see it manifest itself as a reddish pigmentation in the sky that migrating geese instinctively avoided; in silver lightning that crashed down upon the superfluous tower.

He relayed all this to Campbell who ate it up, copying down everything that Lampo said on loose printer paper stolen from Kinko's. Campbell loved the sinister imagery, the paranoid poetry of Lampo's rants about the Chaos Signal, the looming shadow of the apocalyptic Pelican:

The wind and clouds were very cryptic
In your mind a frightening triptych

Campbell would wax poetic and then shout his ebullient catchphrase: "Thus Spoke Zarathustra!" And so Lampo became Zee, and all traces of his former life were washed away as he reckoned with the Chaos Signal, which meant working on his opera.

Together, in Toronto, the duo mapped out all the soup kitchens and men's shelters. Eventually they decided that Saint Christopher House was the best. It was almost next door to a beer store, and the volunteers didn't condescend. Over the next fifteen years, drinking strong beer and bad coffee in the nearby parks, Zee completed and then endlessly refined his final gift to the world: an opera called Bluebeard and the Swan. He stored it under whatever he was sleeping on at the time, and on the day that he finished it, he happened to be sleeping on a mattress at Saint Christopher's across the street from Charlie's apartment.

It might have been lost forever if it hadn't been for the fact that Zee and Campbell were sharing bunk beds at the time. In the morning, Campbell would wake up and meditate for several moments on the papers that were stuffed into the metal frame above his head. For all his self-absorption and sensual leanings,

Campbell had surmised that his friend was some sort of lost musical genius and made sure that the pages were preserved.

By this time Campbell had lost all his hair and most of his teeth. He'd suffered a bout of syphilis and become impotent. He could still get fucked up and listen to Bob Dylan, but he certainly could not fuck.

When the tall, big bellied man first showed up, everyone was dubious. It was no problem to accept his free booze and it was fine that he stayed and drank it with them, but it was clear that the man had motives. He asked a lot of questions about Campbell's dead friend, who's loss still tormented him. The tall man was affable and funny, he told good stories, Campbell grew to like him. Eventually the tall man presented a tempting offer: one case of strong beer, delivered to the steps of the shelter once a month for a calendar year in exchange for any papers that Zee had left behind. Campbell could distribute the beer as he saw fit. This was a once in a lifetime offer and one that Zee would have heartily supported. The pages were handed over – the opera as well as the Chaos Signal transcripts – and a celebratory bottle of rye was opened. There was shouting in the street, and eventually the staff came out and chastised Greg for buying the homeless men liquor.

Tears formed in Errol's eyes, "Gregory, this is the greatest gift that anyone has ever given me. I love you, son."

"I love you too, Dad. Really you should be thanking Charlie, he figured out where Lampo had been living. I just had a hunch that maybe those rumours about his lost opera were true."

"Are you fucked?" Charlie said. "Are you completely, thoroughly and irredeemably fucked in your stupid balding head?"

Greg winced at the insult. "I know, it's a lot of money and hassle to deliver the beer, but I'm almost finished with my mortgage. Besides, it's not too far from the opera company."

"That's not what I'm talking about. You can't take them beer you idiot, they're alcoholics."

"So what? I'm basically an alcoholic."

"You're an affluent alcoholic. You drink Scotch that starts with 'Glen.' Liquor ruined these peoples' lives. You just use it to dull your bourgeoisie sense of self-hatred."

Greg and Errol exchanged glances, unsure of how to proceed in the face of this short-sighted sanctimony.

"Look, Charlie, I appreciate your sense of pathos towards your fellow man," Errol said, "but they'd find liquor one way or another if they really wanted to. This way at least it's good, clean beer."

"For an entire year," Greg said. "They're getting a great deal out of this."

Charlie scowled at them. His phone buzzed in his pocket. It was Noodles. "This conversation is not over," Charlie said, going down to the basement to take the call. "Noodles?"

"Charlie! I love this new picking up your phone thing. Makes my life much easier. Sorry to interrupt your holidays, but I've got a Christmas present for you... several, actually. Manic Toads has a release date; we're putting it out first week of January. I know it's short notice but the time is right. We sent out advanced copies to the blogs, and they're losing their shit. We're hoping to have you on the road by February, if you're up for it. Oh, and the AGO people are creaming their pants over the Algonquin sessions. How was the cabin by the way?"

"Actually, it was a lot like a Stephen King novella."

"Weird, I'd love to hear about it sometime. Oh! They wanted me to ask you about a missing painting though? You know what, fuck it. I actually don't give a shit. Anyway, this is shaping up to be your year, Potichny. Hope you're ready for the spotlight."

"Noodles, February is really soon. You know I've never performed in front of an audience, right?"

"Just use backing tracks or something, I don't care, just figure it out."

"God damn it Noodles, it's not that simple – "

"Actually have to run," Noodles cut him off. "My dealer's downstairs. Tell Errol squash is off next week; I'm checking into rehab again on Monday. Merry Christmas. And a happy new year!"

"What did one snowman say to the other snowman?"

They were sitting at the dinner table now and Sebastian –

one of the twins – was testing out a joke he'd just learned.

"What did he say?" Charlie asked.

Sebastian scrunched up his face – couldn't remember the punchline to his own joke.

"Do you smell broccoli?" he finally said.

Esmé – Greg's eldest, who had taught him the joke – laughed mockingly.

"It's do you smell carrots," she said.

"Because his nose is a carrot?" Charlie said. "That's funny."

"If something's funny you don't say that's funny," Esmé replied, "you're supposed to laugh."

"Ha-Ha-Ha."

"You didn't mean that. That was a fake laugh. You're being a dick-weed."

"Esmé!" Maggie said. "Never, ever use that kind of language. Especially at the dinner table."

"It's okay," Charlie said. "I was kind of being a d-weed." He winked at Esmé and sloshed hot gravy over a mound of dark turkey, mashed potatoes, and Errol's famous stuffing. He was on his third glass of red wine and feeling especially fine.

Greg was starting in on his third plate of food, and Errol was taking turns quizzing his grandkids about their favourite subjects in school. Maggie was catching up with Charlie, exuberant to see him looking so energized.

"Have you been seeing anyone?" Maggie asked, "now that you have the energy to tackle the horrors of online dating?"

"As a matter of fact, yes." This caught the whole table's attention. "And you know her. Sophie Rénard, from Saint Mathilda's. I ran into her on the streetcar. You know she sings at the COC with Greg, right? Anyway it's going really well – "

" – Sophie Rénard?" Maggie cut in suddenly. She reached out her hand and grabbed Greg by the arm. "He's dating Sophie Rénard?"

Greg looked up miserably from his mashed potatoes, a faint smear of cranberry sauce on his upper lip. "Yeah," Greg said. "It's going really well. I think it's cool, old friends reconnecting and all. It's romantic."

Maggie was glaring at Greg, creating an uncomfortable tension. Finally, she collected herself and smiled. "I'm glad you met someone that makes you happy Charlie. The four of us will have to get together sometime soon."

"Sounds great," Charlie said, oblivious to Greg's discomfort. "I'll ask her when she's back from Quebec."

"Oh, and Charlie, I meant to ask you, what's this new speed metal thing you're into? Greg is completely mad for it, but you never struck me as a fan of aggressive music."

In a split-second Greg gave Charlie a look like play along. Maggie swiveled her head, but Greg had relaxed his features.

"I started getting into hard music because of this band from Montreal called Death Grips," he said, improvising. "The speed metal scene in Scandinavia is really cool because you've got these big muscular Viking-type guys that look like murderers, but actually they're very gentle. They get all their aggression out in the music and then go home and cook dinner for their parents."

Maggie looked dubious, but let it drop. The conversation turned to topics concerning the children: science projects, book reports, dinosaurs, and ancient Egypt. Greg was quick to clear the dishes when everyone had finished and soon after, Bouche de Noël, coffee, and hot chocolate were served. The children, who'd opened their presents that morning, retreated to the basement to play with their new toys. Errol and Maggie lounged in the living room sipping herbal tea as Charlie and Greg stripped to their underwear, rolled around in the powdery snow and jumped in the backyard hot tub squealing with delight.

In the tub they sipped Scotch and surreptitiously took hits from a dugout. Fat, cartoonish flakes of snow fell around them.

"What was that about Swedish speed metal?" Charlie asked.

"I'll explain, but you have to promise not to judge me."

"If I judged you for all your weird shit, we wouldn't be friends."

"Alright, whatever. Every Sunday when Maggie and the kids are at church I snort a ton of ketamine and go into a k-hole."

"Ketamine? Horse tranquilizers? Is a k-hole where you forget that you're a human and think you're a mountain or something and can't move?"

"Sort of. I think of it as an inter-dimensional drug, but sure, you basically forget that you're human. When I first listened to the demo for your new record I got stuck in a k-hole for way longer than normal. . . but this wasn't your average k-hole, it was like. . . I'd call it a Cathedral. I fell through this massive space surrounded by a crazy waterfall. There were these big aubergine coloured spheres connected by bridges, pillars of light holding them in the air. I dropped down into a rough, salty ocean, and I felt something come towards me, something ancient and massive. My whole spirit caught fire and I started to scream. That's when Maggie found me. I was screaming in reality and all I could come up with was speed metal. Thinking back now though, the music felt tied to the Cathedral – your music I mean. And then, when we were at the Bartók opera I thought I heard the same music. It's that haunting lead melody that's threaded through your album – it sounds almost exactly like Bartók, there's no mistaking it."

"Impossible. I've never listened to Bartók in my life."

"I know. I'm not accusing you of anything, I'm just telling you what happened. It's a trip man, it's a total fucking trip."

Charlie saw a window here to open up about the weirdness, to try and put into words the surreal melodrama that had invaded and transformed his life. Him and Greg had tapped into a channel of psychic weirdness, a spectral universe that weaved and floated just beyond the observable limits of reality. But then again, if, as Charlie suspected, that universe had been restored to order when the portal zipped shut behind Philip, then there was no sense in exploring a phenomenon that sounded plainly insane.

"I think you need to take less drugs," Charlie said lightly. "It sounds like you're losing it."

Greg sighed and dunked his head under the bubbling water.

"You know what, you're right," he said once he'd surfaced. "I'm stressed out lately. I'm not happy. I've been a shit father and a shit husband. I'm going to make a new year's resolution to stop taking drugs. Just a couple drinks a night from now on. If I'm craving drugs, I'll just binge eat or something. All the most famous bass-baritones are fat anyway. With the exception of that Adonis, Dietrich Eichelberg."

"Forget Eichelberger, you should be proud to be Greg Chest. You're a great fucking guy. Be a little kinder to yourself, it's going to be a great year."

Greg was still frowning. In the distance, through the massive maple trees, the CN Tower glowed red and green against the skyline.

"Remember what Errol always taught us?" Charlie said. "Life moves in cycles; when you're winning, you think you'll go on winning forever, when you're losing, same thing. It's impossible to understand that you're going through a phase when you're in it. You can only see it in hindsight."

"You think I'm going through a phase?"

Charlie deliberated.

"I guess everything's a phase. We look at our lives as one big homogeneous thing, but everyone's a different person moment to moment. I've been at least two different people in my life. You've probably been many more than that. Maybe you've been a hundred people."

Greg sat up on the edge of the hot tub in a cloud of steam, snowflakes melting on his flushed body. He tried to calculate how many people he'd been. Charlie let his thoughts float freely, mesmerized by the lights of the massive tower.

After Maggie and Greg had herded the kids into the van and headed for home, Charlie sat with Errol by the fireplace. They were both concerned about Greg: Greg, who sucked up all the attention and energy of his family without even realizing it; who could not seem to appreciate the good fortune and abundance in his life. But now Charlie's star was rising after over a decade of patient, melancholic solitude. And so, they toasted Manic Toads and talked of Noodles, of Enemy Airship, of the prospect of touring and the Yana Potichny retrospective that would take place in late summer.

Once Errol had retired, Charlie strolled aimlessly through the neighbourhood carrying a bottle of Scotch. Cujo bounded around off leash diving snout first into snow banks and rolling around happily. The multicoloured lights on the huge evergreens tickled Charlie's iridescent mind, and it occurred to him that he had only ever been two people and that now he was becoming a third. It was only this third person who was truly happy and although, by his own calculations, he still had a multitude of drastic transformations ahead, he succumbed to an instinctual belief that he would be able to navigate these twists in such a way that would preserve the contentment that he was presently fostering. He was overwhelmed by the sensation of his feelings turning outward, like a telescope that had accidentally been pointed at the ground, suddenly spun towards space and taken up with the purpose for which it had been created.

The lights, the snow, the hits from the dugout, the aftertaste of Errol's stuffing, and a sudden flash of the flavour of Sophie's perfect vagina became, in that moment, the foundation of a profound euphoria that grew and proliferated in his soul as he wound through the bright, silent streets.

CHAPTER 15

IN JANUARY, ANTIDOTES for Manic Toads was released to universal acclaim. Charlie's record quickly became ubiquitous, pouring out of speakers in coffee shops, bars and trendy boutiques across Toronto and beyond. Between fielding calls from journalists and preparing his live show, all of Charlie's energy went into meeting the popular demand for Cave Music. As a result, he became increasingly self absorbed. His focus, which had blossomed outward in the early days of his recovery, now bent inwards with a sense of narcissistic self-love.

Throughout this frenzied period, Charlie continued dating Sophie, who was performing the title role in Vincenzo Bellini's Norma through January. They saw little of each other, meeting up a couple nights a week for athletic lovemaking sessions and a quick glass of wine.

In late February, Charlie embarked on a cross-Canada tour. Midway through those dates, he booked a European tour opening for a musician named Tatiana Tataru (aka, Space Pussy), who Noodles managed as well. Serendipitously, Sophie signed a contract for a role in Paris that overlapped with Charlie's Europe dates, and the couple looked forward to spending several nights together in the City of Lights after being apart for two months.

Also in January, Greg and Maggie made the official decision to separate on a trial basis. Greg put most of his personal belongings into storage and left for a string of gigs that would take him to Dallas, Sydney, and finally Bulgaria. It was generally understood that Maggie and the kids would remain in their house and Greg would find alternative accommodations when he returned. Neither of them said the word divorce, but it loomed large in each of their minds.

$\diamond$

If Charlie had not been so preoccupied with himself that winter, he would surely have noticed a change for the worse descending on his city – a change that he himself had set in motion. By the time things got really bad, he was long gone.

A subtle shift had occurred in the balance of energy that pours into the world through imperceptible channels. This shift gradually caused communication and empathy to break down. There was a massive rash of nasty accidents caused by commuters fixating on their smartphones. Car accidents increased ten-fold, cyclist deaths spiked, and several hapless pedestrians fell down manholes or walked into traffic.

Strange meteorological events materialized. At dusk the sky turned odd hues of red, gold and turquoise, and though people could see this, nobody commented on it. Clouds formed in the sky like corkscrews and sometimes became translucent, as if a network of rivers were spinning through the air. Astronomers observed that Mercury had stubbornly changed its trajectory: it was stuck in retrograde.

For a few weeks, birds vanished entirely from the city, but then, smack in the middle of winter, huge flocks appeared from every corner of the earth. With the birds came an unprecedented thaw; February grew alarmingly warm. A sinister gang of pelicans took up residence in the tourist area of the harbour, occasionally attacking humans. The city's animal control department was totally overwhelmed. Avian hobbyists lobbied on behalf of some of the rarer species that had overrun the city, arguing that they had a right to nest there.

Perhaps the most notable change that came over the city was the manner in which people began to walk past each other and outright failed to notice the sinister spells that were affecting their home. If the citizens of Toronto were becoming more and more oblivious it was partially due to a tacit collective agreement not to upset the status quo. People wanted to be left alone to tap away at their smartphones, lost in a technological amusement park that promised tiny, steady hits of dopamine.

By March the climate was downright tropical, and still, somehow no one said anything, save for the odd mindless comment along the lines of isn't global warming great!? It was as though the tacit agreement of non-communication categorically excluded discussions concerning the rapid decline of civilization. Sales of wireless devices went through the roof. Fundraising for charities and the arts dropped to virtually nothing. Everyone stopped recycling and the landfills spilled over with outdated electronics. Organic food waste mixed indiscriminately with Styrofoam and broken iPads and stank in the strange winter heat. Commuters decided, as if by agreement, that public transit was for poor, crazy people and anyone who owned a car drove it everywhere, creating citywide gridlock, emitting shimmering waves of burnt up fuel that mingled with the liquid, corkscrewing clouds.

Animals were impervious to the spell but suffered because of it. Hundreds of pets died of starvation or from ailments that went unnoticed across the city. Pet owners largely grew annoyed with their animals, suddenly seeing them as a hassle rather than a comfort. A company that developed phone apps and toys observed this phenomenon and began manufacturing hyper-realistic robotic pets that did not require feeding or walking but were programmed to show affection, fetch, and play dead – no training required. The robot pets were a massive success.

Throughout these months of entropy, Errol looked after both Cujo and Goblin, who'd formed an unlikely alliance in the house at Wychwood. Errol mostly worked from home, and that winter, observing the madness of the flooding wind that had overtaken society, he scarcely left the house, ordering most of his groceries online and trading equities and index funds by phone. He read long neglected leather-bound classics and rekindled his love of literature. He found that Charlie had underlined passages and made notes in the margins of all his books – he came to see Eliot, Tolstoy, and Fitzgerald through Charlie's lens, and realized how utterly isolated and depressed the boy had been. He recalled the strange, haunting noises Charlie had made on his baby grand piano and finally understood that it had not been random key mashing, but a subtle expression of despair; a cry for help.

Along with Lampo's Bluebeard opera – which Melody and the rest of the opera board had fast-tracked for the autumn season – Greg had also given Errol his writings on the Chaos Signal. Errol had the writings translated into English and initially assessed them as the writings of a deranged lunatic. As the months went by, however, he realized that these strange pages constituted a set of prophecies that were now coming to pass. Errol grudgingly took over the responsibility of delivering beer to the men at Saint Christopher's house and became friends with Campbell.

The homeless and the mentally infirm were dying off and disappearing, he learned, obvious fodder for the flooding winds of madness. Lampo was the only guy who'd known what was going to happen – who'd seen what was coming with clarity – and yet, he'd been unmistakably insane. Based on his conversations with Campbell, Errol developed a theory: if the Chaos Signal was a disease, then Lampo's opera was the antidote, an artistic expression with the power to scramble the enemy's signal. It struck him that his life was turning into a way-too-long episode of the twilight zone. He felt that the plot would not be resolved until his boys returned from Europe, where he imagined they were gallivanting carefree, without a worry in the world.

PART TWO:

DECAY

CHAPTER 16

BEFORE HE EVEN had a chance to take the artwork into consideration, Charlie decided that the spacious atmosphere, natural light and rich acoustics of the Musée D'Orsay were already worth the price of admission. Once he was done marvelling over the majestic ambiance of the museum, he took in the statues, busts, and paintings casually, not looking at any of the names or dates. He wanted to let the impressions simply wash over him.

It was only when he reached the Van Gogh area – several small interconnected rooms – that he realized how sharply the acoustics shifted from the main hall to the smaller galleries. In the small rooms the sonic landscape tightened and clarified, individual voices were discernible. The main hall – a huge train station built at the turn of the nineteenth century – transformed all vocal and ambient noise into a massive wash similar to the churn of the seashore. Charlie weaved quickly in and out of the Van Gogh galleries, effectively opening and closing a filter on the ambient noises of the space.

The sound of the museum comprised what seemed like an infinite spectrum of frequencies and textures. Charlie closed his eyes and smiled in a blissed-out trance. A young, pretty woman knocked into him. She was about to cuss him out when a change suddenly came over her.

"Martha, Tracy," she cried, "come over here, you won't believe who I've just bumped into." Her friends came over. They were college girls from London. "This is so weird; we were just talking about you. You're opening for Space Pussy at Golden Arrow tonight, yeah? We're dying to get tickets, but it's been sold out for ages."

A feature article on Cave Music had been posted recently on a popular website, featuring a handsome press photo of Charlie.

It had increased his visibility greatly. The girls looked at Charlie expectantly.

"I can probably put you on the guest list?"

"Is that a question or a statement?" The girl asked, smiling.

"Well, I don't really know anyone in Paris, so I'm sure I have some free spots. Write your name down, and I'll give you three spots."

She wrote her name down in his notebook. It was Natalie.

"Can we get a picture with you?" Natalie asked.

"Yeah, sure," Charlie looked slightly uncomfortable, still acclimatizing to his minor fame.

Natalie placed her hand gently on the side of his neck and looked into his eyes. "I'm so sorry I walked into you."

They used a selfie stick to take a picture of the four of them in front of an iconic self portrait of Vincent Van Gogh. Charlie had no idea whether or not he should smile, but the girls commanded him to make several different faces ranging from sultry to silly. Natalie gave him the name of their hotel, told him to come by for a drink and kissed him on the cheek. When they parted ways, he felt pangs of guilt rushing through him on several different counts, but mostly he felt guilty because of Vincent.

On the Wikipedia page for clinical depression, there was an image of one of his paintings. Charlie had been doing online research lately, trying to figure out his mother, trying to figure out himself. The contours of the buildings and figures he painted all aligned with the brushstrokes that composed the landscape and the sky, as if he were creating a sense of cohesion between people and things that did not exist in reality. It was as though his imagined worlds were submerged in liquid, frozen in celestial jelly. The paintings drew Charlie's attention to the fact that people are made up of the same stuff as objects, and that only empty space is truly exceptional, since it has the potential to be filled with something new. Only new things, novel things, were beautiful. All things, Tatiana had taught him, are most beautiful in their inception. He turned his focus back to the paintings. Spending so much time with his tour partner had caused him to extrapolate and philosophize from basic experiences in a way that was perhaps unhealthy.

In the famous self-portrait, Vincent's face was sallow and

his neat red beard trimmed close to the lines of his face. One could argue that self-portraits were the original selfies, but their value wasn't quantified by likes on social media. Likes had been different in the Belle Époque: a well-placed bon mot, perhaps, in an influential salon. He'd cut his ear off and killed himself. Charlie was pretty sure he'd killed himself. He'd probably be mortified if he knew that people were going to take smartphone selfies in front of his painted selfies.

Charlie imagined that every time someone took a smartphone photo of a painting it died a little bit. If this were true, then the self-portrait was a corpse hanging on the wall. He studied Vincent's face closely. His blue eyes matched his blue jacket, which matched the blue background, once again suggesting congruity when there was only incongruity. Vincent looked impatient and anxious under the gaze of all the tourists jostling to get a closer look. Could he have known that this was his fate? To be captured by horny, vainglorious teenagers on holiday, subjected to a plethora of digital filters and regurgitated, out of focus, onto a thousand tiny screens that people looked at while they were defecating or procrastinating?

As Charlie studied his face carefully, tenderly, the painting came alive and blocked out the surrounding tourists, closed the sound filter completely, enveloping Charlie in total silence. Him and Vincent were the only two beings in the universe, locked into a mutual understanding. All other space was empty, an infinite field of possibility.

Charlie felt the molecular makeup of his body change, felt the lightness of the brushstrokes transform the contours of his soul into something that fit with the rest of this new reality. He felt bright, happy and wise. Charlie thought it was strange that he didn't want to ask him any questions, didn't want to speak to him at all, really. It struck him that in this field he had no questions. Language was superfluous. Experience coiled itself into a warm hug. He zoomed out and saw himself and Vincent in matching rose-coloured jackets, floating against a slightly darker rose-coloured background. Vincent smiled wide with no apprehensions, as if to say now you see why we make art, because it is a sanctuary where you can live forever in ease and comfort, apart from the awfulness of the world. Charlie nodded, Vincent folded his arms smugly. He was alive, hiding out in his own painting, shielded from the public in a way that Charlie could never have understood.

He left the Musée D'Orsay and walked along the bank of The Seine feeling light and joyful. There had been a time when he thought he would never leave the country he was born in, a time when he didn't know if he'd live past thirty or if he even wanted to. But now he was off on a grand adventure that still felt completely surreal. The world was magical and mutable, expanding infinitely outward in a network of tantalizing possibilities.

Everything stirred him; everything he saw seemed to possess a secret message, just for him, that pointed towards life. It was spring and sticky green buds were sprouting from the soil; colourful flowers blossomed in front of the little shops along each street. He was struck by how much sadness was contained within each grain of happiness, how paradoxical it was to truly feel the world. Everything was a swirling Manichean dance of joy and sorrow, small victories and small defeats, connections and missed connections. People coming and going in and out of his life so quickly, as if through a revolving door. He would die someday, everyone would die someday, but to drink from the cup of life unrestrained for a time? What a privilege!

He came upon Notre Dame Cathedral from the rear, bought a cup of wine and a croque monsieur and sat on a bench. The silvery clouds cleared, and light shone down as if in a single concentrated ray on the dusty courtyard. Charlie thought that the heavily buttressed cathedral resembled a sort of living fortress in a symbiotic relationship with the chipped gargoyles perched along its flanks. A dry, dusty aroma presaging rain wafted up his nose; the density of the air changed. He finished his sandwich, pulled out a copy of A Moveable Feast and read half a page, chugged the last sip of his wine and fell peacefully to sleep on the bench. He was awakened after twenty minutes by a light rain and walked in a pleasant daze towards Le Marais to meet Greg for a coffee.

Chapter 17

"I wish you weren't so late. I accidentally spent two hundred dollars on socks," Greg whined as they wandered the narrow cobblestone of the colourful shopping district.

"Sorry pal, this whole European boozing in public thing leads to a lot of napping in public."

"Don't even talk to me about napping. I've barely slept in weeks. This King Lear shit is dark. I feel like Heath Ledger playing the Joker. I've run through every sleeping pill, from Ativan to Zopiclone and back again. Nothing works anymore."

A wispy, black beard had sprouted on Greg's face, dark pouches hung beneath his eyes. He was hunched as he walked, wearing a long wool trench coat. Charlie, who'd mostly known his friend as a bon vivant, was slightly worried, but also believed that Greg was hamming it up a bit. His turn in Bulgaria as the Dutchman had been very well received and sharpened his ability to sing in German. When Eichelberger had bailed on his engagement to sing the title role in King Lear, Greg had been the first choice to replace him. Where Eichelberger had disappeared to was unclear. He'd had a nervous breakdown in the middle of his run in New York; it was rumoured that he'd retreated to a monastery in Nepal indefinitely.

They emerged from the narrow lanes into a busy roundabout. The sun was trying to break through a light layer of grey clouds. Greg shielded his eyes as if the sunlight were burning him and donned a pair of aviators. They sat down at a tiny table at a sidewalk café. Charlie ordered a coffee, Greg ordered a ginger ale in bad French and lit a cigarette.

"Ginger ale? That's a first."

"If I start hitting the bottle right now, I won't be able to stop. The rehearsals have been so fucking stressful. I can tell that everyone wishes Eichelberger were here. The damn opera was written in Bavaria. This role has never been performed by a singer from outside Germany, let alone an American."

"You're not American," Charlie pointed out.

Greg shook his head. "It's the same to them, Canadians and Americans. Semantics."

"I don't think that's how you use the word semantics," Charlie said grinning.

"Whatever, you know what I'm saying."

"Well anyway, they cast you. You got the part. This is your chance to tackle a serious dramatic role. All you have to do is get out of your own way. You'll do great."

Greg lit a fresh cigarette off the end of his old one and looked at Charlie for a long time. "You seem good. Seems like you've been able to get out of your own way, finally," he said with an ironic grin.

Charlie ignored the hostile tone and crossed his legs. "I've been great, yeah, touring's been really fun. I missed Sophie though, so excited to finally see you guys on stage together. It's kind of funny that she's playing your daughter. You know, because you guys fucked?" He stared into the reflective surface of the aviators, trying to read Greg's face.

"It's not really funny," Greg said. "It's pretty tragic actually. Lear really is in love with Cordelia in a kind of incestuous way. Listen, it's been disturbing putting this production together." He took off his glasses and pinched the bridge of his nose. "Honestly, even I wish the kaiser of darkness Dietrich Eichelberger were here to tackle this one. I don't feel right singing this role. I know he really wanted to do it. He owns this territory. I'm out of my depth."

A thick silence hung between them. Greg sulked for a moment and then looked up at Charlie with his sad, beautiful, bloodshot eyes.

"I'm not giving you the talk that you want me to give you right now," Charlie said finally.

"What?"

"I'm not going to do that thing where you're depressed and acting like your life is over and I comfort you and tell you everything's going to be okay and that you're great. I'm sorry that you and Maggie split, but you said it yourself: it's for the best."

The waiter finally came over with Charlie's espresso and set down a baguette stuffed with ham in front of Greg.

"J'ai commander un boisson gingembre, monsieur," Greg said.

"Oui, c'est ca monsieur! Sandwich au jambon!" the waiter cried, rushing off.

Greg picked up the sandwich and chewed lazily at it.

"Why is this so confrontational?" Greg asked through a mouthful of ham. "Shit's been weird between us since you got here. I'm sorry, look, I am having a hard time, but I don't necessarily need a pep talk or anything. I'm glad we get to hang out, so can we just be friends, please?" He waved his napkin as though it were a white flag.

Charlie rolled his eyes. "I guess I just feel like we got into this routine where I never had anything going on so all we talked about was you. And now things are going well for me, and you just want to keep treating our friendship like a series of free therapy sessions."

Greg took too big of a bite from his sandwich au jambon and coughed violently.

"You're right. I'm sorry. It's just a big shift. You're suddenly this ultra-hip cult phenomenon, you got on this amazing European tour, I'm sure you've got pussy falling out of your pockets – "

"I'm with Sophie."

"Oh whatever, I don't give a shit. You barely know Sophie. Like it matters if you fuck a groupie or two."

"Watch it. Look, you chose to get married, you chose to have kids. Nobody forced that shit on you, okay? It's not my fault you treated your marriage like a prison." Charlie looked fixedly at the revolving traffic.

"Fame really is turning you into an asshole, you know that?"

"Just following in your footsteps, I guess."

They sat in uncomfortable silence, Charlie checking his phone while Greg finished his sandwich. Greg walked inside the café and helped himself to a ginger ale. "Sandwich au jambon," he said to the waiter, holding it up.

"Oui, bien-sur, boisson au gingembre," the waiter repeated, smiling. Greg sat back down and took a long sip.

"Remember that conversation we had in the hot tub? At Christmas?" Greg said, finally. "You said that we always become several different people within our lifetime?" Charlie nodded. "I was thinking about it, and I agree with you, but I feel like beneath those inevitable shifts, you have to have one unchanging self to keep it all together. Like if you were a boat, you'd have the freedom to travel the whole world, but maybe there's an anchor you're attached to and the chain is just long enough that you could go anywhere. It doesn't infringe on your freedom, but it's important to remember it's there. Do you see what I'm saying?"

"Are you thinking about taking up sailing? That is classic mid-life crisis."

"I'm serious, Charlie, don't joke around, this is important. Do you understand what I mean?" Greg had become excited, even a little desperate.

"I don't know, sure," he sighed. "Maybe. Not really. Listen, I'm going to be late for sound-check, but I'll think about the anchor thing, I promise." He threw some coins on the table and stood up to go.

"Have you heard about everything back home?" Greg asked. "All the weird shit? Did you hear about the birds and mercury retrograde?"

"I saw some headlines, something to do with climate change? Mercury retrograde is a bunch of bullshit. I'm sure it's fine."

"Where did you get that sample from by the way?" Greg asked suddenly. "I know you didn't make it – it's been driving me crazy."

Charlie pretended to watch the foot-traffic.

"It's not in your sonic language, I know your style inside out, it's distinctly classical."

"That's an interesting note, actually," Charlie mumbled.

"Just please tell me. I won't rat you out, but I need to know."

Charlie blushed all over, got up to hail a taxi, and looked down at his friend's anguished face. "I thought you were going to lay off the drugs. That includes sleeping pills. Please Greg, get some real rest, get a massage and take a bath or something. Stop worrying about me and get your own head right. You're opening tomorrow night."

He got in a cab and shut the door. At Charlie's command the driver raced towards Belleville, taking a detour through Place de La Bastille where the beastly modernist opera house stood ominously in contrast to the bright beauty of the July Column: the golden, glittering figure of the winged statue perched atop its bronze drums, holding the torch of civilization aloft.

The details of the city, which had seemed so enchanting an hour earlier, blurred indistinctly now as he became absorbed in his own racing thoughts. Greg's comment about pussy falling out of his pockets had hit a nerve. He had, in fact, cheated on Sophie twice while touring Canada. Once with a curvaceous, red-headed bartender at a club in Saskatoon, and once with a fashionable, eccentric college girl who lived by the ocean in Vancouver. These one-night stands had not been satisfying or enjoyable. He'd felt as though he were acting out these trysts as part of a script written by a hack.

He'd tried to drown his guilt and shame with alcohol, which worked as a temporary Band-Aid at night, but left him nauseous and irritable in the daytime. He had to be sober enough to perform, and the right amount of alcohol – about three drinks – helped to temper the inhibitions that would have prevented him from giving his all onstage. Afterwards, hanging out at the merch table, he would accept drinks from enthusiastic fans and grow drunk, demonstrating a healthy and genuine affability; though his mind was always drifting in several directions at once.

When the offer came in to tour Europe with Space Pussy, Charlie was so caught up in the daily repetition of self-hatred (during travel), self-effacement (while performing), and self-love (holding court after the shows), that he couldn't imagine going home to straighten himself out. Errol could look after Goblin for another month. Besides, Tatiana was a big-time talent. She was one of the original architects of Space Disco who could also, on the other end of the spectrum, throw down soulful minimalist piano compositions. She even had a few rap mixtapes in her discography that were pretty decent.

As Charlie's transatlantic flight had lifted off, he'd closed his eyes and prayed. Not to the birds, but to the sea dragon who'd healed him in his sleep. He'd been dreaming about her every night, but it was never quite as real as it had been that first time; it was weaker, a sort of distant facsimile that grew more distant with each passing night. The birds were multiplying, roosting all over his hometown, wreaking chaos and havoc, and he could feel the dragon diving deeper and deeper, its healing effect on the fragmented, vibrating world growing feebler with each passing day.

There had been a great deal of turbulence during the ascent. Charlie had prayed for a reversal of the chaos, vowed to behave himself, vowed to be temperate and kind. But even as he prayed to the dragon, he was airborne, leaving his native country behind. His distant prayers grew more and more distant from their target as the airplane lifted above the clouds and strayed out over the yawn of infinite ocean.

When the turbulence ended he'd stopped praying. As if immediately forgetting the noble intentions he'd just set for himself, he ordered a Bloody Mary with two extra ounces of vodka. He swallowed a valium pill, popped his ear buds in and gave himself over to a compilation of psychedelic funk. By the time the stewardess shook him awake in Dublin he'd forgotten the prayer. After that he stopped dreaming about the dragon.

CHAPTER 18

TATIANA TATARU WAS precisely the type of person who makes you feel that there is an elevated class of human beings, of which you will never be a part. She was stunningly beautiful with green eyes, light brown hair, and a well toned body. She wore endless variations on an outfit combining slick boots, tight black jeans, blazers, and colourful, elegant blouses. It was difficult to tell how old she was – she emitted a youthful glow, but her wit and encyclopedic, polyglot knowledge suggested the wisdom of age. As an adolescent prodigy, she'd studied music in Munich and literature in Paris with students twice her age. By the time Charlie met her, she'd already had a long, storied career in the industry, establishing herself as a musical chameleon.

Tatiana's father was a handsome, famous architect who had fled Soviet-occupied Romania in the 1960s and landed in Sweden; her mother was an intensely beautiful, intelligent woman who'd been left to run the most popular newspaper in Stockholm when her first husband died unexpectedly of a heart attack. Tatiana had travelled a lot as a child and took up the piano at the age of four. In her late teens she moved to New York and started a trip hop band called Zamboni. They were briefly signed to a major label, but a dispute between Tatiana and the execs led to a termination of their contract: the only radio-friendly single on the album was called Lick My Throbbing Clit. Her bandmates had pleaded with her to change it, but she hadn't budged.

Disillusioned with label politics, she'd relocated to Berlin in the mid-90s when it was still genuinely seedy and cheap. In a shabby apartment, overlooking the grey flatness of East Germany, she'd mastered two genres that were almost diametrically opposed. One was an elegant, minimalist imitation of the Parisian pianist Erik Satie that drew inspiration from Brahms and Chopin as well. The other was a slow-burn, highly danceable blend of funk music and deep house with subtle elements of ambient interspersed throughout. Along with several other producers working in isolation, Tatiana was credited as one of the founding architects of Space Disco. She was known to stay in her apartment for weeks at a time, barely eating or sleeping, subsisting solely on green tea and fruit. She would emerge every once in a while, in bright, loose fitting jogging suits and crash her friends' shows, freestyling as MC Bolkonsky, dropping such gems as:

> I'm Like a combination:
> Gordie Howe, Chairman Mao, uh-huh,
> I score goals, yeah I fuck cows,
> Then I'm like, James Joyce in a Rolls Royce,
> I make the ladies moist with my gold voice

She would proceed to take ecstasy and dance for two or three days straight, often retreating to some dark corner of whatever warehouse party she was at to fornicate, releasing the tension she'd built up in her marathon work sessions.

In the mid-aughts one of her classical piano albums caught like wildfire, selling half a million copies internationally. Having no interest in wealth or financial matters, Tatiana rented a castle in the northern mountains of Romania for a summer and spent the money on drugs and recording equipment. She invited half the musicians in Berlin to party and make music on the compound of a dead prince – Mihai the Penetrator – who had had a penchant for torture devices and raucous bacchanals.

In recent years, she'd relocated to Toronto and begun working as a producer for indie musicians and best-selling pop artists alike – she'd even won a Grammy for her contribution to a massively successful electro-pop crossover record. Her adventures in pop music, and the naturally calming effects of aging, had finally compelled her to craft her own version of a straightforward pop album: a collection she'd titled Tender Fjords and released under the alias Space Pussy. The album was a bizarre mixtape of piano ballads and dance tracks.

The album was good, but the live show was amazing. As Space Pussy, Tatiana was finally free to combine her many talents into a single spectacle, taking the audience on a wild ride through many different genres, sometimes encoring with an hour of Space Disco and carrying the party well past the noise curfew. She always paid the fine out of pocket.

✧

Tatiana's green room at Flèche D'Or had once been a wine cellar. The venue itself, like the Musée D'Orsay, had been a train station in the early-twentieth century. The walls of the cellar were composed of huge, old stones with moss growing between them; the room was lit mostly by candles, the way Tatiana liked it. Charlie knocked and was bade to enter. She had her boots up on an antique trunk, reading Huysman's Against Nature. She set the book down and poured them each a glass of sparkling wine. Her eyes were a dark, almost black, shade of green, indicating a pensive mood.

"How was soundcheck?" she asked. "You look a little off. Nothing like bubbles to raise the spirits."

Charlie sipped the cold fizzy wine. It was sweet but had a strangely bitter aftertaste. His spirits rose a little. "Check was fine. I had a fight with my best friend is all. I'm worried about him. Worried about everything back home."

"You're playing a sold-out show in Paris, and you're stuck in your head?" she smiled, amused. "You realize that's completely ridiculous. You can let go of your worries, you know. My god, since I met you, you've been a knot of nerves and stress. Let's have some fun tonight."

Charlie forced a smile. "You're right. I need to stop resisting the flow."

"Incorrect!" Tatiana yelled, draining her glass excitedly (Charlie had observed that she had an absurdly high alcohol tolerance). "Resisting the flow is the name of the game. You know who goes with the flow? People who work for banks and PR companies. People who pay their taxes and complain interminably about their phone bills – normies, they're called these days, though once upon a time it was petite bourgeoisie.

They think that artists have it easy, that we get to sit around all day having fun, funny little thoughts and playing around with crayons. But to be a true artist you have to swim upstream vigorously, against the flow. You can pander to the masses but, in my view, that disqualifies you. Commercial artists may not swim in the same river as the ignorant rabble, but they're still flowing in the same direction, using the same force of momentum to carry them along. I consider that shameful. I'd rather be a sewer rat than a commercial artist. Never go with the flow Charlie. If you ever see me going with the flow, put a gun to my head and pull the fucking trigger."

"Jesus. That's pretty extreme."

"Did you see the Bouguereau?"

"Huh?"

"Bouguereau? Danté and Virgil? I told you to look out for it."

"I'm not so sure." Charlie took a small sip of his wine. "I didn't look at any of the artists' names. Van Gogh was the only one that really captured my attention."

"Pffft, Van Gogh, what a hack. Flashy colours, fancy little flicks of the wrist. Glorified postcard artist. Candy for the eyes that rots the brain."

"Don't talk about him like that," Charlie said, reflexively.

"Oh, I'm so sorry," Tatiana's lips curled into a grin. "I didn't realize he was a personal friend of yours."

"He suffered for his art is all. I mean, he killed himself, right?"

Tatiana shot him a grave look. "Is that what you think? That he was a martyr to his art? Let me explain something to you: suffering for one's art is a fallacy. We may be a little loftier, a little more sensitive than your average normie, but that doesn't change the fact that art is simply our job. You punch in, put in your time, then punch out. It's not personal; it's not special; it's just work. If you make it personal you'll lose your mind like your precious Vincent." She was silent for a moment, allowing Charlie to absorb this. "My god, do you know how he died?" she didn't wait for Charlie to answer. "He shot himself through the chest, but the bullet missed his heart. He walked, bleeding on himself, to the doctor. He was treated, but died from an infection the next day. His final words were 'the sadness will last forever.'" Tatiana paused and then broke into mirthful laughter. "The sadness will last forever? Have you ever heard anything so pretentious, so melodramatic? Fortunately, his sadness was terminated, and he was set free. Shuffled loose the mortal coil."

She saw that Charlie was upset and changed her tone. "For some people, the human body is a torture chamber. But usually this type of suffering can be avoided if the subject is reasonable. Some people are more attached to their suffering than we could possibly imagine. Once the attachment takes root it is difficult to sever. This is how some people end up in Hell."

Charlie balked. "You believe in Hell?"

Tatiana's eyes had brightened slightly to a forest green, accented by flecks of gold.

"Not in the traditional Judeo-Christian sense. I believe that people often make their own lives a form of hell. That's even the driving idea behind Inferno. The inhabitants of Hell could be saved if they allowed for it, but they've conditioned themselves to suffer. As Thom Yorke says. . ."

"You do it to yourself," Charlie anticipated the lyric. "That's what really hurts."

"Precisely. Now, if you'd taken the time to inspect the Bouguereau you would have seen a masterful portrayal of Schichhi the usurper sinking his fangs into the neck of Capochhio, the heretical alchemist. Bouguereau emphasizes the straining tendons and muscles of the two men as the usurper seems to drink from the neck of the alchemist. In the painting, Virgil has adopted an air of stoicism; he gazes into the distance, taking in the panorama of Hell, indifferent to this specific, disgusting scene. Danté, on the other hand, stares directly at the damned souls in front of him, feeling shame for the one man and pity for the other. Virgil is wary of getting involved with the individuals: you can't do anything to help them; you can only allow yourself to be pulled down. This is not Virgil's first rodeo. As artists, we are not special. Don't think for a second that we are. However, we do have a privileged vantage point. At the cost of being on the sensitive end of the spectrum, of having the broadest of souls ourselves, we receive the ability to see into the hearts of our fellow men. We take what we find, organize it in a way that is aesthetically pleasing – or at least that elicits a powerful reaction – and for this work we are worshiped. There is an occupational hazard however: that we may get sucked into the affairs of normies and egoists, our soft bones crushed beneath the hooves of earthly devils."

Tatiana grew more and more excited. She stood up and emptied the last of the champagne into her glass. Her eyes were emerald now, positively shining with joy. She paced for a moment and then sat down, crossed her legs over the trunk.

"There's an apocryphal story, more of a folk tale really, in which Jesus goes to Hell. He's fresh from the cross – and isn't it amazing that back then a cross was simply a structure that was good for nailing people to – but rather than catch his breath in Heaven he bee-lines it down to Hell. What a go getter! What virtue! In Hell he liberates all the sinners, zaps them up to heaven, and Hell, that big fat glutton, let's out a groan because it thinks the party is over and there will be no more sinners. And would you believe it, Jesus, people pleaser that he is, actually comforts Hell! Says something like 'Don't cry Hell, for powerful men: judges, lawyers, politicians will come to you from all over and down the ages, and you will be as full as ever until such a time as I rise again.' How great is that? You see Charlie, those who are most suited to participate in our society are precisely those who are the least suited for happiness and fulfillment. Artists get sucked into the act of self-loathing when they over-identify with their work. You need to keep a cautious distance from the mundane affairs of the bourgeoisie – that ridiculous zoo of insecurity and posturing – while giving the false impression that you are participating."

Charlie wrestled with all this and mulled it over as Tatiana stared at him expectantly. "But don't you think that a living piece of us nests inside of our work?" he asked. "Isn't that what makes art exciting? If you can actually impart some morsel of your soul into the work, isn't that what makes it compelling?"

"What, like a Horcrux?" Tatiana laughed.

"I'm serious."

"No. I don't believe that. And I also don't really believe in Hell. Which means, if you are smart and talented, then everything is permitted and the world is like an amusement park, and every ride is Space Mountain and there is never a lineup."

"I still think Van Gogh is brilliant."

"So do I. I was just fucking with you. Your naïveté invites deceit. You should be conscious of that."

There was a knock at the door. The promoter informed Charlie that he was due onstage in fifteen minutes. He finished his wine, left Tatiana, and went to his own separate green room which was lit by fluorescent bulbs and smelled of bleach. He stretched, peed, cracked a beer, and walked out onstage in front of a packed house.

Chapter 19

Charlie's stage rig consisted of a digital piano (he typically laid the foundation with piano loops), a synthesizer, a sampler, and his black bass. He had a plethora of beats stored on his MacBook after Tatiana had patiently taught him how to run digital tracks. He did not sing and specifically asked that a vocal mic not be put on stage. He did not address the audience except with his music. His set consisted of one very long song that loosely resembled Antidotes for Manic Toads, but the music evolved in a different and unexpected way each night.

That night, Charlie was distracted as he took the stage. He gazed out over the black blob of the audience through the massive arched windows. The crowd was a variegated cross-section of enthusiastic Parisian hipsters; they swayed to the rhythm of the tremolo as he twisted the knob on his keyboard and slowly built up the foundation of his set. It was a slow start, but the crowd was boisterous.

Sensing that they wanted to dance, Charlie chugged greedily at his beer and brought in a heavy kick drum. He grabbed the little black bass, plucked a few notes, and signaled the sound-engineer to turn it up. He pulled a pick out of his back pocket and started riffing, fingers dancing around the neck, avoiding the root note, stuttering and punctuating. Suddenly he jumped up high on the neck and landed on something crazy funky. Cries of joy erupted from the audience and Charlie cracked a smile. He walked over to the MacBook and turned up the beat, adding some hi-hats and snare hits.

He walked to the centre of the stage and lost himself in the bass part, slapping and popping, shifting his weight from side to side. Something was growing inside of him – nocturnal, glowing, jungle fungus. He floated out of himself and swirled like a ghostly blanket around his own body. He looped the bass, swung it behind his back, and just danced. His eyes were closed, elbows going up and down in front of his face like a pop star possessed. He chilled the beat out, stepped over to the synthesizer, and started ripping monster leads with a sawtooth signal.

The fungus was spreading, growing brighter and hotter. He was not in control of himself, but he could do no wrong. The whole room had started to vibrate and shake. He was fucking with the beat, fucking with the synth, opening and closing filters, jumping up and down with the crowd. He'd never felt confidence like this in his life. When he brought in Philip's track on the sampler the crowd erupted, and Charlie thought the windows were going to break. He looked over and saw Tatiana standing stage-side with a sly smile on her face. Something clicked: there was something in his system, something more than adrenaline; the wine had had a bitter aftertaste, but he hadn't thought anything of it at the time. He began to suspect that he was high on ecstasy for the first time in his life in front of a thousand strangers. Still, he wasn't nervous, he felt like he was in his own living room. He kicked his shoes off and slid around the stage carpet in his tattered socks.

He knew he should've been angry at Tatiana for drugging him, but the sublime torrent flowing through him drowned the anger. He wanted to isolate each moment and each instant between each moment. He thought about time and how it was indivisible by nature, despite the human impulse to chop it up like a carrot on a cutting board. The past was in the present, the present was in the present, and the future was in the present. He wanted to lock himself into a single moment – isolate and loop it. He wanted to be like Vincent, hiding inside his own painting. The Tortoise and the Hare, Zeno's Paradox, Schrodinger's Cat, Pavlov's Dog. The wild threads of his thoughts were splitting and proliferating. The feeling of harmony drilled into the depth of his cells and expanded outward like an invisible force field. Each time he took a breath his whole body shook violently, and still, he manipulated the sounds expertly without thinking for even one second about what he was doing.

Next thing he knew, Tatiana was onstage behind him, attacking a drum kit. She was mimicking the kick pattern and playing Keith Moon fills with her hands. People started pulling out smartphones, capturing the moment for their socials as the audience heaved forward as a single sweaty, homogeneous organism.

Charlie turned his back to the wild audience and ambled over to Tatiana, who settled into a straight beat.

"Am I on drugs?" Charlie yelled.

"What?" Tatiana yelled back.

"Am I on drugs?"

"I don't know," she said. "Are you on drugs?"

Charlie shook his head. His hair, which had grown long on tour, went all in his face. "Just enjoy it," Tatiana yelled. "This is fun."

"You're right. This is fun. It's funky. People like it."

Charlie felt like recording Antidotes for Manic Toads had resembled a journey to the centre of the earth. With Philip's help, he'd meticulously drilled clear through the crust, the upper and lower mantles, straight into the core. The second he touched the core, the journey was over. Everything reset. Each night he tried to recreate this journey systematically. At the Flèche D'Or, having tossed out his usual map, and with the help of Tatiana, he felt like he'd uncovered a cheat, by which he'd teleported from the surface of the earth directly to its core. Upon touching the core, the journey continued. He was scattered across the galaxy in an explosion of shimmering flakes; an intergalactic diaspora of living space dust. The music was saying that we are made up of everything else and that everything else is made up of us. That's all it was saying. That was all it could ever say.

Charlie looked at the digital clock displaying the time side-stage. He'd played well past his allotted time. He realized that Tatiana had begun signaling the sound techs, they were putting up a vocal mic for her. She was going to segue straight into her own set. Suddenly she was up off the kit. The beat was still playing as though she were holding it in place with her mind. She picked up a green guitar and started aping Charlie's bass riff. They stood in the centre of the stage, facing each other. Whatever Charlie played, Tatiana was right on top of him, biting at his heels. Then Charlie became Tatiana. They swapped bodies. Charlie was playing the green guitar, watching himself play the black bass. He looked into his own gleaming grey-green eyes as Tatiana smirked at him from behind the veil of his own face. The riffs were synchronized perfectly now, their hands sliding around in a mirror image (Tatiana was left handed). The roar of the audience nearly overtook the sound coming out of the PA.

Charlie as Tatiana raised the guitar and watched Tatiana as Charlie raise up the bass, as though he were controlling a marionette; it was as if he were playing both instruments. They locked into steady eighth notes on the twelfth fret, pulsing like a siren. Something whispered in his ear: You can see through other people's eyes; you can hear through other people's ears.

The space dust coalesced into a silver pelican that swallowed up the earth, and for a second, the silence was so deep and complete that Charlie truly believed that the world had ended.

He opened his eyes. He was back in his own body. Tatiana had somehow killed all the tracks simultaneously, and they'd stopped playing on a dime. The whole room had gone quiet, as if they were hypnotized. Tatiana stepped up to the mic, which let out a sharp squeak.

"Charlie Potichny, everybody, Cave Music, give him a hand, tout le monde, donner lui un coup de main. Ladies, he's single and ready to mingle, il cherchez la femme, il est vraiment si beau, si gentil, nous sont tellement chanceux ce soir."

Several women in the audience let loose cat calls. Charlie blushed and stumbled off stage, forgetting his shoes. He was completely disoriented, glowing from the ecstasy. Tatiana had to wait a moment for the applause to die down before she could launch into her own set. Back in his dressing room, Charlie chugged two bottles of water. The cold water hurt his throat, but he didn't care; he'd never been so thirsty in his life. He walked out into the old train station and snuck over to the bar at the back of the room with the hood of his sweatshirt pulled up over his face. He drank continuously from a jug of water the bartender had set out and watched in exaltation as Tatiana sang and danced.

After a moment, he felt a hand on his shoulder; it was Natalie, the pretty British girl from the museum. She'd done herself up with eyeliner, lipstick, and a light coating of glitter was causing her whole body to sparkle – or was that the drugs? She was smiling at him, pupils dilated, definitely on drugs as well.

"Hey arsehole, thanks for putting me on the guest list!"

Charlie clasped a hand over his mouth. "I'm so sorry, I had a really weird day, it completely slipped my mind."

"It's alright. They had a few tickets at the door." She was looking at him intensely, her warm breath sweet and minty on his face and neck. It was such a hungry, unmistakably sexual look that he had the instinct to pull his head inside his body like a turtle.

"Where are your friends?" he finally sputtered.

"They're up front dancing. We were all going mental when you two were onstage together. The chemistry was incredible. I've never heard anything like that. I saw you sneak out here. I wanted to say hi. I've kind of been thinking about you all day to be honest."

She reached up and pulled his hood back. His hair was still all in his face. He was at a loss, turned away from her. He'd had a point of reference when he was performing but now he felt vague and confused. He felt he shared a deep intimacy with this sparkling girl, except that he scarcely knew her. And what he did know wasn't very enticing: she liked to take selfies in museums. His mind was at odds with itself, at odds with his libido, anyway.

"I'm not wearing any shoes," he said finally.

She looked down and laughed at the exposed big toe on his left foot.

"I'm not wearing any underpants," she whispered in his ear.

He took Natalie by the hand and led her backstage towards Tatiana's vacant, candlelit cellar.

Thirty minutes later he was in a taxi on his way to Greg's hotel. He was sticky and anxious. He'd been too high to come and generally felt that the whole episode had been darkly farcical. He felt he needed to come clean with those who were truly closest with him. He needed to talk to Greg and tell him about Philip and Mizza, about the purple spheres beneath the frozen lake. He'd done something horribly wrong, something that had set off the recent events in his hometown. Together, him and Greg would figure it out. Then he needed to talk to Sophie and tell her that he'd been sleeping with other people, consequences be damned.

Maybe they'd break up, but at least he might feel halfway human again. He longed to wash his heart clean and make it a blank slate. He shuddered and resisted the urge to slap himself in the face.

CHAPTER 20

L'HÔTEL PAPILLON WAS located on the south side of a small square comprising a park where Parisians walked their little dogs and neglected to pick up their excrement. It was Greg's favourite hotel in the city, and though he'd ruined several pairs of nice shoes stepping in dog shit, he always insisted on staying at the Papillon, smoking unfiltered cigarettes in the park while practicing natural repose and feeling very continental.

The small square felt hidden and cozy, but as soon as you passed through any of the several cobblestone paths that squeezed out through the ancient brick buildings, Paris opened up in all its ornate grandeur along the banks of the Seine, inducing a sensation similar to vertigo. It was perhaps that very sensation – the feeling of the mind trying to switch gears faster than possible – that Greg was attracted to: for him, Paris was an urban gestalt that triggered a pleasurable confusion in the brain.

At the very moment that Charlie pulled up to the Papillon in his cab, Greg was slipping out of the square into the city and down to the river for a late night walk. He'd taken Charlie's advice to abstain from sleeping pills and, predictably, he could not sleep.

Oblivious to his friend's wanderings, Charlie punched in the security code Greg had given him, causing a sleek set of frosted glass doors to slide open. The dimly lit lobby was silent. Charlie called the lift, which was waiting on the ground floor. Reaching Greg's floor, he jumped as the elevator lurched and hung in the air for a second, trying to identify and freeze the present moment. In the dimly lit hallway he felt a wave of relief wash over him. In twenty steps, fifteen steps, ten steps he could pour his heart out to his best friend. He was like a shook up bottle of champagne ready to explode. There was so much to confess, so much to resolve. He was feeling, prematurely, the relief of unburdening himself of everything that had been weighing on him and the shame that had been gnawing at him for months. Four steps, two steps. He knocked gently at the door, heard the ruffle of the sheets and light footsteps. As the door opened, a woman's voice said: "Back already?"

Sophie stood in front of him in a much too large bathrobe. Reality rearranged itself. He remained surprisingly calm.

"I suppose it was only a matter of time," she sighed. "Why don't you come in? Jesus your eyes are like saucers, let's get you some water."

He walked in a stupor and sat down in an armchair. Sophie handed him a glass and sat on the edge of the bed. Several memories fired in sequence: Greg's reluctance to set them up, Maggie's reaction to the news they were dating and Sophie's recent coldness.

"I cheated on you," Charlie said, surprised by the sound of his own voice.

Sophie smiled sadly. "I sort of assumed," she said.

"Why would you assume that?" Charlie asked. Reality was just barely holding itself together, he thought he might faint.

She shrugged, "Sex, drugs, and rock 'n roll. Oddly I didn't mind, I've never been much for monogamy."

"And you and Greg? When did this start?"

"It's ancient history, as you know. But we also had an affair a couple years back, contributing to the slow decline of his marriage. And then when he came in to replace Dietrich, with him and Maggie separated. . . it was the perfect storm, so to speak."

"So what?" Charlie asked, "you're in love with each other?"

She laughed, "Oh dear me, no. More like an unhealthy obsession, accessories to each other's fucked up patterns. I can cope, but he's in a dark place right now. I know he feels terrible about all this," Sophie sighed, her head dropped, and she studied the carpet for a moment before continuing, "look, he really needs you, Charlie. I propose we use this awful situation as an opportunity to exercise good moral and emotional hygiene. The three of us are all quite frankly a little damaged. We all have mommy-daddy issues and shitty artist egos."

"This is a lot for me to handle. I think Tatiana drugged me. I. . ." Something expanded and cracked in his chest. "There's a weird rainbow around you." His breathing had become irregular.

Sophie cocked her head and gave him a funny look. "You were such a curious little guy when you were a teenager. I don't think you remember how much we hung out. You were shy and gentle when you were sober, but you couldn't handle your liquor all that well. There was a sadness that came out when you drank and some anger. You and Greg both have a penchant for self-destruction, I think."

"Maybe don't do this right now?"

"We were both on the ski team. I remember one weekend in Collingwood, the time we all stayed at Maggie's cabin. You were late to your race and forgot to put on gloves. Halfway down the hill you fell, rolled down the icy course, smashing into all the gate flags. You tore the skin up on your hands. It was awful. Remember?"

"Yeah, sure, I remember," he held up his scarred hands. "What's your point?"

"I was on the hill, right where you fell. You did it on purpose."

"What are you talking about?" he asked, annoyed.

"You threw yourself down the hill. You didn't slip. I know what I saw. You wanted to hurt yourself."

He thought about his mother's presumed suicide, about the frozen lake, about how he'd walked right out on it.

"You saw wrong," he lied. "I slipped. You're changing the subject. Were you just using me this whole time to make him jealous?"

"A little bit, yeah."

"Then why are you lecturing me about good moral hygiene?"

"I don't want this to end badly. I've hurt every man I've ever been with. I'm trying to change."

"Give me one good example of something you're trying to do to change."

"Dietrich," she said. "He's like a little boy. So pure, so serious."

"I don't follow."

"He's in love with me, and I have feelings for him but. . ."

"You're afraid you'd chew him up and spit him out."

"He has the constitution of a Teutonic Knight and a voice that moves heaven and earth, but in truth he's as fragile as a butterfly."

"That's why he's not here, isn't it?" Charlie said. "You kept rejecting him and he couldn't take it anymore. That's part of what makes this easier for you, isn't it? You're hoping he gets over you so you won't hurt him."

She nodded. "It's not working though; he still loves me. He's in Nepal now, hiding out at some monastery. He won't sing. I think he's contemplating a lifelong vow of silence. It'd be a crime if I deprived humanity of that voice."

"Don't be so dramatic. That's on him. Anyway, who gives a shit, it's just opera," Charlie couldn't help but smile. Sophie smiled too.

"You don't seem that upset," she said.

"I guess I'm not. I just wish we'd been honest with each other."

"It's not always easy, being honest. You look like you know all about that."

"What do you mean?"

"Something happened right when I met you, something you've been keeping to yourself. I can read it in your body language: you've got a secret. Look, you don't owe me shit, and I'm not asking you to tell me, but talk to someone, alright?"

"Are we done here?" Charlie stood, growing suddenly defensive.

"That's up to you. Is there anything else you feel like you need to say?"

He considered briefly and shook his head.

He walked into the bathroom and closed the door. He peed, drank from the faucet, and pocketed a bottle of Ativan. Wiping his mouth with his sleeve, he walked back through the hotel room and tried to leave, but Sophie blocked his path.

"At least take these," she said, handing him a pair of way-too-big slippers.

CHAPTER 21

A ·LIGHT, SWEET mist had gathered in the square. He half expected to run into Greg, but didn't. In fact, as he passed out of the square and into the main part of the city, it struck him that no one was around. Crossing to the other side of the river towards the Eiffel Tower, a creepy sensation overtook him: the feeling that he was alone in the city, that Paris had been evacuated, and he'd somehow been left behind. There were no stars in the sky, but hundreds of lights shone out through the mist as he walked towards the tower, his slippers getting increasingly grimy.

He walked back past Notre Dame Cathedral at the front this time, the flat façade of the edifice rising above him in judgment – or so he imagined. He scratched his crotch and walked away from it towards a small greenhouse where flowers were sold during the day. Through the glass of the greenhouse he saw a bright lit up sign for the Métro. There was a set of stairs descending into a dark tunnel. He waited for the pull of the irresistible force that would draw him down into it, and sure enough, his body was tugged forward. He made his phone into a torch and descended the stairs, passing under an archway into a chamber.

It was an odd little room. A massive Turkish rug lay across the unfinished gravel floor. The ceiling – vaulted panels again – was very low; a little chandelier was affixed to it, emitting a rose-coloured light. There was a double bed in the far corner with navy sheets, which all had a matching pattern of mallards on it. A small stereo sat on a hand-carved bedside table, emitting Satie's Gnossiennes at such a low volume that it was nearly imperceptible; the walls were warm, brown bricks. At the opposite end of the room from the bed, a small, black wood-stove emitted a great deal of warmth. Where the smoke escaped to was a mystery. One of Van Gogh's paintings of workers napping against hay bales hung above the bed.

Charlie was still quite high, too high to sleep, so he sat on the bed listening to the piano, glancing at the painting every so often. At some point a large water jug and a glass appeared on the nightstand. He took the Ativan out of his pocket; the pills looked like tiny little mints. He swallowed three of them down with the cool, refreshing water in a single gulp and stared at the fire blazing inside the stove.

After a time, he heard the clink of the glass. When he looked over, the water had been replenished, and Mizza was standing by the bed, stooping slightly under the low ceiling. Charlie's gaze darted from Mizza's wings to the handle of the jug.

"How did you. . .?"

"As per usual, Mr. Potichny, you've become fixated on a most trivial detail."

A faint smile played across Mizza's face. He looked beat up and exhausted. Charlie was so happy to see him that his eyes welled up with tears.

"You died! I literally watched you explode."

Mizza grimaced. "Your generation's overuse of the world 'literally' is incredibly aggravating. As you may have observed, the laws that govern reality are quite different in the realm where I exist. When I exploded in your world I immediately regenerated in that - that. . . place." Mizza spit the final word out with vitriol. "Deprived of death's sweet embrace once more."

Charlie balked at the diplomat's sinister tone. "Miz, what are you saying? I thought you had a wife and kids? What happened to early retirement?"

"Oh, Mr. Potichny, it was a ruse, a clever ruse to deceive you. He chose me because I was an actor once   in your fair city of Toronto. Most would say I gave my best years to the Stratford Festival, but I always felt most at home treading the boards at the Winter Garden."

"You were human once?"

"Yes, I was a human, and what a humanly human I was: prey to vanities, vices, and delusions that would disgust you Mr. Potichny, I have no doubt."

"What was your name? Your human name?"

Mizza opened his mouth, and an alarming squawk pierced

the air. He put his wing-tip over his mouth, embarrassed. "As I suspected, there are certain things I cannot share with you. In fact, we haven't much time, it's a miracle I was able to set this up. Listen to me carefully: there are realms and forces beyond naked perception or scientific measurement that play a hand in determining the fate of life on Earth. When you turned over that painting, when you threw it into that unspeakable realm, you upset a balance that was already teetering perilously. My lot is already lost, Mr. Potichny, but if you do not remedy the situation, all life on earth will be plunged into a dark age from which humanity shall never recover."

Charlie opened his mouth to ask how, but instead a long exhale escaped and his head fell heavily onto the pillow. The light from the chandelier flickered and dimmed; the massive slippers dangled off his feet as the Ativan plunged his comprehension into darkness. The gentle piano music, which he'd forgotten about, gave way to an unpleasant, off-key mutation of Debussy's nocturnes.

He could hear Mizza exclaiming urgently as the walls, floor and ceiling of the cozy room were stripped away. Through the veil of sleep, he sensed that the little bed was floating inside a cylinder so vast that he could hardly make out the walls. The cylinder was rotating, its angle constantly shifting ever so slightly. He sensed the walls breathing and opened his eyes a crack: the walls were moving grotesquely, flapping and malting. He could see orange beaks and shining avian eyes. The walls were composed of giant blackbirds; he could hear them cawing all around him. They'd sensed his presence and called out to him for help.

He heard a crack like a lightning bolt. The sound and the force of the thunder were perfectly synchronized, the texture of the air changed, loose electrons were stripped from the atmosphere. In the darkness, at the foot of his bed, a light came on. It was a giant eyeball opening. Charlie perceived a second eyeball as the first drew back; they were focused on the bed. Thunder and lightning crashed all around him, emitting a blackish, dark-violet light. Gusts of wind flooded the tunnel. Through the flashes of light, Charlie could see what looked like a large raft, a floating island with a little mountain on it, being tossed around in the storm. He willed his little bed towards the land and saw that it was attached to something. The gigantic eyes opened up again. To his horror he realized that what he took for an island was the beak of this great beast. It was a pelican the size of a mountain. Coral-like rocks and crystals grew out of its disfigured body. Pink and green light spilled forth from several of the crystals, and a hairy black braid ran down the length of its back.

The birds were squawking uncontrollably now, tremendously excited by Charlie's presence. He continued floating towards the flying monster who held him in its gaze. How would one battle this beast? It was not possible. Suddenly he heard Philip's Windsong; the sound was muffled and seemed to be coming directly from the monster before him. As he recognized the sound, the beast's eyes widened with fright and then closed abruptly.

The thunder and lightning shut off, and everything went dark. The birds quit squawking. Charlie could still hear the Windsong faintly, but it kept changing direction. Colours and shapes emerged and melted away all around him hypnotically. Maybe it would be best to just nod off, drift into the wall of the chamber and join the ravens. He clung to the sides of the mattress and focused on the Windsong like a thread tethering him to sanity, and just as he felt the thread being cut, the sound morphed back into recordings of Satie coming from the little radio on the nightstand. He was lying in bed, comfortable and unscathed in the warm little underground room.

He put on the filthy slippers and groaned. He looked at the time – it was six in the evening; the premiere of Lear was in one hour at Palais Garnier.

Lear. Greg. Sophie. Backstabbers. The memories of the previous night came rushing back to him and swept away what faint recollection of his dreams the Ativan had left behind. Had Mizza been there with him? It was all a blur.

The buffer of gentle sympathy that the drugs had provided was gone, replaced by bitterness. Greg's a lying piece of shit he thought, as he rose and stretched. The intense clack of Parisian foot traffic was audible just up the steps. He walked outside, unthinkingly, into the fading orange light. He went into the flower shop, bought a bunch of Chrysanthemums, and turned back towards the Métro only to find that it had disappeared. He found the nearest station and squished in amongst the evening crowd. A pair of young men were taking turns freestyling over the beat from Chronic 2000. He splashed a handful of coins into a hat when they came around to collect. The train slid along the tracks, raised above the city on stilts like a flat rollercoaster.

He arrived back at his rental just after dark. Greg would already be onstage. He took the lift up to his floor, entered his apartment, and put the Chrysanthemums in water. He poured himself a huge glass of brandy and went out to the narrow porch. Up the street the sky sucked up the tremendous glow produced by Gare Du Nord, as the building's thick, squat exterior slowly darkened against the ever-brightening night. Charlie sipped his drink and sat staring for a long time, tangled in his wild mind.

CHAPTER 22

FOR TATIANA, PARIS was like a second home. Her on-again, off-again supermodel girlfriend, Marie, lived in Monmartre, and she'd ostensibly booked four days off to spend time with her. When it came to light that Tatiana had rented out a local recording studio for three of those days to cut a new single, Marie threw her out. This was a familiar stop in the neverending merry-go-round of their relationship, and Tatiana was utterly unfazed.

For his own part, Charlie had planned on spending the break hanging out with Sophie and Greg, but after the night of his gig at the Flèche D'Or he didn't want to see either of them. A self-pitying paralysis set in, and he did what any musician does when they feel spurned: he made music. There was a piano in his rented apartment, and he set to work on a series of ugly, brooding compositions he titled Anecdotes from Tantric Shoals.

He lived off of Fanta, cheap wine, bread, and shawarma from the shops across the street. The spring weather took a turn for the worse, and a damp chill set in for the duration of his stay. The apartment was not well insulated, so he draped himself in wool blankets. It didn't help that he insisted on leaving the windows open despite the rain. There was a leak in the closet in the bedroom, and a fragrant fungus had begun to grow there.

The perpetual rainstorms darkened the daytime hours considerably, and Charlie lost all sense of time. Between sessions on the piano, he would lean over the railing of his balcony, surveying the street which was obscured by massive, leafy trees. The crowns of the trees were at eye level with him on the ninth floor, and he started talking to them as though they were people. Sometimes he felt that the trees were his guardians and other times, his captors. Through the trees he could only make out a small patch of the road, which was perpetually slick with rain.

He was drunk and disoriented round the clock for three straight days. Anecdotes from Tantric Shoals was almost certainly the worst music he had ever produced. The day before the tour was set to resume, Tatiana tracked Charlie down. The weather had finally cleared, and they sat outside on his porch drinking espresso in the warm midday sun. Charlie was greasy and stubbly, crumbs of sleep clinging to his left eyelid.

"Did you drug me the other night?" Charlie asked.

"Of course," Tatiana replied, smiling. "You needed it. You were all bottled up. It was fun, wasn't it? And it probably showed you some truth about yourself. Or didn't it?"

"I got more truth out of that night than I really cared for, actually. Turns out my girlfriend was cheating on me with my best friend."

"Okay, so whatever," Tatiana said, swatting the air with the back of her hand. "That's a tale as old as time itself. Ecstasy tends to clear up whatever sediment is clouding your life. I take it once a month like clockwork. Now we go back on tour; we have fun; you are unencumbered with no constraints. Next, we have Amsterdam and then four shows in Germany, all sold out and all crowds of over a thousand. The internet has been buzzing about our performance the other night. People are going crazy to see us on this tour. Life has a funny way of working in this pattern: your personal life goes to shit, and professionally, you have great success. Don't quarrel with the way of the world, just accept it. If you want, we can even keep going after Italy and do some club shows in Eastern Europe. The boat parties along the river will be starting soon in Belgrade. Have you ever been to Serbia?"

"No, listen, I left home for the first time two months ago, and I feel completely fucked up and lost. I hate to do this, but I need to get off this tour. I need to get home and sort some stuff out."

"Charlie, listen to me very carefully. You can't just quit because a girl broke up with you. My girlfriend broke up with me not two days ago. You don't see me whining!"

"I'm not whining! And she didn't exactly break up with me, I mean, it was more like a mutual – "

"I don't give a shit. Listen: remember we were talking about Hell the other night? Well monogamous love, romantic love, is its own form of hell: a sophisticated method of self-torture that developed out of the Romantic movement in the eighteenth century. Historically, marriage has been a pragmatic arrangement between a man and a woman with the goal of perpetuating the species. But our culture, with its idiotic values, somehow came to assert that all of your most intimate feelings need to be channeled into a single relationship that is typically poised on a teetering foundation of animal attraction that will burn out in a few years. These relationships, with very few exceptions, lead to betrayal and disillusionment. You should be so lucky. You don't really seem that upset. Trust me, I've seen much worse. Now, in terms of avoiding this problem in the future, you need to exercise emotional discipline. Fight this fallacious idea that society has planted in your primitive brain of a fairytale love with one person. Don't put all of your emotional eggs in one basket. Cultivate many relationships; come travel the world with me; you'll make many friends, some platonic, some sexual. Don't talk any more about quitting the tour. It's ludicrous. It's precisely the opposite of the correct course of action. And wipe that gunk out of your eyes, it's disgusting." She passed Charlie some tissue.

"I dunno," Charlie said, dabbing his eyes and sipping his coffee. "I hear what you're saying, but there must be some meaning, some greater purpose to life, no?"

"It's just a matter of adjusting your attitude. Of course, you want to feel like you have a purpose. Newsflash: you don't. I promise. But you're lucky enough to have a job where business mixes naturally with pleasure. Epicurus had it right thousands of years ago: what is pleasurable is good. You need to wring every last drop of enjoyment out of this lonely, fucked up world, or it will have its way with you. You go around once, and then you die. And then nothing matters. So: live well, make music, take drugs, and fornicate. You will not get better advice. And you will not find a better springboard for pleasure than what we have lined up for the next few weeks. So, my dear boy, I suggest that you take a shower, and then we'll go buy you some new shoes. I threw your old ones into the audience during my encore. I did, however, retrieve a pair of underpants that I think belong to you from my dressing room. They are washed and folded in my suitcase."

He showered and they took a cab to the Marais where Charlie bought a pair of gorgeous matte black oxfords. They went on a shopping spree, spending thousands of dollars in all the best shops, flirting with saleswomen and intermittently stopping for espressos and pastries in fashionable cafés. They got drunk at a wine bar and proceeded to a party in the Latin Quarter. Finally, they ended the night at Tatiana's boutique hotel, goofing around and debating the great mysteries of art and life on a resplendent white terrace that overlooked the filthy, glimmering river.

Charlie awoke the next morning with a smile on his face, convinced that what was pleasurable was good, looking forward to touring interminably and sucking the marrow from the bones of life day after day, night after night until such a time as he was dead and buried.

CHAPTER 23

ARIBERT REIMANN'S OPERA was dark, dissonant, technically demanding, and grating to the unrefined ear. The people who showed up, who really showed up and gave a shit, were a rare breed of modern opera nerds, fans of the avant-garde, enemies of those played out Franco Zeffirelli productions cherished by old American blue-hairs. This was dirty, risky, deep-cut opera. Everyone had expected Eichelberger to play the role, and anyone who cared was deeply disappointed that this clown from Canada had usurped it. It was a great surprise then when the Canadian's voice rumbled forth that first night, nearly overpowering the orchestra and causing veteran opera fans to grab hold of their armrests as if an earthquake had begun.

The voice that boomed forth from the stage of the Palais Garnier in the two weeks that followed seemed foreign, even to the human who happened to be attached to the voice. Greg felt possessed, somehow not himself, enshrouded in a thick darkness and depression that eclipsed his true nature and allowed him, for that brief run, to inhabit a manic and insane character to the delight of the opera nerds who had assumed he was second rate. If the human voice resided, as he suspected, in the seat of a person's consciousness, then his consciousness was oozing with angst and self-loathing, discharging the sum total of every mistake he'd ever made.

As positive reviews, praise, and offers for more serious roles poured in, and as he received all the validation he'd ever desired, he hit a personal rock bottom. From this rock bottom, his voice took on a three-dimensional quality, which was accented at times by a unique comedic tone of self-pity and self-deprecation. Afterwards it would come to be talked about as a career defining role: the one time that Greg Chest stepped up and proved to everyone that he had heavy tragic chops.

If it hadn't been for the opera house, for the bright chandeliers, the soft velvet seats, the glimmering gold trim, and the opportunity each night to ejaculate his sorrow onto the audience, Greg may well have drowned himself in the Seine. Him and Sophie were sharing a bed nightly at the Papillon. She had told him about her conversation with Charlie – how he hadn't seemed all that upset – but Greg knew better than to take that at face value. The fact that he wasn't upset was disturbing in and of itself. Greg had always observed in his friend the most intense and delicate sensitivity regarding matters of the heart. In high school, Charlie had hidden his sensitivity behind books and resorted to excessive boozing at parties as a defense. Girls had been surprised by his earnestness and poetic intensity if they got to know him; he exhibited an acute melancholy upon rejection despite having barely known the object of his affection.

If Charlie was acting cavalier about a break up, that was an indication that something was very, very wrong. As much as Greg had dreaded hurting his friend, getting caught, being chastised, and beginning a road to reconciliation had also been part of the script. But Charlie had left Paris without even confronting him, depriving Greg of the prospect of catharsis that he craved.

All this left Greg in a state of inner paralysis. They had been best friends from such a young age, and that whole time they had always been in touch. And while it was true that Greg had often treated their friendship as a series of free therapy sessions, he also felt that he'd offered his friend a lifeline, a series of exotic, comical vignettes, and meditations on the struggles of his career and family life. He could see now that he'd been unfair at times and took Charlie for granted. Charlie's sudden recovery, followed by his sudden success, had thrown off the well-established balance of their friendship. He needed Charlie. He loved him more than anyone, save for his family. But Charlie was family; they were brothers – this thought flashed through his head, blinding him for a split second onstage one night. Family was the most important thing in the world. How the fuck had he strayed so hopelessly far from this core value?

He sang and made love to Sophie and traced and retraced the streets of Paris interminably, smoking cigarettes and drinking ginger ale with a grim stew of anxiety simmering in the dark cavity of his chest.

✧

By the night of the final performance, the cast was exhausted. It had been a taxing production, and no one was especially in the mood to celebrate, least of all the brooding titular king. Greg and Sophie showered at the Papillon and ate at a small bistro on the square that was open late. Greg drank down two glasses of Hennessy and then asked the waiter to leave the bottle. He had not had a drink for weeks, but still the alcohol had little effect. He was wearing sneakers, blue jeans, and a Cave Music T-Shirt beneath his velvet blazer. Sophie wore jeans, a black V-neck, and a cream cardigan. There had been an unspoken agreement that as long as the production continued, they would perpetuate their tryst. Now that Lear was dead and buried, it was time to talk.

"We need to stop this," Greg said, sheepishly.

"We've been here before." Sophie replied. "I'm happy to stop, but as long as we keep working together. . . " she trailed off.

The waiter came by and asked for their orders; the kitchen was closing.

"French onion soup," Sophie said in English, although she spoke perfect French.

"Veau de vache," Greg said. The waiter gave him a funny look but wrote it down and hurried off to tell the chef.

"Wouldn't it just be 'onion soup'?" Greg said. "Seems redundant to have to say 'French.'"

"You're an idiot. You always insist on ordering in French, and you always screw it up. Watch what they'll bring you."

"I was in French immersion until grade six, but mostly it's all gone. Charlie's really good at French, but he won't use it; he's too self-conscious."

They sipped their drinks for a while. Out in the park a fat woman was walking her Dachshund.

"Have you spoken to Charlie?" Sophie asked.

Greg shook his head. "You?"

Sophie shook her head.

"And what's up with Eichelberger?" Greg asked, brightening

slightly. "Up in the mountains singing shanti ohm? I always thought that guy had his shit together."

Sophie tensed. "You think because you pulled off one single powerful performance you can talk shit about Dietrich? You aren't half the singer he is, and you know it."

Greg sipped his drink in silence while Sophie scanned her phone. Finally, the waiter set down a pot of melty, cheesy soup before Sophie. A jiggly, white lump of mystery meat was placed in front of Greg next to a pile of sautéed snails and potatoes.

"Cerveau de vache!" The waiter declared proudly. "Specialty of the house, possibly the best in Paris, served with escargot and pomme-de-terre."

Greg took a swig straight out of the bottle. "I was really hoping I'd ordered veal," he said.

"Don't complain. You need all the brains you can get," Sophie replied.

He scooped the soft white meat into his mouth, tried to figure out if it was necessary to chew, and then swallowed the gelatinous substance down. He gagged a little and tossed a potato into his mouth.

"What does it taste like?"

"Not much. I guess it's a texture thing."

"How's the texture?"

"Pretty gross."

Sophie blew on her soup.

"You're right," she said. "We should end it for good. You should make up with your friend. I should be with Eichelberger. You should try couples' therapy with your wife and never sing in German again."

Greg's eyes shot up from the brain. "You love Eichelberger?"

She flashed him a look of annoyance.

"Of course!" he cried. "That's what needs to happen. Like in Buffa! Like in Mozart! You marry Eichelberger, Charlie and me make up, and I go back to my family! Don't you see? This is why Buffa is so great! Everything works out; everyone ends up happy!"

"Buffa presents life as a game that can be won in three hours by moving a bunch of sexy characters around a chess board. It's escapism; it's like reality with all the rough edges sanded off. What's great about tragedy is that it shows life as it really is and reminds us that suffering is the common denominator that draws humanity together."

"That's a pretty bleak outlook," Greg said, as if he were personally offended.

Sophie closed her eyes tight and took a breath. "It's a bleak fucking world. Look at yourself. Look at your life. Your whole energy is convoluted. You're a suicidal optimist."

Greg was taken aback. He spooned more brain into his mouth and swallowed. "I'm not suicidal." Sophie glared, unconvinced. "Okay," he continued, "well, sometimes I wish I'd never been born or think I'd be better off dead, but I would never actually kill myself."

"You need so much therapy, I don't even know where to begin. You're drawn to those flippant comedies because they're happy and simple while your life is unhappy and complicated. It is so typical of men to just ignore their feelings and blindly believe that everything will be okay."

"Don't make this a gender thing. That's just human."

"You use your sadness as a weapon, you know, against people who are ostensibly your friends. You're violent with your sadness."

"Look, I'm sorry, what do you want me to say?"

"My mother always said apologies are the cheapest currency in the world. And that wasn't even a genuine apology, you frugal piece of shit. I want you to get help, real help, from a therapist. If you keep going hard on the cognac and sleeping pills, you'll end up harming yourself, and I'll feel like trash because I participated in your self-destructive bullshit. Also, when you get the offer from the Germans, I want you to turn it down outright. It's not for you."

Greg, wanting to get the hot mush off his plate for good, swallowed a much-too-big piece. The soft, silky brain matter pushed out within his throat. As he forced it down, it seemed to expand in his esophagus, and he placed his hands on the table, clinging to it, as the discomfort passed.

"What?" he asked, after taking a sip of water.

"You're going to get a call from the Germans offering you the lead in Lampo's opera, Bluebeard and the Swan. You need to refuse it. It's not for you. It's for Dietrich."

Greg squinted at her. "You know I found that manuscript, right? I had to hang out with sour-milk-smelling, piss-soaked hobos to get my hands on that. If anyone's ever deserved to sing a role in a show –"

"Think of it as an exercise in selflessness. The role isn't you. Plus, I've seen the score. The low notes are. . . I've never seen anything like it."

"I suppose you're singing the female lead."

"Who else?"

"And you want to sing it with your new boyfriend."

"I want what's best for the opera. They're having trouble raising funds for next year's season. This may be the last well-funded new production we see for a while. It needs to shine. Look, if you want to be a selfish asshole about it, go right ahead. But if you do the right thing, it could be the first step to fixing your broken heart."

"Whatever, let's pay the bill and get out of here. If I need to barf up this brain, I'd at least prefer to do it in the comfort of my own hotel room. Garçon!" he yelled. The brains mushed and sloshed in his stomach as he rose to look for the waiter.

"I'm sleeping at my hotel tonight. Might as well use it once before I fly home."

"Don't do that. Don't leave me alone tonight. And please don't make me beg."

"You are so fucking afraid of being alone. It's pathetic. We both need the space. You've got some thinking to do. Don't bother begging. And don't try to pull off some lame stunt that looks like attempted suicide. I flushed all your sleeping pills and removed the hotel razors. You can drink like a horse; I know booze alone won't do it."

Greg's face sank and darkened, but he forced a smile. "Well. . . fuck me, I am right?"

"That's right Greg," Sophie smiled. "Fuck you."

After Sophie left, Greg took the Hennessy down to the river where it reeked of piss and stale beer. He was in a vindictive, self-pitying mood. She thought he wasn't serious, that he couldn't do it, that he was too much of a dumb, golden retriever of a man. He was sucking back three or four ounces per gulp. His vision blurred and he went off balance, staggering like a punch-drunk fighter. Although he did have the tolerance of a horse, the rapid inflow of liquor caused him to black out for a moment. He danced a jig and pitched head-first, heavily into the water, his clothes absorbing the cold grey wash of the river, shocking him sober and pulling him downstream hard.

The faces of his children flashed through his head. He thought of good sushi, beef tartare, of rich blue cheese, and the way its flavour lingers pleasantly on the palette. He did not want to die. Sophie knew he did not want to die. Why had he thought it was a dare? Why was he so manic and impulsive? He hadn't gotten it from Errol. Errol was the very image of good sense. He must have inherited the death drive from his mother or the universe.

In the end, he finally supposed, it was not relevant from whom he'd inherited what. He was the way he was, and wasn't it even amazing that he existed at all? That he occupied space where there might otherwise simply have been nothing? And here he was in the act of returning to that nothing that he'd often longed for: oblivion. As the river tugged him along like a doll, as his heavy clothes pulled him down, knocking his body against the bottom of the river, he gave up, lazily, thinking that he'd prefer to live, but then that didn't seem realistic. He thought about the boat metaphor he'd come up with and realized he'd lost his anchor; something about psychological degradation had to do with becoming a million different people all at once.

He closed his eyes and gave in to the flow. He went partially into a sleep state and felt as though he were being sucked into a long, stormy tube. He felt like he was going into a k-hole, lost all sense of his body, lost all sense of agency. All around him there was thunder and lightning, and he wondered how there could be a thunderstorm underwater. He tried to move his arms and found that there were black wings in their place. He stretched them out and pecked at his speckled breast. Something like a giant orange sailboat floated on the dark horizon in front of him. What was it attached to? Was that a face? Eyes like marble boulders floated high above him. It was all too much.

And then something strange happened. Within his death hallucination, he heard an ethereal melody; it was the same sound that he'd been obsessed with on Charlie's album, Manic Toads. He rolled his avian eyes as if to say even in death, I've got to deal with this shit? But as the melody unfurled in all its clarity, in stark contrast to the terrifying, soul-disintegrating chaos around him, he felt reality beginning to reconstitute itself. He felt the soft squish of mud beneath his back. He heard a slurping noise as several thousand tons of moving water drained out into some unseen source, and the weight of his body returned. He rolled onto his side and threw up a gallon of filthy water. He gulped a lungful of sweet, pollen-filled air. The brain stayed put.

Broken boats and a piano littered the riverbed. The night was gripped in total silence. Astonished and panting, Greg lumbered to the wall of the river. How the fuck was he supposed to get up? As if answering his thoughts, several bricks noisily slid out, forming a vertical path. He hauled himself up with great determination. As he was climbing, he observed the water level rising beneath him. By the time he was back on land, the river had returned to normal, as if nothing out of the ordinary had occurred.

He walked back towards his hotel, eliciting murmurs from passersby: he was drenched, caked in mud, and smelled very bad. He imagined he would have to throw out all his clothes. He would be very sad to see the velvet blazer go. A strange numbness set in. The miracle that had just saved his life had undoubtedly happened. He'd been in the river, he'd been resigned to death, and the water had drained out. He'd been spared. And yet, it was impossible; it defied all logic.

He wondered if he had in fact died and if this was some sort of split reality, like a death dream that resembled life. Or what if life had always been a death dream, and in death one passed into real life? Wait. No. That was too convoluted. He'd just have to soldier on and trust experience. He'd loosed a sort of prayer, and the prayer had been answered. He'd been given a second chance. He walked along the gravel path in his hotel square, smelled the fragrant roses, and decided to embrace this second chance, this fresh start. He stepped in dog shit. Bad omen. Or maybe it was just chance. He picked up a stick and scraped the shit off his wet sneaker.

CHAPTER 24

GREG SLEPT IN late the next morning and ordered room service. He went down to the hotel bar for a second coffee and lingered over the newspaper. A calm, peaceful feeling was blossoming in him. He had a flight in the evening direct to Toronto. He was determined to try and work things out with Maggie, determined to turn down whatever role the Germans offered him. He basked in that peculiar glow experienced by someone who has resolved to do something just and difficult but has not yet carried it off.

In the afternoon, as he was packing, the phone rang in his hotel room. It was Errol.

"Have you got the offer yet?" he asked bluntly.

"Hi Dad. Love you."

"No time for warm fuzzies dear boy, I need you to turn down the offer. We need to get Eichelberger back."

Greg's good mood eroded slightly. "I haven't received any offer yet, but this is ridiculous. I don't particularly care one way or the other, but Dad, I'm getting the best reviews of my life. My stock is at an all-time high, and my voice can do no wrong. Why is everyone so fixated on Eichelberger for this role?"

He could hear Errol breathing pensively on the other end of the line. "Something's afoot. You've been away for too long to understand but things have been very strange around here. There's more at stake than you could possibly understand. I need you to go get Eichelberger and bring him to Toronto."

"Dad, that's crazy. I need to see my family. I don't even know where Eichelberger is."

"He's at the Namo Buddha Monastery. In Nepal. I booked you on a flight to Kathmandu tonight. It's paid for, non-refundable. You can take a bus or a taxi from the city."

Greg let out a long breath. "Is this about Mercury

Retrograde?"

"It's about the Abyss, the Whirlpool, The Flooding Winds. The birds, Greg, their migration patterns are all askew. I've scarcely left the house in weeks. Thank god Cujo and Goblin are here. Thank god for Kintsugi."

"Kints-what? Errol, you're not making any sense. Should I be worried?"

"Yes, but not just for me. For the city. For your family. Possibly for the entire world."

"You're being very dramatic. Maybe even hyperbolic."

"I am not being hyperbolic," Errol said evenly. "You are going to Nepal."

The flight connected through Istanbul. Without his sleeping pills Greg dreamed in fits and starts through the hellish travel days, drinking heavily at airport bars, engaging in idle chatter with everyone around him.

Kathmandu was cool and dusty. The smell of sandalwood mingled with exhaust on the breeze. Walking through the narrow streets he was perpetually startled by honking motorbikes brushing against him and men whispering the word hashish in his ear. He ate a dinner of momos and vegetable soup on the roof of his hotel and then drank from a bottle of Royal Stag watching TV until the power abruptly shut off. He ordered ginger tea from the front desk and went back up to the roof.

The ruby red sun was making a valiant effort to pierce the thick smog that hung in the air, obscuring the surrounding mountains. On a cursory glance through the Wikipedia entry for Nepal, Greg read that Kathmandu was the third most polluted city in the world. India was enforcing a trade embargo that had hobbled the economy, and the government was in constant flux. Working in tourism was the only feasible method of income in the country. Greg took a long swig from the bottle and watched a pack of monkeys tightrope across a network of sketchy electrical wires. The sky darkened considerably as an adolescent boy brought out the pot of tea.

"What's your name?" Greg asked the boy, removing the lid

and spiking the tea with a considerable wallop of stag. The boy looked around, unsure if he should engage. "Paddam," he said, finally. "And your name? And where are you from?" The boy's eyes brightened, he grew confident and excited as he asked the questions.

"Greg. I'm from Canada."

"Canada?" The boy said excitedly. "I will move there soon. My cousin is in Regina. He is sponsoring my visa. I want to work with computers."

"What about Nepal?" Greg asked. "You don't like your home?"

The boy looked shocked. "It is very bad to live here. We have earthquakes and pollution. No way to make money. Government always arguing. You want to stay here? Give me your passport, I will go to Canada. May I add you on Facebook?"

Greg rubbed his weak beard. Reluctantly he took out his iPhone and passed it to Paddam. The boy tapped the screen expertly, his pleasant face lit up by the blue light. His lips were pursed in concentration. He added himself on Facebook, opened YouTube, and pulled up an explicit hip-hop video. He smiled wide and sat down next to Greg, face glued to the screen. "This is a good phone," he said. "Look how clear the picture is." He punched at the screen some more, pulling up the phone's specs. "I hope to have a phone like this someday. Maybe we will be friends in Canada. Do you live in Regina?"

Something about the boy's demeanor, the confluence of his youth, competence, and hope tugged at Greg's heartstrings and made him ashamed of his arbitrary wealth. The red sun filtering through the haze leant the world a rusty ambiance.

"I live in Toronto."

"Toronto? Very big city. All different people there living together. Like paradise. After I go to Regina I will go to Toronto. I will get a good job and marry a Canadian girl. You can come to my wedding."

Greg sipped the ginger tea. The spice masked the bad whisky that was making his head swim. Now Paddam was playing a video game where he was a ball, rolling around absorbing trees and houses, becoming bigger and bigger. The ball was like the way of the west, Greg thought. Collect things, absorb things, grow larger, ever larger, always hungry, never satiated. But here in Nepal, the mere presence of prayer flags, rounded stupas, and monks in their maroon robes had had a calming effect on Greg, causing him to breathe the polluted, dusty air deeply and reverentially. He had spent his whole life filling himself up, always wanting to be better, smarter, funnier, to sing better, and to make more money. It was as though he wanted to fill all the cracks and empty space inside himself. But all that wanting led to was more wanting. He felt a desire now to drill apart his dense inner self and let in sunlight and cool air.

Paddam's ball was absorbing skyscrapers and Godzilla monsters now. Tiny, diamond shaped kites clung to its exterior. Greg had spent his adult life shuttling between rarefied zones of affluence in Canada, America, Australia, Europe, Japan, etc. drinking good liquor, charming old blue hairs, and flirting with women in wildly expensive dresses. He thought he was worldly, but really, he knew so little of the world. He'd never been to a place like Nepal: it was a place that was spiritually rich but afflicted with a vicious material poverty.

"Keep the phone Paddam. I can get a new one when I get home."

The boy looked up, his gargantuan ball rolled off a cliff into a quarry. "You mean it?"

"Sure, why not? I barely even use it anyway. You're like a wizard with that thing."

Paddam pulled a paperclip out of his pocket, unwound it, popped out the SIM card, and handed it to Greg. He thumbed the screen and restored the factory settings. He hopped out of his seat and sprang towards the stairs. Just before he disappeared he turned to say something, staring at Greg with a troubled look, worried he would change his mind and demand to have his phone back.

"Seriously, it's fine," Greg said. Paddam grinned and bounded off down the stairs, leaving Greg phoneless and alone in the darkness. He sat sipping whisky tea under the rusty sky, tracking his racing thoughts until he fell asleep.

✧

The next day, a hired car transported Greg along a treacherous two-lane highway and then up a unending series of goat-strewn switchbacks. Eventually he arrived at the end of the road: a tiny village with cafés and apartments dug into the hillside. Greg walked with his luggage down a long footpath. He came out into a square and saw a round, smooth belly from which a golden spire protruded, prayer flags hanging all around it, fluttering in the wind. The site of the Stupa looked out over a sea of terraced hills; the evening had cleared somewhat, and Greg could see the colossal, ancient ranges surrounding him.

"Monastery?" he asked the first person he saw. The man pointed towards a stone stairway that climbed up and around the side of the mountain. Greg grumbled, already sweating profusely in his linen shirt, and started making his way up the stairs. By the time he reached the gates of the Namo Buddha monastery he was ready to collapse. He'd tied a bandana around his head to keep the sweat from his eyes, and his skin was splotchy and dark around the face.

The monastery was a huge structure sitting at the peak of the mountain, surrounded by smaller buildings that served as dormitories for the students, a guest house for tourists, and a small café. As Greg walked up to the main building, where the dining room and prayer hall were located, he heard the pleasant pop-smack of a ping pong ball. Peering over the edge of the path, he saw a cluster of students in their maroon robes engaged in a tournament, bricks laying across the table in the absence of a net. Some of them were drinking Mountain Dew and eating potato chips. A Justin Bieber song was playing from a smartphone speaker. Greg shook his head in amazement.

Entering the main building, he came across several older monks with cropped, greying hair. He asked them if there was a big German man around. They all spoke good English and drew some information out of him before answering his question. The big German, they said, spent most of his time meditating in a cave just outside the monastery grounds. One of the monks took him outside and pointed up the stone steps that led to the roof of the temple. Before Greg turned to climb the steps, he asked the monk if it was normal for the students to eat junk food and listen to pop music. He shook his head smiling: "They are on holiday this week." The monk turned briskly and jogged back inside.

Greg climbed up to the top of the temple and out through a set of wooden gates onto a grassy hill that rolled off the back of the monastery. He looked ragged and slightly insane, his shirt was stained with dust and curry, and his bandana had come partially undone. He dug his hands into his hips and leaned over, lightheaded and nauseous. Hundreds more prayer flags hung from tree to tree forming a colourful, swirling network of webs. Down a small embankment, on a shady plateau, he found the entrance to the cave. There was a boulder blocking the entrance from the inside. Greg nudged it and then slapped his palm on it, but nothing happened. He pushed against it with all his might, grunting and yelling, but it was no use; it was an immovable object. He could feel a presence on the other side, breathing gently, absorbed in a deeper reality.

Greg re-entered the monastery and found the older monks. They told him that sometimes the German man practiced silent meditation and fasted for days at a time, sometimes for over a week. They invited him to stay in the guest house; he would be allowed to join them for meals while he waited for the German to emerge.

He walked down to the restaurant and ate some gristly momos and soup. Under the crepuscular sky, he traced a wandering path through roving chickens and goats to the gated guest house. The room they'd assigned him had three beds in it, none of which were big enough for him. He pushed the beds together and slept across them, sinking down into a gooey, soul nourishing sleep and remained unconscious until late the next day, awakening to the sound of dinner bells.

CHAPTER 25

AT THE MONASTERY, meals were invariably some combination of chickpea stew served with rice and bland, doughy tubes. Everyone in the dining hall was meant to sit cross legged on benches, but Greg found this uncomfortable and splayed his legs out underneath the table, signaling servers to top up his plate again and again, downing half a dozen cups of hot yak butter tea.

There were other westerners there as well: a couple of young Dutch men who smoked hash and sketched all day, an American woman who was interested in sustainable agriculture, and, coincidentally, an old Buddhist man from Toronto who bore a striking resemblance to a turtle. Greg avoided the other visitors as much as possible, and other than the old turtle man, they mostly left him alone.

"I don't see you at the prayer services," the turtle man said to him one day. "What are you doing here?"

"Just killing time waiting for someone," Greg replied.

"You know killing time is an extremely anti-Buddhist phrase," the man said. "You should try to find beauty and meaning in each moment."

"I guess it's just that most of life is a bunch of bullshit, realistically, there's only a couple good moments here and there."

"You're not even a little bit Buddhist, are you?"

"Quite the opposite."

The man looked at him funny. "I'm not sure there is an opposite to Buddhism. It would be like trying to fast forward life and not pay much attention to anything or give a shit about anyone."

Greg nodded noncommittally. He opened his mouth to make some sort of confession and then changed his mind.

He slept a lot and did push ups on the roof of the guest house.

He went for long walks through the hills and found a tourist resort that served cappuccinos and beef. Without a phone, he had no method of distracting himself. He read whatever Buddhist texts he could find in English at the school's library and started keeping a journal, writing down why he hated himself so much and trying to figure out why he had tried to kill himself.

The days stacked up. He visited the cave several times. He couldn't explain it, but he knew Eichelberger was back there behind the boulder. Greg had to admit that he was impressed with his rival's endurance. His experience in the hills of Namo Buddha started to feel transformative. He found that sleeping nine hours a night, abstaining from drugs and alcohol, and eating well allowed his feelings towards the world to soften and grow positive. He hadn't been sober this long since childhood.

He learned from his reading that suffering was, as Sophie had declared, the common link between all living things. He read about the importance of pain, of acknowledging and transforming pain into something tender, something meaningful. Without pain, he read, we cease to identify with our own physical selves, which is to say, pain is the very thing that gives us a sense of self. He ceased to feel like an island, or at least, if he remained an island he began to recognize other landmasses in the archipelago beyond his own craggy shores.

On his sixth morning at the monastery, Greg discovered that the boulder had been pushed aside, and the cave stood empty. He stepped inside and examined the space. There didn't seem to be any human excrement, and he wondered if Eichelberger was some kind of android. He tried to move the boulder to see if he could do it, but he could not. It must have weighed a ton. He was incredibly annoyed that Eichelberger, even in a weakened state, could perform this feat of Herculean strength. He pushed and pushed, putting the strength of all of his life's frustrations into it, until he felt it move. He yelped victoriously and stumbled to the ground, watched helplessly as the boulder rolled down into a divot, blocking the cave's entrance. He realized that, once again, he'd done something incredibly stupid.

He spent the next few hours in a panic with no sense of the passage of time. Sitting in the low divot, the boulder had once again become an immovable object. The darkness of the cave was complete; the atmosphere was damp and humid. He hyperventilated for a while and blacked out. When he woke up, his disorientation was complete. By this time, he'd missed a meal, and his stomach was screaming. Even a bowl of the bland rice would have been a great relief. He started bellowing and yodeling, but the sound simply bounced around the small chamber.

Finally, as he lay slumped against the back of the cave defeated, he heard the sound of footsteps approaching. Heavy, self-assured footsteps.

"Gregory?" a lightly accented voice called out. "Are you in there?"

"Eichelberger?" he cried. "I'm trapped in here. Can you help me move this boulder? I think I'm going to die."

There was a prolonged silence from outside, he heard the large man shifting his weight pensively. "I cannot help you. The boulder can only be moved from the inside."

Greg let out a desperate sob. "I'm going to die in here. Why the fuck did you block yourself in like this?"

"Why did you?"

"I just wanted to see if I could move it. I guess I wanted to see if I was as strong as you."

"Do you always measure yourself against the accomplishments of others?"

"Yes. Don't you?"

"No."

Silence.

"Why do you hate me?" Greg asked.

"I don't hate you. I've always admired you. You have an incredible voice, and your comic timing is exquisite. But you've always been standoffish towards me. I am not so much an extrovert. People mistake my seriousness for rudeness."

"Ass Panda!" Greg shouted, banging his fist against the hard ground. "There's been a misunderstanding. I was always jealous that you got the serious roles; you're the darling of the critics. I'm just a clown. I have self-esteem issues. I assumed that you thought you were better than me."

More silence. More shifting of weight. "What good is the praise of the critics? You make the people laugh; you bring them joy. I wish I could do that. My voice is technically impressive, but I hide behind it onstage. I've never had a talent for acting. I have always been jealous of you. Your easy manner, your effortless talent. Life has been difficult for me. I never felt like I quite fit in."

"I'm sorry I was mean to you," Greg said.

"I'm sorry too. I could have made more of an effort."

On either side of the boulder the men started weeping.

"Are you crying?" Eichelberger asked after a time.

"No," Greg lied.

"If you are, I would advise you to stop. You'll dehydrate yourself."

This only made Greg cry harder. "I'm going to die in here aren't I?"

"No. You won't. Listen to me very carefully. You need to be silent. You need to focus on the power of your voice without using it. A man with such a powerful voice as yours will build up an immense amount of strength. You will use the strength to push the boulder out of your way. If you believe in yourself, you will accomplish this."

"What? What the fuck are you talking about? This Buddhist mumbo jumbo won't work for me. I'm an atheist; I can't perform a miracle. I'll probably be dead in a few hours from hunger."

He could sense Eichelberger shaking his head outside the cave. "I will visit you each day and keep you company, but it is imperative that you not speak. I must go, or I'll be late for prayer service. I recommend you focus your energy inward and gather your strength. It's going to be an uncomfortable few days."

The first twenty-four hours were agony. His mind raced, his mouth was dry, and his stomach rumbled angrily. He napped intermittently until he had no idea if it was day or night. Eichelberger came down and told him stories, told him of his youth in Bavaria, and of his working-class parents who'd been raised and flattened by the somber post-war generation. It had been a lonely childhood – singing in the local choir had been a cherished form of escape. His parents had not wanted him to become a professional singer, and his father had been furious with him when he left on a scholarship to Munich. After he left they never spoke, and his father died of a massive heart attack when Dietrich was only twenty-two. Since then he visited his mother often and sent her handwritten letters almost every day.

He'd become interested in spirituality while performing in Philip Glass' Akhnaten in Los Angeles. At the end of the run he had an emotional breakdown and checked himself into an expensive psychiatric hospital. Watching the waves break on the facility's private beach and reading the teachings of the Dalai Lama, he'd come to understand that resisting feelings of pain and regret only created tension. It was the strain from this tension that had caused his breakdown. After a month of group therapy, swimming, and reading he checked himself out and booked a flight across the Pacific to India, travelling on to Tibet and Nepal over the course of a year, going from monastery to monastery and learning different meditation techniques. He eventually ended up in Namo Buddha Monastery and did a solid month of silent meditation in the cave where Greg was now trapped while students brought him rice and water every few days. He was able to accept his father's death and forgive him and also to forgive himself. At that point Eichelberger was very close to giving himself over entirely to monastic life. His mother had encouraged him to do whatever would make him happy. In the small room at Namo Buddha where he slept on a thin mat on the cold stone floor, his father's spirit appeared one night and told him to return to the world, to sing, and make him proud. That settled it.

Listening silently from inside the cave, Greg felt a deep sympathy for Eichelberger. He realized that he probably owed the man a lot. Without a rival, without someone to compete with, he might have grown lazy and complacent over the years. Not that he practiced much or took care of his voice. Singing had always been a matter of mojo for Greg. His philosophy was you either have it or you don't. Eichelberger mostly abstained from alcohol; he drank tea and honey constantly and wouldn't even allow people to smoke around him. All of that together, Greg reasoned, might make a slight difference, but it would only be perceptible to the most astute connoisseur, and of course, to Eichelberger himself.

Then it struck him: what set Eichelberger apart, what made him a truly unique human being and performer, was that he aspired to a higher standard, not for recognition, but for himself; for his own satisfaction. Eichelberger was surprised that Greg measured himself against others, but that's what everyone did. It was an unhealthy, unsettling habit of humans to constantly compare themselves to others. But if the grass always seemed greener on the other side, often it was only a trick of the light. Even Dietrich Eichelberger, who Greg had imagined led the most satisfying, fulfilling life imaginable, was miserable. The details of his misery were distinct from Greg's, but it was misery all the same.

Time continued to pass, and though Eichelberger continued to visit, his voice grew fainter and fainter as Greg lost almost any sense of physical self. Prior to being trapped, he'd believed that human consciousness resided in the mouth, but there in the cave he came to feel like he was inside the mouth of some greater being and that his body was formed of pure consciousness. He remembered a quotation attributed to the artist Artemis Gwillimbury about a transparent eye: an instrument of pure awareness, utterly unconcerned with its own existence.

He passed through the phase of physical discomfort into transcendental bliss. He understood that it didn't matter anymore whether he lived or died, though he was still aware of his family and his responsibility to them. He clung to that responsibility like a life preserver. He'd ceased to be at all aware of his body and could not say if he were dead or alive or healthy or ailing. Once in a while he still heard Eichelberger's voice outside, but it was all gibberish now. When he went away all was silent, and the silence was perfection. This continued for some time.

At some stage in the wandering of his consciousness, in the adventures of the transparent eye, he saw a tiny version of himself. His mind lit up the cave like an emergency flare. It seemed that he himself was the mountain, that the cave was his mouth, and that the tiny version of him was a little avatar representing his will. The experience was dissociative like a k-hole, except everything was sharp and controlled. He watched himself with great interest. Greg-as-the-mountain was calm and perfectly relaxed. Greg-as-tiny-avatar, lit up by the flare of his own mind, was straining, trying to accomplish some great physical feat.

What the little avatar was trying to accomplish was beyond the comprehension of Greg-as-the-mountain. The project seemed to lie within the petty realm of men and their concerns. He sensed that Greg-the-tiny avatar was eager to re-enter the world of human affairs, to return to his family, but additionally – and this was something drawn from an esoteric field of knowledge – that Greg-the-tiny-avatar had an important role to play in a great drama that would have far reaching consequences. There was a sense that the little guy was an integral piece in a slow game of chess that had begun thousands of years ago and was just now reaching a crucial turning point.

The little guy grunted like an animal. The transparent eye popped out of its socket. A burning orange light flooded the little cave and then invaded the whole mountain as though its insides were on fire. The avatar expanded rapidly, filling the whole mountain, and then the mountain shrank down and found itself to be balancing on unstable, wobbly legs. Greg-as-tiny-avatar fused with Greg-as-mountain and the whole package almost tumbled off a cliff in the blinding light. But there was someone there to catch him: a Bavarian Adonis with a voice like a thunderstorm.

It was a few days before Greg was able to travel. There were big bright gobs of light in his eyes from leaving the cave abruptly at high noon, and he was weak from fasting and dehydration. Dietrich kept him company in his guestroom where Greg rested across the three beds. They conversed lazily, talking shop, talking shit, and quickly forming a friendship that felt as if it were decades old.

Dietrich waxed poetic about his recent breakdown: no matter how much time he spent meditating and taking care of himself, his mind always succumbed to the dark entropy of his nature. He knew Greg had slept with Sophie and stepped lightly around the subject, but it was obvious that the man was lovesick. He had returned to Nepal in an attempt to wash his heart clean, and when Greg had arrived he was, in fact, seriously contemplating a lifelong vow of silence and celibacy once again.

"You know romantic love is just an illusion, right?" Greg asked him one day.

"I understand the argument, but for me it is real," he replied firmly.

"You won't give up on Sophie then?"

Eichelberger turned pale and then flushed red. "No, I could not. I would prefer to stay here and live a life of celibacy."

"Jesus. I can't even go a day without jerking off. I even rubbed one out in the cave."

"You should try celibacy when you're doing a show, it builds up lots of good energy in the diaphragm."

"Hmm. Not so much my style. Anyway, buddy, I think you should come back with me. Errol wants you for this Luka Lampo opera. Sophie wants you too. It's why I came all this way."

"Are you authorized to make this offer formally?" He asked him point blank.

"No," Greg said, digging deep, trying to find a reserve of humility. "They want to offer it to me. But I can't do it. I did alright as Lear but it was a fluke. I can't do that again; it'll destroy me. Please, I am begging you, do me a favour, do yourself a favour, come with me, and take the role. Your story doesn't end here, please believe me."

"What about Sophie?"

"What about Sophie? Jesus Eichelberger, you've got a big ol' pair of German balls, why don't you act like it. Roll in hot and sing the part, let your passion spill onto the stage, don't take shit from anyone, and see what happens. You believed in me when I was trapped in the cave, and I trusted you. Now it's your turn to trust me."

Four days after Greg emerged from the cave, the two men walked out to the dirt road and began the long journey back to Toronto.

CHAPTER 26

BY THE MONTH of July, Toronto and the surrounding region had experienced nearly five straight months of summer, as if the land existed in a meteorological bubble created by a comic book villain.

The city had been in a mindless frenzy for nearly half a year. Many of the robotic pets had begun to malfunction, attacking real animals and sometimes their owners. Live cats and dogs who'd once enjoyed a spoiled, domesticated life replete with organic dog food, perfumed shampoo, and regular chuck-it sessions had been thrown aside and left to fend for themselves in panting packs, covered in the filthy lather of an endless summer under thick fur that would be clipped and groomed no more.

And then there were the portals. The spike in missing homeless, it could now be reasonably shown, was due to the dark, horizontal pancakes that materialized at random throughout the city. While the black holes were perceptible from far away, people would often fall into them while texting. In theory, you could avoid them, but they stirred up enough collective anxiety that folks rarely went outside except to go to work or buy groceries.

Once they'd consumed a few victims, the portals snapped shut like Venus flytraps. No one had come back yet, not even the famous entertainment journalist who'd fallen through a pancake while posting a picture of a macaroon (the post itself had found its way online and received 'likes' to the tune of 30,000). The police had referred to the X-Files at the press conference to discuss the journalist's disappearance (the dozens of missing homeless had barely registered), suggesting that these cases fell more within the jurisdiction of a paranormal branch.

The birds were still a big problem. The airspace above Toronto has always been a migratory super-highway for birds, and because of the anomalous climate, thousands of winged creatures were thrown into confusion. As they flew over the city, flocks were drawn down and compelled to take up residence. By this time, the animal rights people had pretty much forgotten their cause, and there was an all-out war between humans and the birds who shit all over their property, scavenging their garbage and from time to time physically assaulting them. The pelicans, who seemed to proliferate and grow larger and larger with time, were certainly the worst – by October they'd carried off seventeen babies in unmonitored strollers (whether they ate them or raised them as bird-people was a matter of great speculation).

A breed of pinkish-red herons who flew around in sharp formations terrorized teenagers and young lovers, descending quietly upon make-out sessions in parks. The majority of the herons would beat up the teens with their beaks while one or two of them snatched up wallets, jewelry, and phones, which were then carried out over Lake Ontario and dropped from great heights. At the press conference, the chief of police referred to Hitchcock.

In August, the weather abruptly turned cold, and all the leaves died on the trees, lighting up the city in a flash of orange-yellow-gold. Cafés abruptly started advertising pumpkin spice lattés, and everyone in the city pulled out their mothballed sweaters. There was a brief moment when everyone thought that life would somehow be normalized, that they'd have a longer than average fall and then a normal winter, but it was quickly shown that this was not to be. Within two weeks it had turned so cold that deciduous trees were completely naked. Snow started to fall, and a gnarly frost set in. Mercury, it should be noted, was still in retrograde.

It was possible that throughout all of this chaos, Errol was the only person who had a proper grasp of what was actually happening. At the same time, by all outward appearances (or at least by the standards of the society in which he lived), Errol had completely lost his mind. At first it had just been the Kintsugi: a Japanese art whereby broken pottery is repaired with a special lacquer blended with gold dust. The obsession had begun in February, and by now there were hundreds of bright vases, bowls, and plates scattered around the mansion like Easter eggs, glittering in the buttery sunlight that filtered through the Venetian blinds.

Errol had also installed a sensory deprivation tank in the house, a white, egg-shaped chamber so large that the wall separating the on-suite from the spare bedroom it inhabited had been knocked down to accommodate it. When he thought he felt the Chaos Signal readying itself for another assault on the city he would hide out, floating in the pitch-black womb of the tank, sometimes for several hours at a stretch.

When he wasn't hiding in the giant egg or assembling Kintsugi, he played with Goblin and Cujo, attended conferences with the opera board via speaker-phone, and cooked for the thirty-odd homeless people who were living in his house. There were thirty-odd homeless people living in Errol's house, because he'd feared that their lives were in very real danger.

Campbell had noted that it seemed like more than coincidence that homeless people were at a higher risk of disappearing through the portals. He'd seen a portal open up on Beatrice Street one night as himself and a companion named Fefferman – a bear of a man who'd run away from his Hasidic community – were collecting empties from recycling bins. As soon as the portal opened up, Fefferman took off at a sprint and lunged through the dark pancake, as if he were possessed. Campbell had to admit, he'd wanted to go too, but he'd restrained himself.

"I stared into the abyss and the abyss stared back – as it always does," he had told Errol. "But then the abyss beckoned me, which it's never done before."

He hadn't gone through. In fact, he had walked right up and peed through it, watching his urine silently disappear into darkness. It was rather curious.

The suggestion was that the homeless had a predilection for the portals; they were drawn to them by some strange force, like sailors to sirens. Errol knew he couldn't house all of the city's hungry and destitute in his house, but the remainder of Saint Christopher's House he could manage. He provided them with no rules or guidelines; he simply asked them to respect the house as best they could.

The liquor cabinet, which he'd kept stocked for guests, was long depleted and most of the silverware had disappeared. The many men and a few women who constituted the new residents of the Wychwood mansion spent most of their time gathered around the big screen in the basement watching sports and movies. For sustenance, Errol ordered groceries by delivery from Whole Foods, and everyone took turns cooking and doing dishes. When they ran out of food, Errol called Domino's. Kintsugis were constantly being knocked over and broken, but Errol didn't mind. Gluing together a vase that had initially arrived from Japan in fragments made it a double Kintsugi. There were even a few rare triple Kintsugis after a time.

The wealthy residents of Wychwood were appalled by their new neighbours, some of whom liked to drink into the early hours of the morning on Errol's porch, and a few of whom would stagger through the streets screaming at hallucinations, but the city was in such chaos that the police refused to respond to their complaints and these individuals were mostly left alone in their new sanctuary.

Errol had become paranoid of the outside world, but he held out hope. He knew the opera was the answer. The one thing that had been a stable source of joy and stability in his life for as long as he could remember was finally going to do something real: it was going to save Toronto. He didn't know exactly how, but he had faith. He often drank espresso with Campbell, going over Lampo's papers again and again, noting the similarities between the mad genius' prophecies and what was now coming to pass. Errol was convinced more so than ever: the opera – Bluebeard and the Swan – was the antidote. As per his instructions, Greg had refused the role and Eichelberger would play the lead, Sophie had taken a leading role, and a full-scale production of the opera – complete with expensive sets, costumes and effects – was underway.

If Errol's past was riddled with regrets over his failed marriage, if his life up to this point had been wasted (as he often suspected was the case), he would at least do this one thing: he would see that this opera went off without a hitch, and in doing so he would save the day. They could put that on his gravestone: here lies Errol Chest, who saved his city by loving opera.

Although his boys had returned from their adventures abroad, it seemed, curiously enough, as though they wouldn't play a role in his grand scheme. Greg had been a trainwreck since Maggie had filed for divorce. He was living out of some filthy motel and had made himself unreachable, seemingly by design. Charlie had disappeared again almost as soon as he'd returned. He'd arrived at Errol's house blathering about a sea dragon, borrowed the four door Porsche and roared off hastily. He'd offered no explanation, but was so adamant that Errol couldn't refuse. Errol had insisted that he at least take Cujo – some lake air and forest free-roaming would serve him well. That had been two months ago. He ought to have been mad about the Porsche, except he wasn't – he didn't care in the least.

This lack of concern was tied up with a strange idea that had overtaken Errol recently: the idea that the concept of ownership was ludicrous. He'd spent his entire life accruing nice things and gathering status as if it mattered, as if he didn't have to give it all up when he died and life trundled along sans Errol, as it had for aeons before he was born. He'd dabbled with socialism as a student – timidly, in the same way he'd sampled same sex romance – but this was different; it was spiritual, rather than intellectual. He knew in his heart that nothing he owned belonged to him. The only thing that mattered was stopping the abhorrent Chaos Signal that was wreaking havoc on his beloved Toronto with its flooding winds of chaos and its appetite for the destitute and downtrodden. That and his boys, wherever they were, whatever demons they were battling.

PART THREE:

METAMORPHOSIS

CHAPTER 27

CHARLIE REMAINED ON tour with Tatiana through the end of May. They played blistering club shows through eastern Europe, drinking tremendous amounts of vodka and kirsch, taking whatever drugs they could get their hands on, sleeping with groupies and trashing hotel rooms. They parted ways on friendly terms after their final show in Warsaw, although Charlie could sense that Tatiana was impatient to strike out on her own again.

From Warsaw, Charlie flew to New York City for a lengthy U.S. tour with a band called The Hoarse Whisperers, who were promoting their third album: One Hit Pony. Despondent and disheveled, Charlie put on a good face and joined his new tour mates in nightly binge drinking and casual drug use. Antidotes for Manic Toads was a cult sensation in the States by that time, and the shows were packed with hipsters, as well as a new-age spiritual crowd who'd discovered the psychedelic, soul-soothing properties of Charlie's recordings. He had no trouble making fast friends and meeting eager sexual partners to soothe his wounded ego.

When Charlie finally arrived home in July, his immune system collapsed from the extended abuse. He fell into a fever for a week, slowly nursing himself back to health with chicken soup and orange juice. When he felt well enough to go outside, he observed that Toronto had become a sort of zombified wasteland. Queen Street was largely vacant save for a few vagrants and harried looking pod people. Walking through Trinity Bellwoods, Charlie watched in horror as a pair of monstrous pelicans dive bombed a pack of dogs, scooping up a corgi and a pug in their mouths and flying off into the distance.

As he turned and sped back towards his apartment, he saw a squat hipster coming down the sidewalk trying to eat a hot dog while scrolling on her phone. Charlie called out as a portal opened up in front of her, but it was no use – she had airpods in.

Back at his apartment a feeling of guilt and shame spread through Charlie's nervous system. All of the reports were true: Toronto was in a severe crisis. The flooding winds of madness that Errol described, the aggressive birds, the vanishing people – it was all real. He couldn't suppress the truth any longer: it was all his fault.

That night he dreamed fitfully of the sea dragon: she was calling to him, pleading with him for help. But where are you? Charlie asked. At once he was presented with an image of Canoe Lake, of Yana's Cabin. He understood that he had to go back into the lake and back to the Cathedral where the furry people lived; he had to find his mother. Then the sea dragon used her elegant tail to punch a button in Charlie's mind that released the memory of Mizza from Paris. Charlie started to get the bigger picture: there was another creature, a gargantuan pelican, that exerted his sinister powers over the world through imperceptible channels. Charlie was caught in a struggle between ancient powers. "Poor Mizza," Charlie thought, as he recalled the horrific Chaos Dimension full of lost, flapping souls.

He woke up fostering a strong sense of purpose. Being on tour for so long had made him restless and the prospect of more action and travel excited him greatly. He dressed, had some breakfast, and checked his email. There was another apologetic email from Greg, detailing his impending divorce. Charlie had been ignoring his friend out of a vague sense of retribution, but now, infused with a sense of catharsis over the hazardous quest he was about to embark on, he drafted a quick note pardoning Greg and explaining that he was going away for awhile and might not make it back.

He clicked send, packed a bag, and caught the subway up to Errol's, keeping his eyes peeled for malevolent birds and hazardous portals.

✧

A short time later, Charlie was piloting Errol's Porsche up the Trans-Canada highway with Cujo panting happily in the back seat. Charlie used his phone to locate Yana's cabin – he was consulting the GPS when the dirt road suddenly spat him out on the embankment. He slammed on the brakes to avoid careening straight into the lake. Fortunately, Errol kept the machine in excellent working order, and the car clung to the dirt beneath its wheels.

As he unloaded the groceries and Cujo bounded into the lake, Charlie heard the creak and slam of a door and perceived the shape of Artemis Gwillimbury coming towards him from her home. Charlie noticed that she was moving slowly, bent over a walking cane and graying all over. In his peripheral vision he saw a blur of red circling over the lake – red herons. Even up here, he thought. Finally, Artemis was standing right in front of him. She knocked on the hood of the Porsche with her cane, "From behind the wheel of this machine you bear an uncanny resemblance to a particular asterisk shaped orifice."

Charlie rolled his eyes, "Nice to see you too Artemis."

When he'd finished unpacking the car he joined Artemis on her screen porch, accepting a glass of cold green tea. Looking out on the choppy, glittering lake a feeling of frustration came over him: the lake wasn't frozen. But of course the lake wasn't frozen, it was the heart of the summer – this never-ending summer. The blazing heat of the sun dominated the sky for fifteen hours a day.

He knew instinctively that the lake would not serve as a gateway to the Cathedral in liquid form; he needed something solid to pass through. He needed a layer of ice. With an urgent sense of purpose burning in his chest, he'd planned to pull up to the cabin and hurl himself into that other world and complete his epic journey, but now he realized this was impossible. He crunched a cube from his drink between his teeth as the heat of the sun mocked him, and Artemis told him stories from her youth.

". . .Georgia was always made out to be this prickly hermit, but she was quite warm when I visited her at Ghost Ranch. Her caretaker scrounged up some peyote for me, and I spent the night creating my own constellations in the New Mexico sky. Charlie? You seem preoccupied."

He turned to look at her, she seemed to have aged a decade since he'd seen her the previous winter. The look of pity was not lost on her.

"I know what you're thinking. You're wondering what's happened to me. Truth is Charlie, I'm an old woman, I've been old for such a long time. Something about these woods kept me vital, but I always knew it was only a matter of time. Whatever magic kept me young has been siphoned out of this place."

They sat in silence for a time. The sun had slipped down below the tree line, and the sky was smeared with cotton candy clouds. The first loon cry of the night drifted through the air.

"It's my fault," Charlie whispered.

"What's your fault, dear boy?"

"You should have let me drown."

"Charlie!" Artemis exclaimed, taken aback.

Charlie's frustration melted into anguish. He set one fist over the other, bent over on top of his hands, and sobbed uncontrollably. It was a powerful sobbing, as though some unquantifiable substance were pouring out of him. The realization of how much tension he was holding in his body was itself overwhelming – he was dubious that he would ever be able to flush it all out.

When he'd stopped sobbing and recovered himself, Artemis had Charlie light some lamps. He fetched himself a glass of water, feeling dehydrated, but buoyed by the crying endorphins.

"It's our nature to blame ourselves for things that have nothing to do with us," Artemis said. "Whatever it is Charlie, you have to forgive yourself."

Charlie smiled and shook his head. "It's not like that," he said and began to explain.

When he finished talking it was nearly midnight. A pensive silence descended on the screen porch as the lamps continued to flicker.

"An immortal beneath my lake," Artemis thought out loud. "It actually explains a lot."

Charlie's chest swelled; she believed him.

"It would account for the magnetism that drew me here, that drew Yana here. That drew you here." Artemis reached out and rubbed the back of his neck. "You did the right thing coming back," she said.

"You think I should go through with it? You think I can make it right?" Charlie asked, desperate for validation. The rhythm of their dialogue was slow, and Artemis lapsed into thought before responding to his question.

"I think that making things right is a fallacy. Even in this case, where it's all laid out tidily like an adventure novel. I believe in divine beauty and the universal wisdom of nature, but as far as individual actions go, well, I would just say don't assume that pursuing a decisive course of action will change anything in a greater sense. We never understand the true effect of our actions, and reading the world as if it contained sign-posts to our destiny is solipsistic and self-destructive."

Before Charlie could reply, Artemis continued. "I don't think anything in the universe will stop you from trying to get to that seadragon, but right now you've got no doorway; you said as much yourself. If you're going to try and read the universe like a book, try this for interpretation: there's nothing you can do, so relax. You're all keyed-up Charlie, I can feel your heartbeat from here. You need to let things take their course."

He realized how hard his heart was thudding, how quickly he was breathing.

"My city is dying," he said. "How can I do nothing?"

A strong breeze blew across the lake, and Artemis closed her eyes, listening carefully.

This whole wretched world is built on an ideal of persistent, decisive action; patience is seen as a weakness rather than a virtue. That's what got us into this whole mess to begin with. Maybe the catfish won't let you into her realm until she senses a different signal from you. Living things are just reactive energy patterns when you break it down, and you probably scan as hostile right now. You need to activate your parasympathetic nervous system: rest and digest. Develop some congenial energy."

"And what the hell am I supposed to do in the meantime?" Charlie asked.

"Chop wood, carry water."

The entire first week at the lake was laced with bitter frustration. He could barely sleep at night, tossing and turning in the musty old bed. Artemis indeed put him to work chopping wood, cooking, and performing a number of other manual tasks. Charlie wondered what she would have done if he hadn't shown up just then, how she would have survived. Somehow this question didn't even seem to have occurred to Artemis. As Charlie went through the motions of the day – reading novels and working – Artemis mostly sat on the screen porch, contemplating the lake in a Zen-like trance. He envied the way she could just sit, seemingly contented, resting in the present moment like it was a La-Z-Boy.

For his part, Charlie felt as though he were constantly banging up against the present moment, as if it were an invisible glass wall that could not be broken. Since he'd been cured of his condition, since he'd been released from the cocoon, his life had assumed a perpetually stimulating trajectory. Though it had been miserable at times, the misery had been counterbalanced by moments of euphoria. The idea that this trajectory had come to rest, that there was nothing to do in an immediate, physical sense was greatly disturbing and ignited an anxiety in Charlie the likes of which he'd never known.

He stomped around in an irritable, insomniac trance for a week as the days grew hotter and hotter. He almost left several times, but a faint instinct told him to stay. Besides, where else would he go? What else would he do? Beneath the uncomfortable thoughts creeping through his mind like a parade of millipedes, a steady hum held him to the spot and told him to bear the discomfort and be patient.

At the end of the first week he drove into the nearest town to buy more groceries and some supplies. He bought himself a bright orange hunting cap at the general store, a tin of Italian coffee for the stovetop and a bottle of decent brandy. At the local butcher he offered extra money to buy some bones for Cujo, but the burly, mustachioed man told him to put his money away.

"Nice cap, you a hunter?" The butcher said.

"No," Charlie replied. "I just like the colour."

"Hah!" The butcher said. "That's rich. You hipster kids from the city are a riot. Say, you've got a mighty familiar look, you from Finland by chance?"

"My mom's Ukrainian, not sure about my dad." Charlie said, blushing and growing slightly uncomfortable.

"You've got some Fin in ya for sure. My wife's from Thunder Bay; the place is crawling with Fins, trust me, you've got the look. Speaking of which, have you heard the one about the Finnish man?"

Charlie wanted to leave but felt indebted to the man on account of the free bones.

"No, I don't think so."

"He was neither Swede, Nor-wegian!" The butcher said triumphantly.

Charlie couldn't help but laugh. He racked his brain and dug out an old joke: "I've got one: two cannibals are eating a clown. The first cannibal says to the second: 'does this taste funny to you?'"

The butcher guffawed and doubled over, slapping his knee, laughing disproportionately hard at the simple joke.

"Tell ya what bud, take this big ol' trout fillet as well. Never frozen. You gotta cook it tonight though, won't be fresh tomorrow. Cast iron, butter, onions, and garlic. Little bit of salt and pepper."

"I couldn't," Charlie said. "You already gave me the bones for free."

"It's the end of the day, I'm about to close up. Look there's two fish left, one for you and one for me to take home to my family. It's no big deal. Don't look a gift horse in the mouth."

"Or you might say. . . don't hook a gift fish in the gills, right?" The words escaped Charlie's mouth spontaneously.

The butcher laughed in a more restrained way this time but clearly appreciated the effort. Charlie accepted the fish, and on his way out, the butcher got the door for him.

"Hope your dog enjoys those bones," he called. The butcher flipped the sign to Closed and clicked the lock. The meat was the last of the groceries. He loaded the final bags into the back seat and headed back to the highway.

On the drive back to Canoe Lake, he realized that a change had come over him. That the simple exchange with a stranger, the basic kindness he'd been shown, and the stupid jokes they'd shared had pried open a little window for positive feelings. He'd been grumpy on the drive out, but as he passed the same trees and divots in the Canadian shield coming back, it was as though he were seeing them for the first time, as if he now inhabited a completely different world.

When he arrived back at Canoe Lake he noticed things that had completely evaded him all week. The sunset was splattering the clouds with joyous colours, and the loon calls seemed extra clear and sonorous, mingling with Cujo's handsome bark echoing across the lake as Charlie got out of the car and tossed him a bone.

Though the days had been hot, the nights were cooling off, and the number of mosquitoes had dropped drastically. The air was clean with a sweet, subtle hint of pollen and pine. Charlie listened to Glenn Gould on his phone (Errol's efforts had not been completely in vain), humming along as he chopped vegetables for a salad and heated up the cast iron with butter for the trout. The knowledge that miles away the friendly butcher was cooking trout with his family elicited a pleasant, tender pang in his chest. At dinner he was expansive, regaling Artemis with stories from the road, discussing the art in the Musée D'Orsay, his encounter with Vincent Van Gogh, and his favourite American gigs.

After dinner, he let Artemis lead him through a guided breathing meditation, lying on the floor of the screen porch with a blanket over him. Afterwards, when he was half asleep, Artemis recounted various episodes from history where no action was the best action. Later on – he drifted off a couple times during the history lecture – he mostly remembered the story about the Roman general Fabius Maximus holding off Hannibal's Carthaginian hordes.

As Artemis continued to speak, the rhythmic patter of her voice took on the synesthetic quality of a stone skipping across the ocean. Eventually the stone dove beneath the surface of the water. Charlie was pulled into the dream world, and his perspective shifted so that he was staring down a vertical chain of Portuguese man o' wars – a pathway of diaphanous parachute bodies tinged with pink and blue – leading deep into an ocean trench. The man o' wars were like markers in a ski race – he was skiing down through the ocean at a speed that was dangerous and out of control.

Although he'd had an intense phobia of jellyfish as a child, he knew these colourful ghosts were benevolent, lighting a pathway to his reunion with the Feline. Don't be a sea fish. Don't be facetious – echoed through the water like sonar. It occurred to him then that humans were arrogant for thinking that their senses delivered unto them an accurate depiction of the world: a dolphin's sonar, an insect's segmented eyes, a canine's sense of smell were all just different ways of relating to the world of living matter. Colours, smells, and sounds refracted through consciousness in a million different ways dictated by the giant prehistoric snail's pace of evolution.

As his descent slowed and he sank back into the dark chamber he'd visited the previous year, where the tube worms sucked him clean, he grasped at a slippery, wordless notion that Artemis had tried to articulate: living things are just reactive energy patterns, eternally bristling at external stimulus: feels good, feels bad, feels neutral. To imagine that human beings were somehow above other forms of consciousness was illogical. Humans were undoubtedly the most complicated form of life on the planet, which meant humans were special, but not necessarily in a good way.

Charlie couldn't help but suspect that the human race, as it was presently poised, was special in a bad way. His purified dream form was released into the chamber of the catfish, but something was off; he shouldn't have been thinking so chaotically, not in a dream, not in the equanimous lair of the sea dragon. He waited for the warm buzz, for the benevolent presence of the catfish, but instead he floated alone in darkness, his doubts concerning the fate of humanity spinning faster and faster as a fear of death took root and grew.

He became aware of his body in the physical world where Artemis had slipped a pillow under his head and covered him in a blanket. His body was asleep but his mind was awake, wreaking havoc. Nonononono, he whispered to himself. He'd been anticipating the Feline, her healing presence, and the restoration of an internal sense of harmony he had not experienced in what felt like a century.

A mosquito was at his ear like a buzz saw, he was awake, shivering slightly. He needed to pee but knew it would be cold without the blanket; he resolved to wait until the need to pee grew unbearable. It had been less than a year since he'd visited that place; that mystical grotto in the depths of the ocean of his unconscious. It had been a fluke that first time, brought on by anomalous circumstances. In this case he would need to cultivate the appropriate energy if he was to be admitted, and for that, he needed to cure himself of his death mind.

He finally got up and peed, shivering violently and cursing under his breath. He rifled through an antique chest in Artemis' living room for extra blankets and made his bed on the green sofa. He lay awake for a long time pleading with his racing mind to calm down, drifted into a shallow sleep and dreamt of the Carthaginian hordes on their elephants coming down the mountains.

CHAPTER 28

AFTER THE GRILLED trout in butter night, his sleeping got better. Sometimes he would drift in the shallows of the ocean, sometimes he would float down to the tube worms, and once in a while he'd be admitted into the lair of the Deep Sea Feline. Typically, he'd wake with a start at three or four in the morning, and when he resumed sleeping he would have predictable stress dreams of Tatiana chasing him through the jungle with a machete, or Sophie as a boa constrictor, slowly eating him alive. If he slept clear through the night, he would sometimes feel the Feline's energy brushing gently against him, but the sea dragon never revealed herself. She was maintaining a guarded presence.

In August, it grew unseasonably cold and Charlie noticed that the leaves of the deciduous trees were changing colour, transitioning rapidly to a golden ginger. In the fall weather, he'd dawn his flannel jacket and orange hunting cap and go on long walks with Cujo, who bounded through the forest with endless energy, terrorizing the squirrels who'd busied themselves stockpiling acorns for the coming winter. He borrowed a meditation book from Artemis and began practicing something called no-mind, wherein the subject empties themselves of all knowledge, takes nothing for granted, and experiences phenomena without attaching any meaning to it. Thus, if he were to think, I wonder how my record sales are doing, an inner voice would interject, saying, What's a record? What's a sale? You don't know anything about any of that.

On those long walks with Cujo, eventually this external voice dissipated, and he was left with mere impressions: smears of colour and light; the feeling and sound of the wind; the soft touch of Cujo's luscious mane when he wrestled with him. Late at night, when total silence descended on the forest and he was tucked into bed, he found he could expand his consciousness and subsume large swathes of the world within it. Rather than giving him an inflated sense of self, he actually found that in this process of expansion, he became much smaller, as if he were a tiny little Waldo in a massive panorama. Finally, when he relaxed his mind and then refocused it, the little Waldo was gone; reality existed independently from Charlie Potichny. And yet the lights were still on; he held reality in his mind without existing in it; he'd smudged himself from the canvas and painted over the smudge to camouflage his very being.

The cold snap continued and Artemis put Charlie to work chopping wood and stockpiling it indoors. They both had to feed their woodstoves to keep warm as the trees hemorrhaged golden leaves. Over morning coffee one day, a high wind whipped across the lake. The morning dew on the leaves had frozen, and they were coming off in such great numbers that Artemis remarked that it looked like the forest was crying.

"I love this time of year," she said. "The trees weep, they let go, they do it so easily without any prompting. I wish it were as easy for humans. We have such trouble crying, we spend our whole lives clamped up and clinging."

Charlie didn't say anything, but he felt like his gradual letting go, his discovery of a universe that existed independently from him, had precipitated the premature change of seasons. They were heading towards winter; the ice would soon be frozen. He could not meet the catfish in his mind, but she was building him a gateway, a portal to her world. As he'd suspected, it was not going to be so simple this time; he'd have to risk his life. He could feel the catfish exerting her power, understanding that he wished to co-operate with her. The red herons had fled the lake, and Artemis was in better health; she'd ditched the cane, put on some weight, and had a brighter complexion. The passage of time took on a fluid quality, and Charlie relaxed back into it, as if he himself were now reclining in time's La-Z-Boy. Artemis noticed the change, and although she did not express her approval vocally, he could see it in her eyes: he'd found her wavelength; he'd begun to unlock the magic of the lake.

The first snowfall of the year occurred in mid-August. They were sipping brandy and playing crokinole in Artemis' cabin, as was their habit in the evening. Her cabin was the warmer of the two, and Charlie had been sleeping on her sofa at night to conserve their shared wood supply. Cujo was splayed lazily on a mauve shag carpet that he favoured; the burning wood filled the space with a pleasant aroma. The flakes were fat and juicy and easy on the eyes. Charlie was so relaxed that he didn't even equate the snow with ice and what it meant for his journey. He looked up from the tan wooden puck he'd been on the verge of flicking and allowed himself to be hypnotized.

He thought back to his life before Mizza, before fame, before the insanity. He remembered endless nights spent cooking variations on a stir-fry, cuddling with Goblin, watching classic films, and getting lost in a world of sonic exploration. At the time he'd believed that this was not real life, that it was a pale imitation, a dance of shadows. Now he missed those days, and he missed the cocoon. In particular, he thought of the quick walk to the corner store to buy penny candy and root beer midway through a film, and how on those rare nights, when the city was quiet and he'd been granted a merciful respite from his chronic pain, the haloed glow of the streetlamps seemed to saturate his body, causing him to become so light and buoyant he believed he would shed his earthly form and dissolve into the night sky like sugar in hot coffee. He was so lost in his thoughts he went temporarily blind and when Artemis called his name, he was surprised by the blizzard beyond the window.

"Charlie," she snapped. "Are you lost in thought, or are you merely stalling on account of I'm destroying you, as per usual."

He came back to himself and smiled. "If I played as defensively as you, I'd always win too. I like to take chances."

"The objective of the game is to win, no?"

"That's a pretty aggressive stance for someone so Zen."

"I spend most of my life painting and looking at a lake, one needs an outlet for one's more aggressive tendencies."

Charlie flicked a piece at one of Artemis' black pucks, nestled safely towards the back of the board. It clipped a peg and bounced harmlessly out of play.

"Four to two," Artemis said, gleefully. "I've got you up against the wall, bitch!"

Charlie was staring out the window again, lost in thought.

Artemis flicked a puck so that it flipped up out of the centre hole and knocked him on the forehead.

"It's no fun emasculating you if your heart's not in it. It's finally snowing, you should be ecstatic; you'll have your gateway soon. What's the trouble, Chuck?"

"I was just thinking about when I had chronic fatigue, when I felt cut off from the world," Charlie said. "I thought that my life wasn't real, but that monastic life was much more real than touring, fame, and travel. When I arrived here at the lake, I felt alienated from myself and out of touch with reality. Let me put it another way. Imagine reality as a massive painting: when I was sick I felt like the paint was wet, and it was constantly being smeared into different patterns; sometimes I was afraid I'd sink right into it and become lost – that was kind of scary.

But when I was healed, when I started to live a so-called normal life and the paint seemed to dry, that didn't seem right either, it was too far in the other direction. When the paint was dry, events unfolded as though they'd been decided in advance, as if they had nothing to do with me. There's a danger in that, because you start to blame external forces for the whole of your destiny and forget to factor in your own will-power."

"I think that makes a lot of sense," Artemis replied. "For most people in our society, the paint is completely dry, there's no room for numinous experience. If you're of a painfully sensitive nature, or perhaps if you're mentally ill, the paint is too wet: you need reality to provide some comfort and stability, but at the same time it's nice if you can see how fluid it is, that it's meant to be played with. Our modern lifespan – eighty to a hundred years, god-willing – is a flash in the pan of evolutionary history, of human history even. Folks these days think they're liberated, that science and the free market is a logical outcome of the historical process, but we're slaves to consumerism and cultural values, living in a spiritual vacuum. Christ, just look at the suicide rate; contemporary western society, as it stands, is not the logical outcome of humanism. Or perhaps the outcome of humanism is a mirage – if so, we'd better figure out a new agenda and quickly. For most people in your world, Charlie, the paint is not wet enough. You've seen it from both sides, now find the middle path. Work with the provisional reality of your culture, but don't

176 | Dave Hurlow

be afraid to reach out and smear things around, better yet if you can show others how to play with the paint."

"Whatever version of reality I'm working with right now," Charlie said, "seems pretty out there, a little too numinous."

Artemis splashed some brandy into their glasses.

"It seems like your lot is to restore a balance that you've upset; the thread leads back to Yana, a juicy mystery. I don't believe in fate, but sometimes an irresistible path reveals itself."

"I could die."

"So, the worst thing is you could die. That's not so bad. You've had an interesting life, thirty whole years of the stuff."

"I don't want to die. I feel like I just started to understand something true, but I can just make out the edge of it."

Artemis sipped her brandy. "I don't think you're going to die. I'm just making a point: behave as if you'll survive, and you'll survive. There's an old saying: go towards death and death retreats. It means don't falter, don't be squirrely."

A shiver passed through Charlie. He glanced at the big thermometer hanging in the screen porch, and Artemis caught his line of sight.

"If this cold keeps up, the water will freeze quickly. It's not a very big lake."

"How long?"

"Two weeks I'd say."

"Two weeks before I go towards death."

"Two weeks before death retreats," she countered.

Charlie's heart was beating out of his chest. Artemis sensed his panic.

"I have anti-anxiety meds in the bathroom. Two orange pills plus the brandy and you'll have a long, dreamless sleep. We need to keep you calm for the freeze to set in properly."

Two pills, one brandy, and half a round of crokinole later and Charlie was sawing logs on the chesterfield.

In the following days it continued to snow, so that tremendous white slabs lay atop their cabins like buttery layers of icing. After a few days, the temperature dropped to a vicious minus

30, and the sky cleared, revealing a bright but ineffectual sun. Charlie scraped the ice and snow off of the Porsche and drove on the mercifully cleared highways to town for a double load of groceries.

It was so difficult to generate and maintain heat that Charlie moved into Artemis' cabin, where the woodstove was well fed around the clock. Cujo, who looked as though his wild canine ancestors had thrived in the ice age of the Pleistocene era, seemed to enjoy the cold when he wasn't lounging on the shag carpet. Charlie made great sport of throwing snowballs for the beast. Cujo would root around with his snout in the snow for a while and then trot back to Charlie, shrugging as if to say disappeared again!

Despite the cold, he continued to walk every day. The squirrels had retreated to the nooks and crannies of the forest, and save for the crunch of snow, the purity of silence was complete. Charlie noticed that a copse of birch trees was gradually being chewed up and downed by beavers. He quickly made a connection between the aquatic rodents and Philip – whatever or whoever Philip really was.

When he strained his mind to recall what the visitor in the painting had looked like, and what he himself had briefly become the night he'd fallen into the lake, he remembered webbed feet and furry faces on the otherwise humanoid bodies – a sort of anthropomorphic mashup between a beaver and a human. He realized that he'd been tempted to dive off the rickety suspension bridge; longed to propel his furry form through the ocean below. He nudged these tangled thoughts aside and returned to no mind, erasing himself from the forest. In walking and meditating, he could temporarily generate inner peace and tranquility, but in the in-between, his mind raced back and forth between a fear of death and the fear of facing his mother – he couldn't decide what scared him more.

By the end of August, the lake appeared to be frozen over, but when Charlie tested it by throwing large rocks, it caved quite easily. He wasn't sure how the rules of the game worked: now that there was ice, could he just waltz out and fall through in the shallows? No, that didn't make any sense. Talking it over with Artemis, they agreed that the lake had to be well frozen before he made a move – the whole point of the exercise was patience, refraining from action.

Soon, however, it became clear that they'd been too patient. The cold was so deep and consistent that the ice had grown thick and completely safe to walk on. In the previous years, the rising temperatures in the region had meant the ice always had intermittent weak spots. It seemed as though the elemental force the catfish had exerted had been too effective, perhaps lacking in precision due to her diminished powers.

CHAPTER 29

THE FROZEN LAKE was like a desert, wind whipped, and inhospitable. Artemis accompanied Charlie on several long walks on which they surveyed the lake for weak spots, wrapped in scarves and sweaters like fat Egyptian mummies. Artemis had an ice auger for measurement; everywhere they looked it was half a foot thick – strong enough to support a small car. Charlie briefly considered driving the Porsche out onto the lake, but Artemis set him straight over brandy one night when the wind and snow had died down and the moon was bright.

"Isn't that a John Prine song? You can't get to heaven in a Porsche?"

"Who's John Prine?"

"A very good songwriter. You're not taking the Porsche, it's too dangerous. If the portal doesn't open, you'll die, and I doubt an ancient god is going to invite a douchey luxury car into their realm." Artemis swirled her brandy. "If only we could find a beaver. . . they build their lodges near moving water. That'd be your best bet in a deep freeze like this."

Charlie's face lit up. "I saw a bunch of trees downed by beavers not far from here! Just yesterday I noticed they'd taken down another one."

"Dear boy, why didn't you tell me?" Artemis said. "Winter came in so fast and hard, they must not have had time to prepare."

"Prepare what?" Charlie asked.

"In the winter, beavers fortify their lodges with mud that freezes; the mud walls are thick enough to keep them warm in their state of semi hibernation. Ideally, they'd have a big stash of aspen and birch chopped up to feed themselves through the winter, and they wouldn't have to venture out. If they do need to venture out it can be deadly, they don't move so well on land and the canals they build in the summer are all frozen over, so they're at risk of being gobbled up by hungry winter predators: wolves, owls, and such. If they're coming out that much they must be in a real bind."

A shiver passed through Charlie. "There are wolves in these woods?"

"You haven't heard them howling?"

Cujo stirred, gazing at them with his light blue eyes. There was a rustling in the forest, and he started barking.

"There's plenty of life in the forest in winter, it's just hidden from us: secret and sleepy. Beavers are nocturnal so keep an ear out at night... not that they'll be too eager to meet you. I'll come walking with you tomorrow, and we'll see if we can track them."

But they didn't have to track them, that night the beavers came to Charlie.

He was deep in a dream when he woke up: a memory of him and Yana playing frisbee in the backyard on a sunny day. She was in a good mood and kept tossing the frisbee so that he had to dive to catch it. Her eyes were sparkling and alive, he was laughing, covered in grass stains and dirt. Eventually the sun went down, she ruffled his hair and they went inside for a glass of chocolate milk. She listened attentively as he sat at the kitchen table, talking about this and that.

He awoke in warmth, and then, with sorrow, registered his mother's absence. Specks of light punctuated the darkness in strange patterns. Something was calling to him. He rolled out of bed and rapidly threw on several layers of clothes. His body felt light and limber, free of any tension. As he opened the door, Cujo's shadow ran out, dashing off into the woods. The dog's footsteps faded away into silence. Towards the forest, closer down to the lake, Charlie made out the silhouette of a beaver, crouched in the morning light waiting for him. There was something simultaneously comical and heartbreaking about the animal, with his chubby face and flapjack tail. He exuded an anxiety: a desire to accomplish his mission and get back to safety.

The beaver trundled into the woods, moving slowly and

awkwardly on the frozen snow. Charlie followed behind. His eyes were sore and he wanted a cup of coffee. The light was turning pink and it was all a bit much. The beaver had picked up some momentum and was moving quicker now towards the picked over copse of birch trees. When they arrived, Charlie observed that the beaver had spent his night dicing up a tree to be hauled off. He used his dexterous five-fingered hands to gather a pitiful load of wood into its arms and then stood staring impatiently at him. Charlie took the cue and picked up as much wood as he could carry. The beaver immediately started moving again, through a dense thicket of white spruce that scratched Charlie as they went. The rodent was moving fast now, eager to get home, leading Charlie into a section of the woods that was unfamiliar to him.

As they rambled further into the tangle of dense spruce, Charlie wondered why the beaver had built his home so far from a reliable food source. Maybe he was young and inexperienced, or maybe there was a good reason involving canals. Time took on a fluid quality – it was hard to say how long they'd been walking when Charlie made out the lakeshore through the trees. This was a secret place he'd never been before, where a break in the land allowed a large bay to mingle with a smaller one, making it harder for the surface to freeze.

The sun was slow in rising and it was still freezing. Charlie had somehow imagined he'd drop off the wood at the lodge and return to the cabin to get Artemis' help, but as he reached the forests' end, it dawned on him that the beaver had led him to a place from which there was no return. The light and air were different here, and he had the sense that he was in a children's fairy-tale. He was caught up in this thought when a massive blur of feathers swooped from the sky, with screaming, angry talons. A great grey owl, with its majestic patterned wings and Rorschach face had landed on the beaver, causing the bundle of wood to spill, and was on the verge of tearing into his flesh.

Before Charlie had time to process the scuffle, the shadow of a wolf streaked through the trees, smashing into the humongous owl and sending up a cloud of feathers. But it wasn't a wolf – Cujo had followed them, lagging silently behind. The dog and owl wrestled in a blur of blood, fur, and feathers. For a suspenseful second it was impossible to tell who was winning, but it was over quickly. Cujo had separated the owl into two large halves. He'd been cut up badly on his right side and had a deep gash on his nose running up to his eye. He was panting heavily while looking at Charlie and then nodded towards the beaver, who was gathering up his wood, somehow unscathed in the fighting. In this new fairytale land, animals had more agency and clearer intentions. He felt bad for the beautiful owl, but he also knew that it had been an agent of the Pelican and had meant to prevent him from returning to the Cathedral by destroying the helpful beaver.

"Thank you," Charlie called loudly to Cujo and immediately felt silly. The dog barked and nodded urgently towards the beaver who was sprinting towards the lake.

As he descended the rocky embankment down to the water in the beaver's wake, the dome of the sun cleared the trees, and everything exploded into a fierce hue of rosy purple. Even the trees seemed to absorb the colour, their needles turning a warm violet. Charlie was so distracted by this phenomenon that he didn't notice the beaver slipping through a tiny gap and into the water, he just heard the slap of its tail, warning his family of predators. Charlie turned back towards the forest and realized that the violet pine trees were bursting with owls, gazing silently at him with quiet disdain. Still, he felt safe; he knew that they couldn't come any further, and he'd reached the sacred portal to that other world.

As soon as he stepped out on the lake he heard the ice creak and shift like old floorboard. He stepped slowly, deliberately, breathing the cold air into his diaphragm and trying to relax in anticipation of the frigid water. When the ice gave out he hovered for an eternal second over the water, wondering if he'd ever make it back. Go towards death and death retreats. He was outside the water until he was inside of it, but rather than cold he felt warmth – he felt almost instantly the fur growing over his body and the seal forming over his mouth. The fur was heavy with a thick oil that protected him from the cold and caused him to sink. He realized he was still holding the load of wood and released it. His new eyes could see clearly and his body moved well in the water. He saw the male beaver swimming towards him, joined by his wife. He recognized immediately that they were a young couple who'd just found each other; they were building a home here and hoped to have children soon. They moved so beautifully in the water, with such grace and purpose that he could see the elegant pathways of their evolution. The barriers between human and animal were stripped away and he felt a deep love for these beings, as if they were family. They gathered up the wood, gave Charlie a look of gratitude, and then propelled themselves towards home with their powerful tails.

Gazing up, Charlie observed that the crust of the lake was frozen over. Either it had closed its wound instantly, or he had already drifted from it in the moving water. Whatever the case, the lungs of his new body seemed to hold an extra reserve of oxygen, and he was not panicked. On the contrary, he turned calmly away from the lake's surface and dove down into the darkness. Moving through the dark, propelled by his strong furry legs, he eventually lost all sense of physical reality. It was as though time itself blinked, and when it flicked back on there was an emerald light in the distance.

He moved his arms and legs in a frog-like breaststroke towards the light. As he grew closer and closer he felt the expanse of blackness closing in behind him, heard the sound of grinding rocks forming the walls of a tight cavern that would crush him to death if he slowed his pace. Returning to the Cathedral, he was not subjected to the body squeeze that had caused him so much pain the last time. He'd undergone part of the transformation in the outside world, providing a level of acclimatization to the dimensional shift.

Reaching the small pool in the antechamber leading out to the Cathedral, he pulled himself out of the water and shook the moisture from his fur. He breathed deeply through his snout and caught a whiff, once more, of that wet dog smell. He turned around to examine the pool that had been his entryway and saw that a tiny stream fed into it through a hole in the rock no more than six inches in diameter. The light was from a candle in a tiny niche, burning a shade of green that made Charlie think of Tatiana's eyes. He felt much more in control than on his first visit and was able to observe things calmly. Thoughts moved through him with limpid clarity, like a train through a pleasant landscape.

He could observe his stream of consciousness without becoming tangled in it. He felt warm and hopeful.

As he moved towards the mouth of the anteroom, where the suspension bridge led through the sheet of falling water, he realized that words weren't important here. What are words worth? And just then, he felt the texture of exterior thoughts and moods brushing against his own; colourful plumes of smoke drifted through his mind without disturbing anything, like stones sinking through clear, bottomless water.

He stepped through the water and out onto the suspension bridge into the expansive chamber. It smelled of salt and pine. The beauty of the huge Cathedral, circumscribed by the waterfall cascading from the darkness above, shocked Charlie even though he knew to expect it. The shock almost caused him to slip and tumble down the suspension bridge. Previously, the bridge had been slung loosely to the network of violet spheres, which had levitated at the same height as the antechamber. Now, however, the bridge was pulled tight, almost like a slide leading downwards.

Charlie grabbed the railings to prevent himself from slipping down the bridge. The pillars of light that held the spheres in place had grown weaker – they'd been slightly translucent but mostly opaque before. Now they were mostly translucent and slightly opaque, and the spheres had sunk low, perilously close to the ocean below. He squinted with his new eyes, which he realized were slightly impaired and blurry out of the water.

There were no other creatures milling about like last time; there was a presence, though. The plumes of smoke that drifted through his mind were drifting through the air as well, swirling in patterns up through the Cathedral's expanse. When they came into contact with Charlie, they passed through his physical body and his mind simultaneously so that external and internal consciousness were indistinct. It was as though the Cathedral was the inside of a collective cranium, and the plumes were thoughts, flitting up and up into the darkness and eventually disappearing.

On the edge of the suspension bridge, Charlie grew dizzy with vertigo. He looked back towards the emerald light and then down into the stormy ocean below. He felt a sudden desire to leap off the bridge into the water and this desire frightened him. Get yourself together Potichny. He started shimmying down the bridge, meticulously making his way towards the sunken spheres. His arms and legs were much longer than in his human form, and it was difficult to coordinate. He longed to be back in the water. Every once in a while, a ghost passed through him and made his mind into a mirror. Studying the sphere that he was bound for, he noticed that it had a chimney where the smoke was coming out.

A third of the way down a wave of fatigue and loneliness overtook him. The vertigo had dissipated, and he grew anxious for company. He loosened his grip and slid rapidly towards the wooden platform that ringed the sphere he was bound for. He hadn't realized how fast he would move with the momentum. Fear and adrenaline washed away the fatigue; he landed hard on the wood, flipped forward, and rolled into the side of the sphere with a thud. He lay supine for some time, staring into the darkness listening to the sound of the water. I have never been so supine, he thought. After a time, he realized there was a steady hum that accompanied the waterfall, similar to the sound of cicadas, coming from inside the sphere.

He gathered himself up and made his way along the rounded wall. On the far side from where the suspension bridge hooked on, he found a large, arched doorway. He walked through the doorway and entered the floating, humming sphere.

Chapter 30

Greg was on the escalator again in a mall that was under siege by zombies. His mother stood at the top of the escalator – just as she had when he'd first started having the nightmare in college – accompanied by a faceless man in a tweed sports coat, who promptly began making love to her. The man began undressing her, peeling off her blouse to reveal a pair of large breasts. As the man took off his tie and they began the carnal act in earnest, the escalator carried Greg down towards a pack of hungry zombies – his feet frozen in a pair of ski boots for some reason – and the last thing he discerned was his own face, buried in his mother's breasts. As the monsters bit into his flesh, as the scent of his own blood mingled with the scent wafting from the Cinnabon, he jerked violently awake and cried out.

The room possessed all the hallmarks of a sad motel: hot plate; broken coffee maker; dirty carpet; lumpy bed. It was midday, and a washed-out yellow light filtered in through the stained curtains. Greg reached reflexively for the bottle of bourbon on the nightstand and took a long pull. His head swam for a moment as he tried to cut the dream loose.

Upon returning from Nepal, Greg's overtures for Maggie to take him back had been met with indifference. It was too little, too late. She appreciated that he wanted to be there for the kids, but she also reminded him that he'd been out of the picture for the past several months and that that wasn't unusual for him. She'd started dating an architect who got along with the kids and didn't travel much. With all the craziness that had been going on around the city, the kids needed security and consistency. Greg was welcome to visit at an assigned time once a week until he got a suitable place of his own to host them. And then came the piéce de resistance: Maggie served him divorce papers.

In the bad motel, he sat up, snorted a big line of ketamine, and laid back, hoping to be transported to the Cathedral. Once again, however, the Cathedral lay out of reach and he simply sank down into warm glowing mud and imagined that he was wrestling with Fyodor Dostoevsky before everything – himself included – transformed into bright, shifting geometric patterns that gelled into honeycomb hexagons filled with thick, warm liquid and caused a further sinking feeling, into the silky sub-basement of the hive.

By the time Greg came to he was running late for rehearsal at the Concern. He pulled himself together and opened the blinds. It had begun snowing lightly – this was late August and winter had just begun. Across the street, men in bright ball-caps milled about outside the off-track betting center. A streetcar creaked past, grinding and sparking and halfway rusted to death. The buildings on the block were all one story tall: a quick-loan centre, a discount porn shop, a pet store, and a burrito place. In the distance, down Northern Dancer Boulevard you could make out the subdued glow from the beach and the gleam of expensive rows of townhouses.

He showered and dressed, pre-occupied with the scum he felt coating his insides from the booze and drugs. He was short of breath as he went down to the parking lot. He stopped and shut his eyes hard in the stairwell, clutching his chest, trying not to faint. He'd stopped exercising, had grown puffy and pale, and his hairline seemed to have receded half an inch in the past thirty days. He'd been subsisting on pub food and beer, popping Ambien to sleep. He took a deep breath, quieted the anxious beast inside himself, and continued down the stairs.

In the parking lot next to the coin-op carwash, he found his PT Cruiser parked on a diagonal across two spots. He realized with a sinking feeling that he didn't remember what he'd done the previous night. Someone had keyed the driver side of the car all to hell and spray painted the word "Pervert" on his hood in bright pink. He stood shivering in the cold for a moment, flecks of snow gathering in his beard, trying to figure out how easy it would be to clean off the graffiti. A pinkish blur in the corner of his eye drew his attention to a pack of red herons in the dead weeping willow next to the lot, surveying him with their beady eyes. Their colourful feathers popped against the chipped turquoise paint of the carwash next to the motel. One of them had a human ear in its beak.

Slowly, he reached his frozen fingers into his jacket pocket and removed the key. The beep-and-click of the car door unlocking caused the birds to jump and croak, but they stayed put. Greg started his car and screeched out onto Kingston Road, immediately accelerating up to 120 kilometres per hour, weaving recklessly between lanes as he merged onto Lake Shore Boulevard and then shot up the ramp to the Gardiner Expressway. He flipped on the radio and Eichelberger's voice filled the car – a rerun of his weekend show: "If Tristan und Isolde teaches the listener anything, it's that lovers cannot be joined in the mundane light of day, that it is only by coming together in the shadow of night, of the eternal ever-after, that two can truly become one, merging in a death dance that is at once physical and metaphysical. Of course, without a deep understanding of Schopenhauer the deeper meaning of these words will always elude the listener. Our public libraries are a wünderbar resource, I would recommend anyone trying to get to the heart of Wagner's philosophy – what's that? My producer has just informed me that the city's libraries have closed until further notice. In any case, here's the love duet from the second act, O Sink Hernieder Nacht Der Liebe."

Greg groaned and flipped the radio to the hip-hop station. Eichelberger had sounded like he was on the verge of tears, and the last thing he wanted was some lame Wagner aria flowing through his mushy brain. He hadn't spoken to Eichelberger since he'd been back. He'd heard that he and Sophie were together, and he didn't want to interfere. It was possible that he'd been on a binge because he knew it was a way for him to neutralize himself and prevent himself from meddling. He'd been cast as Basilio in a production of The Barber of Seville that was being revived for the hundredth time. The costumes were threadbare and the conductor – a man named Picard – was second-rate, but the costume folks were tied up working on Bluebeard and the Swan, and Von Strohn's full focus was required to coach the orchestra through Lampo's incredibly ambitious score.

The multitude of reflective condominium towers made the Gardiner feel claustrophobic, and Greg couldn't help but imagine that Toronto would soon be a forlorn wasteland with post-apocalyptic nomads standing on the remains of the elevated expressway, wondering what their forebears were trying to accomplish with all this hideous progress. He piloted down an exit ramp and pulled into his parking spot behind the Concern.

Upon entering the building, he experienced a moment of déja vu, the music being performed by the orchestra was similar to Manic Toads. He longed for the surreal tangent he was trapped in to end. More and more, everything was tied to the Cathedral and the place he'd visited when he'd almost drowned in Paris. He was paralyzed, more paralyzed than he'd ever been in his life. He still hadn't spoken to Charlie, and the unmended rift weighed heavily on him.

As he walked closer to the rehearsal in progress, he noticed that there was in fact a portal open on the stage with pylons and caution tape around it. He rubbed the back of his neck and stared hard: he'd never seen one before. Against the black wall of the concern it almost blended in – it would have been easy to stumble into it if it weren't for the yellow tape. Visually, the hole had a different texture than reality. It was slightly reflective – like the sky on a starry night. Greg shook his head and focused on the music.

Eichelberger was onstage, singing beautifully in Finnish, brooding masterfully as he sang. Sophie stood in the background, waiting patiently. Finally, when she stepped forward, joining him for a duet, something caught in Eichelberger's throat, and he stuttered and then stopped outright, bringing the rehearsal to a halt. Greg's jaw dropped; he'd never seen Eichelberger so much as miss a note, let alone drop the ball completely.

"What's the line again?" Eichelberger called out to Von Strohn, who had buried his face in his hands.

"Dietrich, we're losing our patience. Should I give the orchestra the rest of the day off? You seem like you could use some individual work-time."

Eichelberger's face darkened, anger gathered around him like a cloak, and he seemed to double in size. A volley of ferocious German syllables ripped through the air like shrapnel. Von

Strohn tensed and shouted back in German. He snapped a baton in half, and a tense silence fell as the two men stared each other down.

"Rehearsal's cancelled," Von Strohn finally said. "We'll get back to it as soon as Dietrich can memorize his lines properly."

The musicians bristled uneasily, and a din of whispers grew as instrument cases snapped open and shut. An apoplectic Von Strohn practically ran right past Greg, but suddenly stopped, wheeling around on the spot. "Gregory. What are you doing here?"

"Um, rehearsal?"

"Rehearsal's cancelled. Picard was being chased by a seagull, and he fell into one of those portals. The whole production's cancelled. Didn't anyone call you?"

Greg coughed and looked away. He still didn't have a phone and checked his email every few days at the public library in the Beaches – which, it suddenly struck him, was now closed indefinitely.

"Picard's dead?"

"Didn't say dead. He's just. . . wherever people go when they fall into those things."

"What's up with the portal on the rehearsal stage? Isn't that dangerous?"

"Whenever the orchestra performs Lampo's score, a portal opens up in that same spot. It's consistent at least; we feel it's safe to continue. We're working it into the stage design. Don't you worry."

"I wasn't worried. Anyway, what am I supposed to do now? I was counting on that gig."

"That's what I want to talk to you about. Follow me. We're going to talk to Vogel."

Vogel was the other German, Von Strohn's counterpart – the general director. He was handsome and square-jawed with slick blonde hair and a wardrobe of tastefully fashionable suits. He had a friendly, easy way about him and a wonderful smile, but he was cut-throat beneath the veneer.

They walked across the Concern, past the giant bull from Norma, which was nestled in a field of fake cherry blossom trees from Madame Butterfly. Someone had positioned a paper mâché guillotine from Dialogues of the Carmelites by the door to the administrative offices, so that one had to walk beneath the blade to enter. Von Strohn led Greg through the door and into a narrow hallway. At the end of the hallway they entered Vogel's office: a big, sunlit room with exposed brick and two dark green leather chairs facing his tiny desk. The windows looked out on a gated parkette. They sat down in the chairs, Vogel was having a conversation in Italian on video chat and sipping green tea from an ornate mug. He laughed loudly from time to time and eventually signed off, exclaiming to the computer screen ciao, ciao, ti amo, ciao.

His facial expression sank into a neutral arrangement as he turned his attention to Greg. Greg was silent. Von Strohn was hunched over, rubbing his hands together slowly. "Gregory," he began. "I'm so sorry that your show was cancelled. The company is reeling from the loss of Picard, but it means we can put all of our focus into the Bluebeard opera, which we feel is the right thing. Ticket sales were weak for the Rossini, Lampo's hot right now, it's relevant, most nights are sold out, and we're adding several more. There's talk of sending the production to Sydney next year."

Greg started to say something, but Vogel cut him off. "You know we wanted you for the lead, right? We were surprised when you turned it down."

Greg's stomach churned. He felt like he was going to be sick. "Eichelberger's your man on this one. He has to be."

"Eichelberger is behaving like a spoiled child. He's losing it," Von Strohn cut in emphatically. The Germans had a tense sidebar in their native tongue. Greg gazed out the window and thought he saw something moving in the snow-dusted shrubs.

"Gregory," Vogel finally said. "Your performance as King Lear in Paris was magnificent."

"You weren't there."

"I have it on good authority. Reimann's Lear is no joke. If you were really as good as they say you were, you could be entering a new phase of your career. We love Dietrich, of course we love Dietrich and of course we want him to succeed in this role, but he has been rather – "

" – Unreliable," Von Strohn chimed in.

"Rather unreliable. We've never seen this side of him. We feel it would be prudent to take precautionary measures. We'd like you to learn the Bluebeard role."

Something definitely moved in the bushes, there was no mistaking it. Greg stuttered, then spoke, angrily. "You want me to fucking understudy? You made me learn Czech last year for a role I never sang and now you want me to learn to sing in fucking Finnish? You krauts are god damn sadists."

The Germans shrugged at each other.

"Additionally," Vogel went on, "We'd like you to exercise discretion in the matter. You can use the facilities to rehearse, and we can provide a few musicians to accompany you, but we feel that if Dietrich knew – "

"You want me to lie? He's my friend, you know."

The bushes were trembling like crazy.

The Germans looked at each other and laughed, then held another quick sidebar.

"Sorry, sorry, we are being very naughty, very unprofessional," Vogel said. "Gregory, we've sent the offer to your agent. It's very generous. We're sorry about Picard, but what else are you going to do? The opera company is in a very precarious position; our donations are way down. Melody's money, your father's money, it can only carry us so far. We have to do something spectacular; Bluebeard and the Swan will be spectacular. Don't you want to be a part of that?"

"I'll talk to my agent," he said, suddenly needing very badly to get away from the scheming Germans.

CHAPTER 31

HE WENT OUT of the office feeling nauseous again; he pushed open an emergency door, stepped into the little parkette and gulped down the cold, fresh air. He bent over trying not to vomit, breathing slowly and evenly. When he finally stood up straight there was a dark, Eichelberger-shaped object in his peripheral vision by the bushes. The shape was wearing dark skinny jeans and an elegant black overcoat with the collar pulled up against a face that was coated in a silvery stubble. Greg stood stock still, looking sad and tired. Vogel's brightly lit office had been vacated. The sky had gone dark, and both men were silent, soaking in the gloom. Finally, Greg took a slim joint out of his breast pocket, lit it, and French inhaled.

"You were in the bushes just now, weren't you?"

"You call yourself my friend?"

"Ike, listen, I haven't even agreed to anything. But if you aren't doing your job, they have every right to hire an understudy. Even if you were doing your job – "

"You knew this would happen, didn't you?"

"Buddy, you gotta talk to me: what is going on?"

"You did it to humiliate me; you handed me the role and Sophie together knowing what a problem it would make to have both."

"How can you say that? After everything we went through? I am on your side. I want you to be happy. Can't you see that?"

"Then how could you let me fall in love with her?" Eichelberger's face distorted with pain. He was pale and had dark circles around his eyes.

Greg realized just how out of control things were and shifted his tone, speaking slowly and quietly. "Ike, you're speaking in riddles. I promise I will help you but you have to tell me what's going on."

It had been snowing lightly, but now it started to blizzard. Greg took Eichelberger by the arm and led him in a circle around the parkette to warm up. He brushed out some twigs that had gathered in his hair from hiding in the bushes.

"Love and death are the same thing," Eichelberger said, finally. "I thought wanting someone was bad, but having someone? Possessing someone? In flesh and spirit? It turns life into hell. All I think about is Sophie dying, or leaving me, or making love with someone else. Every moment that we are not together is agony, even when she is with me is still agony – because I know that it is fleeting, that she will die or betray me, or even worse I will die or betray her. If you are my friend, how could you let this happen?"

Greg re-lit his joint, which had gone out and puffed on it. They sat down on a bench beneath a maple tree, somewhat protected from the storm by the foliage.

"Dude, you know you can't possess Sophie, right? Healthy adult relationships are built on independence. I mean, you know you're going to die right?" He exhaled a thick stream of smoke. "And when you die you can't take anything with you. So there's no eternal love, because there's no eternal self." Greg shook his head in disbelief. "What the fuck am I even doing explaining this to you? You know this. From the cave. I know you know this because I know it, and I'm bush league compared to you."

Eichelberger was doubled over with his head in his hands.

"That's the worst part. I know it's wrong to feel this way, but it's out of my control. I'm terrified I will lose her, and I'm furious at her for wanting to have a life outside of us. And now I don't want a life outside of us. I don't even care about this opera. I want death, Greg. I want to die. That's the honest truth. I never should have left the monastery. If I kill myself, will you sing the part? Will you make me proud?"

Greg threw the joint away and slapped him across the face with all his might. Eichelberger cried out. Some of the madness left his face as he recovered.

"Don't you dare talk like that. You're a goddamn international treasure, and you'll be a great lover too once you get your head out of your ass. Goddamn birds. Goddamn fucked up weather," he grumbled to himself. "You can do this. You just need to be strong. Go home, meditate, and eat some vegetables."

"Okay," Eichelberger said, meekly.

Greg took out a ripped up card from the motel he'd been using for filter paper and passed it to Eichelberger. "This is where I am if you need to reach me. If you're having those kinds of thoughts, just call."

"I'm sorry Greg. I'm sorry if I'm letting you down."

"You're not letting anyone down, just get a grip alright? I should go before this storm fucks up the roads. Learn your damn lines Ike, and give Sophie some space."

Greg stood up and let himself out of the parkette through the gate, which locked automatically behind him with a click.

Over the course of his conversation with Eichelberger, the snow had soaked through Greg's clothes and chilled him to the bone; when he returned to the motel, he took a hot shower with a cup of bourbon and fell asleep on the floor of the tub with the water blasting. He woke up twenty minutes later in a literal fog, steamed like a human dumpling. Towel round the waist and one around his head, he poured a fresh bourbon over ice and flipped on the TV. The radiators had been turned on and a burnt, metallic scent filled the air. His plan was to get drunk while watching CNN, but the phone rang instead. He assumed it was Eichelberger, and when it turned out to be Sophie it took him a moment to orient himself, as if the world had flipped upside down. She was waiting for him in the lobby.

He performed his toilette quickly, out of habit, slapping deodorant sloppily on his armpits and running pomade through his hair. He came down in loafers, blue jeans, a white button-down, and a houndstooth blazer. Sophie was wearing a fake fur hat and an elegant white pea coat. He saw her first, looking sad and beautiful in the terrible fluorescent light. He watched her turn and react to the sight of him, and he immediately knew that he looked terrible despite his best efforts.

"You look terrible," she said.

"Thanks," he said, not knowing what to do with his hands. "How did you find me?"

"Once when you were drunk you said if you were ever going through a divorce and needed to have an emotional breakdown, this is where you would do it."

"God I'm a sad old bastard."

She laughed.

They walked down a hallway and through a door into a Pub called Murphy's Law. The pub was elegant and dimly lit with low hanging light fixtures that looked like underwater mines. A dark warmth radiated from the wooden walls and barstools; it was a stark contrast from the seedy motel. They got a table in the corner, snow blowing beyond a small window as if the outside world were a moving picture. Sophie ordered a glass of wine; Greg ordered a pint of stout.

"Not going so great with Ike, huh?" Greg said.

"He's a disaster," Sophie said, sipping her wine. "I thought it would be simpler, but. . . I've never met such a complicated human in my life. So powerful and at the same time so incredibly weak. Every time I think I can see who he is, the bottom drops out again. Sometimes he speaks poetically, makes love beautifully, but more and more he throws tantrums and breaks down into tears. I love him so much, but I don't know what to do. I'm not his fucking mother."

"That's all it is, isn't it? We mistake the women we love for our mothers and throw tantrums when they won't give us what we want. But we don't know what we want. Humans are ignoble beasts, aren't we? We just kill everything and don't know how to be happy."

"Very astute Greg, but not very helpful. He told me about Nepal. He helped save your life. Now it's your turn to help him. You've been on the brink before; I've seen you as bad as him or worse, but he's less solipsistic than you, less afraid of death. That's what scares me."

Greg thought of the Seine: the filthy gray water flooding his lungs and the benevolent force that had given him a second chance.

"He just needs space. He needs to get out of this crazy fucking city. There's something in the air right now, something muy no bueno."

"Oh, you think there's something in the air right now Greg? Really? You think that aside from the homicidal birds, the portals, the robotic animals, and this fucking apocalyptic weather, there's something in the air?"

Greg sipped his beer, licking the foam from his lips pensively.

"Do you know the story of Bluebeard and the Swan, Greg? Have you read the libretto?"

"No. The Germans are keeping it under lock and key."

"It's about a fisherman from a backwater island who travels to the big city and slays an innocent sea dragon as a gift for this stunning princess. . . he sews the scales of the dragon into a dress."

"Didn't Lady Gaga wear a fishskin dress to the Grammys one time?"

Sophie ignored him. "The princess refuses the dress, but when the fisherman turns off his obnoxious big dick energy and sings in his 'true voice,' she concedes to be his wife."

"Happily ever after?"

"Unfortunately, no. After a few years of domestic bliss back on the island, the fisherman gets restless and blows things up. He takes off to an enchanted forest region in the north, sleeps around, goes on adventures taming possessed demon animals. He tries to get the queen of the forest to betrothe her eldest daughter to him, and she just keeps sending him on these crazy missions. Finally, on a quest to slay the sacred swan of Tuonela, the fisherman is murdered by the husband of a woman he'd seduced. There's a long final scene as our hero is dying, where these opposing forces are fighting for his soul: This creepy, raven-headed demon named Lempo on the one side and the slayed sea dragon and sacred swan on the other."

"Sounds trippy," Greg said. "Way fucking cooler than a Wagner plot."

Sophie's brow was furrowed; she was deep in thought. "It's ridiculous to even consider," she muttered.

"What?"

"When we're rehearsing, I can feel the way the music is tied to the battle for our souls and the trouble here in the city. The line between reality and fantasy dissolves with the music, especially in that final scene. It makes me think of something Charlie said when I first met him: 'it's as if somewhere along the way reality was swapped out for something nearly identical but not quite the same.'"

Greg took a long sip of beer and mulled it over.

"I hope we can pull it off," he said finally.

"We?" She arched an eyebrow.

"We've got to get Ike out of the city. It'll help him get his head straight. He needs to go to a meditation centre. There's one he likes just south of Barrie; I was looking at going there myself. You want me to help him or what?"

"Even if you think you can get him to walk away, how do you know the Germans will let you sing the role?"

"They met with me today; they're begging for an excuse to fire Ike. They want me to be a sort of unofficial understudy."

"Sneaky krauts," Sophie said. They both sat in silence a little longer. The same thing was on each of their minds.

"Greg," Sophie said, sadly. "We can't sleep together anymore."

"I know," he replied, quietly. "It's for the best though; I heard if you go celibate you can build up lots of good energy in the diaphragm."

"He told you that, didn't he?"

Greg nodded, fighting back tears. It felt like the end of something.

"Let's be good to him," Sophie said. "Let's do one good thing together out of this toxic fucking wreck of a relationship."

She stood up, buttoning her jacket.

"Better start learning Finnish, you sad old bastard." She smiled at him, turned, and walked out into the blizzard. He ordered another pint and sat puzzling things out until the bar closed.

CHAPTER 32

"IT'LL BE A miracle if we can pull this thing off, I mean it: the blocking, the set, the costume changes, the lighting cues; it is by a wide margin the most complicated stage production I have ever heard of – let alone been a part of," Greg said.

"Everything's a miracle, dear boy," Errol replied. "Picasso once said: it's a miracle that we don't dissolve like a lump of sugar in our own brains."

They were sitting in the hot-tub at Wychwood on the eve of the opening party for the Yana Potichny retrospective: Mythical Landscapes. Errol wanted to have a pre-party, but his guests from Saint-Christopher's had deterred the likes of Melody Greyhound and Hounslow Hathaway from attending. Only Oliver Noodles had accepted the invitation; he was accustomed to being around hobos from several months-long sprees he'd been on, sleeping in shelters and alleyways.

"Errol, I think the quote is: it's a miracle we don't dissolve like sugar in our own bathwater," Noodles said.

"I don't think so."

"Dad, it's definitely bathwater. The other way doesn't make any sense," Greg said.

"I thought it was like a Zen koan. I could imagine dissolving in my own brain, in the sense that we get so caught up in our thoughts."

"I guess it makes a kind of sense," Noodles said, taking a sip of his non-alcoholic beer.

"No. It makes no sense," Greg said. He was drinking the non-alcoholic beer as well.

"Why are you two drinking that stuff?" Errol asked, irritated. "I'm sober, and I just drink ginger ale and tea like a normal person."

"A frosty brew in the hot tub always hits the spot." Noodles said. Him and Greg clinked bottles. "Plus, we're not exactly sober." They'd been passing Greg's little vaporizer back and forth.

"Shouldn't have glass in the hot tub," Errol mumbled.

At that moment Campbell stumbled out the backdoor, peed at the base of a Japanese Maple, and fell forward into the snow and his own urine.

"Should we do something about that?" Greg asked.

"He'll be fine like that for a little while," Errol replied.

It was mid-September – exactly a year since Lampo had completed his opera and jumped in front of a streetcar – but the weather had settled into a mid-winter mood: the city was frosty and covered in thick snow; long icicles hung from Errol's eaves troughs. It had been a month since Greg drove Eichelberger up to the meditation centre and took over the Bluebeard role. He'd given up drinking but kept up with a bit of pot smoking to maintain his sanity.

The role was challenging in every aspect – movement, singing, acting, and pronunciation – that he had to give all of his energy to it every day. This was helpful, it took his mind off the divorce. If he had any energy left over at the end of the day, he'd stroll across the boardwalk on the beach listening to early Wilco and late Radiohead on repeat.

This particular evening – the opening party for Yana's exhibit – marked a welcome night of recreation and distraction. It was so difficult lately to actually enjoy anything with the psychic blanket of gloom and doom that lay over the city. He hadn't seen much of Errol or Noodles or anyone, really, other than opera people since his return. Worst of all was the absence of Charlie, who he missed more than anything else.

In Nepal, he'd felt enlightened; he'd felt secure in a sense that he had undergone a permanent change of character that could not be undone. But it had been undone; he had backslid and succumbed to all of his worst habits. It was goddamn Flowers for Algernon.

"It's a damn shame that Charlie's not around," Noodles said, hopping up onto the side of the tub. "Would've been cool for him to open the show tonight. No one's heard the music he wrote for the exhibit, aside from the art gallery. At least Tatiana was available to play this gig. She's adapted some arrangements from Manic Toads into Space Disco, which will be a big hit with the crowd."

"Where do you think Charlie went?" Greg asked no one in particular.

"I don't know, but I hope he's taking care of that Porsche."

"You leant him your Porsche? Why didn't you tell me, Errol?" Greg almost howled. "I've been worried sick about him."

"Dear boy, this is the first time I've seen you in months. Don't you dare take a tone with me. It's all I can do to keep the financing for this opera from falling apart, not to mention fielding phone calls from your ex-wife."

"You talk to Maggie?"

"I'm gonna give you guys a minute," Noodles said, retreating into the house to dry off.

"Gregory, I'm sorry I said anything. I think you just need to keep your head clear until after the opera."

"Fuck the opera Errol, this is my life."

"I think the opera is more important than you realize," Errol said. "But if you need to know the truth so you can move on, here it is: you were simply less than dependable as a father and husband. It was unfair to put that much stress on Maggie."

Anger flowed hotly through Greg's whole body. "I'm a bad husband? I'm a bad father? What about you Errol? When mom left you just let her go without a fight, and we've never talked about it. Ever since I started singing, you treated me like a prize pig, like something you could trot out to impress guests. You think I didn't notice? We do not have a good relationship and I – I'm probably pretty badly in need of some therapy to be honest."

"Greg, you're right. I'm sorry that we never spoke more openly, and I'm sorry that I put so much pressure on you. It's difficult for men of my generation to open up, difficult for men in general. I'd be happy to try and mend our relationship, but right now I think it's best that we focus on the opera."

Greg wasn't used to seeing his dad's vulnerable side. For a second, he felt a deep sadness, which was quickly supplanted by a further surge of anger: "Oh, I'll sing the damn opera, old man, but I'm not doing it to impress you. I'm doing it for me and for the city, and I'm going to crush this role just in case your crackpot theories are correct. I'm doing this for my family even if they don't want me."

There was a loud cry from the direction of the Japanese Maple. "Goodbye enemy airship! The landlord is dead! Hurrah, hurrah, hurrah!" It was Campbell, rolling around in the snow, calling out nonsense.

"We should help him," Errol said quietly.

"Whatever," Greg said, as he hefted his massive frame out of the water.

On the third floor, Greg changed into a freshly pressed navy-blue suit, rubbed himself with pomades and lotions, and then oiled and combed his beard, which had finally filled in properly. A melody was stuck in his head, from the scene where the sea serpent warns Bluebeard not to murder her. He faintly heard a chorus from within the house and realized that it wasn't stuck in his head; he'd simply heard it drifting up from somewhere in the house. The stunning orange and pink Kintsugis with their trim of glittering metal massaged his brain as he breathed slowly, stepping carefully down the stairs in his freshly polished brogues. He ordered a taxi and stood in the front hallway. Through the door to the kitchen he could hear Errol encouraging Campbell to drink some water. Noodles sidled up beside him, sucking on his vape.

"Do you hear that?" Greg asked. "The singing?"

"Sure," Noodles said. "Jeezus, rehearsal really is taking a toll, isn't it?"

"You know how it is Noodles: the line between reality and fantasy is pretty squishy these days."

"True. I guess I'm used to that though, from all the drugs. I wonder if drugs would make all this witchcraft any more interesting."

"It would probably be confusing. You'd probably walk into a portal; besides, this pot is strong enough. It's the White Cookies."

"What do you think all this salt is for?" Noodles' attention had shifted to a mound of Epsom salt bags stacked in the living room. Errol came out of the kitchen, guiding Campbell towards a couch to rest.

"It's for the float tank," Errol said. "It needs nine hundred pounds of the stuff to work properly. Wish I'd had the damn delivery men carry it up to the bathroom."

"I'd like to try the float tank," Campbell mumbled.

"Not now," Errol said. "You're stinking drunk; you'll drown."

"Yeah, plus he's got piss all over him," Noodles added. Errol groaned.

"Gregory, fetch me a towel from the basement."

Greg went down and was presented with an unlikely spectacle. The folks from Saint Christopher's were huddled together, sharing pieces of photocopied paper. A tall thin woman with short brown hair was conducting them. They were singing the chorus part from Lampo's opera, doing a pretty good job for amateurs. They all stared at him as he walked to a closet and grabbed a towel. In his head he was practicing his own part, but he dared not sing out loud. He felt it would be an intrusion.

"Dad," he said, passing Errol the towel. "Why the fuck are those hobos all singing the chorus part from the opera?"

"Do you know what a radio is?" Campbell blurted out as Errol guided him towards the couch. "It's an old device. It carries signals in the air. They pass through us. All us animals. Do you know what radio waves can do to an animal?"

"Pretty eloquent for a dude who pissed himself," Greg said.

"I didn't piss myself; I fell in my own piss," Campbell said, growing slightly more alert. Noodles laid the towel on the couch, and Errol lowered the inebriated man gently onto it. "I photocopied the music before I handed it over. They wanted to learn to sing it. They loved Zee; we loved him." Campbell started crying. "It protects them from the Chaos Signal. The flooding winds. The quicksand."

"It protects them?" Greg asked.

"It keeps it away. Like the Kintsugi. It makes it so they don't want to go through the holes. Errol's house, it's a fortress against the Chaos Signal. A sanctuary. That's Lisa conducting them. She used to play the clarinet at the conservatory, but her son killed himself and she became a drug addict. Don't you see? We don't know how to hold ourselves together enough to participate in normal life. Our ties are tenuous. Our guts are spilling out. It's so hard for us not to go through those holes. Because almost anything would be better – you think you know heartbreak but you have no idea." And at that he went unconscious.

"Errol, I have to hand it to you, your house is a pretty fucking interesting place these days," Noodles said as they got into the cab.

CHAPTER 33

ENTERING THE GALLERY, Greg felt a wave of relief wash over him. The warm, spacious building was dimly lit and filled with beautiful, impeccably dressed people. He always loved being at a culture party that was not an opera party, because he was a peculiarity, rather than a figure of explicit interest. There was less of a chance he'd get cornered by an opera geek, and there was a much higher chance of meeting young people with fancy careers and sexy problems. Somehow, however, he ended up packed into a little group comprising himself, Errol, Melody Greyhound, and Hounslow Hathaway. Noodles had run off to check in with Tatiana and although Greg was scanning the crowd aggressively, he could not pick out any familiar figures to glom onto. He was trapped in the opera clique.

"How's the role coming Gregory?" Melody asked. "You really feel that you're up to the task of filling Dietrich's shoes this time? Hounslow and I have a wager on whether or not you can pull it off."

"She thinks you can do it," Hounslow said with a wicked smile. "I'm dubious. Then again, I didn't see you as Lear. To be honest, I hope you prove me wrong."

"The loser has to give the victor a full body massage with warm coconut oil," Melody whispered in Greg's ear and cackled.

Greg shot Hounslow a quizzical look, and he turned bright red. He'd always thought Hounslow was gay, but it now occurred to him that the foppish intellectual might be into older women, or maybe he was just a gold digger. Either way, Greg wasn't one to judge. They started asking him very specific questions about the opera, and although the questions were insightful, he had the unpleasant feeling that he was being cornered all the same.

He took one last look around to see if he could see anyone he knew and then resigned himself to discussing opera. He was experiencing high levels of anxiety regarding the role, and he found it was actually a relief to be able to express the challenges to people who could understand.

They were standing in the main atrium, where a stage had been erected for Tatiana to perform. In recent years, it had become common for the gallery to host musical acts, and since the retrospective incorporated a sonic element, it was a logical fit. While it should have been Charlie taking the stage, Tatiana was a reasonable substitute; she'd shared the stage with him most nights on the European tour, and the public had formed an association between them. She'd lifted all the stems from Antidotes when she taught Charlie how to run tracks on his laptop and planned to use them in her performance on this particular occasion.

Shortly before Tatiana was scheduled to play, Greg released himself from the opera clique and headed upstairs. The Mythical Landscapes exhibit would only be opened up after the performance, but Errol had called ahead and acquired special passes, leveraging the family connection. Greg climbed up to the second floor, walking past the glow of the blue Artemis Gwillimbury room and through a collection of vibrant pastorals by William Kurelek.

At the entrance to the exhibit, there was a rare photo of Yana at her cabin, smiling, paintbrush in hand. There was a strong resemblance between her and Charlie, and he was reminded of Charlie at 13, when he'd secretly enrolled in art class at school but was so incredibly sensitive about anything he drew that he burned his homework. Greg looked into Yana's eyes, "Why did you do it?" he whispered out loud. "Why did you leave him all alone?"

"Are you going to go in?" The security guard finally asked him.

He cleared his throat and wandered in. The walls had been painted forest green and dark, oceanic blue to complement the colours that Yana favoured. The exhibit was spread out over four rooms that felt like they were isolated from the building, from the city even – the dense atmosphere was downright otherworldly. Greg moved slowly and thoughtfully from one painting to the next. The exhibit began with more abstract work: a series of dragon skulls floating in space; impossible palaces that could have served as prog-rock cover art; bright doughnuts laid against dark; heavily textured canvases. In the solitude of the exhibit, Greg became calm. His mind went quiet.

It wasn't until he reached the landscapes that he noticed the music and realized that the melodies and textures slipping out of the speakers hidden in the ceiling were helping him discard his tension. As he took in a bright painting of the Beaver Valley escarpment, he felt his heart separate from his chest and float freely inside of him. The music and the paintings were inseparable. There was a seamless trick to the way that the eyes and ears processed the sounds and sights of the exhibit, and Greg was struck that this must be Charlie's greatest achievement.

Charlie had used his music to poke a hole through time and space and weave sounds through the aura of his mother's paintings. Tens of thousands of people would see the exhibit and hear the music that was almost hidden in the pictures, making the colours richer and bringing everything to life. What you saw and what you heard could not be separated – it was one unified impression. Greg had been noticing tiny vibrations in the lines of some of the paintings, and now he realized that the music was creating this synesthetic visual effect. The pictures were coming to life all around him; the room swelled with life and sorrow.

He had reached the end of the exhibit: the paintings that constituted From a Distance Trains are Small. He was lost in the texture of the Rocky Mountains when he heard footsteps approaching.

Greg turned, amazed that anyone else existed, and found himself looking into the stunning green eyes of Tatiana Tataru. She was wearing black jeans, a black blazer with floral detailing on the lapels, and a v-neck tee. Her hair was tied back and she was glittering from her moisturizing product.

"You're Charlie's friend: the opera singer. The funny guy," she said.

"Yeah, that's right. Nice to see you again," he responded stiffly. They'd met briefly in Paris and Greg had formed a negative association, triggered by jealousy.

"You know it's strange, I talked Charlie's ear off about art on tour, and he never mentioned that his own mother was a brilliant painter."

Greg shrugged. "I think it's painful for him to talk about."

Tatiana studied his face for a moment suspiciously. "All this sinister business with the birds and the weather. . . the Chaos. You and your friend are mixed up in it aren't you?"

"What do you mean?" The question caught Greg off guard.

Tatiana smirked. She was standing shoulder to shoulder with him now, looking into the painting. "It's baffling, but my ears don't lie. The theme in Charlie's music, it's not his. I studied Luka Lampo at the conservatory, you know. The melody isn't from any recording I've ever come across, but the style is unmistakable. The more I work with that melody, improvise on it, remix it, let it seep into my veins, the more I feel protected from the madness out there. Then I learn that there's a posthumous Luka Lampo opera on the horizon starring you, Charlie's best friend? It's all a bit. . . unheimlich, wouldn't you say?"

Before Greg could respond, the painting they were looking at started moving. Something slid down the mountain, kicking up snow, and landed with a thunk in the trees. They looked at each other and then back at the painting. The little lump lifted itself off the ground and rustled the trees; it looked like a baby bear was lost in the woods.

Noodles jogged into the room, out of breath, yelling Tatiana's name.

"Everyone's waiting Tat, let's go."

Tatiana trotted off with Noodles. Greg started to leave but felt an invisible hook tug him back. He looked back at the painting of the Rockies in confusion, shook his head, and went out through the darkened gift shop and back down the stairs. He was rubbing his eyes, trying to understand what he'd just seen. There was an audible buzz in the atrium as the crowd awaited Space Pussy. The rumour that she'd be performing a cover version of Manic Toads had leaked and caused a small sensation. People were curious.

Greg found his way back to the opera clique. They'd been hemmed in by institutional Toronto hipsters who were chattering away and laughing too loud to show what a good time they were having. A drunken man in a leopard print vest and a porkpie hat kept backing into Errol. As anticipation rose, so too did the volume of the chatter: *"Sold a painting for two million and spent the money on gourmet saltine crackers – ALL OF IT!"*

"His Rothko rip-offs are taking forever; he's a real Mark Slothko"

"Ayn Rand? Objectivism? What does that have to do with your showerhead?"

"The biggest cheese and cracker party the world has ever seen."

"I work for a not-profit, but they pay me a huge salary. I'm fucking worth it."

"My thesis topic? The subtle relationship between Kazuo Ishiguro and jam-band culture."

"They just need to finance the cheese."

The lights went down and the chatter ceased. Tatiana silently climbed onstage and started to play.

CHAPTER 34

TATIANA STARTED WITH one of her own songs and then transitioned into what she'd prepared for the occasion: an epic remix of Antidotes for Manic Toads with live instrumentation on guitar, synth, and drums. The stage was bathed in the same forest green shade as the exhibit, and the lights had come down so low that Tatiana could only make out the silhouette of the audience as a jagged, unbroken, black line. The five floors that made up the gallery each had a wrap-around balcony providing a vantage point to the stage, and Tatiana could make out silhouettes all above her swaying to the music. The way the audience moved in tandem was something she'd noticed when she was onstage during Charlie's sets – it was a strange sight to behold.

At some point, her consciousness drifted out over the audience so that she could make out individual figures. A metamorphosis was occurring: the members of the audience were turning into furry, bipedal creatures with glowing eyes. The whole gallery, packed with over a thousand people, was like a temple to some forest god. She felt like she was either a million years in the past or a million years in the future.

Suddenly, floating three stories up in the middle of the atrium, she became aware of a presence: it was Charlie. She realized – somehow, inexplicably – that it had been him in the painting, not a baby bear. She could feel him beckoning her urgently, beckoning someone, anyone, to get Greg's attention and send him back to the exhibit. He was screaming This is an emergency! Something very bad is about to happen! And as she slowly wrapped her head around these words, as she floated weightlessly, separated from her body, something very bad started to happen.

When she landed back in her body, the furry creatures had turned to birds. All around her and above her, rustling and squawking on the balconies, were a thousand menacing ravens. The sight shocked her so much that she stopped playing altogether. The birds began to transform back into humans. For a second, Tatiana took this as a good sign, until she heard the breaking glass, saw the shadows, and heard the flapping wings. Her pulse quickened with the realization that an assault was taking place.

When the first group of pelicans flew into the atrium, all five floors were in complete confusion. The pelicans were the biggest anyone had seen yet, their feathers tinted light blue. They had cold black and yellow dinosaur eyes and thick, furry braids running down their backs. They flew in formation like warriors, hung in the air for an eternal instant. The winged monsters issued a terrifying cry in unison and broke apart in pursuit of individual targets.

The biggest pelican made straight for Greg, who was standing in a stupor, unable to process what was happening. Tatiana leapt off the stage, moving like a jungle-cat, and tackled him out of the way. The hipster in the leopard print vest was swallowed up in a single gulp as the pterodactyl-like creature swept out its wingspan, lifting itself towards the fifth floor in search of its next victim.

Tatiana was lying on top of Greg, pressed to his chest and panting.

"Thank you," Greg said, stunned.

"Find Charlie," she said, "in the painting. Go!" There were portals at all the exits, people were running into them blindly, spinning into darkness. Get back onstage, keep playing! Charlie's voice was in her head again somehow.

Tatiana sprang to her feet, jumped back up on the stage, and brought in a heavier beat. She started riffing on her green guitar. There were half a dozen pelicans now and they all squawked in anger, dive bombing the stage as the guitar wailed. But the music formed an invisible force-field that repelled the beasts; when they came close to the stage it was as if they'd smacked against a glass wall. In the panicked confusion people were pushing and shoving, and a young woman fell from the third-floor balcony. One of the pelicans, rebounding off the barrier, recovered itself and flew in a neat figure-eight motion directly in front of Tatiana, scooping the woman up in its mouth before she could hit the ground.

From where she was standing, Tatiana was able to perceive a gateway to that other dimension in the pelican's mouth. The birds weren't eating people – they were catching them in the portals. Tatiana hit a bad note and dropped her pick in fright. She started finger picking, but it was too late. A hole had opened up in the force field, and a pelican dove through it. She was exposed now, and the birds were circling, preparing to strike.

The one that had breached the forcefield approached her on its clawed, ugly feet, a speckled galaxy of colour swirling in its primeval eyes. She kept playing as it approached, strumming random chords. The pelican screeched at her and opened its gargantuan mouth. She saw clear through into the horrors of the Chaos Dimension; the collective pain of its inhabitants lit up her entire nervous system. In an instant she spun around and cued one of Charlie's stems – the main theme from Antidotes. The pelican recoiled in shock. She peeled the volume up on the whole mix, dialled in a few more tracks, and jumped behind her drum kit. She started playing rapid fire fills and tapping on a sample pad, making rhythmic magic. The pelican exploded into silver dust.

The remaining pelicans attacked the stage in unison from every angle, but Tatiana's playing integrated the wall of sound, and they bounced off it in confusion. The portals blocking the exits started to flicker and wane, and a few people escaped. Tatiana was tapping the sample pad madly, releasing stems from Manic Toads that unfurled like tentacles, slapping the pelicans out of the air. Everyone outside the force field was still at risk, but the tides were turning.

The special exhibit was empty and calm against the chaos in the atrium. Greg was out of breath from running and slowed to a trot as he approached the Trains Are Small series. He found the picture of the Rockies and advanced towards it, calling out his friend's name. At first there was nothing, just dry paint on a canvas. He listened for the music, heard the ambient noise oozing out of the overhead speakers like molasses. Unheimlich, he thought. Unheimlich X-Men. He'd just seen pelicans eating people. Pelicans. Eating. People. He tried to relax and steady himself. He closed his eyes, then opened them and stared into the painting.

The baby bear made crunching noises in the snow and something stepped into the foreground. It was wearing a cloak, eyes glowing like coals under a dark hood. It reminded Greg of the faceless mage from early Final Fantasy games. The entire room was humming, a shiver passed through him.

'Is that Manic Toads I hear?' Charlie's voice was inside Greg's head. 'Is that Tatiana on drums? She's fucking crushing it!'

"Charlie?" Greg said, creases forming in his forehead. "Is that you?" He put his face right up to the little creature in the painting.

'Wow, gimme some space,' Charlie's voice echoed in his head. 'You've got some pretty nasty blackheads on your nose there. Also, you don't need to talk, I can see your thoughts... oh... shit dude I'm sorry about Maggie.'

"Get out of my head you fuck!" With a tremendous amount of force Greg punted the voice out of his head. The little creature in the painting fell over, stood up, and shook a furry fist at Greg. It was as though the little guy was trying to talk but he was stuck on mute. Greg relaxed his mind and felt something slip into it.

'We can only talk if you let me in. I'll try not to look too hard at these insane Freudian junk heaps, but you need to listen up and listen good.' Charlie's voice was back inside Greg's head. He took a deep breath and listened.

'Shit, I tried to script this out, but it's tough,' Charlie's voice said. 'I don't know where to begin.'

"Where are you?" Greg asked.

'I'm in the Cathedral: the ocean beneath the lake. There's a battle going on between the sea dragon who lives here and that. .. pelican monster.'

"What are these things? Gods?"

'They're immortals, yeah, ancient gods. Almost nobody believes in them any more so they only exist on the fringes of reality.'

"Dude, I've been worried sick about you. You said in your

email that I might never see you again, I – I don't want to lose my best friend."

'I'm trying to figure out if there's a way for me to come back. I think I have a solution. . . thing is, it sort of involves you risking your life.'

Greg beat his fist into his palm. "Dude, that's the shit I'm talking about. I'm sick of feeling fucking useless. I barely even feel like I'm alive right now. Hit me with the plan."

'Division of labour. I navigated the Cathedral, you're going to tackle the big bird. And I'll tell you right now, it's not going to be easy, and there's a good chance you'll die or lose your mind or both.'

Greg mulled this over. "But it's the only way to bring you back. And I imagine it's the only way to stop the city from being destroyed."

'Right on both counts.'

"We're going to be heroes!"

'Alright, just be cool man.'

Greg could feel Charlie smiling at him from beneath the dark hood. He felt a deep wave of love wash through him. 'Lay it on me,' Greg said, without opening his mouth, and Charlie started to explain.

Five minutes later, Greg was jogging back down to the main floor with the painting tucked under his arm; Charlie was still in his head.

'Are you sure about this? Frankly, this plan seems insane,' Greg had switched to thought-speech.

'What about all this isn't insane?' Charlie countered. 'The music will only hold them off so long; you've got to give them what they came for.'

'This is some Isaac Asimov shit,' Greg said.

'More Ursula Leguin, more fantasy.'

'Leguin wrote sci-fi too!'

Reaching the ground floor, Greg found that Space Pussy was keeping the pelicans at bay. The force-field was strong and whenever the pelicans attacked the audience, Tatiana swatted them with a sonic tentacle. As she drummed, diaphanous limbs swished through the air and slapped the birds, who grew increasingly furious in turn. As soon as Greg was out in the open, the pelicans all shifted their attention to him. They gathered in formation and circled, building up momentum. The force-field around the stage started to flicker, and the portals at the exits grew stronger. There was a low rumble, something audibly brewing. As the space darkened the pelicans glowed blue, flying faster and faster until they were diving towards Greg at full speed.

'Last chance,' Greg thought at Charlie.

'I'm sure, I'm sure. Focus. Don't fuck this up.'

The birds opened their beaks wide, revealing the portals: reflective black against the blue glow of their feathers. Tatiana reached out with her phantasmagorical arm and knocked down a few birds, but it wasn't enough: the majority of them were descending upon Greg.

'See you in the Chaos Dimension,' Greg thought.

'See you in the Chaos Dimension,' Charlie thought back.

Greg chucked the painting into the gaping maw of one of the birds with all his might. He closed his eyes and threw his arms over his head.

The music stopped. For a second, Greg wondered if it had worked, or if he'd fucked it up and been swallowed up into that other place. He felt his arms, his legs and his torso and gave a tug on his beard. He opened his eyes; everything was in stillness. People were picking themselves up off the ground, emerging from hiding places where they'd been cowering. The portals had disappeared, the pelicans were gone, and the attack was over.

Errol, who'd taken cover behind a sculpture of a polar bear, came running out and embraced Greg.

"Thank god you're alright dear boy," he exclaimed. "You were very brave just now. I don't know what you did, but you stopped them. Magnificent."

Behind Errol, Hounslow was wailing. "She's gone," he shrieked. "The beasts devoured her." It was Melody. The pelicans had eaten Melody Greyhound.

From the stage, Tatiana had watched the pelicans burst into silvery dust as soon as the painting passed into the monster's beak. She was in shock, everyone was. Before, the city had been fucked up in a way that seemed like bad luck, like a fairytale version of a natural disaster. Now it was clear that there was an intelligence behind the deepening disaster. They'd experienced an attack, a violation. Tatiana jumped off the stage and started comforting those who'd lost loved ones. All up and down the atrium people were holding each other and crying. The authorities started pouring in, but there was nothing to be done. In addition to the innumerable people who'd already disappeared, one hundred and thirteen more had vanished into the pelicans' mouths.

CHAPTER 35

A FEW DAYS after the attack, Errol organized a crisis meeting at Wychwood, which was fast becoming the headquarters for the resistance. He'd been working day and night on Kintsugis since the attacks to calm his nerves, and the massive, high-ceiling living room was packed with bright little vases. The attendees sat around a massive sectional in the following order: Oliver Noodles, Sophie Rénard, Tatiana Tataru, Greg Chest, and Errol Chest. The idea was to sift through what they knew, or thought they knew, and figure out a strategy. Goblin was purring on Greg's lap; once in a while she would jump onto his chest and burrow into his beard.

Tatiana had helped herself to some Beaujolais from the wine cellar (Errol maintained a respectable collection despite his teetotaling), but no one else drank. Every once in a while, Tatiana stood up to stretch her legs, staring out the floor to ceiling windows at the trees, the falling snow, and the brightly lit tower beyond.

Greg shifted uncomfortably on the couch, and Goblin sank her claws into his thigh. Charlie's plan, with all its moving pieces and the unlikelihood of its success, weighed heavily on him. He glanced sidelong at the bottle of Beaujolais and started to sweat. Goblin pushed her fuzzy snout into his beard again and purred deeply.

Errol was the first to speak: "With Melody gone, the opera company will soon be forced to file for bankruptcy. That snake Hathaway got her to sign over power of attorney a few weeks ago; he flew to Antigua the day after the attack and I don't expect we'll be hearing from him again. I've begun liquidating my U.S. securities in order to make the necessary payments for Bluebeard and the Swan, but it looks like this could be our – no pun intended – swan song. I hope I'm wrong though, I hope the opera is the antidote."

"Look, I understand that we're all a little out of our depth here," Sophie said. "But how can any of you claim to have a clue what you're talking about?"

"You weren't there," Tatiana said. "You didn't see the way these creatures exert their force; it has to do with subtle, invisible vibrations. Their power comes from a different dimension, it seems ineffable, but it's not."

"Eff the ineffable," Sophie exclaimed. "I'm a singer, not a sorcerer."

Tatiana turned red with anger. "If you aren't going to contribute, then what the fuck are you doing here?"

Sophie blushed. "The man I love has been affected by this black magic. I'll do whatever I can to help."

Greg nodded in support. "We'll need Eichelberger to pull this off. I faxed him a copy of the score and libretto. We need two bluebeards."

"The meditation centre has a fax machine?" Noodles asked in surprise.

"It's a Buddhist non-profit. Everything is thirty years behind."

"Why do we need two Bluebeards?" Errol asked.

"As far as I understand, Luka Lampo's spirit is trapped with the Pelican in the Chaos Dimension. Now Charlie's trapped there, too. I'll have to leave in the middle of the performance to rescue them, and we'll need a stand-in."

"Can we codify the language?" Sophie asked. "This all sounds super sketchy, like a fantasy novel written by a stoned teenager. What exactly are we dealing with here?"

"They're immortals," Greg said. "Ancient gods that have been forgotten. Well, almost forgotten. There's a sea dragon god Charlie calls the Feline; she promotes compassion, understanding, and healing. Then there's the destructive Pelican god: a force of chaos, the jerk behind this terrible mess. They each have their own realms separate from ours. Charlie got mixed up in the struggle between the two and unwittingly made a deal with the Pelican, tipping the scales in his favour. We have to work with him to shift power back to the Feline."

"Son of bitch," Noodles said. "Bailing on his festival dates is one thing, but selling out my city to an evil god? Weak, Charlie, fucking weak."

"Who invited this guy?" Sophie asked.

"It doesn't matter how this happened," Errol said, twisting his moustache. "What matters is we work together to come up with a solution. Apparently Tatiana has some insight into what's happening to our population on a basic level. Would you care to share?"

Tatiana had been standing with her back to the others, sipping her Beaujolais. Now she turned to face them. "Until the other night I was a staunch materialist, a cynic. I believed the world was total chaos, that there were no repercussions to one's actions. I believed that my intelligence, beauty, wealth, and talent entitled me to put myself above others – "

"What's wrong with that?" Sophie interrupted.

"I don't believe that anymore. I don't believe in a storybook afterlife either, but I can tell you what lies through those portals. You all say you saw a dark, silvery sheen, but I saw right in, into the pain that lies in that realm: it shot through me like a bolt of lightning. I saw how our suffering is all tied together. I realized that I'm like the woman in the story about the onion."

The room waited expectantly.

"An old, selfish woman dies and goes down to hell, to the lake of fire. Her guardian angel visits god to make a case for her, like a pro bono lawyer or something. The angel finds one scrap of evidence in her favour: she once gave an onion to a beggar. God tells the angel to offer the woman an onion. If she can hang onto it, it will carry her up to heaven. So the angel goes down, offers her the onion and starts pulling her up. Just when she's almost all the way free, the other sinners see what's happening and grab onto her feet and legs. The woman kicks them, screams that it's her onion, and of course the onion breaks and they all fall back into the hellfire."

"And?" Sophie said, exasperated.

"I'm that woman," Tatiana said. "I've kept the onion to myself all my life, but it's time to share it. We exist to coexist... with each other, nature, the galaxy. Without that connection, everything falls apart, and we may as well give up as a species. Where those birds live, it's an awful place created to divide us, to transform our complex minds into torture devices. We're dealing with a place that thrives on the suffering that humans create for themselves. It pumps that energy back out into the world and drives a wedge between us, vacuum seals us into our own bodies. If enough of that energy gets out into the world, we'll lose our capacity for compassion. If we don't stop these monsters, they'll help us give in to our worst impulses."

The room considered Tatiana's words.

"It sounds like we understand the Pelican's dimension to some degree," Greg said, breaking the silence. "Charlie's told me about the other one, the Cathedral, he calls it. It's a sanctuary that has to be protected from the forces of chaos. It's hidden, but he found a way in. He's the only one who knows the inner workings, who knows how to help us out of this mess. We're basically his support team."

"In a practical sense, what needs to be done?" Sophie asked. "What can we arrange in the real world, with our given resources and skills, to solve this problem?"

"We need to talk to a radio station that plays classical. We need to broadcast the premiere of Bluebeard and the Swan on a powerful transmitter," Greg said. He was petting Goblin, who was purring quietly with her eyes most of the way shut. In the basement, the rag-tag chorus started singing, providing a triumphant soundtrack to Greg's words.

"We need to make sure that this opera is nothing short of brilliant. We need Eichelberger healthy and ready to sing; he needs to come back as the lead. I'll understudy. We need a portable radio with batteries that won't die, and there's a decent chance we'll need that chorus in the basement. Other than that, it's just a matter of time. The premiere is in a week, if we can't reverse the Chaos Signal by then, it'll be too strong. We won't stand a chance."

"Wait, you don't have a job for me?" Noodles said. "Why was I even invited? This is bullshit!"

"You could find a good radio," Sophie offered.

"You can buy the batteries too," Greg said. "Brand name, please."

The phone rang, and Errol went to get it.

"I have a good relationship with Radio Two," Sophie said.

"I'll reach out to them about the broadcast."

"Anything else, just let me know," Tatiana said.

"What you did at the gallery was amazing," Greg said. "A lot more people would have d– " he stopped himself. "Would have gone through the portals, if it hadn't been for you."

"Maybe we can get them back," Tatiana said, putting a hand on Greg's shoulder. "Maybe we can get him back."

"Gregory," Errol called from the kitchen. He was holding the portable phone. "The art gallery's on the line, they want to know why you threw their painting into that demon's mouth."

"Tell them I'll call them back," Greg said. He stood up and lumbered towards the front door. He wanted to get back to his motel room and work on pronunciation.

On the drive home he tried to imagine what Charlie had been going through, what his journey through the Cathedral must have been like, but it was all too strange, too abstract to conceptualize. He climbed out of his PT Cruiser next to the turquoise car wash. A pack of red herons surveyed him menacingly. "You'll get yours, you sons of bitches," he whispered. He went into the sad dark room, ran through several pronunciation exercises, and then fell asleep dreaming of swans and ravens.

CHAPTER 36

THE FIRST THING that struck Charlie upon entering the sphere
was that its interior was ten times larger than its exterior suggested.
A spiraling wooden platform protruded from the wall, leading
around and around up towards the dome. All the way up there
were triangular niches carved into the walls, which were occupied
by furry creatures sitting cross-legged and completely still, bathed
in emerald green light. There was a single, conspicuous niche at
the very top that was unoccupied. Each creature was producing
a hum that formed a greater frequency, which Charlie found
confusing since they – like him – did not have mouths.

The hum emanating from each individual produced a
stream of light, stretching into the centre of the sphere where a
bewildering phenomenon was occurring. When Charlie looked
straight at the swirl of colours produced by the collective hum,
he experienced a shifting, uneasy sensation. He could feel the
moods and emotions of the creatures permeating his own being
in a process of spiritual alchemy. The colliding streams converged
in a psychedelic fire, burning in the hearth of the Cathedral; its
smoke escaped through the chimney in intervals.

Initially, Charlie averted his eyes from the fire; it was too
intense to take in. Rather than ascending the platform, he
stepped into the basin of the sphere and lay down on the floor.
He lay for a time with his eyes closed, just listening to the hum
which could have been a river, an airplane, or the white noise
of his cocoon. The hum without the accompanying visual of the
floating fire was warm and comforting, and dissolved his feeling
of being a lone individual, categorically separate from the rest of
existence. In this position of repose his human form dissolved
into his mammalian form, which dissolved into a floating energy

pattern: a spacious collective of matter and sensations with no fixed boundaries, a bundle of atoms held together by some strange glue.

After a time, feeling quite safe and relaxed, he opened his eyes and tried to make sense of the floating fire. It was made up of different colours and yet it was always one colour: now orange, now pink, now black, now turquoise. No colour ever repeated itself exactly, and each one had a corresponding emotional texture that was transferred to the spectator, separate from any explicit context or narrative. He allowed himself to stare into the fire and experience feelings of jealousy, love, pride, shame, relief, and all of the unnamed territory between the emotions that slip through language like bathwater between your toes. If all this was strange, the strangest thing of all was to experience these phenomena free and clear of the circumstances that produced them, like the aftertaste of a meal one had no memory of eating.

Charlie became completely lost in the flux of the fire, and by the time it extinguished itself he was completely oblivious to the movement around him – of the creatures stretching their arms and hopping out of their nooks. Feeling like an intruder, Charlie expected some sort of hubbub, but the furry creatures simply filed out, leaving him alone in the room, which he now supposed to be a sort of designated prayer room. Following them back out onto the platform, he watched as they dispersed through the networks of bridges and ladders, entering any of the other half dozen spheres of varying sizes. Some of the creatures played on the bridges, swinging on them like a jungle gym, and others sat at the edge of the wooden platforms, staring into the ocean below, seemingly lost in conversation. Although Charlie knew they could not speak, he was struck by the notion that they were communicating without sound. This notion was confirmed almost immediately when a creature that had lagged behind transmitted thought-speech directly into his mind.

'I know you,' the creature said. 'I know you from that other place, from before. You should not be here.'

The thought-speech bloomed in his mind in a way that felt intrusive and made him feel scared and vulnerable. It was formed by something primordial, by a gelatinous shape that rearranged itself, expressing raw thought patterns. The shapes were like palindromes, they bloomed fully formed and symmetrical – they could be read front to back or vice-versa.

They were standing alone, Charlie and this stranger, on the wooden ring around the prayer room. A fine mist drifted through a beam of light, only to be eaten up in the darkness. Charlie hadn't had a chance to examine the creatures calmly before and now he examined this one: thick brown fur, paws that looked like mittens, webbed feet, slim, lanky body, mouthless head with a black snout and a sharp tuft of fur pointing back like a cyclist's racing helmet, bipedal, humanoid body. The glowing eyes differed in colour from one being to the next; this was the one who'd caught him on the bridge last time, the one with his mother's brown-green eyes.

He ventured to enter the creature's mind and speak: 'I'm looking for my mother. Her name is Yana. She's a painter.' These communications were superfluous however, since as soon as Charlie entered the creature's mind, he was met with absolute certainty that this being simultaneously was and was not his mother and also that names, like words, held little significance here. They gazed into each other's eyes for a long time as they came to understand what each was to the other. Streams of thought-speak mingled hypnotically, producing feelings of depthless sadness and joy between them. They sat down on the wooden ring, legs dangling over the edge, and established a dialogue as Charlie slowly grew accustomed to the thought-speech. He kept stretching his legs out in front of him to examine his webbed feet, for which he felt a perverse fascination. In his current mind, which felt so different from his normal one – as though it had been cleansed of anything trivial or unnecessary – he became estranged from his purpose. Seeking an audience with the sea dragon had lost its urgency. All he wanted to do was swim.

'You're the only one who's ever been allowed in here without actually dying,' Yana said.

'I'm not dead?' Charlie asked, punctuating the sentence with an awkward fish hook. Yana contemplated this; he could feel her thoughts churning like a whirlpool.

'You're in the in-between. Neither dead nor alive. It's up to the Feline to decide if you go back.' When she formulated Feline, a golden coil lit up his whole body and the mist passing between them crackled golden-peach and then vanished. Charlie realized he was forgetting his own name and gathered his wits; he had important work to do.

'I need to see the Feline. This place is in danger, look: your home is sinking down into the sea. I came here to help.'

The creature who contained what had formerly been his mother, sensing his anxiety, gave him a look of compassion and formulated a simple shape that meant something like: 'That's not how we do things here. Be patient. You can't fix what you don't understand.'

'So, what am I supposed to do?'

'Explore. There are whole worlds down here. Get to know the place, talk to some of the others. Don't be in a rush, nothing good will come of it.'

Charlie imagined his human body, frozen and lifeless at the bottom of Canoe Lake; a sigh shot from his snout. Yana stood up and made to walk off but Charlie sent out a sharp, angry shape; she turned towards him in surprise.

'You meant to do it, didn't you? You went on ahead and left me behind. Do you know what that does to a kid?'

Her eyes dimmed, and she put her hands on her waist. 'I was in so much pain then. I couldn't think straight, and I was reckless. It was selfish, I'm sorry.'

The apology was genuine and free of shame.

'The sadness took me to the worst places imaginable, did things to my body that destroyed the goodness in me. I didn't want you to be around that. That's why I came here, that's why I became a Diver.' Diver took the shape of the furry, mouthless creatures; the current form of Yana and Charlie. So that's what these things are, he thought, gazing at his webbed feet. Divers.

In the Cathedral there was no time, no sleep, and no meals. The Divers went about as they pleased, sometimes chatting on the bridges and ladders, but more often playing in the half-dozen violet spheres. The spheres each contained environments that, like the prayer room, were much larger than their exteriors suggested. One was a forest populated by ancient red cedars and giant sequoia. The forest floor was littered with hundreds of species of flowers, and there was a humid pocket where succulents and orchids grew. Air plants – curling like miniature dragons – darted between the trees and above the canopy like swallows. The Divers typically walked the labyrinthine garden paths alone, mind shapes crackling in the air around their fuzzy heads. All of the other spheres were filled with water.

Charlie was confused at first as to why there would be four spheres dedicated to water, but as he explored each individual sphere, he found that the texture of their environments was different. One was salt water, another fresh water, and then there was a combination of both: freshwater mingling with the ocean. The lowest, smallest sphere emulated the depth of the ocean with high pressure and low light. Charlie recognized it as a simulacrum of the place where the tube worms had pulled him into the Feline's lair. In the water spheres, the Divers wrestled, raced, and underwent a kind of endurance training to see how long and how far they could swim without resting. The freshwater sphere was the easiest; the deep-sea sphere the most difficult. Initially Charlie thought that the Divers were like monks, but they sometimes wrestled ferociously with each other and trained for hours, like soldiers. He happily joined in the horseplay, working his strong limbs, propelling himself rapidly through the water with his webbed feet, but he wondered what it was all for.

He took many long walks in the beautiful woods, but hadn't reached out to the other creatures with thought-shapes beyond some basic communications in wrestling and training along the lines of 'That was fun, let's go again,' and 'You swim fast, but I'll bet you could swim even faster.'

These thoughts during horseplay could barely be called language. There was a degree of simplicity in the bodily movement and spontaneous choreography that led him to feel the dissolution of the barrier that separated his mind from his body. His mind sank into his body, and the two became one as he moved with a perfect precision that was not unlike dancing. He remembered playing pickup soccer at recess around the age of ten – the split second before puberty throttled him – which, as far as he could remember was the last time he felt comfortable as a human being: the joy of passing, shooting, and sweating, of sprinting and sliding in front of the net to prevent a goal, the endorphin rush, and the laughter.

He realized that sports weren't necessarily stupid; games promoted health and helped draw the mind away from compulsive thinking. Remembering life in his own reality – or the reality he was most accustomed to – was jarring and unpleasant. He didn't like to compare his impressions of the Cathedral to his impressions of the world up top. He felt that if he ever made it back, what he experienced here would turn to sand and slip through his fingers. He realized he had no desire to go back – the warm, playful mood that permeated the Cathedral was a balm – but Charlie made a point of calling up uncomfortable memories from his other life to avoid slipping fully into this new reality. There was an important reason, he knew, that he could not stay here forever: he had a purpose, a responsibility to people suffering on the surface.

He'd been there for what he reckoned was about a week when he found out what the training was for. He was walking in the forest one day, chasing air plants in the garden of succulents, when he realized he was all alone. The other Divers were filing out of the forest sphere. He went out into the Cathedral and saw that everyone was streaming into the middle sphere – the sphere containing the salt and freshwater mix. He followed them in and was struck by how many Divers there were: hundreds of them, moving through the water like aquatic gymnasts.

After a brief warm up, all the Divers sank to the bottom, which was a level field of seagrass. Several of them produced glowing orbs the size of medicine balls from out of thin air. They passed the orbs back and forth, flipping through the water and maneuvering around each other. The Divers divided into two sides of what turned out to be a gigantic playing field. As they divided, half of them took on a glow of violet; the other half took on a glow of dark green. The mixture of freshwater and saltwater created an effect of soft gravity so that the Divers could throw the orbs and run along the field. At either end of the field, goals appeared in the form of small circular frames. During the warmup, Charlie tried to carry an orb right into the goal, but he bonked against an invisible force field, much to the others' delight. This was the rule: there was no goaltending, but you had to throw from several feet out, and the target was very hard to hit.

An especially big, auburn-eyed Diver on Charlie's team – this was the team with the violet aura – began exchanging thought-shapes with him and explaining the rules. The auburn eyes reminded Charlie of his eighth grade English teacher, and he named the Diver after Mr. Frasier in order to distinguish him from all the others. The rules were simple: players passed the orbs back and forth using the scooped paws of their long arms and worked their way down the length of the huge field trying to score. You could run or swim, but you were only allowed four kicks in the water before you were obliged to float back down. There were several orbs in play at once, and the players on each team arranged their minds in a network to coordinate offensive and defensive movements through collective thought shapes. Full contact was allowed, but tripping and interference were not tolerated.

After a lengthy warm up, the greens and violets all dispersed on their respective sides and a horn sounded. Divers who were holding orbs flung them over the heads of the opposing team, igniting total mayhem, and the game was on. Charlie completely lost himself in the ritual for who knows how long. The game was glorious: the physical frenzy, the sneaky strategies, the impossibly long passes, and the assisted goals executed by Divers corkscrewing through the water like figure skaters. It was all Charlie could do to keep up. Processing the complex dialogue that was continuously running between him and his teammates was disorienting, and for the majority of the game he contented himself assisting on the defensive side.

Towards the end he grew bold and went on the offensive, kick flipping himself up through the water with joy. Someone passed him a ball as he soared, and he quickly handed it off, not wanting to botch the play. Emboldened further, he landed in the seagrass and sprinted up towards the goal at full speed. The big, auburn eyed Diver (Frasier) grabbed his attention with a thought-shape and laid out a pattern for Charlie to follow. He skirted towards the side of the field and then bee-lined towards the goal from an angle. A trio of green Divers blocked his path, and he kicked off the ground with all his might. The defenders shot up towards him, but not fast enough. As he soared over them, Frasier flung an orb from the other side of the field in a huge arc. Charlie's arms stretched out with uncanny elasticity and caught the thing. He landed easy down close to the goal. 'Throw it!' mind-shapes exploded from every direction. Without hesitating he cocked his arm back, certain that he would score, but at the last moment something hit him from the side like a rocket and tackled him to the ground. The orb flew up and was intercepted by the other team. When his senses returned, he perceived his assailant's green-brown eyes mocking him playfully. It was Yana. She helped him to his feet and the horn went; the game was over.

Frasier swam over to him and Yana and sensed the strange connection between son and mother. He shot a quizzical glance at Yana and turned his attention to Charlie: 'You're not from around here, are you?'

CHATPER 37

AFTER THE GAME, Charlie, Yana, and Frasier went together to the forest and walked in the shade of the giant sequoias. Frasier was addressing Yana, but Charlie could feel his thought-shapes. The auburn-eyed Diver was excited, confused, and a bit angry. His thought-shapes were coarse and scattered.

'How can it be that we have a stranger in our midst, but he hasn't been a ――― yet?'

Part of the thought-shape was strange to Charlie: a shape that only made sense in the Cathedral, which was something he hadn't experienced yet. It was like the little piece in a light bulb that conducts the light, the filament.

'I'm just as confused as you are,' Yana countered. 'I sense that he's my son, that part of him still exists in that other place, but I have no answers. I don't know how he got in. I don't know why he hasn't been the Filament.' They came to a pond that was completely still, reflecting the trees and the clouds in the rose-coloured sky above. Floating plants danced in the air.

'But you knew! You've known! We need the Filament to keep this place alive, and we have a perfectly good one right here. You've been hiding him.'

'Oh, please. Enough drama. You're acting like you're in the other place. You can sense it yourself, he's not all the way here. We never activate the Filament until they're all the way here.'

They walked a path that went around the pond, Charlie lagged behind and felt like a child, unable to understand much of the conversation.

'The last time we waited, we lost the Filament. You need to tell the others, we need to perform the ceremony soon and send down an offering.'

Growing impatient and annoyed, Charlie jogged up

alongside them, crafting inquisitive thought-shapes: 'Hey! I'm right here. It's rude to talk about someone in the third person when they're present. If I'm going to be a Filament, it's up to me. What in the hell kind of place is this? What goes on here? And what is this weird offering you're on about?'

His questions came out jumbled and misshapen. Yana and Frasier looked at each other with apprehension. They walked through some more trees and came out on the edge of an escarpment overlooking a beach and a velvety ocean lit up with incandescent jellyfish. Charlie was so worked up he barely noticed the ocean. He took a breath and formed a calm shape: 'What is this place?'

The three of them were all gazing out over the ocean now.

'It's a place where some people end up on the way to the long sleep, to reflect and find peace,' Mr. Frasier said.

'In the ceremonies we relive our experiences from the other place,' Yana said. 'Slowly, over time, we nudge the subjective memory of our past away from trauma and come to an understanding, a truce. In contemplation and play we are able to heal ourselves and expel the poison we built up in our other bodies.'

'Poison' flashed an image of a Diver coated in crude oil. Charlie signalled for clarification.

'The poison's different for everyone,' Yana said. 'The first time I felt the poison was in my late teens – it paralyzed me for a time. I worked through it in my first paintings and in my twenties I found success; I thought I had it beat. But after the thing with your father, after you were born, I realized success was a sham. The poison came back and became part of me, like an organ, like my own skeleton. Painting was the only thing that didn't feel like torture.'

The shapes were vivid, clear, and powerful and for a time Yana could not speak. Frasier picked up the thread: 'When someone finds their way here, they act as a Filament at the ceremony. The chaotic energy from the other place is very powerful; it allows us to synthesize the poison into sea-dragon-chow, the waste material is burned off through the chimney.'

Charlie balked and wondered for a moment if Frasier had misspoken, but he hadn't; the shapes were just difficult to read.

When he said 'sea-dragon-chow' all the glowing jelly-fish floated out of the sparkling ocean against the pink horizon.

'The sea dragon gets her energy from our work, that's what powers this whole operation. The Filament helps gather the material, and then the oldest Diver – whoever's been here the longest – delivers the offering. After that they pass on. Once you dive down into the big ocean, there's no coming back. The last Filament we had vanished before the ceremony. Without fresh material from up top, it's no use. The sea dragon's energy is so weak we can't pull in a new Diver. Those who might have come here are going straight to the long sleep... or someplace else. But not here. That's why it's so curious that you've arrived just now. I hate to say it but you may be our only hope, even if you're not ready, even if you're not all the way here... we don't have much time.'

Charlie tried to take all this in. He understood that the Filament who'd disappeared was Philip. He wondered where Philip was now and what lay beyond the portal he'd tossed the painting through. The cold, confused energy of the Pelican's dimension rushed through him. Frasier and Yana took a step back, shaken by the energy. A curious thought-shape bubbled up from Yana.

'It's your turn, isn't it?' Charlie said. 'You're the oldest Diver here. You're stranded because of me.'

'Because of you?' The synchronized shapes crackled forth from Frasier and Yana at the same time. Charlie depicted the events through a rapid sequence of sophisticated thought-shapes. The veteran Divers grew perplexed. Everyone sat down on a set of moss-covered boulders.

'The Filament got out,' Frasier said, dejectedly. 'But that's impossible.'

Somehow, Yana understood. She showed them a diagram that connected her artwork, Charlie's music, and the music of the escaped Diver. The escaped Diver, Philip, was, in reality, the composer Luka Lampo. Charlie noticed that Yana was censoring a swathe of shapes on the periphery of her diagram, but he let it slide for the moment.

'A one in a million coincidence,' Frasier thought, 'but not impossible.'

Their minds converged on the issue of the Pelican's dimension, an enigmatic realm teeming with confused souls.

'It's like the opposite of this place,' Frasier said, in horror.

'I'll be the Filament,' Charlie said, suddenly. 'It's the least I can do.'

'Damn right,' Frasier said.

'No,' Yana said. 'We've never used a filament that's not all the way here.'

'The situation is unprecedented,' Frasier said. 'It calls for unprecedented action. Besides, you've been ready to pass on for a long time, this is your chance.'

'Mom,' Charlie said. 'I can do this, you have to trust me.'

Frasier gave her a look of frustration, and she knew she had to acquiesce. In the time since Charlie had arrived, the spheres had sunk alarmingly close to the big ocean. She made a shape like a green light, and Frasier rose from the boulder and walked off to arrange the ceremony. Yana and Charlie sat in peaceful silence looking out over the velvety ocean and the pink horizon. A huge cloud bulged across the top of the sky like a rolling pin.

'Melodrama doesn't play down here, but I really can't overstate how happy I am to see you, Chuck,' Yana said. She reached out and rubbed the top of his head.

'What were you hiding from us back there? I didn't want to ask in front of Frasier.'

'You'll find out sooner than you think kiddo, just wait. In the meantime, why don't you catch me up. Tell me about your life.'

The jellyfish ocean pulsed with light, and Charlie tried to begin. He used elegant thought shapes to tell the story of his teenage years, the time he spent in a haze of fatigue at Errol's house, the inception of Cave Music (the musical practice that saved his life), of his years in the cocoon, his friendship with Greg. He went into further detail regarding the events of the previous year: a year in which he thought he'd been on the verge of discovering a secret, hidden self. But the secret self was a mirage, an empty symbol that meant nothing. He'd engaged in shameful behaviour and caused pain to those around him.

'But you brought joy and comfort to strangers,' Yana said. 'You can't ever know exactly what that was worth, but don't underestimate the healing power of good art. In my personal life I was so wary and turned around most of the time, that's why I poured all my energy into painting – it was a reliable way to relay something true to the external world.'

Charlie hesitated, then conjured a thought-shape that expressed how ashamed he was of his behaviour. The shape referred to the metaphor of the cocoon, of what he regarded as his metamorphosis gone awry.

Yana took this shape and spun it, creating a gestalt image. She showed Charlie that a caterpillar doesn't magically transform into a butterfly. In the cocoon the pupa undergoes a hideous process of biological decay before reconstituting itself into a colourful butterfly. The ugliness of the pupa is directly proportional to the beauty of the butterfly. The gestalt was a revelation. In the warmth of the Cathedral, Charlie had come to see life not as the rush of sensations that constituted consciousness on a moment-to-moment basis, but as part of a never-ending book that could be read forwards or backwards with equal ease. Existence tended towards entropy, but it wasn't a straight line; the story of his life wasn't linear and it wasn't over. Yana nudged him out of his reveries.

'You're not washed up yet, Chuck,' she said.

Frasier came back out through the brush.

'It's all set,' he said. 'They're waiting for you.'

They retraced their previous path around the pond and past the sequoias. The forest was eerily empty and quiet. The three of them came out into the Cathedral and began climbing a ladder that led towards the prayer sphere. Charlie could see the plumes of smoke escaping through the chimney above. The pillars of light flickered and the structure shuddered and sank. The lowest sphere was partially submerged in water; the big ocean churned angrily.

They entered the prayer sphere. All of the niches save for three were occupied by cross-legged Divers, emitting threads that joined in the colourful fire. Yana climbed into one near the bottom and went into a trance. Frasier ascended the spiraling ramp with him and found his spot about halfway up. Before he went into his trance he indicated the topmost niche to Charlie, just below the chimney.

'Whatever happens,' he said, 'remain calm and observe. Don't get caught up in it, and don't resist or you'll be toast.'

Charlie signalled for clarification, but Frasier's mind had gone blank. Charlie walked the rest of the way up, breathing the salty-piney air through his snout and exhaling slowly. He felt very lonely even though there were hundreds of Divers all around him. It occurred to him that each and every one of them had done this before, and he calmed down a bit. He climbed up into the topmost nook and crossed his legs. He closed his eyes and opened himself up. A thousand broken lives wedged in and coursed through him. He felt as though there was only the slimmest chance that he would not burst completely apart.

CHAPTER 38

As THE MEMORIES coursed through him and gained momentum, the pain quickly became too much to bear. He squirmed and made to get up, but this set off a chain of excruciating electric shocks through his system. Frasier had been right – he wasn't ready. He was tense, clinging to himself desperately in anticipation of annihilation when suddenly he remembered what Artemis had taught him: no mind. If he was going to make it through this trial, he had to say goodbye to Charlie Potichny and smudge himself from reality.

He released the tension and immediately saw that reacting to the memories was a trap. If he'd personally adopted the sorrow and anguish burning off of the Divers, he would have failed spectacularly; if he'd tried to run, he would have imploded. The trick was to observe the memories without reacting to them. Through this method he found he was able to surf the surge of emotions without being engulfed by the wave.

When he channeled the pain through no mind it flipped positive, tenderizing the sorrow and refining it into something obscenely sacred. This ineffable substance was fed into the maypole of swirling energy that was wafting smoke up through the Cathedral. Whatever wasn't burned off was being concentrated into a dense souvenir, a sort of nutritional pellet. 'Sea-dragon-chow!' Charlie finally saw. He was converting the purified experience into food for the Deep Sea Feline.

After a time, he arrived at Yana's living memories – the frigid Saskatchewan winters, a beloved bog where she escaped to draw, the initial breakdown, art school in Toronto, travelling to Europe, a magical night at the symphony in Saltzburg, a handsome conductor on a terrace at sunset, falling in love with – with him!? Charlie almost wiped out before he caught his balance. An affair gone wrong, hard, stubborn feelings, a return to Canada, a baby boy. There were hundreds more to process, and he was obliged to move on.

Elated by the rush of common feeling, he mentally rolled up his sleeves, let his mind go slack, and called upon his full attention. The memories were coming hard and fast; he felt like he was in the late levels of Galaga; to think was certain death, he had to trust his intuition. He was lit up from head to toe, engulfed in a holy fire. The threads of suffering led to a hard, heavy object sunk into his chest: it was him, it was the symbolic monolith he carried inside, the symbol of the self. He concentrated the energy he'd collected into a single beam and blasted it apart.

With the first ecstatic breath of ego free oxygen, consciousness expanded, dancing free of the self – the ego's a yoke; the ego's a joke – filling the Cathedral and the world beyond with a blanket of loosely vibrating atoms, mingling freely with all of creation. Becoming the Filament was alright; becoming the Filament was everything.

The way that Charlie came back to himself was not without its charm. The details of his identity returned slowly, by process of elimination – he did not know he was himself until everyone else had left. The residue that was left behind, the lives of a hundred strangers, sloshed dizzyingly in his mind. He slumped back in his niche and let out a loud, emerald thought-shape, like a groan. He'd never been so tired in his life. He closed his eyes and tried to rest, tried not to get lost in the tangled narratives he'd just absorbed. But soon an urgent thought-shape assailed him like a giant hand snapping its fingers.

'Charlie, get up. It's important.' Yana had come up to the top of the prayer room and was shaking him out of his stupor.

'Hi Charlie. Good work. Are you okay?' Charlie said, sarcastically.

Sarcasm didn't play well in the Cathedral and it fell flat.

Yana looked puzzled. 'Are you talking to yourself?'

'Never mind. Did it work? Was I a good Filament?'

'Of course. You wouldn't be here if you weren't.'

'What do you mean?'

Yana showed him what it would look like if a filament couldn't handle the ceremony. The shape was like a firework exploding.

'Fuck me up! Good thing I'm made of strong stuff.'

'Yeah, good thing you have good genes. Good thing Artemis coached you.'

'Getting cheeky now, are we?'

Yana shrugged, playfully. 'I can relax a bit now. We've got a shot at sending you back.'

Charlie signaled for clarification. Yana gestured at the place where the colourful fire had been. There, in its place, was the white-hot glowing pellet.

'Sea-dragon-chow.' Charlie said.

Yana nodded. 'You're going to deliver it.'

Charlie understood what she meant and shook his head 'Nope. Nonono. That's yours to deliver. You've been stuck here; it's time for you to pass on, to rest.'

'Charlie, listen to me: the longer you stay here the harder it's going to be to leave. You have to go see the Feline, she's the only one who can help you. I can wait a little bit longer, but you don't have much time. I trusted you to be the Filament, now you have to trust me: take that pellet, dive into the big ocean, and ask her to send you back.'

Charlie considered this for a moment.

'I guess now isn't the time to turn back,' he conceded. 'But first you've got some explaining to do.'

'I'm an open book,' she signaled.

'Never date a musician?'

Yana looked up through the chimney, rubbing the side of her furry face.

'I'm sorry I never told you,' she said. 'Luka and I both acted like assholes. Artists have big egos, and we were both pretty famous at the time – we were atrocious to each other at the end.'

'He never knew, did he?'

'We never spoke after the split; we were both so stubborn. I'm so sorry.'

'You loved him though, right until the end. I felt it.'

'Yes.'

'And he followed you here; he found his way into your paintings, into my record, and my life. He loved you back.'

'I wish things could have been different. We might have been a family.'

'We are a family,' Charlie signalled through a wash of tears. 'It's okay now.'

Okay was a big friendly octopus hugging them. Within the octopus hug they hugged each other and fell apart again. A jagged tear that had lain open for years was being patched. Charlie felt alive; he felt sharp and strong and full of love.

'It's time for you to go.' Yana released him from the embrace. She reached out a furry arm and the white pellet floated up, sticking to her paw.

'Go up top,' she said. 'Watch carefully, you'll know when it's time.'

She made her way down the spiraling platform. Charlie hoisted himself up through the hole in the top of the chamber, standing at the apex of the network of spheres. The Divers had dispersed themselves evenly across the bridges and ladders; some of them were gathered on the roofs of the lower spheres. He saw Yana come out the bottom of the prayer room and lob the pellet to a stout, brown-eyed Diver thirty yards away. The stout Diver lobbed it slightly harder and gradually the ball picked up steam, whizzing here and there and emitting a high-pitched whistle. The ocean below glowed a bleached out Caribbean blue, frothing and moaning.

Charlie was stricken with vertigo and almost lost his footing. The pellet zipped faster and faster, describing patterns that hung in his retinas like sparklers in the dark. An animal urge grew in him, and the longer he watched the pellet's movements, the stronger it grew. He felt like Goblin, waiting patiently outside a mouse-hole.

Suddenly, his powerful legs kicked off. He dove gracefully through the air, his arms stretched out and snapped up the chow as he fell through the spheres, maneuvering to avoid the ladders and bridges. A great cheer of shapes swirled all around him; he felt happy and determined. He was going to meet this Feline – the thread that would lead him back to life.

He hit the water and started kicking immediately, using his webbed feet to propel himself downward through the ocean. The pillars of light emanating from some unseen source below allowed him to see clearly, even as he left the Cathedral far behind. There was a long stretch of swimming straight down with nothing to see, and his thoughts naturally turned to Luka Lampo, his biological father. For some reason, the discovery had not come as a shock to him. Rather than flipping reality on its head, the information had simply illuminated a new region of reality that had always been there. Lampo was still Lampo; it just turned out that Charlie shared his DNA, carried a piece of this being's spirit within himself in the same way he carried a piece of Yana. It was at once a novel connection and something he felt he'd always known.

Charlie called up what information he knew about Lampo as a musician, as a figure revered by Greg and Errol, and began to synthesize this with what he remembered of Lampo as a homeless man begging outside of his apartment, as the Diver who'd appeared in his mother's paintings and performed music with him, and as the absence he'd felt his whole life. This last version was the most powerful and least distinct. His thoughts carried on in the same vein for quite some time.

At some point it felt like someone hit the reset button: Charlie did not know how long he'd been swimming for and couldn't remember what he'd been thinking about. It was like déja vu.

He kicked on down, hugging the chow with pride. In the distance there was a golden glow. Turning around, he was amazed to find that he could see all the way up to the violet spheres of the Cathedral. He could even see the surface of the lake above the waterfall, the beavers in their lodge and the great owls circling patiently under a clear, starlit sky. He could see it all with incredible clarity, as if his vision had been upgraded.

"Pretty trippy, hey?"

Charlie started and fumbled the pellet.

"Do not drop that. I am literally starving, and you do not want to be around when I'm hangry."

The massive, golden-yellow head of the Deep Sea Feline had appeared alongside him. She spoke in a deep, husky voice. Charlie kicked backwards a bit and inspected her. The beast's face was symmetrical and feminine, with high cheekbones, pointed ears, cat-like eyes containing vibrant teal pupils, and thin, elegant, slate-coloured whiskers that trailed off into the darkness. She was overwhelmingly beautiful to look at. Her blue-green body, like that of an eel, rippled hypnotically behind her. Charlie's sense of perspective shifted and it seemed as though they were looking horizontally through the ocean and the Cathedral and the lake. The vision slowly darkened, as if controlled by a dimmer switch, and Charlie was left alone with the Feline in her lair.

"Sorry, but it's a distraction, y'know? Hope you took a mental picture, for posterity. Hey, you can just toss that this way," her eyes were fixed on the pellet. "If I bite it while you're holding it, I'll probably take a chunk out of you."

Charlie had been clinging to the pellet extra tight, but now he reached his arm back and propelled it through the water. The elegant sea dragon torpedoed after her dinner and swallowed it whole. Charlie watched in amazement as it travelled the length of her unfathomable body, gradually causing her to glow with an increased brightness. In the distance, Charlie felt a low rumble – the sound of the pillars growing stronger, of the spheres ascending through the Cathedral.

From top to tail she was glowing brighter, looking vibrant and strong. It was as though the water had disappeared and they were floating freely on a dark canvas. She was right up in Charlie's face, burning beautifully against the blackness. He reached out in front of him and realized he had human hands; for the moment, she had returned him to his habitual form.

"You speak English?" he said, surprised.

"I speak whatever language you speak. I'm just projecting concepts into your mind."

"Huh. Well in that case you speak English and bad French."

"Language is overrated. At least you actually brought the goods. Last idiot that visited was empty handed. I've been goddam powerless down here."

"The last idiot," Charlie thought out loud. "Luka Lampo."

"Friend of yours?"

"I just found out he's my dad."

"Hmphh, real piece of work that one. Ah well, we don't choose our parents. And by we, I mean you. I'm timeless. . . and immortal. Anyway, I'm sure you're pretty eager to pass on to the long sleep, I won't waste anymore of your – "

"Wowowow wait, wait. Back up a step. Do not send me to the long sleep. I snuck in here, through a hole in the lake. I'm not even dead." Charlie paused. "I hope."

"Ahhh, you're the sneak! The one I froze the lake for. Sorry, usually I'm all-seeing, but things have been tough lately, mainly 'cause of your padré. I don't have a lot to go on."

"Can I ask where exactly he went?" Charlie said. "Thing is, he kind of found his way back to the surface. And I kind of. . . sent him to the Chaos Dimension."

The Feline opened her considerable mouth, showcasing her sharp rows of teeth and roared loudly. The noise reverberated all the way up through the Cathedral. In her cabin, Artemis experienced a small earthquake, smudged a paint stroke, and cursed.

"You delivered one of my Divers to that fucking Pelican trickster? You really fucked up kid. I oughtta tear you apart."

"Please don't." Charlie was genuinely terrified. "I didn't know the birds were evil; I was just trying to do what I thought was right. Please, let me explain."

"Don't waste my time. If you show me it'll be much faster."

"Show you?"

The Feline flashed a Cheshire grin. "Open up little man."

Her slinky body described a hypnotic pattern, and Charlie felt like he was spinning. His mind vomited up his entire life, all of his subjective feelings, disappointments, and revelations from the time he was born right up to the present moment. He felt as though there was only the slimmest chance he wouldn't burst apart once more. When he came back to himself he was curled up, sobbing in the fetal position.

"Bit of warning would've been nice," he said, putting himself back together.

"Meh," the Feline said. "You're fine; you've been the Filament."

For a moment she sorted through what she'd found in his mind, honing in on the relevant information.

"Ho boy. I didn't think a mere mortal could muck things up so badly. That was a pretty dirty trick they played sending you that phony diplomat though, that Shakesperian rake. I didn't know the Pelican was capable of such sophisticated coaching – that flimsy StormBox premise was straight out of a sci-fi paperback."

Charlie looked sheepish.

"Don't beat yourself up. His power has grown considerably in the last little bit."

"Show me," Charlie said. "Here, I'm opening my mind." He closed his eyes and floated in the darkness. Nothing happened. When he opened his eyes, the Feline was giving him a funny look.

"A human can't look into the mind of an immortal, dummy," she said. "It would drive you mad."

"Could've just said that right away," he mumbled.

"Yeah but it was funny watching you hang there like you were waiting for a tender smooch."

Charlie glared. "Can you take this seriously? I risked my life to come down here."

"Ooh, a solitary human life, sssooo precious."

"Sarcasm? Seriously?"

"Hey, listen, I've been down here in the dark trying to figure out what the fuck is going on like a blind woman reading braille with mittens on. Sorry if I feel like cracking a few jokes."

"Can you just try to appreciate that my life is important to me and that I would love to know, even in the vaguest sense, what is going on here."

"I don't have to tell you," she said. "Close your eyes and follow the thread."

He closed his eyes and everything shifted and re-patterned, causing his stomach to clench. Behind his closed eyelids he saw a tiny version of himself floating in the darkness, and then he merged with that self, eyes wide open. The Feline was nowhere near him.

In the Feline's lair there was no fixed vantage point – everything was mutable. The anthropomorphic being he'd spoken to was a stand-in, conjured by his own imagination to set him at ease and facilitate the feeding; the authentic Feline was a primordial beast, incapable of speech. She was giving him what he needed by pulling images and ideas out of his unconscious to form a coherent pattern.

She uncoiled her endless torso and swam brightly in the distance. Her movement suggested an elegant question mark – the awe-inspiring beauty of the eternal, unknowable mysteries. She was a generous lantern, inspiring the selfless curiosity inherent in all humans by lighting up every scrap of existence with meaning. No one piece of the universe – not even the tiniest most negligible particle – was insignificant. It all cobwebbed together in a perfect balance, an exquisite dance.

A pleasant shock passed through his nervous system, and he felt the connection between himself and everything he held in his considerable field of vision. What this experience was saying to him was primordial and self-evident; it was the feeling that converted the poison into the antidote. The Feline coiled around Charlie and her head passed close by. Her animal eyes trained on him, and he thought he saw the trace of a smile.

As the majestic sea dragon wound away from him and disappeared in the distance, music drifted up from below. His own music. The Algonquian sessions, to be precise. He would have thought it was strange if anything could have been strange at that moment, but it somehow fit perfectly like a puzzle piece. He sensed the presence of Greg and Tatiana down below as well and felt an urgent need to speak with them: a plan had emerged, fully formed in his head. He re-oriented himself (back in his furry Diver form now), flipped around, and swam towards the music.

CHAPTER 39

BACKSTAGE AT THE Four Seasons Centre for the Performing Arts, there were two men in a dressing room sporting matching blue beards.

During his time in silent meditation at the centre, Eichelberger had stopped shaving and by now – the eve of the premiere – his beard had just barely grown to a respectable length. Meanwhile, Greg's beard had finally filled in properly so that they were practically beard twins. They'd gone together to a salon earlier that day for matching haircuts, and to have their beards bleached and then made blue with permanent dye. This had not been part of the costume design and there had been an uproar when they had arrived, but what could Vogel do, force them to shave? They were wearing matching fisherman chic costumes with shiny boots and embroidered jackets. Greg's paunch had retreated since he'd stopped drinking, and the men were practically indistinguishable at a glance. It was Unheimlich.

Greg was pacing nervously in the shabby room and mumbling to himself. Eichelberger was drinking tea and doing breathing exercises with his eyes closed; he hadn't spoken since his return and hadn't opened his mouth except to rehearse. He carried around a notepad and a pen for basic communications, but even in these notes he limited himself to bare practicalities. He'd been sleeping on the floor at Greg's motel room and living mostly off of microwaved soup, crackers, and fruit. The two men had been inseparable and seemed to have developed a way of communicating without using language. They sometimes sang Lampo's score together, doubling each other so that their voices became one, and though the sound resounded throughout the bad motel, no one had ever complained.

In the dressing room, Eichelberger opened his eyes and looked at Greg with curiosity.

"Motherfucking ass panda ass butthole Noodles. One job, you had one job, you Mussolini proto-fascist proto-Marxist, Satan worshipping – fuckfuckfuck."

Greg was mumbling angrily to himself, pleading with no one in particular to deliver Noodles to the backstage entrance with the gear he'd been in charge of securing. Eichelberger caught Greg's eye and gave him a look of annoyance, as if to say "it's not going to help cursing and getting all worked up, either he'll come or he won't. Just sit down and relax."

"No thanks, I'm good pacing," Greg said. "I need to balance out your Zen vibes with raw stress, or we'll just dissolve into the ether."

Greg opened the door to the dressing room and stepped outside, looking around in hope of spotting Noodles. It was total anarchy: the chorus was running around in colourful costumes, a team of dancers was stumbling around beneath a gigantic swan replica, and another set of dancers supporting a giant sea dragon toppled over, knocking a set of cymbals to the ground. They rang out with a clatter and Von Strohn came running over, attempting to reign in the chaos. From down the hallway in the other direction, Greg clocked Sophie walking briskly towards him and tried to duck back inside. In addition to singing the parts of the sea dragon and the swan, Sophie was playing Bluebeard's mother. Her costume was a simple, elegant, cream dress with gold trim. She'd been through makeup and looked twice her age.

"No! Nope! Don't you dare run away from me!" she yelled at him. Greg tensed, his shoulders went up. It looked like he was trying to pull his head inside of his body. He turned and faced Sophie. She jammed a finger into his chest and pushed him back against the door.

"You've been ducking me since we had that bizarre meeting at Errol's house. I held up my part; we're going out on the airwaves tonight, but I have no idea what to expect." She was yelling, attracting attention from the chorus and the dancers.

"Sophie, calm down."

"You don't tell me to calm down you fat, balding baby." She looked down and realized how much weight he'd lost. "Well, you're still a balding man-baby. I have to go out there tonight and sing one of the most difficult parts anyone's ever seen with a portal to some sort of chaos dimension onstage that could release pandemonium at the drop of a pin, and no one has given me any indication of when or how that might happen."

The portal had indeed followed them from the Oil Concern to the Four Seasons Centre and reliably appeared at every dress rehearsal. The crew had artfully worked it into the set as though it were a mirror image of the swan's sacred whirlpool. The area where it appeared had been cordoned off with tape that blended with the colour scheme.

"Sophie, it's a need to know basis kind of thing – "

"Sure, sure keep the woman in the dark. Classic tactics of the patriarchy!"

"You're being histrionic."

"Oh, I'll show you histrionic you little bitch."

She started slapping him, and he held his arms out for protection, sinking down to the floor and curling up in a little ball. Von Strohn had just finished helping the dancers and cleaning up the cymbals. Sophie's yelling drew his attention, and he ran over to them while making tsk noises. He was in his long conductor's coat, swinging his baton wildly, as if it gave him some wizardly authority over the situation. His wispy hair looked as though it had been blown back by a cyclone; he had the air of a man who'd been putting out fires all day.

"Sophie," he hissed. "What are you doing? The curtains go up in fifteen minutes, you should be getting ready." He looked down and recognized Greg's shape, crumpled sadly on the floor. "Greg, what in the fuck are you doing back here? Why are you in costume. . . why is your beard blue? You're just a sub, your involvement is merely symbolic. You should be drinking Champagne and glad-handing donors, not playing dress up."

"It's Brut," Greg said, flatly.

"Pardon me?"

"The bar serves Brut, they make it in Niagara; you can't call it Champagne."

"I don't have time for this, the orchestra is already tuning up!" Von Strohn yelled as Greg slowly rose to standing. "Get this costume off. Better yet, just get out! Stop distracting my leads."

The music director was apoplectic, physically pushing Greg towards the exit and signaling for security. At that moment, the door to the dressing room creaked open and Eichelberger emerged. Everybody froze, rapt in anticipation. The German Adonis' blue eyes were burning with icy resentment.

"On the eve of this historic occasion, a night on which we've been given the sacred opportunity to deliver a spectacle of transcendental bliss into the fraught lives of the public, you bicker like children. Shame on you all. You should be preparing, making yourselves into holy vessels for the music of genius that visits us from a higher plane. I didn't want to sully my voice by speaking words in this circus of ego, but you've obliged me to. Now do me a favour and go prepare for the performance of a lifetime. And leave Gregory alone or I'll walk out, so help me Brahman."

Von Strohn rolled his eyes and stormed off. Sophie caught Eichelberger's eye and the two blushed deeply, overwhelmed and embarrassed by a transparent mutual attraction.

"Uh, I'm gonna duck back inside and try texting Noodles again," Greg said, disappearing into the dressing room.

"Dietrich, I –" Sophie began.

"We should wait until after the performance. It could be distracting – "

"I love you. I want you to remember that when you're singing tonight. I know you think that celibacy and discipline give you power, but love gives you power too. You can stop resisting, I'm here for you."

Something inside of Eichelberger split wide open, and he fought back tears.

"You have so much experience," he said. "You've been with so many men. How could I possibly be enough for you?"

Sophie was fighting back tears as well. "Of course you're enough. You're all I want, none of those other men mean anything compared to you, don't you get that?"

"We shouldn't be doing this right now, so close to the show."

"Don't do that honey, don't wall parts of yourself off like that. Give your whole self to the crowd tonight, give your whole self to me. I'll reciprocate. I'm not going anywhere, and I don't want anyone else. Just relax and enjoy yourself. Who knows what'll happen out there tonight. Could be the end of the world."

Eichelberger grabbed Sophie and kissed her wrinkled face passionately. Dancers, crew members, and singers swirled around them frantically preparing for curtain. When the kiss was over, Noodles' face appeared awkwardly close to them. He had bags under his eyes and looked awful. He smelled of fried onions and cologne and was holding a bright yellow No Frills bag filled with electronics.

"Can you give us a little room, creepo. We're having a moment," Sophie said.

"Sorry. It's just nice. I haven't kissed anyone I didn't hate in years. . . or who didn't hate me."

The door to the dressing room swung open.

"Noodles!" Greg yelled. "Get your ass in here."

"Five minutes to curtain!" someone yelled.

The four of them huddled together in the dressing room.

"Jesus, Noodles, you look like a bunch of snakes having an orgy. You off the wagon or what?" Greg asked.

Noodles' dress shirt was done up all wrong and had mustard stains on it; he had a heavy glaze of stubble and his eyes were having trouble focusing. He held out the plastic bag. "Don't worry about me, I'll be fine. Rehab's like a second home. They have really good cookies, and the lighting is well curated."

"You entrusted this man with gathering materials and I was out of the loop?" Sophie asked in shock.

"Noodles is alright. It's just tough with the Chaos Signal, for those of us with. . . aggressive appetites," Greg said, squeezing Noodles' shoulder.

"It was the full moon that got me," Noodles said. "Made me hungry, horny, and thirsty for booze. I got the goods though, look." He jerked his arm out, presenting the bag to Greg.

They emptied the contents of the bag out onto a table. There was a shoddy boombox that looked like it was from the '80s, a dozen giant, cylindrical batteries, and a large roll of tape.

"What the fuck is this!?" Greg yelled.

"I went to Best Buy, man, the one right downtown. I went in there on the weekend. Do you know what that's like? It was horrible! They said they don't sell radios anymore, they said try a junk shop. I found this stuff in a box in my basement. I'm pretty sure it all works. I lost the piece for the back though, so you have to tape the batteries. It's good tape though, Gorilla brand. I bought it special."

"You're pretty sure it works!? I'm risking my life, motherfucker. You're pretty sure!?"

Greg's yelling could be heard throughout the backstage. There was a gentle knock on the door.

"Um, curtain is in two minutes. Mr. Eichelberger, could you please take your place?"

Sophie and Eichelberger were looking at the mess of batteries and plastic on the table dubiously.

"I could have gotten you a very reliable German radio if you'd only asked, Greg," Eichelberger said.

"Thank you, Dietrich, that's very helpful," Greg replied, barely able to contain himself. "Run along, you two. Sing your beautiful hearts out, everything relies on it. Everything. Don't worry about me and this fucking John Cusack Say Anything radio, it's out of your control."

Eichelberger and Sophie went out holding hands. Greg turned a murderous gaze on Noodles.

"Is there any liquor back here?" Noodles asked. "I thought backstage would be more glamorous."

"Shut the fuck up," Greg said and started putting the giant batteries in the back of the stereo. It needed twelve.

"I used to take chicks to the beach with this stereo and a couple bottles of wine. The beach at the water filtration plant that looks like an Orson Welles movie."

D'Angelo's Brown Sugar was lodged in the tape deck. "Smooth, Noodles, real smooth."

Greg popped the last battery into place and hit power. Miraculously, the stereo came to life. He heard static on the radio, flipped it off again, and methodically laid several layers of tape tightly over the batteries. He turned it back on and fiddled with the dial, trying to find Radio 2. Noodles was sipping tequila out of a flask with a Cave Music sticker on it.

"Chrissake's Noodles, why'd you ask for booze if you had some on you."

Noodles shrugged. "This is my walkin' around booze. It's precious. It's like twenty bucks for a glass of Brut out there."

Greg turned the dial carefully. The tiny, red line floated right on top of 94.1. Outside, towards the stage, Eichelberger's voice burst forth, and the entire building trembled. In his entire career, Greg had never heard a human deliver so much power with their voice. He slowly brought up the volume on the stereo and the same voice filled the room, distorted by static as if it were travelling from the past. There was a lag time of about ten seconds. Greg turned the volume up and down, counting carefully so that he could hold in his memory the exact difference between the live singing and the radio transmission. Once he was satisfied he turned the radio down so it was almost inaudible. He enlisted Noodles to help tape the stereo around his waist, so that it looked like he had a shiny, bulging cummerbund on. Then he sat down with his eyes closed and sang along quietly, skillfully navigating the tongue twisting Finnish dialect.

"I'm going to hang out side-stage and watch the show," Noodles said.

"This isn't a fucking Pearl Jam concert Noodles, sit your ass down," Greg blocked the door. "You know what, give me that flask."

"I thought you were a wagonman."

Greg seized the flask and raised it to his lips. At the last second, he paused, mumbled something to himself, and handed it back to Noodles.

"Are you really going in there?" Noodles asked. "You really going to throw yourself into the Chaos World?"

"Noodles," Greg said. "You ever hit a point in your life where you kind of figure anything would be better than this."

"Oh yes," Noodles replied. "That's what the drugs are for."

"Right. Well that's what this feels like, except it's an opportunity to reach out, rather than retreat inward. I'm finished feeling sorry for myself." He paused. "Besides, Charlie's in there."

"La-di-da," Noodles said, sipping the flask. He pulled out a baggie and did a bump of coke off his hand. "Guess we can't all be Luke Skywalker."

"Are you kidding me? If this was Star Wars, I'd be Han Solo. For sure."

"Can I be Boba Fett?"

"Boba Fett's a villain, Noodles, you're not a villain. How about you be Chewie?"

"Alright," Noodles said, tearing up. "I'll be Chewie."

CHAPTER 40

TEN MINUTES BEFORE the show started, a rowdy scene was brewing on the second floor of the Four Seasons Centre. Tatiana Tataru had purchased two rounds of Brut for everyone in the ragtag group constituting the emergency chorus. Campbell was already quite inebriated and had snuck half a dozen airplane bottles of Canadian Club into the building in his underpants. The bill for the sparkling wine had been well over a hundred dollars, but Tatiana, who was charmingly careless with money, forked it over without batting an eye.

Errol had bought the secret chorus a block of tickets at the back of the Orchestra Ring, despite some serious misgivings. The whole evening was poised to be such a clusterfuck as it stood, but it had also taken on a "the more the merrier" kind of energy: a momentum without logic that could not be reckoned with. At very least, the gaggle of misfits had taken turns showering at Wychwood and then raided Errol's closet with his blessing. They were wearing expensive three-piece suits that were ill-fitting to various degrees; many of them wore tasseled loafers with no socks.

The fact that they were dressed up, plus the giddiness of the buzz from the sparkling, inspired them to roughhouse and sing. Campbell – who was wearing a silver Hugo Boss suit two sizes too large – had been put into a headlock by a muscular Newfie in a tweed Zegna two sizes too small. He was holding his wine out to the side trying not to spill. The Newfie was singing "Living on a Prayer." A small bottle of whisky slipped out of Campbell's pant leg and clattered off the balcony. A teenage boy on the main floor snapped it up and drank it down before his parents could see. Ushers approached the tussling men, trying to break up the fight. Tatiana had moved away from the scene and was standing on a floating walkway that hung in the middle of the cube. Colourful figures moved to and fro; light bounced playfully off of the glass every which way. Having escaped from the headlock, Campbell approached Tatiana. He looked her up and down, rubbing his chin.

"You look strong for a woman," he said. "Your legs are very muscular, that's especially important."

"Is this your way of flirting?" Tatiana asked, bemused.

"No, no, my dick doesn't work any more, you see. It's for the plan, you know, to save the city."

Ushers were directing patrons towards their seats by this point, but the loud banter continued amongst the city's elite:

"The Mayor had his DNA frozen. He thinks they'll be able to extract his consciousness when he dies and upload it into a clone."

"I've got on strong authority that the ghost of Luka Lampo has been haunting this production. I took an Ativan just in case – ghosts trigger my anxiety."

"The Russians are controlling the birds via satellite. The portals lead to a subbasement in the Kremlin where they reprogram Canadians to influence global politics."

"But wouldn't the clone have its own consciousness?"

"They say this is going to be the last opera performed here. They're going to turn it into a self-serve Amazon superstore."

"The libraries were purchased by a huge conglomerate. They've been turned into Virtual Reality arcades where you can sit in an authentic living room from the nineties and watch Friends reruns with the cast of Friends."

"I'm no scientist, but I think the consciousness with the more developed Ego would devour the younger Ego like a bucket of fried chicken. You can't have dueling egos knocking around the skull, it would result in schizophrenia."

"Quickly," Tatiana said. "What do you have in mind."

"If everything goes smoothly, we won't be needed," Campbell gestured to his peers. "But if Greg's not back with those paintings by the dénouement, we're going in, and we'll need someone to act as an anchor, tethering us to this side of reality."

Tatiana's eyes went wide: "I'm terrified of that place."

"If you never face your worst fears, what sort of excuses will you make at the end, when you realize you were never truly alive?"

The crowd had thinned out now and the ringing grew louder.

"Two minutes to curtain. Latecomers will not be admitted and there is no intermission. Latecomers will NOT be admitted."

They broke up the huddle to rush to their seats. Tatiana straightened her back and flexed her muscles as she descended the stairs. She felt strong.

As Campbell and the rest of the secret chorus settled into their seats, Tatiana found her own, front and centre, on the aisle of the Orchestra Ring. Errol had offered her the ticket after the meeting at Wychwood, adjacent to his own seat on the aisle, behind the conductor. The sound wasn't as good this close up, but Errol had a feeling he might need to intervene and keep Von Strohn steady when shit hit the fan.

Tatiana took her seat at eight sharp. Errol glared at her.

"Even when the fate of the city hangs in the balance, you young people can't even leave yourselves a five-minute margin. If you'd been one minute later, they wouldn't have seated you."

"It's not my fault," Tatiana protested. "That crazy man who lives in your house was giving me the plan. I might have to go onstage and act as some sort of anchor?"

Errol was familiar with the protocol. He'd paid off members of the crew to facilitate it if push came to shove, but he did not relish the thought. In his mind the stage was a sacred space during a performance and desecrating it would break his heart in two. He had to remind himself that the lives of his two boys, in addition to the fate of the city of Toronto, hung in the balance and that interfering with the performance of an opera would, in this one singular case, be justified if it came to that.

"There's a rope hidden at the back of the stage. It's been secured to the wall and attached to a harness we used in a production of The Flying Dutchman where the cast literally flew. It's safe, trust me."

The orchestra's tuning ceased, and the lights began to dim.

"Couldn't we have gone over this earlier?" Tatiana asked. "It sounds like a pretty slapdash plan."

"It sort of came together last minute. I think there's a freshness to it though; a je ne sais quoi that gives it a bit of oomph."

"Easy for you to say, old man, you get to sit here and watch."

"I practically paid for this whole endeavor," Errol said, defensively.

"Yeah, sure, with money you made in a system that's rigged in your favour."

"I may be in the one percent, but I pay my share of taxes and donate generously to several charitable organizations."

Lampo's overture announced itself from the pit.

The overture began gently, the violins and cellos creating dynamic swells that were somehow sinister and comforting all at once. Slowly, the rest of the orchestra started to play, revealing the full dimension of the sumptuous overture. Von Strohn's hair was still standing straight up, but he was composed and focused now; it was as though a hundred threads were connecting his baton to each instrument as he conducted.

If Charlie's Manic Toads performances had had the ability to calm audience members and give them a temporary sense of well-being, it was dwarfed by the effect of Lampo's music. Toronto was a city that had been in crisis, in deep spiritual pain for over a year now, but the entire audience in that auditorium, nestled within a glowing cube, felt from the first moments of that overture that they were children again; they were being held by their mothers or fathers; they were completely safe and would always be safe. It was nothing short of a miracle.

When the curtain rose, Eichelberger was standing at the front of the stage against a sparse set, his back to the audience, head in his hands. He stood unmoving as the orchestra brought the music to a rest. For a minute there was as complete a silence as has ever existed on Earth. Then, suddenly, Eichelberger threw his arms out, spun to face the audience and thundered into the crowd. His voice was soon accompanied by the orchestra, playing full tilt at full volume and still, somehow, the vibrations emanating from this one man dominated the space in a way that even the most seasoned opera vet had never come close to experiencing. Errol's eyes lit up and he sat forward; he forgot who or where he was. He was smiling and weeping although he did not know it.

The production hypnotized the audience so completely, it was as though they'd been transported to an opera house in outer space with the set and singers performing against the backdrop of the stars. It was a great equalizer: no one in the audience was capable of calling up the mundane details or troubles of their day-to-day lives or anything that existed outside of that room. Lampo's music was all consuming.

While they were not necessarily impervious to the therapeutic effects of the opera, the cast and crew could not give themselves over to it fully, for they had jobs to do and had to keep their heads about them as a matter of necessity. The set remained sparse only for the first twenty-odd minutes of the opera as Bluebeard declared his intention to set sail to seduce the princess against his mother's wishes. Sophie and Eichelberger's voices coiled around each other like two strands of a double helix and floated out over the audience, inducing mass tenderness with their emotive singing. The opening scene gave way to a bawdy sea shanty in which the chorus of fishermen wished Bluebeard good luck.

Several scenes later, Bluebeard was considering whether or not to dive into the lake and kill the magical sea dragon. As Eichelberger began singing a soft soliloquy, something very strange happened: a second Bluebeard appeared on the opposite end of the stage, singing the same soliloquy, giving it added depth and texture. The voices were so well synchronized, however, that it was almost difficult to believe that they were separate.

There was a rustling and a murmur in the audience as the scene went on. Even the conductor wore a confused look on his face. But it got stranger still: the second Bluebeard clicked a button on the device that was strapped to his stomach and a squeal of feedback peeled off the stage. The doppelgänger then stuttered and jumped backwards in the score, repeating what he had sung ten seconds ago as the true Bluebeard sang on confidently, utterly unfazed. It seemed less and less likely that this was meant to be part of the performance and the murmurs proliferated and rose in volume. But then, just as the conductor looked as though he might explode with rage, the doppelgänger lunged headfirst into the lake's reflection and was swallowed up in darkness.

Eichelberger turned to the audience, subtly breaching the fourth wall as if to say, it's all part of the show, folks, and everything returned to normal. The audience had the memory of a goldfish that evening; they were happy to be re-immersed in the sonic bliss that seemed as though it were raining down from heaven itself.

CHAPTER 41

As HE HURLED himself through the portal, Greg shut his eyes and focused on staying in time with the broadcast. According to Errol's interpretation of Lampo's notes on the Chaos Signal, if the music stopped for a split second, then the spell would be broken; Greg would be at the mercy of the gargantuan Pelican. It had been incredibly challenging to sync with the broadcast while the live performance was going on, and he needed to focus fully to stay with it as the sound of the live performance grew muffled and indistinct behind him. With his eyes closed he could tell that he was floating. It reminded him of the time he'd gone scuba diving in Australia with a hangover so bad he'd vomited through his mouthpiece and watched exotic fish rush to feed on the floating feast. He felt his stomach clench and closed his eyes even tighter. Steady old boy, he thought to himself.

He reached down to the stereo strapped to his stomach and turned the music up. There would be significant breaks where the transmission played without his singing and he needed to be sure it was loud enough. The music was his invisibility cloak and his way out.

Once he was confident in his singing and the volume of the stereo, he allowed himself to open his eyes. He was floating midair in a dark tunnel of unfathomable width. There were wings flapping and giant ravens fluttering to and fro chaotically. The walls of the tunnel appeared to be black, but, with horror, Greg realized that the walls were covered in feathered creatures, clinging to their perches like bats. The air crackled with electricity and smelled of ozone. Greg felt as though he'd be vaporized were it not for the laminar boundary created by the music. The birds circumnavigated him instinctively, cawing and scrapping with their mighty beaks.

Somehow, he managed to stay calm. He willed his body forward, propelling himself deeper into the tunnel. It was like flying in a dream; the music afforded him the power to physically move his body by sheer force of willpower. If there was a problem of navigation and perspective, it had more to do with the fact that the dimensions and molecular makeup of the space seemed to expand and retract from one moment to the next, like a drug trip gone wrong. Or, Greg thought more accurately, like an extra deep k-hole.

He was brought back to his near-death experience in the Seine: the previous time he'd been thrust into this space. But then it had been subliminal, a weak facsimile. This was the real deal, and he could feel it threatening to dismantle his sense of reason: the glued together self which stitched reality together from one moment to the next. He shook it off, focused on singing and propelling himself forward, and tried not to look at the horrific lost souls clinging to the walls. There was only an hour left in the opera. An hour to find the paintings and get out.

Gravity was strange in the Pelican dimension, and he corkscrewed slowly clockwise as he moved forward. He picked up some momentum, trying not to scream or stop singing as birds very nearly barreled into him. He looked back and saw the portal in the distance, the transmission flowing through it, growing longer all the time, tethered to him like a mountaineer's rope. Suddenly the tunnel divided in front of his eyes. There were three paths: two looked like dead ends and the third on the far right crackled dimly, lit up by a path of flickering stars. He went towards the stars, praying it wasn't a trap.

This next tunnel was narrower. The exposed rocks between the birds were cragged like a cavern, and the resonance was much better. It grew narrower still, and he was passing very close to the birds, almost brushing up against them. Seeing birds this large emphasized the notion that they were descended from dinosaurs – there was something cold and reptilian about them. As Greg corkscrewed deeper and deeper, he almost crashed into a crooked rock that was jutting out. On the tip of it was a handsome raven with pied feathers and bright orange rings around its eyes. Unbeknownst to Greg, it was Mizza.

As a result of several recent sojourns outside the Chaos

Dimension, Mizza was experiencing a temporarily heightened sense of agency, which was marked by an uptick in clarity of thought and perception. Seeing this strange intruder, this singer with a blue beard, indicated to him that the humans were finally mounting a resistance effort. As Greg passed by, the handsome bird cawed loudly and seemed to stare in disbelief with a faint smile on his beak. Greg turned himself forwards and cursed. He'd come to another split, but this one went in eight directions that were indistinguishable from each other. He floated in a panic and almost forgot to sing. Forty-five minutes till the big finale.

And then something strange happened: a thread of light appeared out of one of the paths, snaking towards Greg like a tentative caterpillar. It grew less tentative as it approached. Greg felt a tickle in his ears and then a sound so smooth and beautiful it nearly melted his mind: Liquid Legato Liquid Gelato. He stopped singing for a second and felt a gentle tug as if to say: keep singing, moron! The thread had passed through him and connected to the transmission behind him, tethering him back to the opera stage. Now he was like a climber on a zipline: the new thread pulled him down the path it had come from, adding to the self-generated momentum. He was flying fast now down a long, circular tunnel that twisted and turned aggressively like a waterslide and branched off in thousands of directions.

The faster he went the faster he rotated, and he began to grow dizzy; it was tough work singing and keeping his lunch down. He found he was clutching the radio to himself even though it was well-secured. The line pulling him forward added its own part to the orchestra's score, filling it out, making it lusher, and adding tonal colouring. Suddenly, he understood: the thread was coming from the composer; the thread was coming from Lampo himself.

Only the person who wrote the music would have been able to work within it like that, adding a whole new dimension without changing a single note. He sang with renewed fervor – surely he was being drawn towards the paintings, towards the captives. He flew faster and faster, absorbed in the music, letting his fear drop away like a child on a roller coaster. He was performing with one of his heroes! He suddenly understood the method by which Charlie's recent music had been created, and he was struck by a pang of jealousy. Fuck me up, he thought, Charlie was jamming with Luka Lampo, and he didn't even know it. The zipline threaded Greg through a seemingly infinite number of caverns populated by birds who had started to take notice as the volume and intensity of the music increased. The radio seemed to have grown even louder and lost a bit of its static distortion. If he was drawing attention from the hungry ghosts, he hoped that he was still invisible to the big Pelican.

Finally, he emerged into a room that was thick with thunder and lightning. The air was heavy, and Greg knew he had reached the end. There was something colossal in front of him that looked like a sculpture, but it was moving up and down, breathing: the agent of chaos that had been fucking with his city. The zipline was coming from inside of its mouth, and for a moment Greg had the terrifying impression that it had been singing a siren song, luring him into a trap. A flash of lightning illuminated the room, and he saw that the pelican was unconscious; its long neck folded back into itself, its huge, crusty beak running the length of its body, jutting out slightly. It was nestled on a massive rock ledge and gave the impression of being in a deep sleep of the type that might come over a fatigued undergrad who's smoked a bit of pot after their final exam.

The beast's decisively unconscious state calmed Greg. The fact that the thread led inside its mouth frightened him. Nevertheless, the sonic zip line was pulling him on with a momentum that was beyond his control, and as he approached the giant beak he closed his eyes and resigned to follow, quite precisely, the path of his friend into the pelican's mouth.

When he opened his eyes, he was surprised to find that the pelican's mouth, lit up by the thread of light, was as expansive as some of the bigger caverns he'd passed through. Here too, birds fluttered about, and the air crackled and simmered. Lost memories cluttered the space in a way that Greg would not be able to explain. He followed the thread of light down to the floor of the mouth. When he saw the paintings, it was hard not to forget his singing and let out a whoop of joy.

His feet touched down on some soft pink goop, coated in silky saliva. The opera gathered around him like a suit of armour, filling him with the most sophisticated high in the universe.

His heart was free, and his conscience was clear. He picked the paintings out of the goop and examined them: the one from the Rockies that he'd thrown at the AGO and one he'd never seen before of a wheat field in the prairies. As he suspected there were animated hooded figures in each frame. Charlie was jumping up and down and doing a little victory dance; Lampo was barely moving, focused on producing that perfect sound. Beyond the paintings lay the Pelican's throat, a darkened wasteland from which the sounds and movements of even more hungry ghosts could be perceived.

There was a rumble, and the pink goop was sucked violently towards the darkness. Greg fought for balance, gathered up the paintings beneath his arms and turned back. The opera was coming through the radio loud and clear; he and Lampo were fused with it, and the light was bright and clear. He floated up and out of the ludicrous mouth and back into the network of caverns. Only eighteen minutes remained in the opera.

The way back seemed easier: the light coiled through their path – a sonic trail of breadcrumbs. Greg was singing confidently, coming down the home stretch. Somehow, it had all gone to plan; Campbell and his crew would not have to initiate their Barrel of Monkeys protocol, which was pretty dubious in any case, and extremely dangerous.

They passed back through the caverns quickly, but without rushing. Maintaining the quality of their performance required focus, and if they'd broken into a sprint, something would be lost and the Pelican might wake up – it would be a disaster. And though the Pelican slept on, the captives of his realm were paying attention to the foreign presence more and more. The big birds had started following Greg at a cautious distance – just a few at first, but more and more so that as he drifted towards the exit, he felt like the Pied Piper, sneaking the children out of the town.

The inhabitants of the Chaos Dimension had been worn down to varying degrees according to the details of their lives and the length of their exposure. This thread from the outside world, this contraband substance snuck in by a strange, featherless creature, stirred something in many of them, evaporating a portion of the psychological swamp that subsumed them. Many of the older birds who'd been there a long time were unmoved, trapped in a labyrinth of pain and confusion, clinging to the walls desperately.

As he passed out of the final cavern, back into the area where the portal had spit him out, Greg saw the handsome pied bird, clinging to that cragged rock. Mizza saw the paintings, and his eyes shone with hope. He gave a great squawk and jumped free, joining the procession of younger birds. The memories of their human lives were sprouting in their minds like green buds in spring.

Greg came out of the cavern trailed by hundreds of these ravens, hitchhiking on the thread. He'd be able to see the portal soon, and then he'd be home free. On the other side of the portal, Eichelberger and Sophie were singing their hearts out – the opera was headed for its climax. He sang along with his friends proudly. In addition to giving him what he needed for the rescue mission, he was also putting on a career defining performance. It was glorious; their voices were invincible; their voices were one.

Their voices sounded so much as one, in fact, that it took Greg a solid ten seconds to realize that he'd dropped the transmission. He realized this only because the orchestra was conspicuously absent at a crucial moment. His own voice sputtered and stopped, and he was suddenly afraid. Lampo's own contribution also lost its urgency and veered off into dissonant improvisations. The birds behind them grew restless, and they began squawking and fighting amongst themselves.

Greg looked down at the dead stereo. He immediately knew it was broken, but he started punching buttons and shaking it nonetheless. Damn you Noodles. One job! How long ago had it stopped? Could he find his place by intelligent guesswork? His intuition told him that since the thread had been cut there was no way to mend it, someone would have to reopen it and find him, but there were only a few minutes left in the opera. After that he'd be trapped.

As these considerations swarmed his mind, his surroundings began a stark transformation. The laminar boundary was gone – the beast was awake. The complex networks of tunnels and caverns melted away, showcasing the extent of their malleability, until it was all just one massive space. Greg floated in place, still holding the paintings as the Pelican was revealed. The immortal multiplied in size and let out a shrill cry as pillars of lightning crashed all around them, illuminating a space so large it defied perception and logic. Some of the older birds ventured off the wall now, flapping towards Greg as if possessed. As a large, disgruntled raven lunged for the paintings, Mizza swooped into its path and shrieked.

An army of ancient ravens was gathering into formation, ready to apprehend the prisoners and rip Greg to ribbons. For many of the more recent arrivals though – the less indentured birds – the contraband from the outside world had been enough to stir some brave impulse in them, and they closed ranks in opposition with Mizza at the head of the battalion. Greg was shielded by a wall of determined birds. The Pelican screeched and the older ravens threw themselves into the defensive wall. A civil war had broken out in the Chaos Dimension.

CHAPTER 42

WHETHER BY CHANCE or by design, Lampo could not have done a better job providing for the Barrel of Monkeys protocol. From the moment Bluebeard encounters the Swan of Tuonela, the chorus splits in two, coaxing his conscience in separate directions: a show stopping battle between love and hatred that continues to the very end.

At the precise moment that the singers started this epic, fifteen-minute finale, Campbell gave the signal, and the ragtag group in the back row suddenly stood and began singing. As they sang, they filed into the centre aisle and walked towards the stage, their voices joining with those of the professional chorus in perfect harmony.

Over the course of the performance, virtually everyone beneath the roof of the opera house had undergone a transformation and entered a state of hypnosis: the ushers, audience, the orchestra, and even Von Strohn himself had grown lost in the music and entered a peaceful fugue state. Errol had been lulled into a complacent haze as well, but Tatiana – who possessed a strange disposition that rendered her immune to the spell – maintained her autonomy. Seeing Campbell and the other undesirables coming down the aisle, she rose to her feet.

One of the ushers – clearly on another plane of existence – opened a door for the secondary chorus and led them up a staircase towards the stage. Tatiana rushed to join them and caught the door just as it shut. There were two choruses on stage now, forty voices joined in song to support the virtuosic leads.

Tatiana found the harness at the back of the stage. The rope had a bit of stretch in it and just barely reached the glowing portal. Tatiana climbed into the harness, securing and tightening the straps. Finally, she turned to Campbell and gave him a look of bewilderment. She realized with a start that the secret chorus had handcuffed them together, with Campbell on the far end. He was too busy singing to speak, but he gave her a look of mad joy.

Campbell looked out at the audience, slapped himself in the face, and chucked himself through the portal. A gravitational force sucked him in, and the handcuffed singers were pulled after him at an alarming rate, tethered to nothing. It happened so fast that Tatiana was obliged to dive headfirst in order to catch the ankles of the last person on the chain: the Newfie who was built like a brick house. The momentum of the human chain dragged her upper body through the portal instantaneously, and she felt an unpleasant tug as the anchor line pulled taut.

Beyond the dangling chain of singers lay a vision that threatened her sanity: thick, intermittent bolts of lightning crashed in a dark space that seemed to have no definitive boundaries. In the distance a grotesque monster shrieked and flapped its prehistoric wings in a fit of anger. In the brief flashes of light Tatiana made out a battlefield all around her; birds the size of tigers tore into one another, plummeting through the crackling air locked in combat. She was in the midst of the fighting, but the area around the portal was somehow protected. The performance, although it was muffled, could be heard on the other side, loud enough that the chorus could sing along. The chain of singers swung wildly, and she summoned her strength, breathing into her muscles and tightening her grip. This is it, she laughed to herself, this is what it means to share the onion.

When the fighting started, Greg's only instinct was to get clear of it, but this proved to be impossible. The battle soon spread out, and he had a hard time figuring out which side was which. Furthermore, he'd lost much of his autonomy and could not control his trajectory well, if at all. Mizza, however, who'd led the first line of defence, stuck close to Greg now as he struggled in vain to locate the exit. Whenever any of the birds made a move towards Greg, Mizza blocked the way and fought like a maniac – soon he was missing many feathers and bleeding badly.

The first time Greg heard the emergency chorus he thought

he was hallucinating, so little faith he had in Campbell. But the hallucination persisted, faint though it was. He looked to see if the radio had come back on, but it was dead. He wished he could tear the damn thing off, but he dared not loosen his grip on the paintings. He closed his eyes and tried to propel himself towards the sound. Incredibly, he floated into range, close enough that he could pick up his part – the timing made sense: four minutes left in the opera.

Tatiana almost screamed when the light passed through her, threaded itself through the dangling chain of singers, and continued slowly out into the battle like a snake in search of prey. Her stamina was being pushed to its limit. She couldn't hold on much longer. If something was going to happen, it needed to happen now. Just then she heard it: not too far off, a baritone on her side that matched the one beyond the veil, like whales singing the same song from opposite ends of the ocean.

The meandering light had found its target and pulled taut now. The chorus hiccupped in unison and then resumed singing. The singing grew closer, and she could make out Greg – unmistakable with the bright blue smear on his face – making his way towards them, paintings in tow. She laughed with joy and heard the singers and orchestra grow louder behind her, as if a door had opened. Greg was corkscrewing towards them now, hugging the paintings to his sides, still singing despite the intense fighting all around him. He could not see that the pack of birds protecting him were being pummeled, dropping like flies, and that the Pelican was drawing nearer, its reptilian eyes burning with rage.

Though he dared not look back to see, Greg sensed that things were quickly going south. Still, he was so close now, he could see into the mad eyes of Campbell and saw the scallywag reach into his underpants, yank something out, raise it to his lips, and drink. Greg grimaced, but tried not to dwell on it, he was about to pass through the portal. They were in the final minute of singing.

As he sailed towards the portal, Campbell grabbed hold of Greg's ankle and the chain of handcuffed singers doubled back on itself. Greg had picked up a good deal of momentum and fired through the portal like a rocket, dragging the secret chorus with him. From the audience, Errol watched one Bluebeard tumble into the whirlpool that had been installed onstage and disappear. At precisely the same moment, a second Bluebeard tumbled out of the horizontal pool dragging a chain of humans behind him. Tatiana was buried in a huge pileup, but Greg rolled clear.

He tumbled to the floor of the opera house in a wash of light. The orchestra was finished, Eichelberger was gone, and the outline of the portal was diminishing with the conclusion of the opera. The chorus was untangling itself, revealing Tatiana, disheveled and breathless, but safe. Reflexively, Greg resumed singing the final note in the score. The portal expanded and birds started coming through in droves, spiraling out of control and flocking up to the fourth and fifth rings. A dozen, two dozen, a hundred, two hundred birds and more came pouring through until Greg thought his lungs would burst.

As long as he held that note, the hypnotic calm of the audience would hold. The second he let it go, all hell would break loose. The birds stopped coming through, and he held it five seconds longer, his lungs in agony. And then it was over.

He fell to the ground, hugging the paintings like a feral mother protecting her young. There were loud squawks emitting from every nook and cranny of the opera house that were slowly turning into moans, weeping, and manic laughter. As the audience regained their wits, the giant birds began morphing into humans, shedding their plumage and lying naked in the aisles and across people's laps, slick with a placenta-like substance and still moving in a bird-like manner, crouched with their arms folded like wings. Melody Greyhound was strewn across the violins with her mouth open, like a chickadee waiting to be fed. Hundreds of nudes now littered the scene – almost every single missing person had been rescued. Greg's eyes met Errol's and they burst out laughing and crying from relief, and because this was the strangest thing either of them had ever seen.

Hundreds of people were screaming and clogging up the exits, but from the Fifth Ring applause broke out; quiet at first, but then louder. It spread and soon every single person in the audience was on their feet, hollering and slapping their hands together, shouting "Bravo!" The scene was surreal and disturbing, but for those true opera connoisseurs, and those who realized that the missing had returned, the only conceivable thing was to bestow a roaring ovation on those humans who had sung their hearts out and risked their lives.

The cast came out to take their bows, and soon Greg, Sophie, and Eichelberger – the two Bluebeard's and their mother – were front and centre absorbing the love of the audience. Greg handed Eichelberger one of the paintings, and they held them both up over their heads, so that Charlie and Lampo could receive their share of the praise. Though no one in the audience could see, the tiny hooded figures took their bows from within the frames.

In all the commotion, a handsome, pied raven quietly exited the stage trailed by five additional birds. Backstage, he located an emergency exit and herded his companions out into an empty, one-way street. Mizza was cut up and badly bruised, but he didn't care: he was finally free. Even the polluted air of downtown Toronto was sweet to his nostrils: the overflowing garbage bins and hideous financial towers was the sweetest sight imaginable. The four others were still out of it, confused and frightened – it was up to him to lead them. He couldn't know to what degree the Pelican's powers had been reduced, but there was no time to lose. He crowed loudly to capture the others' attention and prepared to take flight.

Somewhere in the fighting, in the dizzying escape onto the stage of the opera house, a notion had drifted into his head: directions to a sanctuary, a place where no one would ever hurt them again. He said a silent prayer, puffed out his chest, and spread his wings. He soared ecstatically up into the sky and the others followed. Soon they were nothing more than specks on the horizon.

CHAPTER 43

FOLLOWING THE INITIAL madness of the premiere of Bluebeard and the Swan, things calmed down. The portals disappeared, and the malevolent birds left the city en masse, many of them heading south for the approaching winter. The missing civilians who'd disappeared into the Chaos Dimension had no solid memories of where they had been, just vague recollections of sound and light and an unpleasant psychic residue, similar to what one experiences after a bad dream. As for the general population of Toronto, there was a subtle awakening that autumn, as if the city's collective consciousness had been thoughtlessly searching for something and then come back to itself, unsure of what that something was, but confident that it no longer mattered.

In the wake of the disaster, and with the reduced influence of the Pelican, people were more open with each other. Intimacy and warmth spread throughout the city's streets, households, and homeless shelters. Crime and car crashes diminished and people stopped constantly taking out their smartphones during social meals to quench their agitated minds.

With the return of Melody Greyhound came the assurance that the opera company would live on, much to the relief of opera fans, the company's personnel and, perhaps most of all, Errol. The initial madness of the opening night produced such a tremendous buzz that the remaining shows completely sold out, and with the company's budget back on track, the Germans could start planning for the following season. Additionally, a decision was made that Greg and Eichelberger would alternate from one night to the next in the role of Bluebeard. This was not so much diplomatic as strategic: the Germans were capitalizing on the already legendary tales of the opening night, during which both singers had graced the stage and somehow rescued the disappeared. On the final night of the run, Eichelberger proposed to Sophie during the curtain call. She responded with an emphatic yes.

After the run of Bluebeard and the Swan was finished, Greg left the motel and rented a two-story house in the Beaches. Maggie softened up and allowed him to host the children on weekends. He took the kids to superhero movies and fed them pasta with meat sauce. In his spare time, he jogged on the boardwalk and went shopping for old records. On lonely nights he trained himself to drink one whisky after dinner and then switch to tea while watching TV or reading.

Through the winter, he often drove to Errol's house where the two men would have long talks while watching basketball on mute, or soaking in the hot tub. The crisis had brought them closer together, and they were learning to open up to each other, making the best use of their time together and speaking in their true voices. They tended to avoid Charlie in conversation as if by accident, and when they inevitably stumbled onto him, it was as if a wound opened up and everything would turn melancholy as they maneuvered towards a different topic. And here was the central problem: they could neither mourn his death, nor celebrate his life, because Charlie was still in limbo.

After Greg retrieved the paintings from the mouth of the Pelican, the AGO had promptly scooped them up and mounted them in their rightful places as part of the Mythical Landscapes retrospective. The painting of the prairies, in which Lampo had been embedded, was a normal painting once more the second it hit the wall, in the sense that there was no furry little dude creeping around in the golden wheat. The picture of the Rockies, however, was a completely different story. Day after day, the gallery received reports from attendees that there was something moving in the painting. Some described it as a little wizard in a hood, others saw a baby bear, and one woman insisted it was Alf.

The painting became famous, the subject of an endless subreddit thread, and people came from all over Canada just to look at the one picture. When huge crowds formed in front of it, security had to shoo people away, encouraging them to pay equal attention to the other paintings. Greg and Errol bought gallery memberships so they could visit as often as they liked, but quickly found that the visits were in vain: even if they could get close enough to the painting and even if it was a day when the hooded miniature chose to reveal himself, he would not respond to their psychic greetings. And so, Greg and Errol would look through the exhibit for the umpteenth time, take a turn about the Artemis Gwillimbury room, and return home with a vague feeling of guilt.

In the new year – and by this time the city had returned to a normalcy so pervasive the birds and the portals had been virtually forgotten – the exhibit closed and the paintings were moved into storage.

✧

Greg took it easy that winter, resting his voice and taking care of himself. He was using a meditation app twenty minutes a day and seeing a therapist once a week. April brought its typical deluge to the Beaches, but his spirit did not dampen. He'd grown used to the idea that Charlie was still alive in some sense, but absent from his life. If a full year passed, he supposed, they'd have a funeral and he could move on. Until then he would try and be open to anything, try and be comfortable with not knowing. Realistically it was anyone's guess whether he himself would live or die from one day to the next; it was amazing that humans were able to accomplish anything with that shadow hanging over their heads.

Of course, all his spinning thoughts and sensations would dissolve back into the great invisible pool of vibrating atoms someday and cease to be his own. In the meantime, all he could do was plan for the future as though it were certain and enjoy the present hour as if it were his last. As long as he had them on loan, he would put his taste buds to use on smoked meat sandwiches and fine whisky. He would pipe J.S. Bach through his ears and Stanley Kubrick through his eyes. He would set his ambition aside for a time and come back to it when it had mellowed and morphed, when it wasn't so urgent and angry and tangled with ego.

CHAPTER 44

THE WINTER HE spent in his mother's painting – hanging on the wall of the gallery, and then later in storage – was certainly the longest winter that Charlie could remember. It wasn't just that it was long, it was that time took on a distinct quality: the experience of being utterly alone with one's thoughts and feelings for that length of time, well, it wasn't quite like anything else. It was, at once, the most boring thing in the world and the adventure of a lifetime. Furthermore, the question regarding the status of his mortality – whether he was alive or dead – was unclear. He felt as though he'd slipped through some administrative crack and the fate of his soul had been buried in a pile of forgotten paperwork.

There were, primarily, two things that allowed him to maintain his sanity: the lives he had absorbed, and the act of walking. In the prayer sphere of the Cathedral, hundreds of lives had passed through him, and the narratives were stockpiled in his mind. He was not familiar with these lives on a conscious level, but the tips of the threads were sticking out of his unconscious, barely visible, and when he tugged on an individual thread, the whole thing unfurled.

Peoples' lives didn't reveal themselves in real-time: there were fat chunks missing and then episodes of shocking clarity, strung together to form the essential narrative. Through the alchemical process practiced in the Cathedral, the narratives had burned off a great deal of the poison that tints the stories we tell ourselves. They were laid out plainly, free of aggressive justifications and other psychological ornaments, though of course some subjective distortion was unavoidable. He'd climb trees or suss out pleasant spots on the mountains and sit for hours on branches and rock ledges sifting through peoples' lives, feeling their pain and pleasure and the vast realms of boredom in between. It was as though a massive biographical library had been implanted in his head, so he could sit and "read" for hours, or even days, without holding a book in front of his face.

Aside from sifting through other peoples' lives, he walked and explored everything within the boundaries of the painting. After he'd been liberated from the Chaos Dimension and taken his bow from the stage of the Four Seasons Centre, the huge screen that allowed him to observe the world beyond had slowly grown more and more opaque until he could only make out shadows moving beyond a frosted wall. He tramped through the trees and over the mountains, the same scenery appearing over and over again: there were no boundaries, just repetition.

Depending on his mood, the world around him would manifest as wet brushstrokes, dry reality, or some combination of the two. It struck him that this was a perfect metaphor for human perception: the world as we know it is simply a product of the human mind. The common phrase "it's all in your head" was somewhat redundant. The entire field of human experience existed solely in the subjective mind. Living bodies were just instruments made up of the earth, which could also perceive the earth. He could feel his mind getting stranger with each passing day, and he wondered if he'd even be able to keep it together if he were returned to the land of the living.

Then, one day, he was returned to the world. He knew something was strange when he woke up, since he never slept. He awoke slowly, groggy as hell, lying naked on the wet, cool earth in a damp chamber. After a few minutes, he raised himself up and took in his surroundings: a small dome-like structure made up of sticks and other detritus and held together by mud. There was a high-pitched chattering behind him, and he turned slowly and saw several baby beavers huddled together in the corner, accompanied by their mother who was eyeing Charlie suspiciously. She seemed oddly calm considering his intrusion.

Suddenly, a large male beaver came splashing up through the underwater entrance carrying a fat armful of softwood and flowering branches. Charlie recognized the male as the beaver who'd shown him to the patch of thin ice: the portal to the Cathedral. The beaver and his mate had survived the harsh winter; it was spring now, and they were a small family. Charlie was overwhelmed with joy to see that they'd made it, elated to smell the wet fur and feel the damp earth with his human body. There was, however, a sense of intrusion, and after a moment in the lodge gathering his wits and reacquainting himself with his human form, Charlie slipped out into the cold water and swam to the rocky bank, hoisting his dripping body up onto dry land.

It was unseasonably hot for May and by the time Charlie reached Artemis' cabin, he was practically dry, his feet bleeding slightly from sharp rocks and sticks. Thankfully the bugs hadn't started up yet. Errol's Porsche was still parked next to Yana's cabin, and Artemis was sitting out on her screen porch staring at the lake. Charlie put his hands over his crotch as he approached, but she'd already seen him.

"You think I've never seen a man's genitals before, Chuck? Limp, hard, half-mast, it's all the same to me. Uncover your shame, feel the breeze, dear boy!"

Charlie awkwardly uncovered his genitals. Cujo bounded out of the woods barking his head off and made straight for him. He covered up again, running into Yana's cabin to retrieve a moth-eaten robe before greeting the pooch. He was glad to see that the wound on Cujo's face had healed, although there was a bad scar down the front of his face.

He joined Artemis on her porch, Cujo lay down at his feet. They sat in silence for a while.

"Took you long enough," Artemis finally said.

Charlie laughed. "As if I had a choice!"

Silence again.

"Don't you want to ask me what happened down there?" Charlie finally asked.

Artemis gave him a scathing look. "Eager much?"

Charlie frowned.

"I think I have some idea," she said. "I listened to the lake every day, it gave me updates."

"So you weren't worried?"

"Worried?" She gave him a puzzled look. "No. No point."

More silence.

"Did you get to see her?" Artemis asked, finally.

"Yeah," Charlie smiled. "Yeah, I did."

"Good, I'm glad. And I'm glad you're back; I want you to take me to the city."

"Seriously? I thought you had to stay here, like an old washed up Jedi. I thought your life-force was tied to this place."

"My dear boy, I've been deep in dialogue with the lake for the past nine months, feeling each and every tiny little ripple. The situation has changed. I no longer need to be here."

"Why? How?"

Artemis shrugged. "It's simply the reality of the situation. Are you ready?"

"I mean. . . I could certainly eat something."

"We'll grab burgers on the way, my treat."

"Do you even have any money?"

"My paintings sell for millions. I keep the cash in several shoe boxes."

"Yeah but, isn't it all from the '80s? The burger place might not take antique money."

Artemis glared at him. "They will accept my hard-earned money and I will pay for the petrol, and I will hear no more jibes about antique money."

Charlie raised his hands in surrender.

"Let me just see if I can find pants and a shirt."

They got in the car and sped south, eventually stopping at a well-known tourist trap off the highway. They sat at a picnic table near a novelty train sipping coke while Cujo ran amok, eating napkins and fast food wrappers. Charlie stuffed french fries into his double cheeseburger, and devoured it voraciously, setting to work on Artemis' fries.

"Twelve dollars for a burger combo!" Artemis lamented. "What has the world come to?"

"Infafunshabish," Charlie said, exposing a mouthful of french fries.

"Ugh, you know your mother talked with her mouth full too. Most endearing."

Charlie swallowed.

"Sorry. I said inflation's a bitch."

But Artemis wasn't listening, she was transfixed by a hipster couple vaping and taking selfies in front of the stationary train.

"What on earth are those two doing? Whatever it is, I hate it."

Charlie started to explain, but a commotion erupted: Cujo had jumped up on a neighbouring picnic table and ran off with a cheeseburger in his maw.

"Who the fuck's dog is that?" yelled a man in a motorcycle jacket.

"You got any more of that antique money?" Charlie asked. "I think we gotta buy that dude a burger."

Artemis rolled her eyes.

Entering the city, Artemis directed Charlie to a quaint side street in the Rosedale Ravine. There was a single, minimalist two-storey house at the end of the row with a plaque out front and tourists with camera's milling about.

"They turned my house into a damn museum!" Artemis cried.

Charlie fought hard to suppress a laugh.

"I'll take you to Errol's place," Charlie said. "There's plenty of room there until you sort this out."

A few moments later, they pulled up in front of the house at Wychwood. Errol spied them out the window and approached, with Goblin lazily bringing up the rear. They got out of the car, Cujo barking like a maniac to greet his old friends.

"You remember I told you about my stepdad, right Artemis? This is Errol."

"The owner of this ludicrous machine?" She gestured at the Porsche.

"Would you prefer I drove around in a beat down Honda like some broke college student?" Errol asked.

"I think you two are going to get along," Charlie said.

CHAPTER 45

BY THE TIME May rolled around, Greg had decided it was time to get back to work. His agent arranged for him to contribute to a Bel Canto greatest hits mixtape: an opportunity to warm up in a closed environment before returning to the stage. The divorce papers had gone through, and Maggie was now engaged to the architect. He was trying to accept this, but he also craved the distraction of work, which maybe wouldn't be such a bad thing. There was also Sophie and Dietrich's wedding to look forward to: they'd booked a fancy resort in the country for the summer ceremony. Greg had chilled out his drinking successfully and was looking forward to the party and a good excuse to get properly drunk and dance spastically to Superfreak.

It was thoughts of the wedding that preoccupied him one evening in mid-May as he sat with his nightly glass of whisky. The Dispossessed was splayed in his lap, Mendelssohn was on the stereo, and a freak rainstorm was cutting through the pink dusk, massaging the slanted roof of his house and tapping on the skylight. He wished that Charlie could come to the wedding with him. There would be opera nerds there, but there would also be eligible women. He imagined him and Charlie in slick suits, sipping cocktails and chatting up culture babes. He grew lost in the fantasy so that when the doorbell rang, it sounded through the fog of his waking dream. He wasn't expecting anyone, and most people texted to announce their arrival. He hadn't even known the doorbell worked.

He lifted his heavy frame out of the armchair and padded in his socks towards the door. He opened it to find Charlie standing on his porch, a sheepish grin on his face.

"Hey man," Charlie said. "Can I come in?"

✧

Down in the Cathedral, the network of wooden spheres had ascended high above the churning water. Divers were scattered about in and outside of the spheres, walking in the forest, playing in the oceans, chatting through thought-shapes on the ladders and bridges between the spheres. There was plenty to celebrate in the Cathedral: not only had the lost Filament returned, but there had been a sudden influx of six additional Divers, carrying chaotic energy from the other place that was off the scales. This material would be synthesized into incredibly dense sea-dragon-chow when the six were ready, providing a tremendous amount of strength for the Feline.

The Diver formerly known as Luka Lampo was perched on the lowest sphere, listening to the ocean below. If he listened carefully, he could make out long complex movements that resembled Chopin's "Étude No. 12", Debussy's La Mer or Wagner's Symphony in C Major. This particular Diver, with his icy blue eyes, was unique insofar as he heard music in the ocean: music that grew tangled in the peach coloured dust that rose from below and disappeared through the lake above.

As the blue-eyed Diver lay there, listening for the music, he felt an intense longing to return to the living world. Accompanying this longing was a quiet sense of shame. By this point, he'd served as the Filament. He'd absorbed the traumatic lives of his fellow Divers and produced the glowing pellet that had allowed the veteran Diver – his former lover – to descend and pass on to the long sleep.

Furthermore, he knew he was privileged above and beyond his invitation to come to the Cathedral. He'd broken all the rules, descended early and empty-handed, somehow escaped from the ocean below, played a part in an epic posthumous adventure, and ended up on the stage of a gorgeous modern opera house, taking a bow during a standing ovation for the premiere of his masterwork. And still he'd been allowed back.

As these thoughts ran through his head, his face reconfigured itself into a smile, minus the mouth. The afterlife, in many ways, had already been more gratifying than life itself, despite the fact that he still harboured mixed feelings. Ultimately, however, he was certain he'd be able to accept death in a way he was never able to accept life, just like all the other Divers.

He gave up his search for a discernable melody and let the sound of the waves wash over him. The ocean's cadence and tone held its own charms without him trying to squeeze something more out of it, without him willing it to be like this or like that. The ocean isn't Chopin, he thought. The ocean is the ocean. He fell lightly into sleep, or something resembling sleep, and dreamed one last time of the great concert halls of Europe.

ACKNOWLEDGEMENTS

First off, I'd like to thank the real-life Goblin – I thought I wasn't a cat person and you proved me wrong. I'd like to thank Dave Bidini, Warren Sheffer and Janet Morassutti at Ballpoint, and Mitchell Gauvin, Heather Campbell and Lindsay Mayhew at Latitude 46. Big thank you to my early readers Rich Light and Dan Latner. Thanks to Ron Eckel for the encouragement and indispensable feedback. Thanks to Phil Deck and Rob Gleadow for a glimpse into the opera world. Thanks to Wenting Li for drawing such a great Feline. Thanks to Liz Haines, Story Planet crew and every single kid from every single workshop – for dreaming so wild and helping me find the fun. Thanks to my dad, Gerry, my mom, Julie, and my sister, Robin – couldn't have landed in a more loving, supportive family. Thanks to my amazing wife, Annie Briggs, for keeping the magic alive, even (and especially) through the tough times. I want to thank all my friends for the laughter, inspiration, co-regulation and dancing. I love you all and I am so, so lucky to have you in my life. Finally, huge shout-out to all of Toronto's artists, dreamers and freaks, past, present and future: you make our city weird and fun.

ABOUT THE AUTHOR

Dave Hurlow is a Toronto-based musician, writer and educator. He was a founding member of the Juno nominated rock band The Darcys, and currently releases music as Decafwolf. A graduate of King's College University in Halifax, his previous publications include the short story collection, Hate Letters from Buddhists (Steel Bananas Press, 2014), as well as articles on literature and music for NOW and The Ex-Puritan magazine. He also develops and facilitates creative writing and music programs for Story Planet, and is currently training to become a teacher. Deep Sea Feline is his first novel.

Learn more at davehurlow.com